Pride Publishing books by Gin Vane

Southern Awakenings
From Bad to Worse
Some Place Like Home

I0563701

Southern Awakenings

SOME PLACE LIKE HOME

GIN VANE

Some Place Like Home
ISBN # 978-1-80250-549-8
©Copyright Gin Vane 2023
Cover Art by Kelly Martin ©Copyright June 2023
Interior text design by Claire Siemaszkiewicz
Pride Publishing

SOME PLACE
LIKE HOME

Dedication

For Em.
I would write anything to make you smile.

This book is for those who enjoy the release found
in rope, dominance, and submission. There's no
one "look" to kink. Find what works for you and
run with it. I hope Carver and Daniel's journey
can be a window into just how caring and
unexpected a dynamic can be.

Part One

UNTAMED

Chapter One

Carver
Fairview, Louisiana
Summer of 2019

"Y'all still open for business?"

Carver looked up and saw someone he should stop expecting to be done with. Hadn't seemed to keep the man from popping up last year either.

Everett Kane stood in the waiting room of his empty auto shop, both hands stuffed in the pockets of khaki pants. Carver sighed, stood from his chair and turned down the narrow hall. He met eyes with Everett on his way to the intake desk to shuffle the first stack of papers he could find. "Needin' the boat again, Law Man?"

The former detective snorted. "Not so much. More cheatin' husbands than serial killers of late."

"A smaller sort of evil, then?"

"Honestly? It's been a nice change of pace."

Everett still smiled like he didn't know it lit up the room. There was a reason they'd met how they had years ago at Jeanie's Western Night. Try as he might to change it, Carver had always been a sucker for a smile.

Everett pointed to the line of chairs against the wall, then back to himself. Carver tipped his head and watched him choose a seat by the cooler. Everett pulled a paper cup from the sleeve and pushed the blue plastic tab. Barely a swallow of water dribbled out. Without his planned distraction, he looked a bit lost.

For his part, Carver took his time "filing" those random papers. After a too long day of too few customers, he didn't have the energy for the light-stepping Everett always seemed to need. "That car in the lot looks fine to me," he said. "What d'you want?"

The other man shrugged and stared at the cup in his hands. "Just…in the area. Thought I'd stop past."

Carver walked to the front of the intake desk and leaned his back against it. He pushed the sleeves of his dark mechanic's shirt up his arms before folding them over his chest. He could wait for Everett to get to his point, but it'd be easier to lead him to it. Easy was the name of the game, these days.

"Look, you don't gotta worry. It's obvious you and Colt are—"

"Water under the bridge, man." Everett swept the rest away with a friendly toss of his hand. His blue eyes creased with embarrassment. "Though I think I still owe you an apology or four."

Carver tried to fight it off but couldn't help his grin—looking at Everett all contrite and shit. Their run-in years back hadn't been *all* bad. He'd had plenty of worse nights. Before and since. But Everett seemed to want to know things were settled between them, and at the end of the day, Ev was a decent guy. Carver could let him off the hook.

"Don't mention it," he said. "We've all been there."

Everett nodded as the flush faded from his cheek. Like he didn't know what else to say, he asked, "How 'bout you? Doing well? You, uh…seein' anyone?"

The fact he'd even ask proved how little Everett knew him. Carver turned his gaze to the parking lot and tried not to think of the whopping *two customers* he'd helped today. "Nah. Work's been too busy to think on much else. What I need to do is hire some help out here."

He ignored the keen look Everett gave the empty waiting room. He didn't contradict him, whatever his detective's eye might've noticed. "Sounds like one of those good problems."

"Maybe, yeah."

Everett knocked back his swallow of water. "Well, if we hear tell of any mechanics worth a damn, we'll send 'em your way."

"Same with any murderers I find. Send 'em right over."

"Hell no, man." Everett's laugh was bright as ever. "Life's quieter on that front than it used to be. Thank God."

Everett stood and fumbled in his back pocket. He opened his wallet and retrieved a business card, running his thumb along the edges as he spoke. "But really, uh… See, me and Colt run our own agency now. Help people lookin' for stuff. Investigative work, mostly."

He took a step toward the desk but pulled up short, like he'd reconsidered, and instead tapped the card against his thigh. "Don't know why you would, but if you needed something checked out or... I mean, you had our back before the cops even, so..." Everett shrugged and met his eye. "Just, don't have that second thought. Call. We'll give it a shake."

He didn't know what Everett expected him to say, but the other man seemed content to leave it at that. The bell chimed as Everett pushed the door open to leave, and without really meaning to, Carver found himself following after.

He braced his arm against the glass and asked, "You come here just to give me this?"

The former detective looked like he wasn't sure himself. He stopped on the sidewalk and shrugged. "Just tryin' to pay it forward, I guess. You..." He worked his jaw and considered his words. "You helped me back when. Whether you knew it or not. Didn't have to, but you did. So...same here, is all."

They held each other's gaze for longer this time. Made it easy to notice how Everett's landed on his bike in the garage—and quickly back again. The man's earlier flush returned to his cheek and Carver wondered how that night years ago looked from Everett's purview...

"Don't mind obvious myself."

"Dance with me some."

"What's it gonna be, Everett? Omelets or eggs?"

"Don't think gay's your problem, man. Heartbroken is."

Everett broke their staring match first and smiled at the pavement. He made a point to reach inside and leave his card on the low table. His eyes shone with humor as he scanned the shop's magazine graveyard. "Besides, Colt will pitch a fit if he has to find a new bike shop. Got his heart set on some road trip, and he ain't gettin' no damn where on his own."

"Thought you didn't care for motorcycles."

"Yeah, well that ain't changed," Everett admitted. "But if I'm going, I'd rather know the thing's been looked at."

Colt could probably fix what was wrong himself, but whatever he'd told Everett, he couldn't afford to turn down the business. And if he was being totally honest, he didn't want to. Things might be strange for a spell, but Everett and Colt? They seemed like decent people. Jeanie was always saying he could use more of those in his life.

"Tell Colt to bring the bikes over," he said. "I'll take a look."

"Will do." Everett turned to leave again, but Carver raised a hand to stop him. He circled back inside to the intake desk, rummaged in a drawer, then jogged back to the door. Might as well get all the awkward out in one conversation.

"Heads up."

He tossed a silver bolo tie at Everett's chest. The man caught it, surprised to see the thing again. But there was a fond sort of *thank you* in his wave goodbye, and Carver figured they were as square as they were like to get.

He watched Everett drive away, unsure why he was doing it. Wasn't like the man held any attraction for him now, though Everett seemed to have gotten better with age — more so since he and Colt got back together. It was strange to think of Colt as someone other than his partner in misery, but the whole *once* they'd seen each other since Foxland, he'd looked better than Carver had ever seen. And it was hard to begrudge someone like Colt a little happiness.

Colt had never talked much when Carver was slinging drinks at Jeanie's. He'd visit mostly in the off-season, when the place filled with locals instead of college kids. The other bartenders didn't like him, but Colt's brand of nihilism fit well with his own views on relationships. People were nothing but tangled webs of need, and he'd never got a handle on being in someone's life long-term. Wasn't worth the bother. He'd been in too many systems to know what family felt like besides suffocating, and the one time he'd thought those days were over...

No. It was better not to get involved.

Still, Carver paused at the magazine table. One stilted conversation with Everett had him wondering on that blank space in his life, where words like *family* were supposed to go.

His phone chimed in his pocket and Carver flinched, startled back to reality. He pocketed the business card and groaned. He needed to close up soon or he'd be late for his shift again. He turned to grab his keys, but his gaze got stuck on a framed dollar bill and the photo mounted beside it.

It was the first money he'd ever made with this shop of his, but that wasn't what stopped him cold. It was the middle-aged woman with her arm around his shoulders, grinning proudly up at him. He sighed. What he wouldn't give for a business partner now.

Denise hadn't been his mother, but she'd been close. Close because of the man he'd cropped from the other side of the photo, the first time he'd let himself think words like "home" might be made for him at all.

Shit. He needed to cool it. He never did well when he worked a shift in this mood. No one liked a sour bartender, and damn if he didn't need the tips.

Carver hit the lights, locked up and pocketed the shop keys. He pulled a black button-up from his cherry-red truck and deemed it suitable for a night in neon lights. As he drove, he tried not to run the numbers of the business in his rearview—how short things were getting, how hard it'd been to reopen in Fairview, how he loved and hated this bar job that kept him from investing in his shop how he'd like.

The photo of Denise flashed through his mind again—the way she'd pinched his side to get him to "*smile for the camera,*" how she'd organize the receipts at the end of the day so he could get home faster. He shifted in his seat, unable to get comfortable. Maybe it was how settled Everett had looked that had him wondering.

Fuck. He knew where this train of thought would lead. As a boy, he'd spent equal time in foster homes and state-run group homes. Neither left much time to think on those real parents he must've had. He'd been too angry at them for dying, for only ever being a mystery. But lost as he was feeling with this favor in his pocket, maybe it was time to put those ghosts to rest. Like he'd done with Denise, with Derek and the whole of the Patterson family.

Derek...

Even years later, the pain was a familiar ache.

Carver turned the radio up as high as it would go and sped the rest of the way to Jeanie's. If some part of him needed family answers, then fine. Maybe he would take Everett up on his offer. But like hell was he bothering with feelings again. He'd found a work-around for that years ago and preferred to keep to routine.

He parked his truck in the lot and slammed the door, yanking off one work shirt to pull on another. He knew how tonight would go and that was comforting in its own way. He'd work his shift. Keep an eye out. Find some company for a night — and wake to an empty bed, his or some other man's.

Another day in paradise. Just living the dream.

Carver pushed the door open and flipped on the neon lights. Alone at the bar, he downed a shot of whiskey and wondered when his life had stopped sounding like fun.

* * * *

Everett
Mason, Louisiana

Summer had always been Everett's least favorite season, but that had been starting to change after his first one living with Colt. Life after Foxland had settled them into comfortable habits. Moving slow in summer heat was one. They worked for themselves now at Harkan & Kane Investigations. If they didn't want to hike to the office on a one-hundred-degree day? Fuck it, then. Call the boss.

Pretty easy, since he slept beside him every night.

Still, years of punching the company clock made him feel like a kid playing hooky. More often than not, he'd spend their days off waiting on *something* to go wrong. But today, Everett was doing all right on that score — enjoying quite the show as Colt worked a wrench on his pair of motorcycles.

They'd known each other over a decade now, but Colt still didn't understand Everett's views on acceptable danger. Sure, he'd ride a bull—for eight damn seconds. But some hog of metal and chrome, zigzagging past cars who weren't ever looking? *Hoo,* no thank you. Everett liked living too much to go asking for a wreck. He'd told Colt as much for weeks, though it had changed fuck-all about his plans for some road trip.

In the shade of their small garage, Everett sat in a lawn chair and sipped his iced tea—a staple since he'd been trying to cut back on the beer. Colt circled the bikes, lost in his project, and Everett swirled the ice around the bottom of his glass. "Just gonna remind the room at large there's no way I'm ridin' that thing. Even if you get both working again."

"All right, Ev. Keep tellin' yourself that."

"I'm serious. It's your fault you let 'em go to rust."

Colt braced dirtied hands on his hips, planning his next move. He wiped a greasy arm across the front of his ribbed undershirt. "Both of 'em need work. Sat idle too long. Couldn't ride around on hot parts while I was some cop."

"Well. Good thing we ain't that anymore."

Brown eyes met his, bright with agreement. "Good thing."

These days, their silent stretches were the comfortable kind of quiet—an opportunity to linger over a shared smile. Colt's curled in the corner of his mouth as he tugged dirty fingers through a shop towel, smearing the grease around more than anything. "I need to stop by Carver's. If we're gonna do this right, I'd like his opinion."

Everett inhaled his next sip of tea and sputtered it into the glass. His talk with the mechanic had gone all right, but personal progress aside, the sound of that name had him diving for the spare fridge and the six-pack on the door.

"Who?" He made a study of the fridge's contents, doing his best to feign ignorance.

Colt walked over and leaned an arm on top of the door. The weight of the man's gaze landed heavy on the back of his head.

"Carver," Colt repeated. "The guy with the boat last year? He runs the only decent auto shop around, near my old office in Fairview."

He could tell by Colt's tone that his mind was shifting gears and spared a moment's sympathy for what those perps must've felt, getting pressed by Detective Harkan back when. He popped the cap on a beer and tugged the door from beneath Colt's arm. He tried his best to look unbothered and retreated to his lawn chair.

Colt took his time retrieving a plastic-covered plate. He sat on his toolbox, knees sprawled, and leaned a forearm on his thigh. "The way I remember it," he drawled, "Carv picked up some hours at a certain establishment in Fairview. Not far from the college out there."

Well, shit.

He mentally cursed his partner for looking so like a kid in a candy store. Colt would find a way to gloat about this. His ears burned hot, so he took another pull from his beer. "You're gonna make me say this, aren't you?"

"If there's somethin' to be said."

He lasted a whole seven seconds under Colt's even stare.

"Jesus, fine." Everett threw his hands up in defeat. "I went once, all right? Well, twice."

"Get your story straight, Ev."

"Shut your goddamn mouth, you," he snipped, aware how embarrassed he sounded. "It was once. For a case. And then…"

"Then?"

Everett studied his bottle. "Yeah. The once. I might…*know* Carver. A bit."

He chanced a look up, unsure what he'd find. For once, Colt cracked first.

"Fuckin' knew it."

Everett blew a long sigh from his lips. Relief flooded his body as he leaned into the chair for support. "You— you complete and total asshole. Got me sweatin' over here like some whore in church."

"Should've *seen* you," Colt said, outright amused. He tried to smother his stupid chuckle with a cough, but that'd been clearing up since he'd cut down on the Camels. In time, Everett found himself laughing along, joining in the joke though it was at his own expense.

"Relax," Colt told him once they managed to settle down. "It was clear as day on your face when you got on that boat. Just your luck, right?"

The comment pulled him up quick. How long had Colt known about Carver? "I didn't… I mean, you didn't say—"

"'Course not. What we were facing that day? Couldn't care much about somethin' from those lost years. Not once we'd found our way back." Colt shook his head in that *c'mon now* fashion and tore into the plastic wrap with a smile.

Everett was still amazed at the difference it made when a person heard "*I love you*" on a regular basis. All the worries he'd ever had, the goddamn artful ways they'd managed to never say how they felt—now, none of it was necessary. All that came from the fear, from not knowing if this was really happening, if a love like theirs could be built to last.

Well, it was a year last Sunday since he'd talked Colt into living mid-suicide-run at Keith Edwards'. It was ten months since he'd brought Colt home from the hospital, and eight since they'd been living together as a permanent, on-purpose thing. So at Colt's gentle prodding of, "How'd it happen?" Everett was only a bit embarrassed to have a story to tell.

"It ain't…" He tried, then started another way. "I mean, it's not like it matters."

"Ain't about *matters*." Colt gestured with his chin. "You and Carv? Oil and water if I ever seen it. Bound to be fuckin' hilarious."

He narrowed his eyes. "I hate you, you know that?"

The tilt of Colt's head was damn-near haughty when he quirked his lips up like that. He popped a cube of watermelon into his mouth and Everett's priorities shifted the longer he watched Colt eat. He licked the juice from his thumb in God's-honest habit before realizing he had an audience. A red flush rose on his cheek.

"Tell me," Colt said. "Before you're sportin' wood over a snack tray."

He knocked Colt's steel-toed boot with the sole of his sandal—a concession to the heat his partner still refused to make. "Yeah? Why should I?"

"Might get something in return."

"Like what?"

"Well right now, the front-runner seems to be watchin' me eat watermelon—"

"There's not a lot I wouldn't watch you do," Everett teased. And having made Colt blush like a schoolgirl *twice* already, he polished off his beer and settled in for some humble pie.

He rubbed his hands together. "You're gonna laugh."

"Hope so. C'mon already."

* * * *

Fairview, Louisiana
Fall of 2016

The first time he went to Jeanie's was for the job. It was necessary, cut and dried—tax deductible, even. Nothing wrong with the trail turning to a certain kind of place. But with views at the station being what they were, he couldn't farm this out to the rank and file. None of that changed how uncomfortable Everett felt, walking up to a campus bar on the wrong side of forty.

In the two long years since Colt had left Mason, there'd been plenty of time for Everett to do some thinking. He hadn't come to any conclusions a label could define, but he was done pretending he knew the answers to all things. Even so, Everett didn't think he was gay. However badly he'd fucked it up, he'd loved Rachael too much for that. But as the months wore on, stretching one year into two, he did wonder if there were other men like him. And if he were even more honest, men out there like Colt.

The shame of how things ended outweighed his nerves for months, but Everett could only distract himself with the coal-raking for so long. A part of him was only human and that part was *very* curious. The dating sites made sense for women, but for men it all seemed so fast. Which had an appeal, sure, but there was no chance to figure anything out. Like a person had to know what they wanted before they ordered.

Too much like a pizza for Everett. But maybe he was old-fashioned that way.

When he arrived at Jeanie's, he was surprised by what he saw. The place seemed…normal. Pretty much what he'd expect for a Thursday night. Not much of a crowd, though the regulars were in. Sure, they were mostly men, but it wasn't anything obscene. Just folks drinking beer, moving to the same music as those line-dance joints Rachael used to drag them to.

He spent an hour getting none of the case answers he needed, but laid down a healthy tip all the same. That was when he saw the flyer — advertising a theme night he might've been too ready for, given previous endeavors in his life. So that Tuesday next, with tawny beard grown-in and a shirt he hadn't worn in years, Everett darkened the door of his first-ever gay bar for Western Night.

* * * *

"Need a light?"

He'd lasted a whole thirty minutes before the heat was too much to handle. Lord, but maybe he just weren't built for this anymore, even as a wallflower. He'd made a break for the smoke deck in search of relief and found one lazy fan and the stillness of the Louisiana summer. He'd also found a man in a dark cowboy hat, flipping a silver Zippo.

"Thanks," Everett said, leaning into the flame.

"I'm Carver," the man said.

"That a first or last name?"

"Does it matter?"

Everett rolled that around in his mind and shrugged. "Fair enough. Nice to meet ya."

"And you are?"

Fair being fair, he gave one name, no explanation. "I'm Everett."

Carver swallowed a smile and took a drag from his cigarette. "First-time jitters got you in your head, if you don't mind me saying. You? Got nothin' to worry about." He coupled the compliment with an appreciative up-and-down of his frame. Everett's face heated further, but he never did get to disagreeing.

He took the opportunity to look at this man with the convenient lighter. Maybe the beer was mixing with that wild blood he'd always had too much of—for Rachael, for most women, it seemed—but when Carver leaned closer, cheating a look from under the brim of his hat, he couldn't help thinking Wrangler Jeans could scout some models from this place.

Looking like *that*? Carver'd do all right.

Everett took another pull from his bottle. They'd only exchanged a handful of words, but this stranger had clocked him easily. "I'm that obvious, huh?"

Carver only shrugged. "Don't mind obvious, myself."

That third beer was making a convincing argument on this stranger's behalf and Everett wasn't afraid to push on his definitions with someone he never planned to see again. Hell, maybe this *was* some mid-life crisis after all. Wouldn't hurt to let his gaze slide over Carver's jeans, fit the right kind of close, snug over boots that looked like he worked in them, a belt with some wear and a simple black button-down. Near his rolled sleeves, there was grease smeared up his elbow.

For a moment, Everett thought he recognized the shape of a familiar tattoo…

He shook his head to clear the thought and focused on the man beside him. Carver was fair-skinned and clean-shaven, his black cowboy hat casting shade over his eyes. Everett couldn't tell their color, but the bit of bright peering down was dark, like gasoline catching the light. Carver's easy smile folded a dimple into his cheek. He had the grace to turn his head as Everett gave him the once-over, but Carver didn't stop him from looking.

So, yeah. Maybe he wasn't too mad about how close they stood, the way their shoulders touched as they leaned against the brick exterior. It gave a convenient excuse to get his feet wet, so to speak. That dance floor had felt too much like floodwaters. Everett wasn't sure he'd ever be comfortable there.

Carver seemed to read his mind. "A lot of guys come here lookin' for a body. Nothing wrong with that. Sometimes, that's all you're needin'. But that doesn't seem like your game. Am I right?"

This whole situation had Everett on his head. Used to be a line like *that* was on the tip of his own tongue, ready to excuse his way into a night of company with a friendly stranger. Usually a woman-stranger, but still. And what was more, when had Everett become the sort of person *not* to have one-night stands? When it had been so important he'd wrecked a marriage and more for such "freedoms"?

When the fuck had *that* happened? He felt uncomfortably old.

Everett drained his beer except for a final sip, then fit the butt of his Camel into the bottle between his hands. Without really meaning to, he'd made the switch from his old cowboy killers. He'd never checked, but if he were a betting man, he'd say the date lined up with a crime scene two years cold. He held his eyes closed and let himself get lost in the scent.

Carver asked, "You wanna talk about it?"

He laughed once, harsh in the back of his throat. Here he was, talking to a perfectly pleasant stranger, and he was mooning after Colt's cigarettes.

Pathetic…

"No," he answered low. "No, I do not."

"Good."

He looked up. Carver's smile turned reckless. There was something rough to how it hung crooked on his face, but it got Everett smiling back — brought with it their earlier humor — and that was a *dangerous* kind of action, the way Carver was responding. He took advantage of his height and leaned into Everett's space, angling his still-burning smoke down the neck of the bottle. The cherry hissed in the warm beer as Everett swallowed hard. Just as he was wondering what Carver's shower might smell like — if what was wafting off the other man's neck was some on-purpose thing — the thought crossed his mind that maybe he should check himself. Maybe Carver was making use of a place to ash, and where would he be then?

Two long strides and Carver stood at the bar's back door. He swung it open wide and held his arm against it. "C'mon, then."

"C'mon where?"

Carver jerked his neck at the dance floor. A familiar fire started low in Everett's belly, but he had no idea what to do with it. "No, I don't think… This ain't really my scene."

"It is tonight. Dance with me some."

Something about Carver standing there, arms crossed over his chest in challenge, just didn't make sense. Flattered as he was feeling, Everett *did* own a mirror. "What is this? There's plenty in there easier than me. More what you're lookin' for."

"How would you know what I'm lookin' for?"

Everett waved the comment away, but Carver pressed on. "Look, I'm not talking about *lookin' for*. I'm talking about tonight. So what's it gonna be, Everett? Omelets or eggs?"

He paused a moment too long. Carver pushed off the door with a shrug.

Then suddenly, without consulting him at all, Everett's feet were moving with newfound speed to follow. Carver winked at him as he realized what had happened. The asshole had played him good and was still leaning against the door, having never intended to leave him hanging.

And okay, maybe he could appreciate Carver's style. It was something like a trick he would've pulled on...

For Christ's sake. He halted his own train of thought. *Stop thinking about him.*

A final look at Carver's dark eyes, and yeah, Everett decided. *All right. For tonight.* He timed his movement with another patron's exit—the perfect reason to slide against Carver the right kind of friendly—and answered the man's question with one of his own.

"Omelets or eggs?"

"You sayin' you do breakfast, then?"

The way Carver grinned at that should have been illegal.

Back on the dance floor, the music thrummed in his chest. The bass, smoke and beer mixed a haze in his head—not hard to see through, but enough to dull the edges. Carver navigated the crush of bodies better than he did, so he followed the man into the far corner. Panic rose in his chest when they stopped beside each other, but the feeling eased as a confident hand rested in the small of his back.

Carver angled his head down. "All right?" he asked in his ear.

Everett could only nod. Carver stood close with just enough distance not to assume anything, but there wasn't exactly space for that length-of-a-Bible test either. Of course, that wasn't all those early lessons taught him not to want— until he'd tripped face first into a relationship with another man.

Goddamn it, hadn't he settled the score on thinking about that tonight? Besides, there'd have to be something proper wrong with him if Everett couldn't focus on the man in front of him. Carver led him in a dance little more than an excuse to press close and breathe together. He mimicked the swaying pattern and found it easier to follow than he'd thought— easier all the time. He fit his thumb around the leather of Carver's belt and pulled him in, closing that final distance with a sigh.

Dancing like they were, he could feel the effect they were having on each other, that press of obvious desire Everett was afraid to admit he'd missed. Carver slid a hand from his hip and up his back. He wound around until fingers fit to his neck, rubbing his thumb at the top of Everett's spine. Carver's nose brushed his in time with the music, side-to-side as their heads swayed with the beat.

And it was almost too easy for Everett to tip his chin up. Felt almost natural the way Carver traced his scruff, fingers too tender for the room around them. He wanted to close the distance between their mouths — surprised him, how much he wanted so fast.

He brushed his lower lip against Carver's and thought, *Okay. So this…exists. Without Colt.*

It was information. It was good to know. It was exhilarating.

Carver caught his mouth once and pulled away, returning to the dance like it could be an accident, if he wanted.

Not tonight.

Everett met his second kiss head-on and yes, there was something familiar about the embrace, yet blessedly not the same at all. There was the taste of smoke and the tang of beer, but beneath it all was something warm and honey and oat — sustaining and steady, tinged with spice. Wasn't long before Carver was pulling them firmly together, their swaying attempts at *not* calling this what it was falling fast by the wayside.

Carver stroked his tongue with his own and Everett was glad then for the noise — for the smoke machines and every bit of this dive meant to make private bubbles in public space. Thanks to the racket of the club, he could moan the way he wanted as Carver tasted him, as the fervor of the kiss grew near combusting and *shit,* they needed to cool it before this went any further.

Before Everett couldn't stop, staring bar patrons be damned.

As soon as he'd had the thought, Carver was pulling back. He brushed a kiss to the high point of Everett's cheek and nipped his ear. "Follow me home?"

It wasn't really a question.

Closing Everett's tab took no time at all, then Carver was leading him out through the back and into the parking lot. He didn't stop at any of the cars. Everett groaned under his breath.

"You fuckin' *would* ride a hog."

Carver smirked and grabbed the helmet off his bike. "You're talkin' like you know me."

"Not pretending to. I just notice things."

"And why's that?" Carver tossed him the helmet— another dare, as there was only one. But if he thought Everett was going to ride on the back of a *motorcycle* with another man in plain view of *anyone*, he had another thing coming. Besides, he wasn't sure how to bring up his profession. Not like cops were most folks' cup of tea for plenty of reasons, most of them good. But he liked Carver, at least enough to get on with, and the thought of lying outright didn't sit comfortably.

"I'm police," he said. "Detective, actually. Hope that's okay."

If Carver had opinions on the matter, he didn't voice them. He seemed darkly amused and not the least bit surprised. "No use tryin' to hide my secrets then? Law Man?"

"See, that's why I don't say nothin' —"

Carver laughed outright, like his discomfort only made this better. "Calm down. Shit, everybody's gotta make a living." He draped clasped hands over the edge of the bike and rested his forearms on the seat. Something shifted in his stare. "You help people?"

Everett shrugged. "I try, yeah."

The other man nodded and threw his leg over the leather. "You gonna get on this bike then, or what?"

* * * *

Carver's place looked more like a home than his own two-bedroom, but it was still working its way from *functional* to *lived-in*. A stack of boxes in the corner made him ask, "You new in town?"

"Nah. Just a new place."

He noticed the phrase *Shared DVDs* crossed out to say *Clothes* and Everett figured that was enough of asking questions his host might not want to answer. Before long, Carver was beside him again, popping two bottlecaps and handing over a cold beer. Even in his own house he kept his hat on, like he'd forgotten it was there.

Unsure what to do, Everett stared out of the window and drank. Carver mirrored his pose and did the same. He must've started talking because Carver was nodding, though he kept his gaze distant and set his beer on the cabinet. Everett continued with his story about who even knew what and, without even having to look, Carver snagged the neck of his beer and set it beside his own.

Carver cut a glance sideways and with no further warning, Everett was being pulled into a kiss. It was exactly like the bar—rushed and rough and *right*. Carver held them together with an arm around his back as they swayed for balance, and thanks to their height difference, that black hat of his wasn't even in the way.

He got his hands on Carver's hips and walked them to the nearest wall, ready to do this shit on purpose. Carver peeled out of his button-down lightning fast. Everett ripped off his own bolo, letting it skid to corners unknown. The other man flicked a finger at the pocket of his rodeo shirt. "You ride any? Or just like the fancy clothes?"

The way Carver teased made it easy to return the favor. "Keep that up, you might find out." He pressed his hips against Carver's and slid a hand around his back.

"Careful, Law Man. Starting to make me like you some."

"Wouldn't want that, right?" he asked.

"Course not."

Everett pulled at Carver's belt and worked the leather free, pushing down the zip and cupping him through his jeans. Carver knocked his head against the wall and his hat fell to the ground—revealing chin-length, sandy hair of a color to Everett's own.

The man caught his mouth in another kiss as he fumbled with the remaining belt. "How'd you want this?"

He swallowed hard against the nerves. "I, uh... I only ever done this the one way."

Carver stayed quiet, but Everett hadn't a clue what the man was thinking. He'd been unable to string two words in his mind since Carver started kissing his neck—but as good as it felt, that bit of blond in his periphery was *very* distracting.

Before Everett could think of a way to break the tension, Carver pulled back to meet his gaze. His eyes were bright with mischief, but Everett wondered if that knowing smirk hid something less self-assured.

"Nothin' wrong with that," Carver said, breathing harsh. "Except I don't know if I can wait that long."

Everett shrugged. "Ain't gotta be a whole thing."

"All right."

He took them both in hand. No more words were needed.

* * * *

He was doing up his belt when Carver asked, "So, you married?"

The *to a woman* his tone implied was obvious, if unspoken. Everett leaned against the wall and kept focus on his hands. He couldn't say why the thought of eye contact left him so unsteady. "No. Why you ask?"

"Seems like you're hating yourself for somethin' over there. Took a shot."

"Hating myself?"

"Won't look at me now."

Everett closed his eyes, ashamed to be so obvious. It was fine, it was all *so much more* than fine — until it wasn't. He couldn't say why, but the second they'd finished pressing close, Carver had sensed the shift in his mood immediately. The taller man shook his head at the ground and sat on the couch alone. Everett found he actually missed the crap music from the bar. Anything would beat this silence.

He recovered his shirt from the ground, but couldn't find his bolo. Carver watched him search with harsh eyes. "No offense, Law Man. But I've been to this rodeo before. I'm gonna give you some advice for free." Carver shoved off the couch and retrieved their abandoned beers. He handed Everett's off and said, "Don't think gay's your problem, man. Heartbroken is."

Everett almost dropped the condensation-slick bottle. The whole *point* of this was not to think — about his feelings, about Colt...

"You don't... Look, you don't fuckin' know me."

"'Course I don't. Got no idea what I'm talkin' about." Carver returned to the couch and sat with his legs spread wide. He leaned against the sofa, arms draped along the cushions like he couldn't be bothered. He tipped the neck of his bottle to where Everett stood frozen. "Yours was darker, wasn't he? Haven't liked me so much since I took off my hat."

"That isn't—"

"It's not your fault," Carver interrupted. "Hell, I started it. Got what was comin' to me, chasing the lost ones." He shook his head, voice low in his chest. "Fuck if I don't learn."

Everett felt like he'd stumbled onstage without a script, but Carver's guesses were hitting too true a spot. "Screw you, man."

"Fine. Yell if you need to, but I'm not your goddamn Band-Aid."

There was plenty he could say in self-defense, but it all felt like too much for some one-night stand to handle. "I didn't..." he heard himself stammer. "It's just, Col was..." He scrubbed a hand down his face. This was useless. "Fuck me." He sighed. "Never mind."

Carver stared at the blank television and pulled hard from his beer. He asked like he knew the answer, "You need a place to crash?"

"Hell no. I need to, uh...need to be gettin' back."

"I'll take you over," Carver offered. He didn't stand up.

Everett knew this line, at least. "No need. Ain't far. I saw the way."

He pulled his shirt across his shoulders, looking a final time before giving his bolo up for lost. He stopped at the door and rubbed the back of his neck. He hated that he was stuck being Carver's bad night, that Carver had wound up as his nicotine patch at all, but...it just wasn't right. Wasn't the same.

They both knew it was a lie when Everett said, "I'll see ya."

He wasn't halfway down the porch steps when the door locked fast behind him.

* * * *

Mason, Louisiana
Summer of 2019

The rest was harder to tell.

Everett didn't like to think about those years apart. Not now that he finally had all he'd ever wanted. But the ache in his chest didn't remember the date — that it was no longer a lonely morning in 2016, that he didn't have years of penance to pay before fate would force them together. His throat constricted as he remembered the desperation, how it had driven him from Carver's house and straight to the station. He remembered the burn of the whiskey while he searched up Colt's business for all the wrong reasons — and freezing when the right ones were all he wanted to say. Because after two years of silence, Colt had answered his late-night call, and it had been all Everett could do to keep his breathing steady.

"...Ev, is that — "

Before he'd thought to do it, he'd been staring at the phone in its cradle. In the morning, there was a hole in the company wall to explain to Stapes, but bloody knuckles in the name of Colt Harkan weren't a surprise by then. Even now, sitting in the garage of their shared home, the ache was palpable. Like a clenched fist shaking in his chest.

Everett swiped his eyes with the back of his hand. "See?" he forced out, trying to make light. "Fuckin' hilarious, I am. Always good for a laugh."

Colt was across the garage before he took another breath. He hauled him into an embrace. "Don't, Ev. Just don't."

They swayed together in the heat and didn't worry over the sweat. Everett toyed with the loops around Colt's belt and focused on controlling his breathing. Colt traced a hand soothingly down his spine. In time, he asked in his ear, "I ever tell you how you callin' helped the case?"

He shook his head against Colt's shoulder, but didn't otherwise move. Familiar lips pressed a kiss to his temple. "I kept expecting you to stop, but…you just kept calling. So I got a better phone. One with a proper machine."

"Fancy."

Colt laughed lightly, like he'd expected the interruption. "Not long after, I got a message from someone who wanted to hire me. They put me on the trail of those burner phones." Colt pressed his nose into his hair and breathed. "We never would've solved it if I'd missed that message. If you — if you hadn't called when you did…"

He felt less silly about his own damp face when he saw Colt's glassy eyes above him. "You weren't even trying," the dark-haired detective choked out. "And you were leading me through the dark. To solve the case. To bring me back to you."

And really, it was when Colt said things like that Everett knew he was different — that *they* were different this time. So he didn't stop a single word from rushing past his lips when he said, "Babe, you better shut up and kiss me right now, 'cause —"

As usual, Colt was two steps ahead of him.

Colt claimed his mouth like it was his God-given right, and wasn't it amazing how this was familiar now, that *this* was really his normal — how the only lips he ever wanted on his again were perpetually rough, but full and ever-warm. He sighed at the taste of smoke and watermelon, and that deeper bit of earth that clung to everything Colt did. The heat of their kiss grew until it rivaled the climbing thermometer, and the metallic *clink* of Colt's belt prying free was about the best sound he'd ever heard.

Everett sighed as he pressed his hips against his partner's. Colt really was a genius. This was exactly what they needed. He reached inside Colt's jeans to get a hand on him, stroking with the firmness he knew the man preferred. "We ain't really goin' to the office later, right?"

"Hell no."

Everett spared a thought for their part-time receptionist, who'd be turning away walk-ins, after all. "We gotta stop lyin' to Martha."

"Like she didn't already know."

He laughed into the kiss and Colt drank the giddiness from his lips, turning it to a needy groan he only just held back. Colt palmed him through the thin fabric of his shorts. "We may not go in tomorrow either. Not now I've got competition."

"Got no such thing and you know it," he shot back, barely tracking the conversation as Colt kissed down his neck. He paused to lick over his pulse and Everett did his best not to shiver. His breath hitched in his throat but he forced out all he was feeling, aware by now how badly Colt wanted to hear it. "The whole reason I went to Carver's was 'cause I was so fucked up over you. Missed you so much it ached."

"*Fuck*, Ev."

And yeah, maybe a confession like that shouldn't do as much for Colt as it clearly did, but a love like theirs was always going to be a bit twisted. Wasn't much to be done about that. Colt kissed him again and brushed a thumb along his cheek. He fumbled for the doorknob at Everett's back with his other hand. "Guess I ought to thank him. If it weren't for Carv, we never would've —"

He cut Colt off with a kiss. How the man was still focused on *talking* was truly beyond him. "Maybe you ought to finish that other idea you were havin' there."

Colt shot him a look, then nodded at the open garage door. Everett shrugged and threw his hand backward, hitting the button beside his head. The sound of grating metal over a track filled the garage. He smirked at Colt's surprise. "Well, go on then."

"Really?" Colt teased as he stroked. "Can't wait thirty seconds for me to get you in the house?"

Everett pushed Colt's jeans over the curve of his ass, sliding the pants to the floor in time with the closing door. "Nah. Always best to go with the first thought."

Chapter Two

Daniel
Mason, Louisiana
Late August 2019

He read the sign again—Harkan & Kane Investigations. He pushed rounded lenses up his nose and shuffled his travel papers. He was meeting his new landlady…at a private investigation office?

He found the right bit of correspondence and reread it. Martha said he should take a cab from Edwards Regional Airport and meet her at work for the keys. The address was right, so this had to be the place. Though it certainly wasn't what he'd expected.

By the time Daniel Henning had fumbled his way out of the car, rearranging confirmations and ticket stubs from his journey stateside, the cab driver was standing impatiently beside his luggage. Daniel shouldered his duffel from the backseat himself, releasing a deluge of dirt and sand. Embarrassed, he rummaged through too many pockets for the cash he was looking for. Except when he unfolded the crush of paper, the money was all the wrong color.

Right. American bills are on the left.

He corrected his mistake and tipped the disgruntled driver. He rolled his luggage to the door, where a small blue sign at eye level read "Open." He pushed inside with his shoulder and tugged his bags in after.

So close. He was *so close* to done with this leg of travel. All Daniel needed were the keys to his rental and the car he was borrowing for his three weeks in town. Then he could finally take a shower. Maybe do something about his hair. It had grown impressively long in the two months he'd spent overseas.

Near the office door sat a woman with silver hair and kind eyes. She peeked out from behind an old computer monitor. Beside a coffee machine in back stood a blond man in a jacket, tie and jeans.

Daniel addressed the woman at the desk. "Martha Bennett?"

Her smile was welcoming, crinkling the corners of her lips. "You must be Professor Henning."

"Please. Call me Daniel."

The blond man turned from his mug to look at him—and spilled half his coffee in surprise. "Jesus, Martha. I thought you said some professor was stoppin' by. Not Daniel fuckin' Boone."

Like I've never heard that before…

"Everett Kane," Martha reprimanded. "Don't be tellin' me that's how you're gonna greet my new houseguest."

The blond's face reddened as he set his coffee down. He grabbed a handful of napkins and dabbed at his shirtfront. "I'm sorry, Martha's right. I shouldn't have—just startled me, is all."

"It's fine," Daniel said automatically, apologetically. Then, before he could stop himself, "I mean it's not fine, but I don't really know you so..." He let the sentence taper off. "This is awkward."

"These those people skills you're famous for?" a new voice asked from deeper in the office.

Another man turned the corner, dressed similarly to the blond. He had dark hair, tan skin and a deeper voice—and while his tone stayed even-keel, his brown eyes looked amused. "Thought that was the deal," he said to Everett. "You talk to folks. I do the rest."

"Yeah. Because *that's* how this has always worked."

The two men stood rather close, clearly accustomed to being in each other's space. The dark-haired one pushed a wad of napkins into Everett's jacket, like there was nothing strange about the gesture. Daniel remembered a line from one of Martha's emails.

You can meet me at the office, but don't worry yourself. They're sweet boys who work with all types.

Apparently, "all types" didn't include someone with his amount of facial hair. Or head hair. Or maybe it was the khaki vest with its many oversized pockets. More than a few passengers during his travel had asked if he was military. He knew it was rude, but it was hard not to laugh. Nothing could be further from the truth.

Still, it was nice to know that, even this far from a college campus, maybe things really were changing. Two men in a relationship, running their own investigation firm? In Louisiana? And they stayed in business? Daniel wouldn't have thought it possible.

He realized he was staring and returned his attention to Martha. "I'm sorry. Were there keys I might be able to…"

"Of course. You'll want to get in and settled. Shower the airport off you."

"Oh, this is more than airport. I'll be finding dig dirt for weeks."

"What brings you to town?" Everett asked him, like he was determined to prove he could, in fact, handle small talk.

"I'm giving a lecture series at Fairview College," Daniel answered. "I'm borrowing one of Martha's rentals for a few weeks."

"And the car." Martha placed another key in his open hand. "As promised."

"Right." Daniel pursed his lips in apology. "About the car?"

"She's old, but she made the drive fine this morning."

"It's not that."

Martha's brow furrowed. "You don't drive?"

"No, I do. It's directions that are more the problem."

"I can get you the address—"

Daniel held his brick of a phone up for inspection. He'd found this an easier solution than explaining to *everyone* that he didn't have GPS. He pocketed the device and adjusted his glasses. "So unless you've got an actual map, I really don't know where I'm going."

"Jesus, he's worse than you," Everett told his partner. "But with twice your old hair."

The dark-haired man knocked into Everett's shoulder, intentionally spilling the rest of the coffee in his mug. Everett sputtered and waved a hand at his wet-again shirtfront. "Really, Colt?"

"Seems like." The man moved to stand behind Martha, flipping through notes in what looked like a sketchbook. "How were you plannin' on getting home?"

"It's not so far," Martha said, copying down directions from her computer monitor. "I'll call a cab."

"We'll take you."

"You boys don't need to worry. I'm the opposite direction—"

The dark-haired man placed a gentle hand on her shoulder. "We'll take you," he repeated.

Martha set her palm over top and patted twice in thanks.

"Well...that's good," Daniel offered, feeling out of place. "I'll just go?" He gestured over his shoulder to the parking lot.

"Here." Martha handed over a page of handwritten directions. "It's an easy drive if you're paying attention. And just call if you get lost."

"Nice to meet you, Professor." Everett waved.

"Sure," Daniel replied, aware how short he sounded. He was too tired to pretend at niceties. "Same here, I guess."

He could tell his manners were rusty by the room's reactions. Everett flushed an even brighter red. Colt smirked, like watching his partner try too hard was a common pastime. Martha looked disappointed in all of them—and though he'd known her for all of five minutes, it still had a surprising effect.

He shook his head and decided Mason was a strange little town. He could only hope that Fairview would make more sense.

* * * *

The first thirty minutes went easily enough. He only got lost twice, which for him was pretty good. But as always, that third time was the charm and near the end of Martha's directions, he missed the turn for Fairview. He tried to backtrack, though all he accomplished was driving in circles for twenty minutes. In theory, that shouldn't have been a problem, but Daniel was starting to think Martha's definition of *"making the trip just fine"* was different from his. Granted, he didn't know much about cars, but that much smoke couldn't be normal.

He pulled onto the shoulder of the rural highway and opened the hood. Nothing was on fire, but if the temp outside was below one hundred degrees, Daniel would eat his hat. And the humidity? How did anyone deal with this? He'd handled summer in Qarah for eight weeks without issue, but ten minutes of Louisiana were already doing him in. He dialed the only number he had and hoped Martha was still at the office.

"Hello?"

"Hi, again."

"Professor Henning?"

"Daniel. And yes." He breathed out slowly. "How attached are you to this car, exactly?"

"What happened? Are you all right?"

"Yes and no," he hedged. "I'm fine and the car is in one piece, but it seems to be smoking. That's not good, right?"

Martha laughed. "I'm sorry. Give me a moment." He heard the muffled cadence of a conversation, then she returned. "The boys are gonna call you a tow. You got any clue where you are?"

"The last road sign I remember was for Henley, but it was a while back."

"That's nowhere near the directions I gave you."

"I got turned around." Daniel took in his surroundings and winced. "A lot."

"It's all right. Help's coming, dear. You hold tight now."

Daniel opened the trunk and fished out his canteen. He hadn't expected to need it now he no longer lived on a dig site, but he was grateful for the few swallows of water that remained. He wiped his mouth and dabbed his forehead with a sand-colored bandana. He tied it over his head to get some shade without the heat of a hat. He couldn't fathom staying in the car right now. At least being outside provided the illusion of a breeze.

Fifteen minutes later, he'd sweated through his long-sleeved T-shirt and tied his thin jacket around his waist. His thick, lace-up boots were a practical choice, but "breathable" wasn't a word he'd use to describe them. Add to that the sweat caught in the extra five pounds of hair he was toting around, and by the time Daniel spotted the red truck in the distance, his mood was well and truly sour.

The muddy vehicle stopped behind his sedan and the driver jumped down from the cab. He wasn't dressed like any mechanic Daniel had ever seen. His straw cowboy hat seemed par for the course, but not so much his dark button-up, even rolled at the sleeves — and those jeans were too close and too clean to work in.

It would be just like today if Daniel got stuck being someone's first call. He'd heard the old phrase about "dressing for the job you want," but this guy was taking it way too literally. Like he'd heard Daniel's thoughts about his wardrobe, the man opened the buttons down his chest and tossed his dark shirt over a sunburned shoulder. His thin undershirt looked no better than

Daniel's, sweat-damp and more than a little see-through.

The mechanic looked under the hood and leaned his weight into his back leg. "What's wrong with it?"

"Couldn't tell you if I tried," Daniel admitted. "It was smoking, so I pulled over."

"Figured that out yourself, did you?"

"Well, as *fun* as it sounded to meet my maker in a car fire in the middle of nowhere, I thought I'd pass."

The mechanic eyed him, then returned his gaze to the engine. "You're a lot."

Daniel sighed, trying to calm himself. This guy was his only way out of the heat. He could play nice for a few more minutes. "You're not really catching me at my best, okay? At least I knew enough to call a professional." He closed his eyes and rubbed his brow with thumb and forefinger. "I *did* call a professional, right?"

The mechanic slammed the hood shut. "The call I got was about a car that needed towing. Didn't say nothin' about a Sasquatch with a smart mouth."

"So professional's out the window, then. That's great."

The man grumbled as he walked back to his truck. Daniel didn't catch it all, but thought he heard, "Gonna be late to work because of this." He watched the other man pull something from the cab of his truck, then stick a toothpick between his teeth. There was some judgment in his tone when he asked, "What were you doin' this far from anything?"

Daniel sighed and leaned his hands on his hips. "I got lost, okay? And what's this if not work for you?"

"That's a bigger question than we've got time for." The mechanic tossed a plastic water bottle at his chest, then made quick work of hitching up the car. He was briefly interrupted by an alarm blaring in his pocket. He flipped the toothpick over in his mouth and cursed when he checked the time on his phone.

"C'mon, I got places to be. Up and at 'em, genius."

"Professor, actually." The correction came as natural as breathing. He opened the passenger door and couldn't help but add, "Well, technically also genius, but that doesn't seem especially relevant. At the moment."

The mechanic struggled with the ignition, cranking his wrist twice. On the third try, the truck sputtered to a start. He rolled the toothpick between his back teeth. "Must be nice not to have to work two jobs."

He laughed once, humorlessly. "You'd be surprised. Adjuncts don't get the fancy salaries. I bet you make more than me with this truck."

Daniel pointed the air vents at himself, dabbing his heated face with his soggy bandana.

Beside him, the mechanic huffed and shook his head. Sweat-damp hair stuck to his neck, the same burnished gold as his straw cowboy hat. He hadn't said much, but Daniel could tell the guy was frustrated with him. He recognized the expression from his students, colleagues and co-authors—and every local guide that'd ever tried to give him directions.

The mechanic hooked a wrist over the wheel and cut off his next attempt at pleasantries. "Look, I'm gonna stop talkin' now. I'd appreciate if you did the same."

The frankness of the statement caught him off guard. "And you say *I'm* a lot."

"I'm serious. Can you just—" The mechanic mimed a zipping motion in front of his mouth. He turned up the radio. "For like, two minutes. Can you do that?"

"That's pretty presumptuous—"

"*Hey.*" He made the zipping motion again, dirt-brown eyes staring straight through him. Daniel pushed his head into the seat and decided to ignore the rusting roof. He swallowed his comments on the state of the vehicle and didn't even ask if they should call another truck to tow this one. All things considered, he thought he was doing well.

Ten minutes down the road, they turned at the sign he'd missed for Fairview. Not long after, the mechanic parked beside an old cement building with large glass windows. If a person didn't know what they were looking for, they might never know it was an operating business. There was no sign anywhere, no lights on inside. The only thing in the lot was a motorcycle.

Hopefully, that meant this guy could fix the car quickly. He was only in town for the three weeks of his series, then he'd be back on a plane to do it all again elsewhere. The less time he had to spend carless on a college campus, the better. He'd done those grocery trips before—squeezed on a bus with a bunch of undergrads, young and privileged enough to think it all a "novel experience."

Daniel broke the silence as they entered the shop together. "So...how long do you think this will take?"

"Dunno. Can't look now." Carver tossed his keys at the front desk. "I told you. I got places to be."

God, was he *ever* going to get out of his travel clothes? "Then how the actual hell am I supposed to get to my rental?"

The mechanic huffed a laugh. "That just ain't my problem, man."

Daniel took a deep breath and tried to wrangle his temper. He couldn't remember the last time he'd gotten off to such a bad start with someone. "I'm asking if there's a taxi service I could call."

"Not many of those this far away from the airport." The mechanic rebuttoned his dark shirt over his chest. "Most of that's over in Mason. And before you ask, there's no ride shares around. Even with the college nearby. Your apps won't do any good here."

Daniel held up his low-tech phone for inspection. "I wouldn't know what to do with them." He braced a hand on the edge of the desk and tried to think. His options were dwindling fast. "Look, uh—" Daniel paused, only now realizing he'd never asked the mechanic's name. He winced. That...wasn't great. Talking to people outside academia had always been challenging, but even for him, this was bad.

The mechanic piped up from behind the intake desk. "Call me Carver."

"Right. Look, Carver, we've clearly gotten off on the wrong foot here. Maybe we just start over." The man stayed silent, so he kept on talking. "I'm Daniel Henning, and believe it or not, I'm not usually such—"

"A pretentious asshole?"

He could tell the mechanic was waiting for him to rise to that. He opted to ignore it as he worked up to the question they were both knew was coming. "I'm at the end of eighteen hours of travel. I have never needed a shower so badly *in my life.* Is there any way you could drive me to campus? I'll pay you."

It seemed like Carver wanted to roll his eyes, but he crossed his arms and shrugged. Then he nodded at the empty desk. Daniel plucked the thinning fold of cash from his left pocket. He put a twenty on the desktop. Then another. And another. And—

Carver swiped the cash and grabbed the keys to his truck again. "Where you goin'?"

Daniel handed him the directions Martha had written. Carver raised an eyebrow at the address, but said nothing. "You ain't far and it's on my way." He sighed. "Guess today's your lucky day."

Yeah, this is luck. I just paid eighty bucks for a ride with someone who hates me.

The drive to his small rental house was short and silent. Carver told him to come by the shop after the weekend for updates, and no sooner had Daniel grabbed his luggage, than the mechanic was out of his narrow driveway and speeding around the corner.

He took a deep breath of relief when he stepped inside — Martha had turned on the A/C in anticipation of his arrival. He dumped his suitcase in the bedroom and immediately started the shower. By choice, he spent his life immersed in ruins of the past. He didn't miss much about the present when he was gone from it.

But today? Good water pressure made the list.

One very long shower later, Daniel unpacked his conference clothes into unfamiliar drawers. He caught a glimpse of himself in the mirror on top of the dresser and shook out his overlong hair. He looked like a muddy sheepdog. He'd trusted himself enough to handle the beard, but now his clean-shaven face looked like a stranger's. Like it belonged to someone else. Or a younger version of himself...

"You're hilarious with that thing," Aminah chided.

Daniel flipped the flimsy pages of the instruction manual. He didn't usually care for gadgets, but considering how many conferences they had on their schedule, the refurbished

Garmin made too much sense. "With all the travel we're doing this summer? You'll be eating those words within the week."

"We don't need a GPS," Aminah said, almost sing-song. Daniel eyed her over the frames of his glasses and she reconsidered. "Okay, you need a GPS. Desperately. But that's what you've got me for, right?"

"Until we split for the European conferences. Leaving me alone in – "

"Berlin. One of your favorite cities where you absolutely speak the language. You'll be alone for three days, most of it at a Hilton. You can handle it." She paused beside the bed where Daniel sat reading. She pushed gentle fingers through his long brown hair, then sat beside him.

She rested her head against his shoulder and he leaned down to meet her. Her black hair felt silky against his cheek. The lamp on the nightstand highlighted the gold in her russet-brown skin.

There was definitely something he'd planned to say before he looked at her. But even after so long together, just the sight of her was enough to distract him. "Besides," Aminah continued, "this way, we talk to twice the audience. Address the problem from multiple sides."

"I know." Their eyes met and Daniel smiled. "You're right. It's important."

Aminah beamed. She loved to travel more than anyone he'd ever met. It was hard not to be excited when she was clearly ready for adventure. "There's this hike my advisor recommended to see the Pico del Cielo. It's supposed to have amazing views."

"You should definitely do that before I get to Malaga."

"I know better than to ask you to hike with me." She plucked the Garmin from his hands and lay back on the mattress. "Maybe I should take this."

"I bought it for me."

"I'll bet any amount of money you'll break it within the week."

"So little faith in me, love?"

She gave him a look that had them both grinning. "The only thing you're worse at than directions is technology. Tell me I'm wrong."

He couldn't, so Daniel pulled off his shirt and tossed it at the open drawer. Aminah's clothes were neatly placed inside, and feeling guilty for his mess, he stood and folded his too. He grumbled as he did so, mostly to amuse her. "This purchase changes nothing. I still say the only technology worth a damn is from years with 'BCE' at the end."

Aminah laughed, musical as ever. "You have to live in the present sometimes, Daniel…"

Alone in his rental, he dragged his fingers across folded clothes he rarely wore. There were dress shirts and sweaters. A few pairs of non-cargo pants. Maybe half of each drawer was full by the time he'd emptied his suitcase. Standing in front of the mirror, he stared at his reflection and rubbed his freshly shaven chin. He'd considered keeping some of the length on top, but…

He closed his eyes. He could almost feel the touch of Aminah's hand, combing stray hairs behind his ear.

"My sweet Daniel…"

No. The hair definitely had to go.

He shelved his grief and pulled into his sleep clothes. He'd do his best with the clippers tomorrow and find a barber before orientation.

Chapter Three

Carver
Fairview, Louisiana

"Hot damn, but they got the pretty ones out tonight, huh?"

Jeanie winked his way as she dried a pint glass. She tossed the rag over her shoulder and nodded at the door. "Incoming."

Carver looked at her with suspicion, but he knew better than to bicker. Jeanie might play for the other team, but she was rarely wrong about this.

He spotted the group at the corner table and took stock. Professional shirts and dresses. Light knit sweaters and varied shades of khaki. They were lucky to find a table so big. The place was pretty packed for a Monday. Then he did some mental math and remembered the date. The awful traffic he'd sat in all day began to make sense.

He asked Jeanie, "New semester started?"

"Surely did. For the next few months, our scenery's 'bout to get a lot better." Jeanie popped the tops off two bottles. "Gonna have all kinds around. Even if half of them are straight."

"Shame."

It wasn't until the corner group settled that any of the "Ivy Leaguers," as Jeanie called them, caught his attention. When the last man slid into the end of the booth, Jeanie nudged his shoulder, but Carver was already watching. The man was gorgeous. Couldn't call him anything else. He smiled at the woman sitting beside him—a pleasantry, but his blue eyes shone all the same. Almost like he was apologizing in advance. No one at the table seemed to mind.

This guy had "book smarts" written all over him. His brown hair was short for style, not regulation. His warm beige skin was smattered with freckles, most heavily on the backs of his arms, and round-framed glasses covered too much of his face. He adjusted them often out of nervous habit, like he was having a good time and that was the strange part. Carver wondered how long it would take for the rest of the bar to notice him—because his short-sleeved, thin-striped button-down *had* to be two sizes too small.

The stiff fabric strained across his front. He wasn't broad chested, but had the lean sort of muscle built by repetitive movement. A runner, maybe. The sleeves fit close around his biceps and drew Carver's attention lower. Since the man was sitting on the end, he could clearly see the slacks riding tight across his thighs.

Jeanie waggled her eyebrows in that *"What'd I yell ya?"* sort of way and continued filling their order. "Gonna help me with these, Romeo?"

"You know"—Carver sighed—"I've lost track of how many times I've told you to not to call me that."

"If you'd stop takin' home half the bar every night, I wouldn't have to."

"Like you're any better."

"Take it up with the owner. Oh wait, that's right." She pointed at herself in mock surprise, mouthing the words, *"That's me."* She flipped him the double bird and grinned. Multicolored neon reflected in her silver rings. As though she'd made her point, Jeanie stood up straight and hefted her tray on her shoulder. Carver shook his head and followed in her self-important wake.

Once at the table, he picked up snatches of the group's conversation. Sure enough, Jeanie had them pegged. Young professors and TAs, if Carver had to guess. He didn't recognize anyone enough to remember a name, but there were benefits to living in the revolving door of Fairview. There was always something new showing up in his own backyard.

He helped Jeanie shuffle drinks around and handed a beer to Mr. Tight Shirt. As he did so, he looked up at the man from under the brim of his hat. A strange expression passed over his face. "Uhm, thank you."

Carver let his eyes drop low and flick up again. He licked his lips. "Any time."

The man's lack of accent meant he wasn't local, but besides that, Carver couldn't place him. He felt the man staring at him as he picked up some empties. Maybe the prof had a thing for cowboys. Plenty did. He could work that angle.

He left the table first, but Jeanie caught up fast. She reached up to swat the back of his neck, but he managed to dodge her follow-up coming for his ear. She shook her head. "Starting early tonight, aren't you?"

"Why'd you point him out, then?" She rolled her eyes and rounded the bar, but Carver called after her. "Don't play innocent with me. I know you too well for that."

Another middle finger pointed his way, but any more razzing would have to wait. For the first time in months, there were lines at the bar. It was time to work.

As the night wore on, Carver didn't have time to help with tables. He left those to the other servers and stayed in his preferred territory behind the bar. The place had a different energy this time of year. Jeanie's was about the only place that felt like home, but now it was like company was over. Like he had to impress or be on his best behavior. Reminded him of those first days at a new foster house — how a strained formality settled over everything, making it hard to get comfortable.

He'd finally cleared the bar when Jeanie returned and stood beside him. She took a long drink from her water bottle and smiled. "Didn't miss the noise, but I did miss the money."

"Welcome to the on-season," he said. "Let's hope they come back for more."

Jeanie leaned against the wall and nodded to their left. "Speaking of which, your secret admirer's over there without a drink."

"I noticed."

"You gonna help him?"

He smirked. ""Eventually. It's better to make 'em wait."

Jeanie snickered, quieting when the short-haired man set his glass on the bar. "Uhm, excuse me? Could I get another?"

He winked at Jeanie as he turned away. He ignored her mocking groan and pressed his palms to the wood, leaning forward with a smile. "Another what?"

The question tripped the stranger, like he hadn't thought that far ahead. "I...don't know, actually. I didn't order this one. What've you got?"

"I thought you looked new here." Carver waved at the list of beers on the wall while the good-looking stranger weighed his options. To his practiced eye, the professor seemed ripe for a good time. It was a little early, but no sense in not shooting his shot.

"You might as well wait to order," he said.

"Wait for what?"

"Lookin' the way you do? Here? Won't be long before someone's sending you drinks."

The man adjusted his glasses and looked down — pleased, if embarrassed by the compliment. He placed his arm on the bar. "How exactly am I looking?"

"Don't act like you don't know."

The stranger smiled again, but it was sharper than the one he'd caught at the table. Or maybe it just felt different now the man's focus was solely on him, eyes too blue to believe — two bits of sky snatched from a sunny day. He let his eyes trail over the man's chest and arms. The guy noticed that he was staring, but Carver wasn't trying to be subtle. "You can't tell me you didn't wear a shirt that tight on purpose. Which of your friends over there are you tryin' to impress?"

The stranger ran a hand through his hair, pushing it nowhere. The blush on his cheeks deepened. "It's just an old shirt."

"You must work out, then. Doesn't look old."

"I don't get out much." He edged closer still, like he didn't want to be overheard. "Look, what are you trying to do here?"

It was a stark shift in tone from the banter Carver expected. He slid the empty glass away and shifted his weight into his hip. "Right now, I'm tryin' to figure out what you'd like to drink. Because that guy over there?" He pointed a few stools down. "Asked me to send you something."

Carver's answer didn't seem to satisfy the professor. He wasn't offended by the idea, but he clearly wasn't interested. Typical. These college types were all the same. They were happy to go to Jeanie's like they had something to prove, but at the end of the day they only cared what their straight-laced families wanted.

"Look," he said, ready to lay it out for him. "You come to a gay bar? Can't expect to be catered to, man." He crossed his arms over his chest. "I won't bother you with any more drinks from admirers, but you'd cut your work in half if you put on a fuckin' jacket. Just sayin'."

He opened a cheap domestic and set the bottle down, waving for the stranger to take it away. Mr. Tight Shirt seemed to find his backhanded compliment and narrowed his eyes. "Thank you? I think?" He took the beer, looked at his friends, then quickly back to Carver. "I'll see you...later?"

"Whatever," he grumbled, rinsing a glass. "I'll be here all night."

Around then, Carver was glad for the crowd. It gave him something to focus on instead of licking his wounds. Not that he had them. Some half-baked rejection wasn't about to sour his mood. He'd find someone willing to get caught in his snare eventually. Wasn't hard to do at Jeanie's.

Still, Carver caught himself glancing at the corner table all night—and more than once, the stranger was staring back. He did put on a jacket somewhere near his third round, but he didn't return to the bar. Probably for the best. Carver never meshed well with the bookish crowd, even back when Derek's friends "from his program" would come around. He'd do his best to be social, but always felt on the outside, looking in. And it didn't help that they were all his age, working on second and third degrees while Carver trudged his way through a bachelor's, pulling doubles at Jeanie's to make ends meet, thinking every day about the dream he'd left to do so.

He should've noticed the way Derek had clammed up when his friends were around. How they had rarely gone out in public, and when they had, it had always been a mixed group. How eventually, Derek's friends had stopped coming by altogether. How it had gotten even worse when Derek's father had come to visit...

To be honest, it was a lot like how he was feeling now. Like he wasn't even a person. Just a body, taking up space.

He didn't notice when it happened, but the next time he looked, the corner table was empty. He sighed and wished his head wasn't so stuck in the past today. Between his own ruminations and this distracting stranger, he hardly remembered any other customers. That'd probably be reflected in his tips.

He dug the metal scoop into the ice bucket harder than necessary. Jeanie took notice of his mood as she mixed a round of shots. "Someone turn you down for a change?"

"Nah. He's straight."

"You sure?"

"Don't care to find out. I've spent my time chasin' what would rather not be found."

Jeanie tried not to laugh, clearly of a different opinion. "He got under your skin fast, sugar."

"Save your *sugars* for someone who'll enjoy it." He pointed out a woman in a short sundress who'd been eyeing his friend all night. "Over there, three o'clock. Got *experimental phase* written all over her."

He took the shaker from Jeanie's hand and filled the shot glasses she'd laid in a line. She pushed hasty fingers through her straight black hair, combing it so the shaved side of her head was visible. She unfastened her own black button-up until the band of her sports bra was visible, exposing tawny skin darkened to amber by summer sun. "Just my type. How do I look?"

"You're terrible."

"You're worse."

He tipped his hat. "And proud of it."

It was a common exchange of theirs, comforting in its own right. He watched Jeanie flirt and tried not to be bitter. At least one of them had had some luck tonight.

Carver stayed behind the bar and started scouting again. There was still an hour until close. Tonight didn't have to be a loss. He made eye contact with another guy at the bar and a smile spread across his face. He had brown eyes and dark curly hair. The red and yellow neon danced across his light brown skin. Looked to be a local—sort of like the cute Creole waiter they'd had a couple months back.

Yeah. Something familiar sounded nice.

Carver snagged two beers and waved down the other bartender. He needed this more than a couple hours' cash. Besides, Simone was used to closing alone. He set a full bottle beside the man's empty and asked, "You waitin' for someone?"

"Not anymore."

Finally. Somebody out for the same reason he was.

He leaned close and took the empty barstool at his right. The man shifted in his seat and returned his heated gaze, saving them paragraphs in the process.

Carver adjusted his hat. Yeah. He could play this game tonight.

* * * *

The small bell on the shop door was always loudest in the mornings. Carver massaged his forehead and gulped down more coffee. A late night with little food had left him more hungover than usual. He flipped a page in a magazine he'd memorized and looked up — to find none other than the cute professor from the bar.

Carver tried not to let his surprise show, but his shoulders hunched all the same. He'd hoped the man wasn't as attractive as memory had painted him, but if anything, he looked *better* outside the dim lights of Jeanie's. And he hadn't half the reason this time, wearing a loose gray tee and olive-green shorts.

Carver tugged the brim of his hat lower. Maybe he could get out of this unrecognized. "Can I help you?"

"I take it all back. You're very professional."

"Excuse me?"

The man rummaged in his pocket, then laid down a set of keys and folded, handwritten directions. Carver recognized the address…but could it really be the same guy?

Daniel laughed. "Do you remember me now?"

The first thing he thought was how different Daniel looked with short hair and no beard. The second thing was how in the *hell* he was going to talk his way out of this one. Couldn't seem to catch a break, these days.

"I've got to say," Daniel joked, his tone friendly, "it put some things in perspective. Once I realized you didn't recognize me."

It was probably about time to extract the foot from his mouth, especially since the news on the car wasn't good. "Right. About that..."

"Let's call it a wash, yeah? Neither of us gave a great first impression."

"Which time?"

Daniel shrugged. "Either of them?"

He dug a toothpick from his pocket and propped it in the corner of his mouth. When he looked up, Daniel was offering his hand to shake. He eyed it warily. "You might win by default after Jeanie's. Some would say I owe you an apology for tellin' you off like that."

"Why do I get the sense that's not something you often do?"

He snorted once. "Because it's not."

Daniel smiled at the floor and retracted his hand, placing it back in his pocket. Carver searched for his notes on the sedan to distract himself. Was he supposed to notice the other man's covert glances? He didn't know what to do with the attention — especially since it seemed Daniel liked what he was seeing. Talk about some mixed fucking messages.

Was Jeanie right about him after all?

"Do I get to hear this apology?" Daniel asked, his blue eyes laughing. "Or merely be comforted with the knowledge it exists?"

The prof was doing a better job hitting back what he was serving today. And maybe it was because they weren't nearing heat exhaustion, but he was funnier than Carver remembered. And a lot less annoying. He swallowed hard and tried to pivot the conversation. "Jury's still out on that. Your car, though." He cleared his throat. "That's more open and shut. The engine's blown, but I can probably save it. Though I'm having a hard time finding parts 'cause it's so old."

Daniel rocked on his heels and nodded. "How long do you think it will take?"

"Conservative estimate? Two, maybe three weeks."

"Fan*tastic*," the professor sighed. "I'll have it just in time to drive back to the airport." Daniel kicked the toe of his shoe into the floor in frustration. "Sorry. I'm not here for a long time."

"Or a good time. Apparently."

A laugh caught in Daniel's throat. "You wouldn't be the first to say that." He scratched his neck and sighed. "Right. Well, standing here's not going to change anything. I should call Martha. Thanks for trying."

Carver rolled the toothpick between his teeth. "How long did you say you're in town for?"

"Three weeks. Until the end of my lecture series."

He pulled the pick from his mouth and tapped the dry end on the desk. He met Daniel's gaze from beneath the brim of his hat, already regretting what he was about to offer. "Look, you paid like eighty bucks for a ten-minute drive the other day. And I'm guessing I threw a wrench into your first night out in a while."

Daniel shrugged. "Maybe a little. Why?"

"I'm not sayin' I've got all the time in the world, but there's not much to do if I'm waiting on parts. So if you're needin' a ride someplace"—Carver sighed—"call it a shuttle fee. We'll settle up once the car is fixed."

Daniel looked at him over the rim of his rounded glasses. "Let me get this straight. The guy I practically had to beg for a ride is *volunteering* to be my personal driver?"

Yeah, no. He shouldn't have offered. This was a *bad* idea. "I was. Until you said it like that."

"It's going to cost extra now, isn't it?"

"Was always gonna cost extra. I'm not running a charity here."

Daniel smirked. "I should probably agree before I find a way to triple the price, hmm?"

"That'd be the smart move, yeah. If you're really some genius."

The prof smiled outright at that, amused by their teasing, and it wasn't fair the way that cut through him — how it made him feel like the center of attention. But not in a bad way. More like Daniel was catching up to the offer he'd missed at the bar.

"Well," Daniel said. "Then thank you. I accept." He pocketed the handwritten directions again. "You wouldn't believe how long it took me to walk here."

Carver blinked at him. "Your place is like a mile away."

"You know, it helps when you point it out? Makes this thing I can't change *much* easier to handle."

He caught the sarcasm and let the matter lie, then scanned the shop for his keys. "You need a ride to your rental, then?"

"My office, actually. Haven't managed to make it there yet."

"Shouldn't be hard to find. I'm pretty familiar with campus."

"You are?"

Now why the fuck had he gone and said *that*? His short time at Fairview wasn't anything to write home about. He usually pretended he'd never been to college — mostly because he wished that were true — but something about this professor was bringing up all his ghosts today.

Yeah, I know campus. I'm a thirty-something dropout and my ex might still work there. I'm a real catch.

The last thing this conversation needed was Derek's shadow. Carver waved off the professor's interest, doing his best to backtrack. "You live somewhere long enough, you pick up a few things." He opened the shop door and waved for Daniel to leave. "You go ahead. Need to lock up if I'm gonna be gone."

The short trip to Daniel's office was tolerable, if quiet. He pulled beside the small campus building, then handed his phone to his passenger. "Put your number in. So I know to pick up when you call."

"Right." Daniel handed over his small, dense flip phone in turn. He eyed Carver's used iPhone as he took it, grasping it carefully with both hands.

He was tempted to ask if Daniel was joking, but his inability to navigate the thing made it clear he wasn't. Carver did his best to swallow any amusement. He never would've thought he'd have the professor beat on something. "I haven't seen a flip phone in a decade. At least."

"It still works." Daniel prodded the iPhone's screen with an index finger. "Why would I get a new one if it works?"

Carver raised his hands in mock surrender, then toggled through the T9 to input his name and number. No sooner had he done so than the phone began to ring. Daniel took his cell back quickly and pushed the smartphone into his chest, glad to be rid of it.

"This is Daniel." He propped the phone between his ear and shoulder, dug a notebook from his messenger bag and started to write. Carver occupied himself by scrolling his contacts. His social life earned him plenty of bedpartners, but not as many numbers. It didn't take long to notice Daniel's name wasn't there. He did, however, find a contact for a "Dangstil Heaving" with the numbers "862" listed in the email line.

He chuckled. It was like this guy was from a whole other time, though if Carver had to guess at his age, he didn't look far off thirty in either direction.

The smartphone buzzed lightly in his hand — two texts, both from Everett.

Colt's gonna bring the bikes by in a couple weeks.

You give any thought to my offer?

He hadn't realized he was smiling until it faded. Since Everett had come to visit, he'd gone back and forth on if his past really mattered. He was already sitting on a campus he'd sworn never to set foot on again and at this particular moment, watching Daniel scribble notes with that focused look in his eye, he didn't feel up for any introspection.

He dismissed the notification and sent no response. Only then, as he tuned into the professor's conversation, did Carver notice that Daniel wasn't speaking English. It wasn't a language he recognized, either. There was a different rhythm to Daniel's speech, his voice lower and more melodic. He had no clue as to the content of the conversation, but he couldn't help but listen as Daniel's voice transformed. He hit the consonants lighter, let phrases blur and mingle with the harshness in his throat. It was almost hypnotic, listening to him speak.

After a few minutes of notetaking, Daniel pocketed his phone. Carver cleared his throat and turned his screen toward the passenger seat, showing him the contact for "Dangstil Heaving."

"Any edits you wanna make here? Professor?"

Even embarrassed and red-faced, Daniel was something to look at. His self-deprecating smile and furrowed brow made it easy to join in the laughter. "*Please* delete that. I'll just text you my number."

"Yeah, all right," Carver agreed. "Who were you talkin' to?"

"Pratik. He's a colleague, still on-site in Qahar. We've been studying the integration of ancient *qahats* into modern irrigation as part of our research."

Jesus...

"I'm not gonna pretend I know what any of that means."

"Well, it's actually—"

"Believe me, I'm not asking." Carver drummed his thumbs on the steering wheel. "So, you were speaking..."

"Arabic, mostly."

"You a language professor?"

"I'm an anthropologist. But it helps to speak more than English when your research predates it by a thousand years."

Carver scratched his nose. "Well. Color me impressed."

He regretted the phrasing as soon as he'd said it. He sounded like a goddamn church lady. What *was* it about Daniel that put him so off his game?

He adjusted the rearview mirror, then tugged on the brim of his hat. "Look, you need a ride someplace else? Or can I get on with my day?"

Daniel seemed confused by his shift in tone, but he shut his composition notebook and tucked it under his arm. He adjusted his glasses. "Yeah, no. I got it from here. I guess I'll...call you later? If I need?"

Carver nodded and stared out through the windshield. From the corner of his eye, he watched

Daniel walk toward the building. He got halfway to the door before turning over his shoulder to jog back. "Sorry, I just—"

Daniel's messenger bag sat in the passenger footwell. He gathered it up and handed it through the window.

"Right. Sorry. Thanks again."

Carver didn't watch Daniel go this time. It was more uncomfortable to be on campus again than he'd thought, sitting in this place he'd tried so hard to call home. The few years he'd been gone from it felt surprisingly short.

If he'd stuck to Derek's plan, he'd be graduating this year. And still working too long on top of the studying—scraping by with Cs, trying not embarrass Derek in front of his peers. He didn't even know if his ex had finished his program. Probably, though. Derek was all about "The Plan," which meant he would've finished his doctorate last year. Always so eager to move on to the next big thing.

Carver never could've kept up. He knew that now. So why had he volunteered to help Daniel so fast? When he was obviously cut from the same cloth as his ex?

Because I'm an idiot who thinks with my dick, that's why.

Had he learned nothing from Derek? He'd ignored plenty of red flags because he'd wanted him too badly. Because he'd made the mistake of falling in love. Of thinking it was mutual.

Fuck. That sinking feeling? That terrible lurch in his gut? He'd promised himself that first night on Jeanie's couch—catching feelings for someone so far above him? Never again. And what had seemed a great way to make some cash now felt downright dangerous. If he was oversharing with Daniel on day one, where would he be after three weeks of his teasing and smiles?

He flipped the turn signal and steered back to the shop. When he arrived, a text was waiting for him.

Daniel Henning. Try not to forget next time.

Carver smirked, realized he was doing it and tossed his phone at the passenger seat. He groaned and leaned his neck against the headrest.

Be careful, he told himself. *You don't need this lesson again.*

Chapter Four

Daniel
September

His first week getting settled in Fairview, Daniel saw Carver almost daily. To his credit, the mechanic held up his end of the bargain, arriving with promptness each time Daniel called.

He was doing his best to consolidate trips, but inevitably, there'd be something he forgot at the office and needed at the house, or vice versa. His first lecture was at the end of the week and after months living on a dig site, he had lots of brushing up to do. He was scheduled to talk about his research to different departments — anthropology, architecture and business classes — but one of those audiences was easier than the others.

Aminah had been good with people in ways he never was. She could talk to anyone, from anywhere. And on the rare occasions otherwise, she had never let them get in her head.

There was so much he missed about their life together, but Aminah's spontaneity, her daring spirit — that was the hardest to live without. She could make anything an adventure. It wasn't just grocery shopping — they were planning brunch and a meal with friends. They weren't doing laundry — they were having a heated, academic debate and happened to be folding clothes.

It didn't matter how long it'd been since he'd got that call, since the day that had turned his life into an ellipsis. So much of life now was like walking through a fog. When he wasn't on-site, Daniel was lucky if he remembered to feed himself more than once a day. It was easier to stay distracted, to get caught up in work. It was the only time he felt normal, and there was always another paper to write. Another journal to submit to. He couldn't remember the last time he'd cooked himself a proper dinner — let alone invited anyone to join. When was the last time he'd even thought to ask someone on a date?

And really, that was what had Daniel stumped about this hot-and-cold mechanic who'd been driving him around. At the bar, before he'd realized who he was, Carver had clearly been interested. He couldn't have been more obvious. And it'd felt nice. A bit surprising, but nice. Yet, the more time they spent together, the further Carver retreated into himself. He was always up for a bit of back and forth — usually about one of Daniel's oddities — but the second he answered a work call, Carver was instantly distant.

It probably didn't help that the calls were in different languages — Arabic, Assyrian, German, Greek and Spanish by his count. But what was Daniel supposed to do? Pretend he didn't speak them? If

Carver was curious about what he was saying, he could just ask. But he never did. Probably another mark in the "not interested" column.

As the days went by, Daniel had even less of an idea where they stood. He almost wished he could have a third chance at a first impression, ridiculous as it sounded. Spending this much time with Carver was reminding Daniel of things he'd long forgotten. Every time he looked at the mechanic in his shop clothes, he couldn't help but picture him in different work attire...

The move was too purposeful not to be practiced, but it caught his attention all the same. He couldn't stop thinking about it — the hungry sheen in Carver's dark eyes, how they dropped low to his mouth, then up again. Like he had a few thoughts about the way the night might go.

The rumble of his voice as he offered, "Any time..."

That small peek of tongue as he wet his lips, giving Daniel too many ideas at once...

The man defied explanation. There was something just under the surface with Carver — and the surface wasn't bad either. He never reacted the way Daniel thought, and it left him guessing in a good way. That was something he used to look for across his partnerships — professional, platonic and otherwise.

He spent too much of their drives together wondering how that night at the bar might've gone. So when Carver pulled into his driveway on Wednesday, calling out, "Where to, genius?" like some kind of nickname, Daniel had to remind himself to *cool it*. Just because he worked at a gay bar didn't mean Carver was interested. Maybe he only flirted for tips. And besides, he'd be leaving soon anyway.

He should ignore Carver's sideways glances, forget the casual hook of his wrist over the wheel and the way his arm flexed as he steered. How he shook his head every time Daniel forgot his messenger bag. On Thursday, Carver got out of the truck to bring it to him on the sidewalk. He lifted the strap over his head, encircling him, then slid his finger beneath the thick fabric. He followed the line across Daniel's chest, joking in a low voice, "Gonna make me think you're doing this on purpose."

Daniel had been too focused on the rush of heat to his face to do more than stutter his thanks. He was famously dense about dating, but that *had* to be a pass, right? And he hadn't been leaving his bag intentionally, but if it got Carver to look at him like that again, he might start. He couldn't remember feeling this wrongfooted around someone since...well, since Aminah had disappeared.

Which was exactly why Daniel was making this trip. One last inconvenience to Carver's schedule, then he'd have less of a need to bother him. These "shuttle rides" were getting expensive, costing money and peace of mind.

They had barely a thing in common. He should remember that.

* * * *

At the close of his first week in Fairview, Carver drove them to his office to get a long list of books he needed. They filled a couple boxes and loaded them in the truck bed, then Daniel handed over the address he'd written down earlier. "You have time for one more stop?" He asked.

Carver checked the time. "I got an hour. If it's close."

"It is. Precision Bikes on 4th. Have you heard of it?"

"There's another bike shop on campus?"

"I guess. Martha recommended it."

Carver looked at the address and nodded, but he stayed quiet as they made their way across campus. For his own part, Daniel did his best not to stare. The more familiar he grew with Carver's crooked smile, the more he wondered what it'd be like to kiss it away—how it might feel to press his mouth to those full lips, to toss his ever-present hat aside and get a handful of golden hair.

Daniel tugged at the collar of his T-shirt. Thank goodness Carver was caught in his thoughts. This unexpected resurgence of his libido was testing his patience.

It wasn't like he couldn't say something. He'd dated some in the years after Aminah but nothing seemed to stick, no matter the gender of his dates. Except Carver seemed exactly the type he could learn to be casual with. Hell, he'd offered it up on a platter—if Daniel had been faster on the uptake. This was all normal for Carver. Maybe he could try something different, for once.

Or, he'd make everything awkward and wind up on the outs with the only person he knew in town. The thought gave Daniel pause.

Carver slowed down by the shopfront of bicycles. "This is the place you meant?"

"Obviously. What'd you think I meant?"

All the tension left Carver's shoulders and he visibly relaxed. He draped a wrist over the steering wheel and laughed under his breath. "Nothin'. Thought I'd missed something."

This wasn't the first clue he'd collected about the state of Carver's shop. Sure, he was waiting on parts for Martha's sedan, but he couldn't have that many customers if he was always so available to drive him around. He wondered if now Carver's mood might return to its earlier levity. And sure, he hardly knew him, but Daniel found himself wanting to be the reason why.

He gestured to his khaki shorts and old college T-shirt. "Take a good look. What part of this says I'd be in the market for a motorcycle?"

Carver cracked a smile. "You want me to answer that?"

"You don't have to. It's that obvious." Daniel shouldered his messenger bag and started to unload the books. It'd be hard to balance both boxes on a bike, but he'd managed worse before.

Carver unbuckled his seatbelt and all but leapt from the cab. The man picked up the box he'd set on the pavement and put it back in the truck bed. "Quit that. I'll drive you back."

"That wasn't part of the deal."

Carver scuffed his work boot against the white line of their parking spot. "I don't mind. Besides, now I'm all interested in what sort of bike would be for you."

Daniel snorted and adjusted his glasses. "Whatever's cheap and dependable. And ideally, nice enough that I could sell it when I leave."

Carver's smile widened. "Should get you a basket or something. You'll break your neck tryin' to cart around boxes like these."

"A trailer would be more helpful—"

"And a ribbon. With a big ol' bow."

"What's wrong with ribbon?"

"Nothing." Carver leaned into his personal space and his mouth dried up. He cleared his throat as the mechanic eyed him up and down. "There's a joke I could make about gettin' you all tied up. But I'm not gonna say it." Carver strummed the strap of his messenger bag against his chest and, still smirking, strolled into the bike shop.

Either that was a lucky guess, or this guy is reading me way too well…

"Real mature," he called after him.

"Yessiree," Carver replied, overplaying his accent. "That's me."

It didn't take long to find something that would work for the next two weeks. As the cashier rang everything up, Carver stepped close behind him. It was a small store, but he didn't have to be that close. Which meant he was *choosing* to be that close, intentionally resting a hand on his back. The heat from Carver's body was noticeable even through his light clothing. Daniel swallowed hard and tried to ignore it.

Then Carver's chest brushed against his shoulder blades, sending a tingle down his spine, and he wondered what would happen if he pressed back — if he dared to offer resistance, even for a moment. Instead, he looked down at the counter and saw a pink wicker basket. Behind him, Carver waited, like he expected one of their serious-but-not-actually-serious fights.

"Joke's on you." He doled out an extra twenty to the cashier. "I'll use the thing."

Carver laughed low and the sound reverberated in his chest. Warm breath tickled the back of his neck — the man's mouth was so close, even Daniel could tell he was doing this on purpose. But to what end? Just to get him hot and bothered and leave the store with a wink?

Apparently, yes. Because that was exactly what Carver did.

The bike rattled in the truck bed as they drove away, but there was no hiding the bright pink basket and Daniel felt he'd come out on top, in a way. They were halfway back to his rental when Carver's phone rang.

"Hey, what's goin' on?"

Daniel watched out through the window to give the illusion of privacy. Carver's teasing mood faded the longer he listened.

"When's the appointment?" Carver asked. He listened then slumped in his seat, flipping the hazards as he pulled to the side of the road. "You're killin' me, Jeanie. I actually have someone comin' to the shop this afternoon—all right. Don't worry. I'm on my way."

Carver dropped his phone in the cupholder and reached around to the sliding window, twisting his body as he searched for something in the back. Daniel tried to give him space, but it was a small truck. Then he noticed that Carver's T-shirt had ridden up as he moved, revealing a flash of sun-kissed skin that made his hands clench into fists. It had been *so long* since he'd felt anything like this. Part of him wanted to just reach out and —

"Damn it. The one time I don't have a shirt in the back." Carver faced forward in his seat again. "You mind if we make a quick stop? I can drop you on my way to Jeanie's."

Daniel nodded as Carver swung the truck around. He'd never been to Carver's place before, but they passed Jeanie's on their way, so it had to be close. He didn't have many landmarks in Fairview yet, but the bar was one.

When they arrived, Carver jumped from the truck to a gravel driveway, yanking off his T-shirt as he jogged inside a small house with gray-blue siding. An off-white overhang shaded a concrete porch with a single chair. The garage wasn't attached and, thanks to the open door, he caught sight of a motorcycle. From the splatters of mud, it seemed to get more use than the truck.

Not two minutes later, Carver was shoving out of the door again. He had the brim of his hat clamped between his teeth while he tugged on an undershirt, trying to walk and change at the same time. But what really struck Daniel was how different the man looked without his straw hat. His blond hair, no longer restrained, fell to his chin, straight and thick. Without that shadowed brim, it was easier to see the richness of his eyes—a warm brown, like cherrywood. Sort of softened the whole of his face.

And yes, he'd assumed Carver was well put together from the glimpses he'd gotten this week, but to have it confirmed so visibly left Daniel at a rare loss for words.

His body, though? His body had *plenty* of thoughts to share.

Daniel shifted in his seat, trying his best to hide how much this display was doing for him. He yanked his messenger bag into his lap as Carver opened the driver's side door. He'd seemed in a hurry before, but now Carver stood still, looking him right in the eye.

"You still want me to drive you back?" he asked.

No, I want you to take that shirt off again.

With the way Carver's eyes darkened, Daniel worried he'd said the thought aloud. But he hadn't, and Carver was still looking at him. He dropped his eyes to his mouth, then back up. Just like that pass at the bar.

Maybe he *could* get another redo.

"You know," Daniel said, not moving his bag off his lap, "I think I could use a drink."

* * * *

Carver

"You. Are. A life-saver."

"Go on," he encouraged, pushing the front door open. "I won't stop you."

"My hero. The best bartender of all. A literal angel on Earth." Carver rolled his eyes as Jeanie popped her dark head up from behind the bar. He walked to stand beside her and pushed her shoulder, teasing. Then he pulled her in for a side hug she eventually returned.

"Seriously, Carv. Thanks."

"Yeah, I got you." He kissed the shaved side of her head. "You know that."

Daniel lingered in the doorway, adjusting the strap of his bag. The place was practically empty—maybe one or two tables, but that was normal for a weekday at three o'clock. Even during the on-season. Carver moved behind the register to clock in and waved Daniel over, motioning for him to sit.

"Now I feel bad." Jeanie leaned close, though she didn't bother whispering. "Didn't realize I was interrupting something."

His head shot up and over to where Daniel was getting settled. If the prof had heard, he wasn't saying anything. "Ain't like that," he whispered back. "I'm fixing his car. Don't be jealous." He gave Jeanie a look that she knew meant *back off, please,* but he wasn't hopeful she would. Jeanie rarely did.

She glanced over to where Daniel was setting up his laptop, then back to him. "Simone was supposed to cover me, but she's not answering my calls. I think she slept in. Since she closed alone last night. Again."

He sighed. "Which is another reason I'm here, so quit harpin' on it."

"I'm not judging. Keepin' you around makes me look saintly." Jeanie circled the bar with a towel in hand. Carver flinched at her honesty, but Daniel didn't react to her claims—not even when she leaned on his shoulder and pointed at his screen. "Damn, I haven't seen slides since I was in high school."

Carver couldn't help but laugh. "Can't imagine you in high school."

"Neither could I. Probably why I dropped out. Still went to the parties, though." Jeanie winked his way. "Nothin' like a game of Truth or Dare. Or Never Have I Ever. Good times." She kept leaning on Daniel's shoulder, including him in the conversation whether he liked it or not. "How about you, smart guy?"

"Daniel," he corrected, eyeing her from the side.

"All right, Daniel. What were you like in high school?"

He didn't stop typing as he answered. "Well, I was fourteen when I finished. So I missed a lot of the social stuff."

Unsurprisingly, their small talk earlier hadn't covered Daniel's schooling. Jeanie raised her eyebrow and played at impressed. "Wow. You were some real-life kid genius, huh?"

"Leave off, Jeanie—"

"No," Daniel corrected with a laugh. "I'm just the asshole who never had to study. There's plenty of things I struggle with. Just school was never one." He adjusted his glasses and looked up from his screen. "I think I've played one game of Truth or Dare in my life? Never heard of the other one you mentioned."

"You kiddin' me? It's a classic, like Spin the Bottle," Jeanie teased. "Somethin' you play in your best friend's basement and pretend you're disappointed when it lands on her."

Carver dropped the shaker he'd been drying. It clanged to the floor, but when he looked up, Daniel was smiling. He turned to Jeanie, face hot with embarrassment. "I thought you had an appointment to get to?"

Jeanie sat on a stool to the left of Daniel. "Shay's not here yet. Why're you freakin' out?"

"I'm not freakin' out."

"Yes, you are." Jeanie reached over the bar and grabbed a bottle and three shot glasses. She started filling the first, mischief bright in her eyes.

"Oh no. You're not draggin' me into this—"

"C'mon, Carv. He's already started and he doesn't even know it." She placed a shot in front of Daniel, who barely closed his laptop in time. "Never have you ever..." She waved her own shot in encouragement.

The professor picked up the small glass. "Never have I ever...played this game before?"

"Exactly. Cheers, bitch." She clinked her shot into Carver's and downed the liquor. She didn't wince as she poured another round, but Carver took the bottle from her hand.

"That's enough of that. If we're really doing this, we're switching to beer. Some of us gotta work around here."

Jeanie pouted. "Fine."

He poured three pints off the tap and passed them around. "We'll start small," Jeanie said, tapping her chin. "Never have I ever…gone to college."

I swear to God, Jeanie…

Daniel took his shot and turned the glass over on the bar. His mouth twisted and he reached for his beer. At Jeanie's nudge, Carver also took a slow drink.

"That ain't fair," he told her after. "Too easy."

"You're just mad you got suckered into it because of—"

"Jesus, *fine*. Shut up and I'll play." Carver eyed her over his beer and tapped his chin the same way she had. "Never have I ever…bribed my ex-girlfriend to drive me all over town, even though we broke up two years ago."

"Okay." Daniel set down his beer. "So this isn't really a game so much as—"

"That's right," Jeanie answered, all bravado. She leaned back in her seat and laced both hands together, resting her head on her palms. "No matter what I do, they can never really leave me." She stretched her neck and smiled. "Look, it's a lesbian thing. It's just what we do."

"Didn't you set her up with her current girlfriend? Who you also dated?"

She shrugged. "And they're both much happier for it. Which is why I get driven around, you ass." Jeanie reached over Daniel to flick him in the ear, but her arms were too short to reach. Annoyed, she turned to their guest with an expectant look. "C'mon, Doogie Howser. Your turn."

"I really don't know what to—"

"Don't worry." Jeanie smirked. "You'll figure it out."

To her credit, the rest of the questions were easy. Nothing too invasive, which he could tell was grating on her nerves. She'd thought herself so clever, making them play this stupid game to learn what was up with him and Daniel. How could a game do that if Carver didn't know himself?

Near the last third of their beers, Jeanie lost patience with their questions about travel and number of siblings. "God, y'all are asking the most PG bullshit," she complained. "Never have I ever sucked a dick. *There.*" She finished the last of her beer and set the glass down hard.

Carver froze, unable to do anything but glare at her. Daniel seemed similarly struck by the question. She looked them over and sighed. "You're both terrible liars."

A car honked outside and Jeanie swiveled over her shoulder. "Well, I think my work here is done. I'll tell Shay you said hi." She stood on the rungs of the barstool to pat him twice on the cheek, obviously pleased with the chaos she'd created. He scooped up their empty pint glasses as she left, opting to refill them rather than acknowledge her final question.

"Soooo," Daniel said, drawing out the word. "That's Jeanie, huh?"

"Yep. My best friend in the world. How I hate her." He placed the beer in front of Daniel and waited for a reaction. He seemed a little thrown, but mostly amused.

"She was right about one thing. I did learn a lot about you."

He very much doubted that. Their questions had stayed very tame. "What didn't you already know?"

"That you'd traveled at all." Daniel sipped his beer. "No offense, but you don't seem the type to summer in Rome."

"Wasn't some big thing." He shrugged. "I was in the Army, briefly."

"Why'd you leave?"

"Not my choice. Medical discharge."

"Were you injured?"

He shook his head. "Nothin' useful like that. They learned some information I didn't mention when I enlisted. Apparently, if you have the wrong sort of concussion in your medical history, it doesn't matter that you were eleven years old. It makes you a risk."

"What happened?"

Carver snagged the towel from where Jeanie had left it and finished wiping the bar. "I got into it with some kid at school. Don't even remember what about. I was pretty scrawny growin' up, so. Didn't go well." He tossed the cloth over his shoulder and lifted the hat off his head. Standing beside Daniel's barstool, he pointed out the scar at his hairline. He followed where it curved around his right ear before covering it again.

"And from then on, the hats?" Daniel flicked the straw brim, jostling it back on his head. Carver smirked as he righted things, but the prof ducked down to keep eye contact. "You always seem to be wearing one. Like you're hiding something under there."

"Hiding something? Does that sound like me?"

Daniel gave his answer more thought than necessary. He said quietly, "I can't tell," and proceeded to stare straight through him. Carver swallowed, but held his gaze. He didn't know how much time passed, but eventually, Daniel shook his head. "I can't figure you out, Carver. I don't even know if that's your first or last name."

"What's it matter?"

"It doesn't. Except I really want to know."

"Why?"

"I have no idea."

That smile of his was back with a vengeance, and Carver didn't want to ignore the pull he felt to lean closer. Daniel looked at their refilled drinks and deliberately picked up his beer. "Ask me something. Anything."

The invitation made his skin tingle. He itched his arm in search of relief. "I'm not like you, Daniel. I don't speak a bunch of languages. I'm no good with words."

"Then don't use words."

Blue eyes dared him forward. Daniel didn't move, but he tilted his chin up. They'd been circling the question of Daniel's sexuality the whole game — for the whole week, if he was honest. It'd be so easy to lean closer, to dip his head and capture Daniel's lips in a kiss. The mantra he'd been reciting all week no longer seemed to apply.

"Ask me," Daniel repeated.

He's straight, don't bother. He's straight, don't bother. He's straight...

The door to the bar swung open, a slice of sunlight cutting through the cozy dark. A small group walked in, chatting amicably. Without a second thought Carver put some distance between them, but the prof looked as caught up as he felt. He couldn't help but push it one step further.

He leaned close to Daniel's ear before circling back to the register. "Stick around tonight. Maybe I will."

It took far too much willpower not to watch for Daniel's reaction, but there were people to serve and it was his job to do it, so Carver turned his focus to the task at hand. "How can I help y'all?"

"Can we get a menu?" one woman asked. She hooked arms with the man she'd entered with, who was glued to his phone. Peak straight culture. It was definitely the on-season if the fantasy football types had found their way to Jeanie's.

Carver walked them through the specials and took their food order. Another woman had entered with them, but during his explanation of appetizers, he'd lost track of her. Whatever. If she wanted something, she'd find him.

He turned to the taps and rinsed out a glass. As he lifted his eyes to the corner of the bar, he found the woman talking to Daniel, who didn't look pleased about it. He was typing again—or trying to. Under the guise of rolling silverware, Carver shifted close enough to listen.

"I just wanted to say how much we appreciate you coming to Fairview. I know it can't be easy, continuing your work without…on your own, I mean." She placed a hand on Daniel's shoulder. "I can't imagine dealing with that."

The professor's back stiffened. "Yeah. It wasn't great."

"And they really never found your girlfriend? Nothing that gave any clue where—"

"I'm sorry, were you saying something useful? Or can I get back to this?"

He'd never heard Daniel snap that fast at someone besides himself. The woman, who Carver had assumed was a colleague, turned away, her face caught somewhere between embarrassment and pity.

"Of course," the woman said. "I'm sorry. I didn't mean to offend you."

"People never do. And yet..." Daniel gestured vaguely in front of him, then rubbed his forehead with his hand. The woman returned to her friends and Daniel looked his way sheepishly. Like he'd been caught doing something he shouldn't.

Don't bother, Carver reminded himself. *He's straight.*

Daniel adjusted his glasses and stared blankly at his laptop. "Yeah, I'm just... I'm going to go." He left some money on the bar and made his retreat. "Thanks for the drink."

Carver stared at the folded bills until the door closed. He watched out of the window as Daniel wrangled the bike from his truck and left. Good, then. That settled things a bit. Whatever he thought he'd seen this week, it wasn't interest. He was glad to know where things stood.

He dug the metal scoop deep into the ice bin. The next time he saw Daniel, he'd go back to keeping his distance. Probably what he should've done in the first place.

* * * *

Daniel

"I feel like I need to explain myself."

Carver shrugged in the driver's seat. "It's a free country."

He snorted at the sentiment and kept loading groceries in the footwell. He'd waited a few days before texting Carver again, but his empty fridge didn't care about his pride and he could only eat pizza so many times in a row. The mechanic had arrived in his truck, timely as ever and twice as silent. The drive to the store was paralyzing, and the ride back was starting to look the same.

Daniel took his seat, closed the door, and tried to steady his breathing. It was time to clear the air, though he was still annoyed they had to have this conversation. "Can I assume you've done a Google search since Thursday, or am I going to have to start from scratch here?"

Carver raised an eyebrow. He was being too brusque again. "Sorry," he said. "You'd think I'd be better at this."

"What're you talking about?"

"What Sarah said at the bar. About what happened to my girlfriend." He stared through the windshield at the half-full grocery lot. "Disappeared without a trace. Topped all the headlines. Not that it mattered."

Carver shifted in his seat, but didn't say a thing. Local news updates played on the radio as they drove, but eventually the question came. "What happened?"

"What happened was her name was Aminah Bashir and not some white-bread, girl-next-door shit." He flicked the radio off. The background noise was too much right now. "I imagine what you meant is if they ever figured out what happened, and no. She just never met me at a conference. No letters, no calls. No body, alive or dead. No ransom. Just gone." He noticed he was bouncing his leg and tried to stop. "Just 'one of those things.' So the authorities stopped looking."

"How long ago was that?"

"Seven years." He swallowed hard and forced himself to continue. "And it's probably painfully obvious, but I haven't dated much since." He chanced a look at Carver. Now that he'd started, the whole thing came spilling out. "You weren't wrong to say I don't get out much. The academic community is so insular, and everyone knows someone who was at that conference. Or heard about it from so-and-so, you get the picture." He tried to focus on the passing scenery. "I travel a lot, but it's only ever a matter of time before people realize who I am. Why Bashir is the first author on all my papers. It was our research, but it was her passion."

He worked his jaw and chanced a look up. Carver was wearing a familiar expression on his face.

It'd been too much to hope this conversation would go differently. "And then, people look at me the way you are now, and it doesn't seem to matter what I wanted. Even casual things turn to pity." He shook his head at the groceries in the footwell. "And I was never good at casual in the first place."

He caught Carver looking at him from the corner of his eye. His tone was less clipped when he asked, "Why are you telling me this?"

He let out a long sigh, leaning into the embarrassment. "I'm trying to explain what you've seen this past week. You weren't imagining things, and I wasn't trying to lead you on. Not that it matters."

"Why not?"

"Because you're still looking at me like I'm about to break!" He cut himself off and stared out of the window again. He bit the inside of his cheek until he tasted blood. "Look, I'm sorry. Forget I said anything."

Carver remained silent for long enough that Daniel wondered if he meant to stay that way. But as they turned the final corner to his rental, the man surprised him again, his voice softer than before. "I don't know what that must've been like. But you're not the only one tryin' to leave their past behind. Hell, most of the guys I see are doing the same, one way or another."

"Does that include you?"

Carver scratched his nose. "Maybe a bit." He adjusted his grip on the wheel. "It's how I wound up in Fairview. I followed a guy here. He wasn't out, though I thought he was. Apparently, all we'd been doing fit under the label of 'roommate' for him."

"Ouch."

"Yeah." The mechanic laughed without humor. "Last time I even thought about something long-term. It's just not for me." He shrugged, mostly casual. "But hey. Know thyself, right?"

"Look at you. Quoting Shakespeare."

"Am I?" Carver's smile stuck around longer, fading on his face into an expression like interest. The tension in the cab shifted to something more familiar. "So, you're not…"

"Straight?" It was Daniel's turn to laugh. "Hardly. People are usually surprised when they hear I had a girlfriend."

Carver's voice remained low, still unsure. "What is it you want, then?"

That was the question, wasn't it? He'd been trying to find the words all week and hadn't managed any that didn't make him sound like some desperate cliché.

"Honestly? I want what you have. To be able to let go for once. To just let myself be."

He didn't know what to expect in response, but the mechanic's smile widened to something like a grin. "That?" Carver dared to wink at him. "I think we can do." He pulled into Daniel's driveway and shifted into park, turning in his seat to give him full attention. "I work late tonight, but I'm not closing. You should come by. Finish the drink I owe you."

He searched the other man's eyes for signs of sympathy, but Carver shook his head. "It ain't pity, all right? You can trust me on that."

Something about how he said that made Daniel believe it. He crossed his arms over his chest and leaned on familiar territory—talking shit to each other. "What, are you going to show me your moves? How you get all the guys?"

"I could." Carver's grin was sharp enough to cut. "Been going easy on you. On account of thinkin' you were straight."

"Assuming, just like the rest of them." He smiled at the floor. "Fair warning. I'm not going to fall for your cheesy lines."

"My lines aren't cheesy."

"No one ever thinks they're cheesy," he explained. "Just like everyone thinks they're a good kisser."

"I'm a good kisser."

He met Carver's eye. "My point exactly."

The mechanic breathed a laugh and tipped his head away. "All I'm sayin' is I know how to show someone a good time."

"So show me, then."

Carver's gaze snapped to his, amazed. He hadn't expected him to be so obvious—to be honest, Daniel had surprised himself. But it felt good to say what he actually meant. It reminded him of other parts of his life, of times he'd been much more comfortable taking the lead.

He gathered up his groceries and pinned Carver with a stare. A dare, if he cared to think of it that way. "If you weren't just feeding me lines that night, then show me a good time."

Was it his imagination, or was Carver leaning closer?

"Come by Jeanie's and it's a date."

An interesting choice of words, coming from someone like Carver. "A date, hmm?"

"Yessir." The mechanic smiled broadly. "My way."

Chapter Five

Carver

"What's got you all jittery and nervous?"

He punched another order into the register. "I am not."

"Defensive, too. That's new." Jeanie caught his face between her palms and smushed his cheeks together. She scrunched her nose and made the same face back at him. "If I didn't know better, I'd say you had something lined up for once."

He pushed her hands aside and fixed his hat. "If I did..." He emphasized the first word. "*If,* then I'd appreciate you not makin' some deal out of it. Because it ain't one."

"Of course. Mum's the word." Beside him, she quietly made a batch of Long Islands. "It's that professor, isn't it?"

"Jeanie..."

"Called it."

He rolled his eyes. "I didn't say a word, how'd you —"

"No, Carv." She hit his shoulder and waved at the door. "It's that professor. Here. Again."

They were well into the Saturday night rush. The energy in the bar tonight was different from the last time Daniel had come past. For one, it was full to bursting with townies and college kids alike, all looking for a place to dance. The neon lights behind the bar were the brightest in the place. It took a moment to spot him in the darkness, even with Jeanie pointing through the crowd.

Daniel wore the same shirt as the first time he'd come in — that white and blue striped, short-sleeved button-up that had no right looking as good as it did. Dark slacks fit tight to his legs, cuffed over black leather shoes. He remembered what he'd told Daniel that first time at the bar, but to Carver's eye, he didn't seem to be carrying a jacket. Maybe Daniel was done trying to hide. Seemed like, because his jacket wasn't all that was missing.

The prof wasn't wearing his glasses.

Daniel spotted him and walked to his corner of the bar. He grabbed a bottle of something and poured a stream of liquor into the shaker in his hand. "Almost didn't recognize you," he joked.

"Oh, because of…" Daniel waved at his face, then shoved his fists in his pockets. "I used to wear contacts all the time, but the glasses are easier. I just figured…" Daniel looked up. "Might be nice."

"I like it," he told him. "Makes it easier to see your eyes."

Daniel arched an eyebrow his way. "This one of those lines I should expect?"

No, Carver thought unkindly. *It's one of those things I'm not supposed to say out loud.*

He plastered on a smile and poured out a line of shots. "Maybe. But don't take my word for it. A mirror would tell you the same."

"It's nicer when you say it," Daniel replied. They shared a smile, both staring a little too long. Daniel broke away first and leaned on the bar. "So...how's this usually start for you?"

Right. He was supposed to be welcoming Daniel into his world, not being charmed by first-date banter. Because this wasn't even a date. Not really. "Depends on where I see someone. On the patio?" He pointed to the back door. "I bum a smoke. Or lend a light."

"If you're inside?"

"It helps that I work here. But you already know one of my tricks."

"I do?"

"You should." He slid a beer across the bar, overdoing it on purpose. "This guy wants to send you something. What should I have him order?"

Daniel didn't seem to follow. "That's your move?"

"Your reaction tells me a lot. First, if I'm wasting my time." Daniel nodded, conceding the point. He continued, "It also tells me what to get you if, when you talk to that guy, he's waiting for someone and you're left drinking alone."

"That's...wow."

Daniel seemed equal parts impressed and gobsmacked. He wasn't sure if he should be flattered or embarrassed. "It's just a foot in the door. People like to be remembered."

"Then what?"

He shrugged. "Don't usually need much else." Why lie about it? He'd built the reputation. Might as well live up to it. "But you're in luck tonight. I prefer the slow play." He winked at Daniel, pleased to see at least that move hitting the mark. He turned to catch Jeanie's attention and motioned that he was clocking out. She flipped him off, but that was as good as a thumbs-up. He returned to the register and looked Daniel up and down. "I'm off my shift soon. You wanna dance?"

He had said it the same way as countless times before. Usually, that was a winner.

Daniel only laughed. "Too easy. What else you got?"

He played along and dropped another standard. "This doesn't seem like this is your scene. Am I right?"

"Predictable," Daniel told him. "That may, in fact, be the oldest line in the book."

"Still works, though." He circled the bar, noting how Daniel's bright eyes followed. He wasn't wearing anything special—just his regular black button-down and dark-wash jeans—but Daniel was staring like he was something to look at. Like maybe he saw something he wanted.

He adjusted his hat and stepped into Daniel's space. The prof didn't move away as he lowered his voice, asking again, "C'mon. You wanna dance or what?"

This time, his words had the desired effect. Daniel swallowed and nodded. Maybe Carver was imagining things, but when he put his hand on Daniel's back to guide him to the floor, he heard a sharp inhale of breath even through the noise of the club.

He steered them to a corner away from the bar. No need to make it easy for Jeanie to spy on him. Daniel dodged the dancing crowds as best he could, leaning close to be heard over the music. "So you convince a guy out here and what? Go full Swayze? Sweep them off their feet with a dance?"

He tipped his head, amused by the reference. "I'm not that good a dancer."

"Then why—" Daniel gestured between them, but he caught the man's hand from the air. Carver brought it to rest on his hip, then slid his arm around Daniel's back as he angled his head. Using the excuse of closeness, he breathed down the professor's neck. His surprised shiver was easy to feel, standing close as they were.

"Because mostly," he said, lips brushing the shell of Daniel's ear, "it's not just dancing."

"Mostly?" Daniel croaked. "That's the qualifier we're using?" His voice wavered, the slightest bit harsh in his throat. "You know I've got to be different, now. On principle."

"Of course," he said aloud. But in his mind, Carver thought, *We'll see.*

This late at night, the DJ was in the thick of his set. Bass thrummed in the speakers, thudding deep in his chest. It'd be easy to close his eyes and get lost in physical sensations, to rush through this precursor to what they both wanted. But he hadn't been lying when he'd said he liked to play the game. If it was really just sex he was after, he could get it easier than this. Between the apps, bathroom etiquette and knowing the right parts of town, he wouldn't even have to know a guy's name if he didn't want to.

Carver had learned the hard way he wasn't built for the long-term, but he did miss certain parts of it. Mostly the understanding that came with. Even if it was just small talk during a dance, it gave things a more substantial feel. Like an agreement between equals.

People had needs. He'd gotten good at meeting them. And as he and Daniel danced, the prof took all his cues — returning like for like when Carver trailed a hand up his arm, tracing fingers around the edge of his short sleeve. One of Daniel's hands toyed with the back of his jeans. His thumb snuck beneath his shirt to the thin white cotton beneath and even through the fabric, Carver felt the heat like a brand. He tilted his head toward Daniel's neck and breathed out slow.

"Might've been a minute, but you're not missing a step." He spoke the compliment near enough to be heard as he slid a hand up Daniel's back. The nape of his neck was damp with fresh sweat. He rubbed a circle at the top of the man's spine as Daniel pressed their hips together.

"Some things you don't forget," his dance partner whispered back, and Carver had to bite the inside of his cheek to hold back a groan. The way they were swaying, their chests brushing close together...

He pulled back enough to get a look at Daniel's face. His cheeks were flushed, his breathing elevated. He wondered if Daniel realized he was licking his lips like that. So he tipped forward, just enough to share breath, and Daniel leaned to meet him, creasing his eyes closed.

"I've got to be honest. I'm starting to see the appeal of this."

"Thought you might." He crowded closer, ready to bridge the distance with a kiss.

Daniel turned his head, making him miss.

Tease...

Blue eyes lit with amusement. "Starting to, I said."

He exhaled slowly and gripped Daniel tighter. "How're you feelin', then?"

Daniel laughed. "Like I could still use a drink."

"Can do that here easy. Or someplace else." He ran his thumb down the side of Daniel's neck. "I think even you can tell my place ain't far."

"For what?" Daniel's bottom lip brushed his as he spoke. "Wine and conversation?"

"Well," he mused, dragging his mouth over the other man's cheek. He palmed Daniel's hip and pulled him close, whispering in his ear, "A cold beer and a hard fuck's my specialty."

"Ohhkay, that's just not fair…"

The words came out in a rush of breath as Daniel clutched his waist, like he needed help to balance. Time for the obvious question. "Is that a yes?"

Daniel nodded.

"Then let's get out of here."

＊ ＊ ＊ ＊

Even in the truck, the drive was still fast this late at night. He tuned into a different station, trying and failing to avoid ads.

Daniel smirked. "I think you're the only other person I know who still listens to the radio."

"Yeah?" He looked Daniel's way. "Well, tech's expensive."

"And tech is *tech*. No, thank you."

"I think a radio still counts as technology, genius."

Daniel didn't rise to his bait. "You know what I mean."

Carver kept one hand on the wheel and rested the other on the gear shift. He tapped his thumb against the leather stitching, the only sound in the silence. Another commercial later, Daniel asked, "Is the drive over always this awkward?"

He wasn't sure how best to explain that he didn't actually know. He normally brought guys back on his bike, which didn't allow for conversation—awkward or otherwise. But as he met Daniel's eyes in the rearview mirror, he considered a new idea.

"Doesn't have to be."

He returned his gaze to the road and shifted his hand from the center console. He started modest, placing his palm nearer Daniel's knee than his thigh. He froze at first, but relaxed as they turned a corner, so Carver ran the back of a finger along the inside seam of his slacks. Daniel exhaled slowly, hands frozen where they'd rested on his thighs. His arms had gone rigid, like he was doing his best not to move.

"That's quite the counterargument," Daniel managed to say. "And you call me the genius."

He squeezed Daniel's knee, tracing patterns with his nail over the silky fabric. It was hard to tell from a side-eye view, but it looked like Daniel was pressing against the seat, straining for contact as he moved incrementally higher.

Yeah. This would be *plenty* to keep them busy.

Carver let up once they were parked in his driveway. He beat Daniel to the door and held it open, waving him inside. He pointed out the small living room to their left, taking care to mention the record cabinet. He had a hunch it might be the professor's speed.

"Put something on, if you want. I'll be back."

It wasn't often his dates could get the record player to do much, but as he'd expected, Daniel didn't have any trouble. In moments, mellow bluegrass chased away the house's silence. Must've been one of the albums he'd picked up from Derek's family. He didn't remember purchasing this himself.

After a pit stop in the kitchen, he leaned against the living room wall. When Daniel stopped scanning the dust sleeves, he handed him a cold can.

"Fresh out of wine," he teased. "Sorry."

"Not something you keep on hand?"

He shook his head. "Wine drunk's a different kind. Too emotional."

"Sounds like you've tested this theory."

"I'm a bartender. I know what I'm talkin' about." Carver cracked his beer open and sat on the couch, hoping Daniel would follow. "Wine is feelings juice. Don't mess with it unless you want someone's life story spillin' out."

The prof continued to thumb the records on the shelf. "But beer is safe?"

He snorted. "Beer is cheap."

"I think you just called yourself a cheap date."

He smirked and spread his hands wide. "As advertised."

Daniel shook his head, but still came to sit beside him. They both took a drink, then Carver knocked lightly into the other man's shoulder. "I'm just showin' you what to watch out for. Wouldn't want you wasting your time in the next college town you're in."

Daniel narrowed his eyes. "So, you're protecting me from a hypothetical sweet-talking bartender? By running your game as a sweet-talking bartender?"

He grinned. "Is it working?"

"The damsel in distress? Not really my trope."

"But you're still here," he joked back. "Still lettin' me."

A strained expression passed over Daniel's face — gone as fast as it came. "Yeah. So I am." He held his beer between both hands.

Carver didn't know what the professor was stuck on, but clearly, he was starting to have second thoughts. He didn't think he'd pushed Daniel into any of this, but maybe he'd missed something. He flicked the tab on his can. "You know, you don't have to prove anything. If you wanted to call it a night…" He trailed off, unfinished but understood.

Daniel slouched forward and hung his head toward the floor. He turned to look at him, relief and frustration clear in his face. "Are you sure?"

"Nothin' wrong with some catch and release." He leaned his forearms on his knees and mimicked Daniel's pose, ignoring his own disappointment. He bumped the sides of their beers in cheers. "It's fine. Keeps me on my toes."

"Well. Glad I could be of service."

Carver took a long drink — honestly, he needed it — but it was hard not to notice the way Daniel kept staring, the way he watched him swallow with that earlier fire in his eye. So all right, maybe the prof was conflicted. Could be a case of cold feet instead of the full cold shoulder.

Sitting so close, their arms and legs just touching, it'd be easy to lean forward and kick things off, but this needed to be Daniel's call. He wiped his mouth and set his beer aside. "I thought you were leavin'."

Daniel shook his head, like he'd forgotten where he was. "I did say that, didn't I?"

"That's what I heard."

"Right. Yeah, right." Daniel stood and, after a couple false starts, deposited his beer on the coffee table.

Carver followed a few steps behind, showing him out like he assumed a good host would.

When they reached the door, Daniel turned the handle and paused. Unsure what else to do, he extended his hand to shake. "Well. Goodnight, then."

Embarrassment turned to amusement on Daniel's face. "So formal?"

He didn't respond, leaving the other man to fill in the blanks.

"Right," Daniel corrected himself. "Mostly doesn't go this way for you." He didn't argue and Daniel continued to chide, "Don't we think highly of ourselves?"

"You said it. Not me."

"It can't go that way for you every time."

He considered that, tipping his head side-to-side. Daniel sighed. "*Every* time?"

He pushed his shoulder into the wall. He wasn't trying to brag, but the man asked a question, right? "I mean, if we're already here...then, yeah. Pretty much."

"Jeez Louise. Makes you wonder —"

"Wonder what?"

Daniel smiled and looked at the open door. "I didn't mean... It's a figure of speech."

"Mm-hmm."

Carver stared at him from under the brim of his hat. Daniel turned his way in the hall, still not leaving. Blue eyes darted to his lips, then away, and the third time Daniel repeated the circuit he stopped hiding his amusement. He'd been ready for Daniel to be a bit gun-shy, but the desire was clearly there. What was he waiting for?

"Look at you," he teased. "You're dyin' to know."

"Know what?"

"What you're missing." He crossed his arms over his chest, aware what the pose might do for his biceps. "Admit it, genius. You can't stand not knowing."

He expected the professor to laugh. Maybe joke about his cheesy lines. Instead, something in Daniel's eyes flipped like a switch and he closed their distance fast, crowding into his space.

Daniel ducked under his hat to press their foreheads together. "Let's say you're right," he whispered, voice strained. "That I can't stand it. What then?"

Carver hitched up his chin in challenge. "I think you know what."

Daniel's exhalations broke and crested over his face, but he didn't move. He held completely still, putting the ball in the other man's court.

"I think I want to kiss you," Daniel said at last.

Well, that much had been obvious all night. "Just think?" He laughed. "I must be losing my touch —"

Before he could even finish, Daniel's arm was around his neck pulling their mouths together. The professor sighed against his lips and braced a hand on his hip. And damn, but it was a *good* kiss. He was firm but didn't rush, didn't try to take more than was offered. Carver kissed back with subtle pressure and teased his tongue along the seam of his lips, toying with him more than anything. The cool taste of beer gave way to the heat of Daniel's mouth and Carver felt dizzy. He hadn't drunk enough tonight to be this off-balance.

Daniel pulled back first, holding his eyelids closed. He mumbled under his breath, "Of *course* you're an amazing kisser."

"That a problem?"

The prof licked his bottom lip. "Tell you in a minute."

With renewed purpose, Daniel steered them into the house, pushing the door shut as he pressed Carver against his own wall. He wedged a leg between his feet, encouraging Carver to rock against the pressure of his thigh. Their lips met again and this time, he didn't hold himself back. He teased with his tongue when Daniel opened his mouth to him. He'd thought to use the distraction to flip their positions, but that wasn't possible with Daniel's hands wrapped around his wrists. Daniel used the hold to force his arms above his head, taking advantage of his surprise to kiss down his neck.

Well, damn. All right...

Daniel rocked against him and mumbled, "Tell me if I'm doing something wrong here."

"Not at all." He cleared his throat. "Just not what I expected."

Daniel licked a stripe up his neck and *goddamn*, he couldn't help the way his hips jolted at that. "You kidding me? I've barely been keeping a lid on it." Daniel kissed over his collarbone and groaned. "I've been trying not to do this all night. All fucking week." He bit down on his shoulder and tugged at the fabric covering his chest. "Take off your shirt already."

Shit, that's hot.

He pulled the offending garment up and over, shouldering off his layers and dropping them to the floor. After playing the lead all night, he hadn't expected this sort of encounter, but damn if he wasn't willing to come along for the ride. And Daniel just kept kissing him — full and long, like he didn't need air at all, exhaling in pleasure when he broke away to mouth down newly revealed skin. Warm fingers swept across his chest and traced the lines of his pecs. The prof tweaked his nipple, as if to test if he liked the sensation, and he surged against Daniel's thigh, pulling him still closer. The roughness of his jeans slid against the silkiness of the professor's dress pants and *fuck*, that felt *really good* –

He nearly choked on the sound he wanted to make. Daniel was finding too many of his buttons too fast.

"No wonder this goes so easy for you," the man said against his chest. "All you have to do is strip and they're putty in your hands. Who wouldn't be?"

It was a roundabout compliment, but Daniel said it with conviction. Like something he really meant. Intending to silence him, Carver caught the man's face between his palms. "You're talkin' too much."

"Give me something to do, then."

His eyes went wide as Daniel smoothly dropped to his knees. The man tugged his belt open and nosed along the hard line of his arousal.

Carver pounded his fist against the wall. It'd been easy to picture him and Daniel like this, but in the midst of the real thing, he realized how wrong he'd been. With the way he'd gone on about not dating much, Carver had assumed Daniel would play it shy. But he wasn't looking for a guide. Daniel wanted to give the tour himself.

The prof's knowing smile glinted in the low light of the foyer. "Now would be a good time to tell me what's off the table."

He fought off the harshness in his throat to answer, "Very little."

The way Daniel reacted, it seemed he liked his answer. And once he got his mouth on him, one thing was immediately clear. The man wasn't kidding when he said he didn't know how to do casual. He launched into things like a lover, like he might use the information later on. Daniel dragged it out when he found something that pleased him — pulling out all the stops to swallow him down his throat.

He wouldn't have ever known *all this* was beneath the professor's surface. He had no idea why, but Daniel's laser focus had set its sights on him. And while Carver wasn't used to being on this side of the crosshairs, he had to admit that it was kind of nice.

It was also testing every bit of his patience.

About the third time Daniel backed off and left him on the edge, Carver knocked his head against the wall and huffed in frustration.

"You havin' fun? Being the world's biggest tease?"

"That's rich, coming from you." Daniel swirled his tongue around the head of his dick, sending shockwaves of pleasure up his spine. "Can't stand a taste of your own medicine?"

By this point, he'd been hard for who knew how long. Daniel's hands were everywhere, brushing the creases of his hips, the outsides of his thighs. He should've expected the man to be a quick study, but the way Daniel had already learned to tease his balls while he closed his lips and sucked — it was getting more difficult to keep himself quiet. The sounds were creeping into his ragged breathing, desperate noises forming in the back of his throat. He had to be careful, needed to keep the volume down —

"Come on, Carv. Let me hear you."

Is that what he's waiting for?

Carver had hardly got the chance to touch him yet, but as he glanced down, Daniel looked as wrecked as he felt — damn-near desperate for him to comply. Daniel twisted his wrist and stroked his spit-slick cock, reaching between his legs to tease at sensitive skin and *fuck* –

He couldn't help it. His stomach swooped low, a specific desire building that he hadn't felt in years. Despite his best efforts, a rough sound caught in his throat.

"*God*, like that," Daniel rasped. "Do that again for me."

The prof licked him from base to tip, still taking his time about it. His hand flexed where it rested in short brown hair while Carver tried his best not to hurry things along. Daniel teased with his finger again – lighting him up with sensation, just on the edge of enough – and if the man kept making him make noises like *that*, there was *no way* Carver was getting out of tonight with his pride.

He wasn't sure if he cared.

Jesus, Daniel...

Carver curled forward, rounding his spine against the wall. He pushed Daniel away, complaining, "You're gonna kill me if you keep on like that."

Daniel's quickened breath blew warm against his leg. He kissed his bare thigh, but was back on his feet in no time. "Trust me," Daniel said with a smile. "I've barely started."

And Daniel had warned *him* about cheesy lines...

In retribution, he moved his foot behind Daniel's and pushed, flipping their positions for a change of pace. He didn't get to stay in charge for long – just until Daniel leveraged them off the wall, sending them stumbling for the couch. Carver flopped on his back and lay sideways on the cushions, reaching his neck to watch as Daniel shed his shirt. He unthreaded the belt from his slacks and pushed the dark fabric over his hips, not yet removing his close-fitting boxers. Then Daniel braced his arms on either side of his head and lowered down, fitting their bodies together with a sigh.

Carver's hand flew backward and reached for the side table—and more importantly, the bottle in the top drawer. He pushed the lube into Daniel's hand with no preamble. Amusement mixed with desire in his sky-blue eyes.

"Convenient," Daniel said, flipping the bottle open.

He tried to make up some ground by pressing his thigh into Daniel's erection. The man's breath hitched as he handed the lube back, then Daniel's slick fingers were around the base of his cock, applying just the right amount of pressure. And apparently, Carver had stopped even *trying* to keep quiet, because he couldn't help but moan as Daniel got to work again.

The weight of the man above him was a pleasant, grounding sensation. He did his best to kiss Daniel back, to keep his hips still and let the man explore, but he couldn't help himself.

"*Fuck*, Daniel. You gotta..." He pressed his head into the arm of the couch. "You gotta let me do somethin' here."

"Who's stopping you?"

That was a fair point. He reached clumsily for Daniel's waist and tugged his boxers down, taking a moment with the bottle before *finally* getting Daniel in hand. He fell heavier against him in response, but the weight was welcome. Gave him something to push against as he thrust into the vice of Daniel's fist.

He ran his thumb around the tip of Daniel's cock, dipping into the slit. Then he mirrored the other man's technique and kept on with full, long strokes. Daniel broke off their kiss, mumbling something he couldn't hear. Or maybe he just didn't understand it. Who knew what language Daniel might be speaking? And something about knowing he'd driven *Daniel* to such distraction—with little more than accepting his advances—he felt good. Powerful, even. In a way he never had before.

Heat pooled in his belly and Carver sped up his movements, thrusting with more intention as he felt Daniel doing the same. They ground their hips against each other, teasing with their hands as their lips stayed sealed, more breathing into each other's mouths than actually kissing.

He swallowed against a dry throat, tired of fighting down release. "Does that—"

"It feels fantastic," Daniel affirmed. "You're fantastic. Don't stop."

His instinct was to shy away from the praise, but Daniel didn't give him time to think about it. He pushed his forehead into Carver's temple and dislodged his hat, sending it tumbling to the carpet. With the hand braced by his head, Daniel pushed fingers through his hair, so gentle that he almost didn't mind. At first.

Then his spine arched—an instinctive, unchosen action—and of course, Daniel noticed and took it for a positive sign. With a shuddered sigh, Daniel got a proper handful and tugged, moaning into his mouth as he sucked on Carver's tongue. Daniel's other fist stayed tight as he thrust up into it, and before he could even be ready for it he was shaking apart.

"*Fuck—*"

He came with unexpected force, hitching his hips as Daniel worked him through it. He shot halfway up his chest as Daniel kept staring—all blue-eyed intensity and a proud, knowing smile. Carver tightened his own fist, desperate to bring Daniel's attention back to his own body, and with little more than that, the man followed his example. Like all he'd needed was the *fucking show* Carver had put on to finish.

So much for keeping his distance. The first time they fool around at all and he was moaning like a bad porno flick. He closed his eyes and hoped Daniel wasn't looking at him.

Then the prof found a way to make it all so much worse.

Warm lips brushed his cheek as Daniel pushed a hand through his hair again, moving dewy strands from the sweat near his brow. All at once, Carver's mind was anywhere but the here and now...

Harahan. Such a small town. The first place he'd stayed long enough to grow his hair out to cover his scar. He'd slump over his desk in homeroom while Derek flicked paper footballs at his head. He'd pretend not to notice the way his hand lingered, sifting through strands to pull the small triangle free...

Fairview, years later. Back in their old apartment. His head in Derek's lap as they watched late-night TV. Derek traced the scar with his thumb idly. Carver's chest swelled with the intimacy—even if he only got it when they were alone...

Their old bedroom. Derek behind him with an arm around his waist, kissing his neck as he grabbed his hair, pulling at the roots as he thrust deep inside. Pleasure flared at the base of his skull—at the base of his spine—everywhere all at once...

Until there was only distance, both on campus and at home. That space on the couch so normal that, when he reached for Derek's shoulder, he was pushed away.

"God, Will," Derek snapped. *"Give it a rest. Why d'you always have to be so clingy?"*

Tangled up with Daniel on a different couch, blunt nails pushed over his scalp and Carver shuddered.

What the fuck was he doing?

Daniel brushed the other man's hair aside and pressed his nose into Carver's cheek. "Fine." He breathed through the word dramatically. "I'll admit it. A date your way? Pretty fun."

He noted the effect of his comment with confusion. Carver went quiet, then started shifting out from under him. He reached for the tissue box and tossed it at his chest. Then he stood, scooped up his hat and left the room.

The sounds of rushing water filtered from down the hall. Carver was probably just taking a moment to clean up. He used a few tissues himself before pulling back into his pants, unable to keep from grinning. Fuck, if he could remember the last time it had felt like *that*. After a long week of wondering, he finally knew how Carver sounded when he let loose. When he let his walls down.

Daniel smiled and tried to catch his breath in the quiet. The music had run out long ago. As he stood to choose another record, Carver strode into the room. He'd pulled on his pants from where they'd fallen in the hall, but didn't look his way as he settled at the end of the couch.

"Everything okay?" he asked. He had a growing suspicion it wasn't.

"Yeah." Carver lit a cigarette and rubbed his brow. "But you gotta go. It's late."

Based on how the night had gone so far, this wasn't what he'd expected. He didn't think Carv would be the type to cuddle after, but this closed-off shadow of the man he'd driven to distraction? Something was off. Why was Carver so determined to make him leave?

His overactive mind supplied a plethora of answers.

Because this was just a game. A thought experiment taken form. Nothing like you're used to at all.

He cleared his throat. "Did I, uhm…did I read something wrong here?"

"No. Just, we're done now. I'd like my space." Carver slouched and pulled his hat over his eyes. "Been a long day."

"Yeahhh." He stretched out the word in disbelief. "I don't think that's it."

Carver took a drag deep into his lungs and sighed out smoke. "You said you wanted 'casual'. Welcome to it."

"You can be casual without being an ass." Carver only shrugged. It was enough to pique his temper. "Wow. Really digging in here, aren't you? Why are you closing me out so fast?"

"Which one of your fancy degrees makes you think you can talk like this to me?"

Carver was finally looking at him, but he wasn't making sense. "None of them?" he replied. "What's that got to do with —"

"Nothin'. Forget it."

Frustration was clear in Carver's tone. And sure, maybe he was making a big deal out of this, but Daniel couldn't help feeling discarded. Tossed aside. While he'd been on the couch playing it all over in his mind, Carver had apparently decided the night was done. His walls were back again.

Daniel worked his jaw as he gathered the rest of his clothes. This was so stupid. He should've gone with his gut and left when he had the chance. He pulled his shirt roughly across his shoulders, not bothering with the buttons. "I'll tell you one thing for free." He pointed his balled-up undershirt at Carver on the couch. "You? Aren't fooling anyone. The last thing you want is casual."

The mechanic stayed silent, giving no response. And Daniel knew he should cut his losses—just take the embarrassment he'd earned and go—but he'd never been good at leaving well enough alone. Maybe it was childish, but he wanted *some* reaction.

This disconnected playboy act was just that. He couldn't let it stand unquestioned.

He marched to the couch and stood in Carver's line of sight. "The way you talk to these guys? The lines you use? You said it yourself—you prefer the slow play. So why aren't you letting yourself have it? Your ex really burn you that bad?"

"You done yet?" Carver asked, meeting his eyes. "I thought you were leaving."

"You don't even know you're doing it, do you?" He snatched the smokes off the side table, keeping Carver from reaching for another. It earned him a withering glare, but he didn't care anymore. It wasn't his place, and no one had asked him, but at least Daniel could say he'd been honest.

"You don't want casual. That's not what this is about. You're micro-dosing intimacy because you think it's all you'll get."

Carver's brown eyes went hard, no trace of warmth to be found. "Fuck you, man. And get the hell out of my house."

"Not a problem." He threw the pack of smokes at the table. His face felt hot with anger and shame. "These must be those Southern manners I've heard so much about. Great job, Carv. Your mother must be so proud—"

"I wouldn't know!"

The words tore from Carver's throat, loud and harsh. The short outburst rang between empty walls, fading into their least comfortable silence to date. Carver pulled a toothpick from his pocket and ground it between his back teeth.

He might've worked the man up before, but this was the first Carver had actually yelled. He looked embarrassed, a red flush high on his cheek, and Daniel knew he'd taken things too far. "I'm sorry."

Carver's tone was even this time. Detached. "Just leave."

"No, just—I mean, I will but... I'm sorry. I didn't know." He looked at the floor and ran his tongue over his teeth. "You want me to go?"

"Yes. No." Carver leaned his forearms on his knees. "I don't know."

He nodded, then motioned toward the couch. "Can I sit while you figure it out?"

Carver used his toothpick to point to the corner. "Over there."

He crossed the small room and sat in an armless wooden chair, waiting with hands laced for Carver to speak. In time, the man leaned his back against the cushions, apparently resigned to having to talk at all.

"It's not some big thing, but I never really had family. Grew up in the system. No siblings, either." Carver finished his beer and crushed the can between his hands. "Sorta why things were so hard with my ex.

Wasn't just him I was leavin'. We went to high school together." He stared at the ground. "His mother, Denise...she practically adopted me. And that was when me and Derek were just friends."

It wasn't at all what he'd expected to hear. He tried to keep a blank face, unsure how successful he was. "Kind of hard to picture you as the high-school sweetheart type."

Carver waved it off. "Wasn't anything till after my bit in the service. I'd been home a year, no plans on what to do..." He shook his head. "Then Denise said I should open my own garage. Helped me set up, get the word out. She knew everyone in Harahan and we made a decent go of it. Especially in a town so small." He ashed his cigarette in Daniel's undrunk beer. "What I wouldn't give for some fuckin' regulars now."

"So how'd you wind up in Fairview? You said you followed him here."

Carver's straw hat bobbed along as he nodded. "Derek came home to visit a few months after I'd opened. Said he was gettin' ready for grad school and that I should come with."

"And you did?"

A wry smile curled Carver's mouth. "Oh, I went full tilt. Closed up shop and got talked into a business degree. Should've remembered how much I hated that school shit, but it seemed like a plan at the time. Started working at Jeanie's to make ends meet." He rested his arm on the side of the couch and picked at the dark upholstery. "So when his white-collar father came to visit and Derek started callin' me 'his roommate,' I had a problem with that. And the girl he brought home didn't help."

Other people might expect condolences. But even if Carver did, Daniel doubted he'd accept them. So it was handy that blatant honesty came fastest to his lips, because before he'd really meant to, Daniel scoffed. "Well, fuck *that*. What'd you do?"

"What I had to. I left. The apartment, college, everything. I pulled doubles at Jeanie's till I could open again." Carver flipped the toothpick over in his mouth. "But between the house and garage rent, I gotta work too much to get the shop on its feet. Never known a thing like 'family money,' but it ain't even about that." He stared off at nothing in particular, his voice even lower than before. "Would just be nice to know. To check that box. To know for sure." As if remembering he had an audience, Carver looked up. "Anyway. You didn't ask for a sob story."

"We didn't even have to break out the wine." He smiled briefly, and when Carver reciprocated, he took a chance and offered his two cents. "You could pursue it, you know. Hire someone to look up your family. Maybe they could find something through state records."

Carver hung his head in defeat. "Jesus, you and Everett both. He put you up to this?"

"The guy I met once for a whole five minutes? Oh, yeah. We're best friends. Getting lunch next week, in fact."

It was amusing watching Carver try to fight it, but the corner of his mouth betrayed him with a smile. It made him look unexpectedly earnest. "He's just been sayin' the same thing. Says he owes me for helping with a case some months back, but I wish he'd pick some other way."

"Well. Not to belabor the obvious, but you just said you wanted to know. So…" He trailed off, not wanting to push.

Carver tipped his head. "I did say that, didn't I?"

He decided to make the obvious joke. "That's what I heard."

Carver smirked, then blew out a breath. He pointed between the two of them. "This gonna be weird now?"

"Doesn't have to be. You okay?"

Carver adjusted his hat. "I'm fine. You?"

"Of course." Daniel ran his hands over his thighs and stood. "Well. I can head out, if you want."

"Yeah. This sofa's seen better days."

"I think it worked in a pinch."

Carver snorted, surprised yet appreciative of the levity. He pulled a white T-shirt over his head. "You want me to drive you? Since your sorry-ass bike's still in back?"

"You don't have to—"

"It's fine." Carver twirled his keys on his index finger. "Saves me the trouble of finding you in the morning. Middle of some goddamn field."

"Oh, good. More jokes." He buttoned his shirt and followed Carver to his truck. "Lucky me."

Chapter Six

Colt
Mason, Louisiana

Ev was already seated at their small kitchen table when Colt rolled out of bed. A usual Sunday. Nothing special about it. He shuffled into the kitchen wearing the same T-shirt and boxers he'd slept in and stopped at the percolating machine, brewing a pot of liquid sanity.

Behind him, Everett cleared his throat. Something small clicked as he placed it on the table. Colt gripped the edge of the counter and tried to steady his breath.

Not this again…

He'd successfully dodged two attempts so far — three if he counted that time in the bedroom last week — but here Ev was. Bringing it all up, before he'd even had his morning coffee. Not to mention his total lack of a cigarette. Colt sighed and dismissed the memory of the first time they'd broached this topic. He was once again behind the stove — this time scrambling an egg to avoid the silence.

Terms of engagement, indeed.

The first time Everett had tried had been at that new seafood restaurant down the street. Colt had foiled another attempt on their anniversary last month. And he'd thought the topic well-avoided till that third time cropped up, right in the middle of certain...activities. He'd managed to stay ahead of it each time, to not let Everett start some speech or similar nonsense, but now? For once, Everett had got the jump on him. But he wasn't ready for this conversation to intrude upon their routines.

His partner said from the table, "You can look at it, Col. Ain't gonna bite."

Colt turned and leaned his back against the counter. He looked at the box, then to Ev, and tried not to choke on all he was feeling. It wasn't that he didn't appreciate the gesture, just...it was too much to explain. Especially to Everett, who'd mainlined normativity for most of his life.

"Ev. I don't..."

"What?"

He tried to find the words, but Colt wasn't sure they existed. When it came to him and Everett, some things ran deeper than words. Since the first day they'd met, he'd felt the tug of their inescapable bond, pulling them steadily closer until they gave up trying to fight it.

But still. Didn't feel right, somehow. Nothing about their lives should be celebrated with roses and tuxedos.

"Rhett..." He kept his voice soft as he explained. "You know how I feel about you. That's never changed, even when I wanted it to." He locked eyes with the man, staring down those flames of earnest blue. "I just don't know that we're...*that*. That it suits us."

"Don't know if we're what? Officially a couple of old queers?"

Everett made that sound like a whole different joke these days. It was no longer the sort of thing that built walls around what they were doing. He delivered the punchline with the same *"there you have it"* tone of voice he used for other inevitabilities in his life. It made him smirk. That tone was something Ev had picked up from him. Just another sign of how they'd kept on changing each other. He stared at the small velvet box on the table, unsure if this was a change he wanted to make.

He could tell he'd been quiet too long when Everett sighed and leaned back in his seat. "Just say it."

"Hmm?"

"You only ever pause like that when you don't wanna say it, but you always need to. So, say it."

He creased his brow in confusion. "What d'you mean, *it*?"

"Whatever *it* is that's making your face look like that." Everett opened the box and spun it around. A simple, silver band shone from between two bits of dark fabric. "Because not for nothin'," Everett said through a smile, "but you're over there cookin' the both of us breakfast, drinking coffee I made while you're clinging to this argument."

"Ev—"

"You wear my old college T-shirt to a bed we've both been sleepin' in a while. We fuckin' live together. And work together." Everett turned the ring in its setting. "If *this* is about sharing a life, I think we might be arguing over semantics, babe."

"Guess that's what I'm asking. If *this* would be sharing a life."

"Why wouldn't it be?"

Colt chewed the inside of his lip, but Everett wasn't in the mood to wait. "Out with it, Col. C'mon."

Nothing for it but truth, then. Ugly as it was. "Just never thought the institution meant that much to you. The way we started and all."

In years past, a comment like that would've sent Everett on a blame-based tirade. Now it made him somber as he handled his well-worn guilt. "Look, when we started...I didn't know anything else was possible. Had no idea what I was feeling for years and I just... Well, you know. You had front-row seats to that disaster."

He nodded in the following silence. They'd had this conversation in every possible way. This was territory they didn't need to go over again. "I did."

"And well... I mean, things are different now. I'd like to keep it that way."

"So would I." He looked at Everett fondly, wishing there was some other way. But the man was right. A part of him did need to get this off his chest. "That still don't mean the white picket fence suits us any better together than it did apart."

There. He'd said it. Even if it hurt to watch the excitement dim in Rhett's expressive face.

"If it's the fence that offends you, we can get somebody out to fix ours." He recognized that tone, too—the muddy gray of Everett making light through his own disappointment. Colt knew that no one saw the world through colors quite like he did, but there was an extra sort of heaviness to watching Everett through that haze. Made him miss the orange warmth that surrounded his partner in sunnier moods.

Everett put down his coffee, then returned the small box to his pocket. "It's fine. I mean, I don't get it, but you clearly think you're on to something. I guess I'm just lettin' you know... It's on the table. For me."

He removed the eggs from the stove before they burned any worse, setting the pan on a folded towel between their empty plates. He circled the table as Everett picked up the spatula and added food to both. Feeling guilty but not sorry, he stopped behind his partner's chair and stroked the short hairs at the back of his head. "I don't mean to be difficult."

"Just comes naturally, huh?"

He breathed through a laugh. "Somethin' like that."

He waited for Everett to finish serving before he reached for the man's chin, tilting his head up. Everett's eyes so often told him everything he needed to know. He hoped that, after all this time, Ev could read him just the same.

He traced Ev's bottom lip with the edge of his thumb and leaned down for a slow, soft kiss. It was the right thing to do. Everett welcomed it, returned it, and the tension eased in his chest. When he pulled back, the room's colors had gained vibrancy again and Colt allowed himself to smile, to be present in his feelings. He might not be keen on swapping vows, but he could give Everett this.

"It's not the paperwork that makes this real, Ev. I've been a sure thing for longer than you know."

Everett laughed, traces of pride in his eyes. "Oh, I *know*." Then Everett pulled him back in, sighing in contentment as he opened his mouth. As it always did, Everett's kiss had him leaning down to chase it, doing everything he could to keep contact. Maybe they could put a pause on breakfast, warm things up again once they'd finished...

Everett broke the kiss and whispered, "Just think about it, yeah?"

He owed the man that much. He'd stop pretending he didn't know about the ring. No more heading off the conversation before they had it. He nodded his agreement, and Everett still had that look in his eye when his cell phone started buzzing. He checked the ID and seemed pleasantly surprised.

"Carv. Good to hear from you, man. This about the bikes?"

He squeezed Everett's shoulder and took his seat. Seemed like he was eating breakfast after all.

"Yeah, we can do that," Everett said between sips of coffee. "If you've got time to come past the office — tomorrow?" Everett looked at him for confirmation. Not able to hear the other side of the conversation, Colt only shrugged.

"Tomorrow's great," Everett decided. "We'll see you then." He set the phone on the table and pulled a pen from his pocket. He scribbled notes on his paper towel "napkin."

He chuckled at his partner. "What's all that?"

"That," Everett said, popping a piece of scramble into his mouth, "is the start of another mystery."

* * * *

Carver
Fairview, Louisiana

Carver filled his days as best he could, including a trip to Everett and Colt's office to answer questions about his upbringing, now he'd given them leave to look into his family. He had to do something to make

Everett stop with his well-meaning texts. It wasn't because Daniel had suggested it. Or because since Saturday, the man had starred in his every waking thought.

Jeanie had asked him yesterday how it was going with Daniel, but he wasn't sure how to categorize things at all. There was no denying it had been some of the best sex he'd had in a while. In a *long* while. And for a man with his pastimes, that was saying something.

But did Daniel still want it? After the fucking tantrum he'd thrown? He wasn't sure if he dared to ask, and Daniel hadn't stopped by Jeanie's again. So mostly, he didn't think this would be a repeat sort of thing. Which was good. He avoided those on purpose. All was as it should be.

As best he could, he pushed thoughts of Saturday from his mind and kept to his usual schedule. He worked his many bar shifts and intermittently at the shop, doing the best he could not to check his phone too often. After a week of carting the professor around, his downtime felt emptier than before.

His phone finally buzzed in his pocket on Tuesday with a message from Daniel.

Any chance you're free? I could use a ride to the library.

He read it from every angle, but there was no hint to Daniel's mood. In the end, he settled on something casual—since Daniel seemed to think that wasn't something he could do.

Too many books for your basket?

He hit "send" before he wasted more time drafting responses. Daniel's reply was fast this time.

If I say yes, will you come?

Carver stretched his neck and focused on reading the message as intended — and *not* reliving memories of what was clearly going to be their one-off. He ignored the opportunity for innuendo and shot back a simple, *Where are you?*

* * * *

Not long after he was in his truck, pulling up to Daniel's office. He texted to let him know he'd arrived. Didn't usually take long for the prof to make his way down.

Twenty minutes later, he couldn't take the waiting anymore. He wasn't thrilled about having to get out and look for Daniel, but if he wasn't answering his phone, what else was he supposed to do? He spared a quarter for the meter, tugged his hat down and walked inside. He found the nameplate for *Professor Daniel Henning* next to three others on the second floor.

The door was open, and while the room housed four desks with dividers, it seemed a cramped space for so many people. Daniel stood at an honest-to-God chalkboard, writing in what he could only assume was another language. His glasses were halfway down his nose as he consulted the book in his hand.

He wore a thin sweater, somewhere between tan and gray. He set the book on a nearby table, pushing the long sleeves up to his elbows as he continued to read. An old A/C unit buzzed in the window, blowing cool air at the edges of his short brown hair, and it was around then Carver realized he was staring. Which wasn't good for plenty of reasons.

He cleared his throat and knocked on the open door. Daniel raised his eyes to the noise and furrowed his brow. Carver watched as confusion, recognition then embarrassment passed over the professor's expressive face. He scattered a stack of papers with his hand and, when he found his flip phone, a glance at the screen had him swearing.

"Oh, fucking *fuck*. That's just great." Daniel pocketed the device. "I'm sorry, I got wrapped up in this. Totally lost track of time."

"Figured it had to be something." Daniel looked even more sorry, but he waved it away. "It's fine. Just didn't want to keep waiting for nothin'. You still need a ride to the library?"

"I swear, I'm almost done with this translation. Five minutes, tops." Daniel's gaze slid back to the chalkboard. "That okay?"

He shrugged. Sure, it was annoying, but he wasn't going to cause a scene. This time.

"I'm already here," he said, aiming for unbothered. "What's five more minutes?"

Daniel nodded and returned to his work while Carver tried to occupy himself. The other desks were mostly bare, but the one nearest Daniel was covered in folders and assorted dishware. He nudged a coffee mug with his knuckles. It was no longer warm.

"How many people are in this office with you?"

Daniel flipped a series of pages, splitting his attention between the book and the board. "Technically, there's four of us in here. But the others are never around. And we all have our own desks."

"So, these are all your doing?" He circled his finger above a collection of cups. Coffee, water, something with bubbles and what looked like a half-finished smoothie. "You allergic to cleaning up after yourself?"

"Please don't. I'm drinking those."

"All of them?"

"Yes," Daniel answered, an edge of annoyance in his voice. Without looking, he pointed in the direction of the desk, counting off on his fingers as he categorized the beverages. "Caffeination, hydration, carbonation, breakfast. So, leave them."

He held his hands up and stopped fussing with the mug's handle. "You must be an expensive dinner date."

"I'm an excellent dinner date. I share dessert and everything."

He said it quickly, like facts he'd memorized. Daniel's attention was still elsewhere. His head stayed on a swivel from notes to board and notes again.

"That from your dig or something?" Carver guessed.

"No, actually. I'm checking something for a friend." He slid a photocopy of a stone tablet across the table. Carver wandered over as Daniel explained. "Translations of this text have existed for centuries. But modern historians still use those translations, and the result is often taken out of context. What started as Hebrew became Greek, then Latin, and only then early English. So I'm double-checking it."

He raised an eyebrow. It was the perfect opportunity to ask something he'd wondered all week. "How many languages do you speak?"

"Fluently?"

"Sure."

"Fourteen."

He tried not to swallow his tongue. "And not fluently?"

"Twenty something?" Daniel said, nonplussed. "I stopped counting."

Jesus. There was out of his league and there was *out of his league.* Carver wasn't sure he and Daniel were playing the same sport. "Why so many?" he asked, trying not to sound impressed.

"It's easier than reading around the biases of translators past."

"Easier? Learning twenty-some languages was *easier*?"

Daniel opened another book, unfazed. "After the first seven, it's not so bad."

He kept waiting for some reaction, but there wasn't a trace of pride. Daniel wasn't bragging, though he'd be within his rights to do so. He sounded like he always did—distracted, but otherwise the same. Matter-of-factly providing answers to Carver's questions.

"Language is just a puzzle," the professor said as he flipped another page. "The parts may look different, but if you know what you're looking for, they fit together the same."

He nodded along, but he was feeling more small-town by the minute. "Whatever you say, genius."

He returned to Daniel's crowded desk and noticed a small empty cup near the edge. The rough pottery had a border pressed into the clay. He picked it up—no bigger than a shot glass—and ran his fingers over the pattern. Behind him, Daniel made a frustrated sound and closed his book roughly.

"I'm not going to find what I'm looking for here. Not quickly, anyway." Daniel circled the table to stand beside him at the desk. A warm hand gripped his shoulder and squeezed—plenty casual. If Carver had been ready for it at all.

"Good to go?"

Daniel brushed the back of his neck with a thumb. Carver flinched in surprise and lost track of hands, allowing the small cup to slip from his fingers. He reached to catch it but only sent it spinning, bobbling the clay once before it crashed to the floor.

He held his eyes closed and ignored the burning in his cheeks. "That wasn't some super-old, super-important bit of clay, was it?"

"Ancient," said Daniel. "Irreplaceable, actually."

Like he didn't think you were backwoods enough before…

Carver dropped to the floor immediately and tried to gather the larger pieces. He felt a hand on his shoulder again and chanced a glance up as he cupped pottery shards to his chest. Except Daniel didn't look angry. He looked very, very amused.

The professor grinned and braced his hands on his hips. "I'm obviously fucking with you. It was a gift shop trinket. Forget about it."

Relief washed over him, followed by a wave of embarrassment. He didn't get to respond to either as Daniel nudged him with his knee, bringing both their attention to his suggestive position. "I've got to say, though, I'm not mad about the view."

There was pretty much no way this could get worse. The past few minutes had proved again how far Daniel was above him—and now he was literally *on his knees* in front of him, his hat barely poking over top of the desk. Face level with Daniel's belt, he craned his neck to meet the man's gaze.

So, of course, that's when those officemates who were "never there" walked in.

"Oh, hey. You're the new guy, right?"

Daniel snapped his head to the door and Carver ducked his chin. Hopefully, the desk would shield him from view. There wasn't anything wrong with him being in Daniel's office, but explaining why he was *kneeling in front of him* to a bunch of snobby strangers was not on the list of things he wanted to do.

But it was the perfect excuse for a different desire.

Maybe it had to do with wounded pride, but Carver couldn't shake the need to level their playing field. Daniel had surprised him Saturday, taking control the way he had. It threw him off. Made him wrongfooted around the other man. Because Carver was many things, but a lazy date wasn't one. He tuned into the conversation above his head and shifted on his knees.

Time to get comfortable...

A voice at the door asked Daniel, "You stickin' around for the year?"

He wrapped his hands around the prof's calves, rubbing his thumbs up and down the fronts of his shins.

"N—no," Daniel faltered. He braced his hands on the desk. He regained composure enough to add, "Just, uhm...just a few weeks."

Another voice joined the conversation, this one higher than the first. "That's a shame. With Adrien out, we're all helping cover the 300-level lectures."

"Mm-hmm," Daniel replied, his voice strained. "Yeah, that's...awful."

He couldn't help but grin. He slid his hands up and over Daniel's knees, then down again, repeating the slow movements as the people at the door kept talking. Each time he reached his fingers higher until Daniel sank to his forearms, stepping a foot back to lean on his leg, as if stretching. He opened a drawer and noisily filed some papers, turning his face to whisper, "Carver. What are you doing?"

"What d'you think?" he whispered back. "Unless you'd rather I got up."

He shifted as if to stand and Daniel slammed the drawer in panic. "No, don't—you can't—"

Carver slid his knees apart, once again sinking low. He did the same as Daniel had nights ago, taking his time in running his nose along the line of Daniel's cock. "Then I think my hands are tied. So to speak."

"Don't tempt me."

It sounded like he meant that. Interesting.

Carver smirked and leaned slowly forward, asking with his eyes if he should proceed. Daniel creased his brow and muttered something in another language, but the way he was nodding made it clear his advances were welcome. He mouthed at Daniel through his dress pants, the rough wool rasping his lips. He kept on as Daniel rounded his back, exhaling slowly. "Oh, fuck…"

"If you want it so bad," he said, breathing hot along the cloth-covered tip, "Get 'em to leave."

But Daniel was in for the introductions he'd yet to receive as both his officemates chimed in about changes in curriculum, asking Daniel's opinion on who even knew what. Which was fine. It gave him ample time to free the button on Daniel's pants, to slowly lower the zip one burr of metal at a time. The thin fabric of Daniel's boxers was easy to push aside, but he took it slow, curious just how much the professor would let him get away with.

He freed Daniel's length from the layers of cloth and licked up the underside. Daniel's front leg twitched and he kicked the desk, prompting the second voice to ask, "You okay, Henning?"

"Yeah, I just…uhm. Stubbed my toe."

Carver smiled, his lips close enough for Daniel to feel it against his skin. The first voice grew louder — someone was walking closer — but he didn't stop. Instead, he sealed his lips around the head of Daniel's cock.

"You got plans for lunch? The two of us were gonna —"

"No!" Daniel snapped, causing the footsteps to halt. He backed off and tugged the prof's pant leg twice. Daniel seemed to realize his error and stuttered, "I mean — yes. Yes, I do. Lunch plans, for sure. You bet."

A short silence followed, but Carver didn't hear more movement. Eventually, the second voice weighed in again. "All right. Well, good to meet you, Daniel."

"Yep, very good. Real ah…" He cleared his throat. "It's been a real pleasure."

Carver held still as the footsteps retreated, followed by the *thunk* of the office door. Daniel waited without moving, not making a sound — ensuring they were alone before tilting his chin up rough.

Finally. Daniel's focus was back on him.

"No part of that was fair."

"You want me to stop?" he asked.

The prof smirked. "Don't you dare."

He adjusted his neck to hold the man's intense stare. This was his favorite part of games like these, because the way he was looking down at him, Daniel seemed to think he knew what he was in for. Nothing could be further from the truth.

Carver ducked his head and, without preamble, took him down his throat. The tease was over. He was finally going to have the upper hand. Maybe then he'd be able to work this professor out of his system.

Daniel sucked in a breath as he pulled away, leaving off with a slight pop. "Are we really doing this again?"

"Seems like," he answered. "That a problem?"

"No, no problem. I just didn't expect—" He took him into his mouth again. Daniel stopped, interrupted by his own hum of pleasure. "I swear. I never know what you're going to do next."

He kept on until Daniel's legs were trembling, moving as slow as he dared. He wanted to do the same as Daniel had for him and paid close attention to which touches received the best feedback. Daniel rested his hands on the back of his neck, no longer bracing against the desk for stability. He hissed when Carver closed his mouth, using more suction and moving faster. He leaned close enough to nose at Daniel's pants and swallowed, holding his throat tight for as long as he could before pulling off.

He took an unimpeded breath and wiped his mouth with the back of his hand, ready to dive in again—and he would've, if it weren't for the desperate arms pulling him up. He got his feet beneath him as Daniel hauled him close. His cheeks were flushed, his pupils blown wide, as he palmed his cheek and asked, "Can I kiss you?"

He wanted to laugh. This guy was something else. He'd spent the last five minutes with the man's dick in his mouth and Daniel was honestly asking. Like he didn't know this was all he'd wanted since Saturday.

He pulled Daniel's head close. "What d'you fuckin' think?"

And sure, maybe Daniel had been the first to complain, but the way this man kissed should be a crime. He was so sure in his movements, in the way he claimed his mouth — it forced all attention to the sensations in his lips, in his heated cheeks, to the way Daniel's stubble rasped against his chin. The tantalizing pleasure of Daniel sucking on his tongue...

Fuck, if he wasn't careful, things were going to flip Daniel's way again. But Carver knew the signs to look for now. When Daniel pulled him in by the neck, he followed quickly into the other man's space, stumbling them back so Daniel's legs hit the nearby desk chair. The wheels knocked into the wall as Daniel fell against the chairback. His light sigh of surprise turned to breathy profanity as Carver again hit his knees.

He didn't let up this time. He took him down and kept a steady pace, encouraging the rocking motions that Daniel was trying to hide. He let his hand explore Daniel's hips and thighs — surprisingly muscular if all he was doing was riding that bike of his. He curled his fingers in a loose fist and placed it against his mouth, allowing Daniel to thrust in and out of both, moving more as Carver encouraged it. He wanted to see Daniel needy for once, too caught up to care about roughness — all the things he *thought* he was going to get that first time.

So now that he finally was, maybe Carver was showing off. He might not speak fifty languages like Daniel, but hey. Everyone had their talents. He'd been told this was his.

The tremors in Daniel's legs grew stronger beneath his hands. He opened his throat, not moving an inch as Daniel tapped the side of his neck. "Carv, I'm not... *Fuck*, I'm gonna —"

Daniel's spine rounded against the faux leather chair. He hunched forward and threw his arms around

Carver's shoulders, surrounding him in a tense embrace as Daniel came down his throat. He gripped Daniel's hips harder, his nails digging half-moons into heated skin, and focused on bringing him down from the high. In time, he leaned his head on Daniel's leg as they caught their breaths.

Daniel's voice was hoarse and full of humor as he stared at the ceiling. "What was *that* for?"

"Just evening the score." He sat back on his ankles, pleased with himself. "Barely got a word in edgewise on Saturday."

Daniel laughed through his next few breaths and threw an arm over his eyes. "Never done that at work before."

"Yeah? What's the verdict?"

"Well, it beat the hell out of the day I'd planned. That's for sure."

"It's a cliché for a reason." Still kneeling, he nudged his nose into Daniel's thigh. He lowered his head and, since Daniel hadn't put himself away, teased his flushed tip with another slow lick. Daniel jerked beneath him, oversensitive. He leveled a gaze downward that could only be described as feral.

"You should get on that table." Daniel phrased it like a suggestion, but it sure didn't sound like one.

"Thought we were goin' to the library."

"You're not going anywhere."

Before he could react, Daniel was hauling him up again. He fit their mouths together as he steered them to the table. And Carver let him. It wasn't often he found someone who challenged him like for like, but since the first day they'd met, that just hadn't been a problem for Daniel.

Truth was, he'd been fighting his own arousal since the moment his knees hit tile, and having Daniel stand between his legs—tugging his belt away, attending to it himself—was making the ache near-impossible to ignore. He tried to help rid himself of clothes, but found Daniel's hands at his wrists. This time, Daniel held them on either side of his thighs.

"If you keep making me move your hands," he warned, "I may actually tie them."

Something about that image felt right, pinned the way he was. What might it be like to sit there restrained while Daniel had full use of his hands...

He rolled his hips into the other man's. "I mean, if you're offering."

"Really?"

The prof leaned back to look at him, like he'd heard something important. Carver shrugged in affirmation. Daniel ran his thumbs over the sensitive insides of his wrists. His smile was damn-near blinding. "I'll have to keep that in mind."

Daniel kissed the breath out of him before moving to his neck, loosing his wrists to unlatch the belt at his waist. He grazed teeth along the side of his ear, careful not to dislodge his hat. And that voice was just as he'd remembered from Saturday night—that confident, almost smug sort of tone when he'd told Carver to *give him something to do...*

Daniel pulled his belt apart but left his jeans fastened, palming him through the denim. He nodded to the desk at their side. "Is that what does it for you? Wondering if you'll get caught?" His voice went up at the end, like he wanted to know specifically what he'd enjoyed. He was too distracted to test wits with Daniel, but before he could respond the prof had answered his own question.

"No, that's not it," he corrected himself. "It's simpler than that." Daniel pulled back, realization in his eyes. "You just like it, don't you? Being used."

An unexpected, uninhibited, *completely* unplanned noise rumbled from deep in his throat. Daniel chuckled in his ear—and yeah, it was embarrassing, but that ship had set sail their first night.

The prof teased his earlobe with his teeth. "I'm right, aren't I? You didn't care if they heard. You wanted me so far down your throat you could choke."

Oh, God. Now who's not playing fair?

He was close to biting through his tongue to keep the sounds at bay. Something about the way Daniel said that—his quiet confidence that he knew what Carver needed—it had him arching into his body, desperate for more. Daniel held him down on the table while he sucked a bruise low on his neck. Then he wrapped his other hand around his throat, holding firm as he teased in his ear, "You like how it feels, don't you?"

He swallowed against a dry throat and moaned. Daniel's breathing stuttered. At least he wasn't the only one affected by the thought of this, getting worked up just discussing it—

"Don't you?" Daniel repeated, firmer this time.

Right. The prof liked to hear him. Still had to get used to that.

"Yes," he forced out, though it felt dangerous to admit. He waited for the other man to pull away, but the grip on his neck remained firm. Daniel shifted so they were face to face and ran the pad of a thumb over his lips. Fair being fair, he licked the edge of his finger.

Daniel cursed under his breath. "All you had to do was ask."

He pushed two fingers deep into his mouth, pressing his tongue down hard. At the same time, Daniel lowered his head and nosed at Carver's shirt, rasping teeth over his nipple and finally loosening his pants. He opened his throat as Daniel's hand pushed in and out, sucking on his fingers in mimicry of minutes before.

"You like this?" Daniel whispered.

Couldn't he fucking *tell?* Carver was practically whining around his fingers, swallowing just for the feel of it in his throat. And the way Daniel kept talking, that self-assured voice of his...he *had* to know his words were doing as much as his forceful caresses.

Daniel pressed down on his tongue until he gagged around his fingers. "That's it," he murmured. "Like you mean it."

Holy fuck. Daniel definitely knew what the dirty talk was doing to him.

His stomach clenched as Daniel thumbed the wetness at the head of his cock, bringing it to his mouth to taste and *shit,* that was it. Almost without warning he came into Daniel's fist, making more noises he'd probably regret. And in the time it took to settle down after, he wondered if he'd evened their odds at all.

With Daniel, all his old rules didn't seem to apply. He was always coming up short, but not in a bad way — it made him want to keep trying. Like Daniel was a puzzle he had two weeks left to solve. He pushed to his forearms, halfway lying on the table, and found Daniel sprawled beside him looking much the same — like he was that tablet he'd been trying to translate.

Neither man spoke as they caught their breaths and stared. With the way they'd just wrecked his office, it *ought* to have done more to ease the tension. But nothing had changed between them at all. The fact he was pleasantly sweaty, accepting Daniel's help rearranging his clothes, had made the wanting worse. There was a deeper pull when he locked eyes with Daniel now. An informed desire. Like they both knew exactly what they were missing.

He ducked his chin and pulled his belt closed, wondering if Daniel would intervene this time. He didn't, but kept on staring as Carver set his feet on the ground.

"You working at the bar tonight?"

"Why?"

"No reason."

"Mm-hmm." He adjusted his hat. "We goin' to the library or what?"

Daniel hadn't moved from his leaned-back position on the table. His dress pants were zipped but unbuttoned, hanging low around his exposed waist. His sweater was still pushed halfway up his chest. With an edge of their usual teasing, he asked, "Is it too much for your ego if I admit to needing a nap?"

He tried not to grin. "Probably."

"Glad I mentioned it, then." Daniel closed their short distance to cup the side of his jaw. He felt himself flush, but didn't pull away. Sure, he liked the praise—who wouldn't? It was how *much* he liked it that didn't sit comfortably. He was glad when Daniel moved the conversation along.

"Sorry to make you drive over for nothing."

He shrugged. "Wouldn't call that nothin'."

Daniel laughed, so he followed his comment with a wink. Just like that, the fire was back — banked, but smoldering. Hot enough to burn.

This guy was almost too easy to please. Carver shoved away from the table, hoping he didn't look as obvious as he felt — damn-near preening under Daniel's studious gaze. He tipped his hat and smirked. "Well. I guess I'll see you around, Teach."

The professor's eyes darkened, but he didn't move from the table. He should look less intimidating, disheveled as he was, but it had the opposite effect. Like his sense of self didn't come from something as small as rumpled clothes.

In that moment, Daniel looked like an entirely different person. Not some overgrown wild man with a smoking sedan. Not some cleaned-up pretty boy with a shy smile. Not even the bumbling professor who couldn't find left with two hands to help.

Leaving the man's office, Carver didn't know who Daniel was now. But after all of *that*? He really wanted to find out.

Daniel

Fuck.

That was the only word in his head as he watched Carver leave his temp office — because not a bit of the last half hour was stuff that happened in his life. It was like he'd jumped to some parallel universe the moment he'd arrived in Fairview. Like a new entity had taken charge of his fate.

It had to be one of the two. He'd never been so lucky as this.

The A/C blew cool air across his chest and he tugged his sweater down. He'd forgotten he was still half-undressed, sprawled atop a table of books like some letter to *Penthouse*. He set himself to rights and sat in his desk chair, dazed. Maybe it wasn't hyperbolic to say that Carver had sucked his brains out.

After Saturday, Daniel hadn't known what to do. There was no script to follow, no hint from Carver on how they might proceed. They'd managed to leave the ghosts of his past at his Carver's, and once the mechanic had dropped him at his rental, things seemed almost amiable. The usual jokes were there again. So he'd unloaded his bike, waved goodbye—and walked inside to have a casual little freakout.

Carver had let him peek behind the curtain just enough. He worried he'd taken advantage in following the man home. Because he didn't plan on bringing it up *ever* again, but Daniel had completed his analysis and arrived at a conclusion. Carver's casual nightlife didn't give him all he wanted. Maybe it'd worked at one point, but now? It was just a way to cope that no longer functioned.

That was why he'd almost left on Saturday. Once he'd realized what the man was up to, he didn't want to be a tool Carver used to harm himself. But instead of helping him find another way to deal, Daniel had given in and signed up for a tour of the man's self-destructive behaviors. For a bartender, Carver didn't drink overmuch, but that wasn't restraint. Alcohol just wasn't his vice. And Daniel couldn't help but feel that, whatever they'd started, it was the equivalent of a full-blown binge.

He'd texted about the library to test the waters, to see if Carver had spent his time wondering in the same ways he had. If this showing at the office was anything to judge by, he felt confident that whatever this was, it was mutual — and *someone* needed to pull Carver's head up. He'd been walking the same path so long he no longer noticed the blinders he wore, never mind the fact that he'd put them there himself. Just from his short visit with the woman, it was clear Jeanie cared about him. Sounded like those detectives did too, if they were offering Carver assistance with his personal life.

But the real kicker — the real reason Daniel was stuck on this small-town mechanic — had clarified the moment he'd hit his knees. He covered it with charm and cheesy lines, but Carver *liked* it when someone else was in control.

And now that he knew? Daniel wanted to be the one to take it.

It seemed a lifetime since he'd attended to this part of himself. It used to be a perk of his travel-heavy schedule. When he visited certain cities, he'd pack another sort of bag. Different clothes. A few toys. His own bundles of natural hemp rope.

God, but he'd forgotten how *good* it felt. To be of service. To create order instead of wading through chaos. To help instead of endlessly trying and failing. To earn the privilege of hearing how badly someone needed what he gave...

Needless to say, he hadn't packed that second bag for his trip to Fairview. Daniel considered his situation and toyed with the lanyard of his faculty ID, unsure when he'd plucked it from the desk. He wound the long green strap tightly between his fingers. Now that he could see the whole picture, he had a choice to make.

Did he dare use this unexpected connection to indulge this piece of himself? Might he use the full breadth of what he knew to show Carver what he was missing? Was he really going to let himself have this again?

A darker question followed in his mind, steeped in shame seven years cold.

Haven't you learned your lesson? After last time?

Daniel stared at the desktop computer that took up half his workspace. He did his best to swallow old guilt and look at the situation logically. There was nothing wrong with his desires—then or now. And there were certainly stores in town where he could find what he needed.

He pulled his laptop from his messenger bag and set it on the table. This brand of research wasn't the sort he did at work.

Part Two

UNTRIED

Chapter Seven

Daniel

"Hey, stranger."

Carver's head shot up from behind the bar. He'd waited a solid twenty minutes for the line to die down. Now that he'd made his presence known, he noted the change in Carver's demeanor. There was something new in the way their eyes met before the man squared his shoulders and sighed, as if annoyed.

Carver angled an empty pitcher beneath the tap to fill it. "What d'you want? You saw me five hours ago."

"I did." He plucked the strap of his bag over his chest. "Want to see more?"

* * * *

They crashed through Carver's door in a tangle, not separating for a moment. Carver didn't fight him as he steered them to the couch, falling backward when he pushed against his chest. Daniel lifted the messenger bag over his head and dropped it to an empty cushion. He placed a knee beside Carver's thigh and straddled him, only then allowing their lips to come back together.

It would be easy to get distracted with the way Carver answered his kisses, but he hadn't biked all over town today for nothing. He gathered the man's wrists in his hands and slowed their progress, brushing their mouths together until they stopped, breathing heavily in each other's space.

He moved both their hands to rest against Carver's chest. "So. About before…"

His host was still out of breath. "What part of it?"

Now or never, I guess…

"The part where I wanted to tie you." Daniel dragged a kiss over the back of Carver's wrist. "How much of that have you done?"

The mechanic shrugged. "Not more than a T-shirt to a headboard. But I'm open to it."

"Yeah?" He tugged his bag closer and flipped the top, revealing a bundle of rope. "How open, exactly?"

Carver's dark eyes flashed with uncertainty, but there was also something deeper. A sharper sort of interest. "I wouldn't know the first thing to do with that," he teased. "But you look like you've got plans."

"I might. If you'll let me." He shifted his weight, grinding against Carver's already-insistent erection. "I just need your hands. Well, and a door frame."

That earned him quite the look. He didn't drop his gaze. "You game?"

Carver adjusted his woven-straw hat to sit farther back on his head. "All right. I'll try anything once."

He did his best not to show it, but those words sent excitement rippling down his back. He let out the breath he hadn't known he'd been holding and pressed a kiss to Carver's neck.

He shifted off the couch and emptied most of his bag on the coffee table. He'd had to make do with the selection at the hardware store, but he'd bought the softest synthetics he could find—braided black rope that would stand in contrast to Carver's fair skin. He'd taken special care in checking them, bundling each length for ease of use. He grasped one by the knotted ends and let it unwind from his hand. He draped the longer rope over his neck, allowing the knots to drag across the carpet.

When he pulled a small knife from his pocket, Carver shifted in question.

"It's just a precaution," Daniel told him. "Better to have and not need." He scouted the room for what he knew was in the corner—the armless, probably-at-one-time dining room chair where he'd ended his last visit to Carver's.

He pointed to the closed door along the right wall. "What's through there?"

"Bedroom."

"That'll be fine." He placed the chair in the doorway, leaving the door itself ajar. The seat faced the living room. He cleared his throat, but it did nothing for the anxious energy in his chest. His nerves kept trying to tell him it'd been years since he'd done this—even longer since he'd been someone's introduction to it—but given time, he settled into a once-familiar focus. He breathed deep and looked at Carver, sprawled on the couch.

"Come here."

Carver shoved off the cushions in what felt like slow motion. He took his time crossing the small room and Daniel let himself watch the show. His dark shirt was already half unbuttoned, revealing much of his neck and chest. By the time Carver stopped in front of the chair, he'd freed the rest of the fastenings. A smile hung crooked on his face.

"Where d'you want me?"

There were too many answers to *that* question, but most importantly, he didn't want to scare Carver off. Would it be too much to admit this was all he'd thought about since his office—the mechanic's strong hands done up in a pair of cuffs? That he'd been practicing knots in his mind all day?

He tapped the wooden chairback and kept his response brief. "Just sit."

Carver did so, placing his hands on his denim-clad thighs. Daniel left the longer rope around his neck and considered the two small bundles on the table. He held each to feel the texture then dropped one, letting it thump to the ground. The other he unwound and folded it in half. "Hold your arms in front of you. Wrists together, but with space."

Carver complied and he stepped in front of the chair. He reached his fingers through the bite to make a loop, which he fit over both of Carver's wrists. He pulled the tails through and reversed tension. "Hold still for me. I need resistance until I'm finished."

Carver raised an eyebrow but followed his instructions. He gathered up the ends and wrapped the rope around twice, then reached through the secondary bite to tug the tails through. He made another loop around the lines as Carver held them taut, only then cinching the ropes down to create two separate cuffs. As he worked, Daniel's pace of breathing slowed. The muscles in his hands remembered the motions easily.

This felt good. *Really* good. He'd forgotten how much he'd missed this.

"Flex for me?" he asked. Carver did, so he ran two fingers down one wrist, tucking the tips of both beneath the cuff. He noted how the touch coincided with a lovely hitch in Carver's breathing, then checked the other as well. Wrists were delicate. He'd rather be safe than sorry.

Once satisfied, he caught the tails to finish the tie. "Looks good. Still feeling okay?"

"I'm fine." The man shifted in his seat. "Just seems like a lot of fuss over nothin'."

Carver's nerves were overcoming his curiosity the longer he had to sit still. Daniel made sure the lines of the ropes were even, flicked his eyes to Carver's, then returned to the cuffs. "Trust me. It'll be worth it."

"I'll hold you to that."

"You should," he countered with confidence, pulling the remaining rope through the other cuff. The mechanic's arms twitched, though he quieted himself. "What?"

"Nothin'. It just..." Carver flinched again as he pulled, almost laughing. "It sort of tickles."

He spared a moment wishing for what languished in his East Coast apartment, but there was nothing to be done about that now. He finished with a half hitch and pulled, ensuring nothing would collapse. And of course, nothing did. That was the best part about the double column tie. Once set, the cuffs would remain at this tightness no matter how Carver struggled.

He ran the backs of his knuckles over the braided black bands, then tugged the remaining rope, sharp and quick. "How's that feel?"

Pleased curiosity chased the nervousness from Carver's face. His head hung toward the carpet, but he could still catch the edge of a smile. "I'm fine," he said. "Why stop now?"

It was good to see desire returning to the forefront, but Daniel needed to set some ground rules before they went any further. "That's not an answer, Carv."

He bent his knees until he was at the man's level, lifting his chin to ensure eye contact. "I'm going to ask you that question a few different times. And I need to know what your answers mean. So."

He slowly pulled Carver's bound arms above his head. "For tonight, green is good." He stopped his movement and continued to hold the rope tight. "Yellow, we pause." He let the rope slide through his fingers. Carver's wrists landed on top of his legs. "Red, we stop." He searched Carver's face for understanding. "Okay?"

His brown eyes were clear and focused. Daniel tugged his arms up again. "So. How's this?"

Carver's low voice rumbled, "Green." The word buzzed in Daniel's brain, fuel for the fire in his blood. He took a steadying breath and lifted the long rope from his neck, making a loop and securing it to the cuffs. He moved behind the chair, keeping a hand on Carver's shoulder. As he walked, he wound the long rope over his hand, only stopping when Carver's arms were raised above his head.

"Try pulling against it now. How's that feel?"

"Fine." Carver tugged. "Or green, I mean."

His mouth twitched into a smile. "You're doing great." He squeezed Carver's shoulder twice. "I'm not going far, but I need both my hands." He tossed the lead rope over top of the door, tied a square knot then closed it in the frame. Once he stood in front of Carver again, he inspected his work. "Try pulling again."

Carver's elbows pointed up and out, bound hands hovering just above his hat. He could tell the other man was trying to move by the way his fingers stretched and flexed. But no matter how he struggled, the doorframe held him secure. He watched Carver come to terms with the fact that he was well and truly restrained — and as expected, it didn't cause fear. His spine didn't stiffen against the seat. Instead, Carver relaxed into the hold, slouching in a way that forced his arms higher.

Daniel stayed where he was, admiring his work. It wasn't long before his reverie was interrupted by a question.

"You gonna leave me here or what?"

An appealing idea, but no. He slid his glasses from his face and folded them away. "Not this time."

He used his knee to force Carver's apart and stood between his legs. He let the breath fall out of him as he tilted Carver's head back. Such a lovely lack of resistance. "You're already doing so well," he told him. "So this time, you get what you want. Up front."

He cupped Carver's face and brushed a thumb along his cheek. He strummed his bottom lip. "And I know what you want, so. Open up."

Carver

Daniel's hand was hot on his cheek as his other reached for his belt. The man's knee pressed against the insides of his thighs and his stomach lurched in anticipation. It made him lightheaded, made his throat run dry and *goddamn*, but how'd he even get here with Daniel?

And more importantly, why did he like it so much?

Over the years, Carver had explored his interests with more than his share of strangers. No one would ever call him a prude, but this wasn't some accidentally hard smack on the ass. It was all so intentional. Daniel had taken time rigging him in this getup — and not because he'd needed to. He'd clocked the confident ease Daniel used to handle the ropes, the casual way he tossed a bundle to the carpet, how naturally he twisted the black fibers into sturdy knots. And while it felt strange to be the center of such attention, the nervousness passed the moment he tested those cuffs.

He really couldn't go anywhere. And Daniel was looking at him like he'd given him a gift. For just sitting there, leaning his weight into the ropes.

Shit. A guy could get used to this.

Despite the time it'd taken for Daniel to set up, he still looked ready to go—from his licked-red lips to the eager erection in his hand. He stroked himself, teasing as Carver pulled against the cuffs. Desire flared in Daniel's too-blue eyes. He remembered the man's questions from the office and couldn't help but ask.

He jostled the ropes again. "Is that what does it for you? You like watchin' me struggle?"

The prof's cheeks reddened. He looked almost shy. "A bit. But it's not as good as what comes after."

That was obviously meant to bait him, but Carver found he wanted to know. "What's after?"

Daniel tipped his head back and leaned his own hips forward. "You'll see." He brought the tip of his cock to Carver's lips and the shyness was gone. Only certainty remained. "I thought we'd pick up where we left off. Since you liked it so much."

The prof stroked his cheek and his mouth fell open. He closed his eyes as Daniel pushed down his throat, and the sound of his sigh—that relieved little moan— seemed even louder, more needy now he was without one of his senses. Part of him wanted to watch the effect he was having on Daniel, but it was almost too much at once. What if he did something wrong?

He remembered Daniel's earlier praise and shivered.

"You're already doing so well…"

So he fought against the nerves of trying something new, blinked his eyes open and leaned forward. The position forced the ropes to hike his arms higher. Limp as he felt, his body was still upright, and with a hand on either side of his face, Daniel was in complete control. He kept it slow at first, testing how much he could take, holding still as Carver's lips brushed the hair below his navel. He swallowed around Daniel's length, relishing the feel of thick heat in his throat, but this pace wasn't likely to do much for Daniel. Why was he going so slow?

It took a while for him to realize what was happening—because for all that Carver had the man's dick in his mouth, this wasn't about Daniel right now. He was using his arousal as a tool for Carver's pleasure—not his own. Daniel only liked watching him gag because, he'd be hard-pressed to say it, but he craved that feeling. Daniel must've figured that much out from the office.

And so far? So damn good. He wondered how long Daniel could keep this up.

The prof rocked into his mouth with whispered encouragement—first in English, then what could've been one of a dozen languages. But his tone stayed the same, heady and tantalizing. It made him want to take hold of Daniel somehow—his hips, maybe his ass. He wanted skin beneath his fingers, to pry his cheeks apart in search of heat, to make space for all the other things his body desired.

Daniel hadn't done a thing about his jeans yet, so he sat there—trussed up and teased out—waiting for the moment he might steer them another direction. All this lead-up had him in a haze. He pulled against the cuffs for leverage, sinking down on Daniel's cock as he hummed and he could *feel* the stutter in his hips, the way Daniel braced his knee on the seat to keep standing—and if his own dick didn't get some contact soon, he might just writhe to the floor.

Without him saying a word, Daniel pulled out of his throat. He swiped a thumb through the wetness at the corners of his lips, tracing patterns in tacky spit with a look of wonder.

Daniel was breathing heavily when their eyes met. "More like this? Or was there something else you wanted?"

"You really asking?" His voice was hoarse to his own ear.

Daniel nodded. "I'm really asking."

He pulled against his bindings, using the rope to sit up straighter. He leaned forward until his mouth brushed Daniel's hip and hoped. "Then I really want to fuck you."

It was a gamble, asking for that. But Daniel had seemed able to guess what he'd wanted since the start. The look on his face said this was no exception. "Finally making good on that promise, hmm?"

"What'd I promise?"

"You remember." Daniel pushed off the seat and closed Carver's knees. He sat across him as he had on the couch, straddling his lap. Except now, Daniel's long legs touched the floor on either side of him, allowing enough reach for him to retrieve another item from his bag.

"There was something about a cold beer, which I got." Daniel leaned close and nipped his ear. "And a hard fuck that I didn't."

Oh, fuck you, Daniel...

He groaned as his hips hitched upward. He hadn't ruined this by being honest. In fact, Daniel seemed as eager as he was — the man was already pulling his jeans open, tugging them down his thighs.

Daniel teased, "Look who's ready to go," then closed a hand around him. He crooned in his ear, "Ask me for it."

It was just like the man to turn a simple question into a power play, but he was too far gone to care. "Please, Daniel." He stuttered another breath. "Let me fuck you?"

Daniel slowed his movements and their gazes met — locked onto each other like they were the only two people in the world.

God, but his eyes are blue when he looks at me like that...

"I already told you," Daniel said quietly. "Whatever you want."

Yes.

He assumed the ropes would be coming off for this, but Daniel didn't touch them. "I can't," he started, then reconsidered. "How am I gonna —"

"I'll take care of it."

Daniel lifted off his lap and removed the last of his clothes. He folded them roughly, then sat back down atop him — holding a silver metal plug in his hand.

Where the hell had *that* come from? It was all happening too fast for Carver to keep track. Quick as anything, Daniel produced a bottle of lube he recognized from his own side table. He coated the toy, then reached around his body to push the tip inside. Daniel hissed in pleasure, taking it in easily, shifting against his thighs so Carver could *feel* the coolness of the metal, so different from the heat of his skin...

"Fuck all the way off, Daniel." He groaned. "You can't just —"

"What? Prove that I do go shopping without you?" Daniel pressed their mouths together as he ground against the plug. He rocked in Carver's lap and wrapped his hands around his neck, but the kiss didn't suffer for it. Daniel kissed like he needed it more than air, and if it left him dizzy on the receiving end, that was fine. He wasn't going anywhere.

Daniel was using his tongue to stroke his own when he reached for the long rope and pushed. The shortening of the lead hiked both his hands higher. He had to arch his back and crane his neck, but the look on the professor's face overshadowed any discomfort.

Daniel pinched the tips of his fingers and rested his mouth by his ear. "What color, Carv?"

It took a moment for the question to register, but the truth was he felt amazing. He got to sit there and enjoy the show of Daniel getting himself ready — didn't even have to move on his own. Daniel was taking care of it all, and the way his breathing raced since he'd got that plug inside him kept Carver on the brink, desperate for when he could take the toy's place.

Daniel gently tugged his chin down. "Hey now," he said, waiting for his attention. "I need to know. Color?"

Right. Still had to tell him. "Green."

It was harder to form words than Carver had expected. Smart of Daniel to make it so he only had to remember one. Moving at all was like pulling through molasses, but the stretch was delicious. He couldn't remember the last time he'd felt this good.

Daniel must've heard some of that in his answer, because he smiled even as he pulled away. "Hang on for a second."

He twisted his wrists against the cuffs. "Real funny."

It wasn't a great joke, but it got the job done. Daniel laughed and pulled a condom from his bag. He returned to his seat on his lap, then reached behind himself and removed the plug. He dropped it aside and bit the corner of the condom. Holding the package between his teeth, he tore it with a turn of his wrist.

"It's been a while for me," Daniel said as he fit the condom over him. Carver tried not to shudder as he added extra lube, then moved to hover over him. "Might need to take this slow."

"Charmer," he managed to say. Then nothing seemed funny anymore.

Daniel lowered himself and they exhaled in tandem, both of them freezing as he sank partway down. It was like a punch to the gut, knocking the breath from his lungs—all he knew was heat and the tight grip of Daniel's body, so similar to the ropes he'd tied around his wrists...

Despite the warning, it wasn't long before Daniel sat flush against his thighs. He grabbed the lead rope of the cuffs again and pushed, using it to brace as he rolled his hips. "How's that?" Daniel asked, voice tight and strained.

He pushed his feet into the carpet for leverage, pressing deeper instead of answering. Daniel twitched on his lap and groaned. "*Fuck*, you feel good."

It was probably for the best that Daniel had kept him tied, because hearing words like those made Carver feel like he was floating. Each time he pushed up, Daniel's body melted around him, arms thrown across his shoulders as he rode. He kept on with the encouragement, too—raw, choked-off phrases he didn't seem to mind if Carver heard.

"Just...there. Fuck, *there*." Daniel's sigh turned to a laugh. "You're doing so well."

Those words worked their way under his skin as he kept moving, using instinct as a guide. They rocked and moved together as Daniel explained how to use the ropes to assist.

"If you pull against the cuffs, you can — yes, like that. That's... *Oh*, that's deep. *God* — "

Daniel grabbed the chair back and the wood creaked in his hands. He found the right angle and thrust again, amazed how Daniel moaned every time he fucked up into him. It was the first bit of work required of him all night but *goddamn,* he was willing to do it.

Whenever they had to move or adjust, Daniel's hands were there, and it never took them long to return to the pattern they'd set. He'd long ago lost track of time, but now there was hardly a thought in his head. All that mattered was the grind, the strength of the rope, the slick sounds of their bodies and the tenor of Daniel's groans.

Carver had never strung the pleasure out like this, never chased it this long without just getting what he wanted. And what he *really* wanted to know was why the delay made it so much better. How'd this book-smart professor with a quick-witted temper know what he wanted so completely? How'd all this control hide beneath those respectable sweaters?

"Tell me how you're feeling," Daniel choked out, grinding against his cock exactly how he needed. Carver tried to answer but only managed a whine, and somehow that kicked Daniel into yet another gear. They kept matching their movements as he tried to quiet himself — but Daniel noticed. He forced his face aside and buried his mouth in his neck.

"Don't hold back. I want to see you." Daniel licked a stripe over his pulse. "Come for me, Carv. Let me hear it."

Daniel clenched around him — made him see fucking stars — and suddenly, that choice was no longer his to make. He fisted his hands against the cuffs and bucked up into Daniel, groaning as the pleasure built and crested as he came. And it just kept *going*. Longer than he'd really expected. He worried he might shake apart if Daniel weren't holding him down.

Entirely spent, Carver blinked sweat from his eyes. He slouched against the ropes and watched through his lashes as Daniel took himself in hand. The prof stroked himself faster and faster until his fingers tensed on Carver's neck. With his button-up barely hanging on his arms, it was easy for him to hit skin as Daniel rounded his back, curling possessively over him as he finished with a groan.

Slowly, his awareness returned. There was Daniel panting in his ear and the weight of the man's head on his shoulder, proof of Daniel's pleasure warm and wet across his chest. Still held in the tight heat of his body, Carver shifted his hips. Daniel sat back with a satisfied grin.

"Beautiful." He breathed through the word.

He was probably talking about the ropes, but Carver didn't know what to say. Daniel didn't seem to mind and pressed a kiss to his collarbone. "Give me a moment. I'll get you out of that."

"Take your time."

It was easier to joke. That meant he didn't have to think. Because now that he could again, Carver found he had only one thought—how was he going to talk Daniel into doing *that* again?

Daniel

One look at Carver, wrecked against the ropes, and his hindbrain shivered possessively.

"Beautiful," he said.

A different word echoed in his mind. *Mine.*

At least for now. For tonight. Anything else required further discussion. But first, he had to bring Carver down from the high. Then he could gauge his thoughts about a repeat performance.

He almost hated to move him. Carv made quite the picture. A sheen of sweat covered his shoulders as he leaned against the chair back, bound hands reaching to the sky. If nothing else, he'd gotten to have this once — and he'd been right in his estimations. Carver needed this.

And after providing it? Daniel felt better than he had in years. Maybe his strange luck would hold and he could show Carver more. Take him for a turn around the proverbial dance floor.

Then what? Hand him off to another lead?

He halted his internal monologue. Better not to follow that metaphor. Instead, he levered off Carver's lap and set about the business of clean-up. It wasn't long before he was back in his boxers and opening the bedroom door. He kept the rope pulled tight as he lifted the knot from the frame, bundling up the lead as walked. He untied it from the cuffs and lowered Carver's arms.

Carver lifted his head to look at him. Daniel pulled him close, pressing the man's cheek against his thigh. "It's all right. Come sit with me."

They didn't have far to go, but it still took time to get him to the couch. He hadn't bound Carver's legs at all, but even so, his knees were shaking. Daniel got him settled, then rummaged through his bag for his water bottle. "Here." He handed it over. "Bite the mouthpiece and it acts like a straw."

He placed the bottle between his hands, cupping Carver's fingers since the cuffs still held him tight. He seemed surprised to need the help, but working together, he managed a long sip.

"I'm going to take these off now, okay?"

Carver nodded, almost surprised to see the ropes around his wrists. "Sure."

He took the water bottle back and set to work untying. It wouldn't do to release all the tension at once. The last thing Carver needed now was to feel untethered.

Once the cuffs were undone, he looped the ropes over his neck and settled in the corner of the couch. He pulled Carver against his chest and massaged his lined wrists. Somewhere in all the fun, his straw cowboy hat had once again fallen off. He knew better than to linger now, but the way Carver's hair stuck to his forehead couldn't feel pleasant. He pushed a few strands aside and waited for a reaction.

It wasn't what he'd expected. Carver leaned into his hand instinctively. And for a while, they sat together as he toyed with the sweat-damp strands near his nape. He didn't know how long it was before Carver shifted, as if waking, and moved his head away.

He wanted to follow after, but moved his hand to Carver's shoulder instead. "We should talk about that."

"About what?" His voice still had some gravel around the edges, but his eyes were clearer. They could have this conversation now.

It was obvious Carver liked it when he played with his hair, but he was so hot and cold about it. There was likely something to that, something indicative of the larger talks they needed to have. "I don't want to do anything that makes you uncomfortable."

"Who says I'd let you?"

There wasn't much behind the words, but he still gave Carver a look. He trailed his hand from the man's shoulder and followed down his arm, coming to rest at his wrist. "I need to know. Was all of that okay?"

Carver smirked at the ground and dropped the attitude. "Jesus, were you there?"

His good humor was contagious. He tried not to sound too pleased. "So, tying your hands is a yes, then?"

"I'd say so, yeah."

Flushed and embarrassed was a good look on Carver. He licked his bottom lip as he considered his next question. "Would you want to try this again? Another time, maybe?"

"I mean, fuck. If you're offerin'."

And *that* was the best news he'd heard in years.

"What about your legs?" he asked. "Or different positions?" His mind filled with options — other types of ropes, different ties. With Carver on board, his next two weeks in Fairview were now a new kind of interesting. Or an old one, depending how he looked at things.

Carver raised an eyebrow. "Maybe? I'm not sure."

"That's okay," he said, reeling himself in. "You can think about it and let me know. There's no rush."

Carver stretched and put some small distance between them. Their shoulders and legs still touched where they sat on the couch. He rolled his wrists. Daniel did his best not to stare.

"I feel like I should offer to drive you back, considering." Carver breathed through a laugh. "But I don't think I can get off this couch."

"Then don't." That was sort of the point, considering the state Carver had left him in at his office earlier. "I think I've sorted how to get to my place from here. Finally."

Carver bobbed his head in affirmation. He rubbed his hands together, but didn't yet move. It seemed like there was more he wanted to say, but he didn't want to rush him. "Have some more water. I'm just going to pack things up."

In the time it took to bundle the ropes and get himself dressed, Carver had finished most of the water in the bottle. He stood beside the couch an arm's reach away. "You about done with that?"

Carver nodded and he returned the bottle to his bag. When he looked down again, he'd worked up the nerve to speak.

"I, uh…" Carver sat on the edge of the cushions, running his hands over the lines on his wrists. "That was great. And I'd be down to try more, if you wanted. While you're in town."

He smirked. "I think that could be arranged."

"But I don't want to be totally…helpless. Maybe just hand stuff for now? With the ropes?"

Pride burned in his chest. Boundaries meant Carver wanted to do this again. That he wanted to explore. Boundaries meant *next time*.

"That's fine."

"And I'd rather…" Carver cut himself off. He didn't leap off the couch for his hat, but his eyes settled where it rested on the carpet. He pulled the band from his hair and retied it at the base of his neck. "I don't like when people mess with my hair. Just a personal thing."

It boded well that he could set this limit. He noted the tension in Carver's posture, even leaning against his knees. He was waiting for a reaction…bracing for rejection.

He waited until their eyes met to speak. "Thank you for telling me. It's not a problem."

Carver nodded, the barest trace of a smile on his lips. "So...I'll see you around?"

"Yeah." He tilted the man's chin and kissed him again. "You will."

Chapter Eight

Carver

The next day, he got another text from Daniel. It wasn't about transportation.

What are your thoughts on having your arms tied behind your back?

There was no precursor, no lead-in — just a question that overtook his thoughts for the rest of his busy Wednesday. In his brief bit of time between the shop and the bar, he fired off the only response he could think of.

Don't know. Never tried before.

Daniel replied rapidly.

We could try and see.

Carver smirked. Another text bubble followed.

You working tonight?

Yes, he sent back, aware he was dodging the question.

Daniel didn't let him get away with it.

Yes to what?

His fingers hovered over the screen as he considered. Tuesday night had been, well. Eye opening. To say the least. After Daniel had left, he'd sat on the couch and run his thumb over his wrists, tracing the remnants of the ropes. When the marks had faded in the morning, there'd been a bit of disappointment he hadn't expected.

Daniel was always double-checking, always making sure, but a part of Carver wished he didn't have to say what he wanted. It was harder to admit in the bright light of day, alone with the memories of how it'd felt to give Daniel control. He didn't want to look too closely at why, but he wanted it. God, he wanted it. And Daniel seemed eager to oblige.

Was it really so unthinkable that, for once, things might play easy?

He fired off a short response and shoved the phone in his pocket. He didn't check it again until the end of his shift, but Daniel had replied almost immediately.

Same time?

He'd been partway through his delayed answer when Daniel had walked into Jeanie's, messenger bag in tow. And back at his house, Daniel had sat him in the chair again, this time facing backward as he'd laced him in an elaborate restraint. From his triceps down to the tips of his fingers, Daniel had woven the rope around and between his limbs, pressing his cheek into the chairback until he was finished. He remembered the strain of holding his arms behind his body, the deliberate way Daniel moved him when and where he needed, the sliding pressure of hands brushing over his naked chest. Only once he'd finished the ties had Daniel addressed their physical needs, coaxing him to lean into the ropes until he shook apart.

After he'd been untied and unwound, Daniel left him with another soft kiss and far more questions than answers. He'd stood in the stark brightness of his bathroom and looked himself over in the mirror. His eyes followed the red lines that crisscrossed his arms as he remembered all Daniel had said this time…

"That's it. Release into it, Carver."

"That's good. You're doing so good for me…"

"Don't move, I'll take care of it."

"Eyes on me, Carv."

"Ask me before you come…"

He'd shivered beneath the fan and wondered what the rest of the week would bring.

His next day off was Sunday.

He met Daniel at the bar every night.

Sometime during the afternoon, he'd receive a text that would set his imagination spinning. Then Daniel would arrive at the bar near close, that dark olive bag strapped across his chest, and play at casual. To the unknowing observer, it was probably convincing. He'd made the same mistake in estimating Daniel by appearance alone.

But Carver knew there was more than notebooks in that canvas bag of his. He'd tally up receipts as Daniel watched him work, running his thumb beneath the bag's strap and down his chest—a subtle reminder of what he wanted, why he was there. Then they'd throw the prof's bike in his truck and make the short drive to his house, where Daniel used his bag of tricks to take him out of his mind.

Truth be told, he hadn't ever gotten laid like this before. Jeanie gave him all sorts of shit for it, but usually, he'd try his luck once or twice a week. And whatever he'd told Daniel, things didn't always go his way. But the texts kept coming, and the prof kept showing up. The more they incorporated the rope, the better it seemed to get for them both. He hadn't thought that was possible, but he wasn't complaining.

By Sunday, he was expecting Daniel to ask if he was working, but he wasn't sure he dared to break their usual pattern. Their excuse of "meeting at the bar for a drink" had worn extremely thin. If he just invited him over, he was pretty sure Daniel would come.

But why would he ask that now? Daniel had less than a week left in Fairview, and he couldn't spend *all* his time turning Carver's knees to shaky, unsteady things. Maybe a break would be good. A reminder of how things would be once Daniel was gone.

Not entirely pleased with the plan, he replied.

I don't work until Tuesday.

Daniel's response took no longer than usual.

Glad you've got some time off. Enjoy yourself.

He waited to see if more was forthcoming, but his phone stayed silent. It didn't sit quite right. He'd expected disappointment, maybe frustration. He knew first-hand that Daniel had a temper. What he couldn't figure out was why this wasn't tripping it.

Monday came and went without any word from Daniel. Part of him wanted to reach out, but what would he say? Everything he could think of sounded petty or pleading. So when his phone buzzed in his pocket on Tuesday, he was relieved to see Daniel's name on the screen.

Hope you got some rest. You working tonight?

As far as he could tell, nothing had changed. He caught himself smiling and pecked out a reply.

More of the usual. Can't complain. Yes, I'm working.

Tuesdays at Jeanie's were a tossup. Sometimes the place would be dead for hours, but sometimes a theme night packed the house. Tonight was the kind of Tuesday that should've been easy. With only a handful of patrons, he should've been behind the bar, ready to catch Daniel's eye. And he would've been, if it weren't for the fight at the corner table.

Daniel had distracted him all day with questions about tying his legs and something called a "futo." It took one Google search to know *that* was a big fucking yes. He liked being on his knees. This seemed like an intensified version of it, and without really meaning to, he'd been counting down the hours all night.

So when some popped-collar, polo-wearing asshole clocked his frat bro square in the face, it pulled Carver from his fantasies and forced him to intervene. He shoved the drunkest out of the door while keeping pressure on his buddy's shoulder, unkindly turning the arm in its socket. Frustrated for many reasons, he pushed them into the night, kicking the first guy to the ground before turning to the other.

"Don't touch me, faggot."

The humid night faded as he heard that word again—but in a very different voice.

"I always figured your friend for a faggot, but living with him's a different story. You gotta be careful, Derek…"

"It's not like that. He's just my roommate, Dad."

He did his best to shake the memory and tossed the kid at the pavement. "Trust me, shithead. You ain't gettin' that lucky." He crossed his arms and stood in the doorway. "Now get the fuck outta here."

The guys were all bark as they stumbled to their feet. Mumbling curses under their breath, they swayed in the direction of campus. Carver watched them go until they turned the corner. He lit up a cigarette, but it didn't do much to help.

Maybe he could cut out early. He was in no mood to deal with this bullshit.

Then he turned to his truck where Daniel leaned against the door, a dark strap slung across his white T-shirt. His bike was already in the back. And his bright eyes were fixed on him.

The prof couldn't have timed this better if he'd tried. For more than the usual reasons, he wanted out of his head tonight. He strolled over, exhaling smoke, and dropped the cigarette right in front of him. He crushed it beneath his foot. "Hey."

Daniel shook himself to attention. "Hi."

He could tell now when Daniel was holding himself back—the tick in his jaw and the way he tensed his neck. Dead giveaways. Not to mention his usual vocabulary turned to stilted, one-syllable words. Maybe he was still amped from earlier, unused adrenaline firing up his blood, but after two days of wondering what this moment would bring, watching Daniel look at him like *that* was turning his mouth dry.

He leaned their bodies closer and reached for the door handle. He tilted his head to align their lips, just enough to feel the warmth of Daniel's breath across his face.

Then he pulled the door open and climbed inside. "You comin' or what?"

* * * *

"Over there. On the couch." Daniel's mouth was a bruising pressure against his own. It felt amazing. "I want you on your knees."

Fuck. Yes. He was very okay with that.

It had only been two days since they'd done this, but there was an unexpected desperation he enjoyed—in himself and in Daniel. The prof jerked both their belts aside and walked them to the couch, expecting him to be ready when he shoved against his chest. He fell to the cushions and enjoyed the view of Daniel above him—already shirtless, unwinding a bundle of rope and doubling it in his hands.

It really was wonderful watching him like this, all flustered and focused just at the idea of teasing him. He had no idea why someone like Daniel would be so fascinated by it, but he wasn't about to ruin things by asking either.

Daniel gestured with his chin, expecting him to move. "Knees. Now."

He couldn't help but smirk. "Well, yes, sir." He reached up for a mock salute. Daniel caught his hand from the air.

"We didn't discuss that," he rasped, down an octave.

"Discuss what? Manners?"

Daniel held his eyes closed for the space of a deep breath. When he looked at him again, there was disappointment in his smile. "Right. Forget it."

"What?" He waggled his eyebrows. "That do somethin' for ya?"

The prof leaned closer and stared straight through him, oddly serious. "Not if you didn't mean it."

He felt his brow crease and Daniel touched his cheek. "Don't worry about it." His expression cleared. "Right now, I just need you to kneel." He took two steps back and looked him up and down, smirking. "Naked, please."

Daniel didn't have to tell him twice. He yanked off his clothes in record time and, as soon as he was bare, the man was on him. Daniel bound each of his wrists singly in a length of rope. The efficient looped knots took no more than thirty seconds.

And *shit*, but that was doing things for him that he hadn't expected.

"I had a whole other plan for tonight," Daniel confessed, double-checking the ropes. "Then I saw you. The way you handled those two." He added another length and wrapped it twice around his shoulders, trapping his hands against his chest. "Color?"

"Green."

He was starting to tip into that quiet place already. The embarrassment he felt at desires new and old didn't seem so loud. How could they when he saw what it did to Daniel, how the man's pleasure seemed to hinge on Carver's own enjoyment?

Daniel finished the tie around his shoulders and with that, his hands were useless. He needed help to turn and face the couch back, then he balanced his knees on the edge of the cushions. Daniel tipped him forward, forcing his legs apart. Carver found if he twisted just the right way, he could push his bound hands against the couch to brace — but he was far more interested in pushing against Daniel, in rubbing against the erection pressing into his back.

There really was something about how it made the man shiver.

"I couldn't even go in," Daniel admitted in his ear. "I would've caused a scene." He slid a hand across his collarbone, securing his body against his chest. Daniel's forearm fit snugly beneath his chin. "Tell me what happened. Every bit of it." He kissed over his pulse, just beneath the brim of his hat. "No matter what, don't stop talking."

It was a new version of an old request. He knew Daniel liked to hear him, but what was he supposed to say? "What d'you wanna know?"

The arm not looped around his neck circled his torso. Daniel rocked against the small of his back. "Why'd you kick them out?"

He shrugged. "They started a fight."

Daniel's fingers skated over his skin. "What about?"

"Couldn't tell you. Seemed like they were buddies until half the party left. Then they were tanked and at each other's throats." Thinking about those assholes brought back his earlier frustration. There was something special about the havoc of a drunk, entitled rich kid. Came with its own special brand of *fuck you*, in his experience.

Daniel licked the shell of his ear and stopped all possible thought. "I heard what he called you."

He shuddered. Was that what this was about? "And?"

"That ever bother you?"

"Always figured your friend for a faggot..."

His impulse was to adjust his hat, but the ropes prevented that. Instead, he cracked his neck and kept as upright as possible. "Never took much stock in what people thought of me."

"Why?"

He exhaled in frustration. "'Cause people don't usually think of me." He wasn't sure he liked this game as much as the others. Keeping this shit off his mind was the point of hook-ups like this, but their current conversation wasn't allowing for that at all.

Daniel didn't speak for a time. He ran a hand over his back, then across his shoulders. He alternated between skating softness and the sharper pressure of nails, but never more than a tease—a way to prime the skin. Then Daniel fit himself more securely behind him, pressing his thumb into the muscle of his biceps and circling the lines in his arm. "Was it easy for you?"

He didn't answer immediately, enjoying the impressed tone of the professor's voice. It earned him a solid swat to the ass—not really discouraging behavior, but it was a reminder to hold up his end of the bargain. He was supposed to be talking.

"I know how to fight. They didn't. And they were drunk. Was only ever gonna go one way."

"Did you fight a lot growing up?" Daniel touched his thumb to the raised edge of his scar—the bit that curled by his ear—but didn't move his hat. He tried not to want what he couldn't have, but he also knew Daniel was only following his lead. He had one perfect memory of what it'd been like to be controlled that way—of Daniel's fist in his hair, dragging him close as he devoured his mouth. How much better would it feel now that they'd added so much to their repertoire? If he said he'd changed his mind, would Daniel—

Another stinging slap on the ass reclaimed his attention. "You stopped talking."

It was the right kind of pain. He liked when Daniel traded between softer touches and harder impact. Now his focus was back where Daniel wanted it, but he didn't mind. The more he talked, the lower Daniel kissed down his spine. It was a hell of a motivational tool.

"I guess that's somethin' to thank the military for. They cleaned up what I already knew." Daniel didn't move the arm from around his neck as he kissed lower, dragging his tongue down and around the side of his hip. It forced Carver to arch away, pressing his chest into the couch. The muscles in Daniel's arm flexed around his throat. That definitely felt better than it should.

"Do fights happen often?"

"No. But I don't mind helpin' when they do. Jeanie shouldn't have to worry about some bros trashing her place."

The prof nipped his side with his teeth, nearly bending them both in half thanks to the grip around his neck. "You're amazing."

That almost sounded like he meant it. He shivered, though his face flushed hot. "I'm just a guy, Daniel."

"Not from where I'm standing."

The obvious awe in his voice didn't make sense. He was about to ask after it when Daniel slid his hand down his ass, between his cheeks, and brushed two fingers up and down. "Is this okay?"

He tried, but there was no keeping the tremor from his voice. "More than."

"More, hmm?" Daniel's fingers briefly left his skin, returning wet and ready. "Then ask me for it."

C'mon, Daniel. Again?

It was the only thing the professor did every time. No matter the tie or position, even if it was obvious how badly he wanted it, Daniel made him ask. He didn't usually mind, but he wasn't yet so far gone that the words came easily. He licked his lips as Daniel's hand retreated, sliding up his spine the longer he stayed silent.

And he couldn't help it. He twisted his wrists in the ropes, gritted his teeth, and swallowed his pride. "Don't...don't stop. Go back to that."

Daniel's hand paused its upward trek. He heard shuffling behind him, then the tip of one finger pressed inside his body. Daniel urged the tight muscle to relax as he kissed the back of his thigh. Damn, but he must've been kneeling himself to pull that off. The muscles in his legs jumped at the unexpected sensation.

"Need to hear you," Daniel murmured. "If you want it."

For fuck's sake...

He'd already asked once. He wasn't going to beg. "Goddamn, just do it already—"

Before he could finish Daniel took hold of his hips, hiking them up as high as he could. And by the time he'd realized it wasn't just Daniel's finger ready to work him open, he was moaning freely into the cushions, willing to say any damn thing so long as Daniel kept doing *that*. All he knew was heat as Daniel's tongue circled his entrance, prodding alongside his fingers to make himself at home.

There was no way they'd last long enough to try that leg tie tonight. And as much as he'd been looking forward to something new, knowing he had the power to change Daniel's plans—that simply doing his job was enough to get the man *this* desperate…it just did things to him, okay? All Daniel had to do was talk in that confident voice and something inside him perked up and paid attention. He didn't know why. He just knew it was true.

It was the only reason he could figure for why he'd suddenly become such a quick shot.

Pleasure-drunk and fully spent, he slumped over the back of the couch. Daniel dropped to the carpet near his feet and kissed his knee. Like he was coming back for it later.

"Tomorrow work for you?"

It was the first time Daniel had confirmed their unofficial schedule aloud. It was kind of nice.

He pressed his forehead into the cushions. "I'll be here."

* * * *

Carver spent the next day in a haze. He knew this thing with Daniel was unsustainable, that it flew in the face of his hard line against relationships. But he also knew he didn't care. Sure, their thing had an expiration date, but he'd be damned if he missed a minute of it. It just felt too damn good.

He spent all his time at the shop that day reliving the past night over. When he got to Jeanie's, he was anxious and needy, like his skin was a size too small, and it wasn't until Daniel followed him home that either of those feelings eased.

True to form, Daniel had checked in via text about the tie they'd discussed and ditched yesterday. The futo was new territory for them, but Carver was game to try. Once back at his place, he followed Daniel inside like usual. He'd been headed for the couch when a hand on his shoulder pulled him up short.

"Since I'm tying your legs tonight, a bed might be better." Daniel waved at the door he'd only opened once. "If that's okay with you."

He shrugged. No skin off his back. "Sure."

Carver was well used to bringing guests into his bedroom. It didn't usually bother him if he'd remembered to "clean" or not. But this time, he looked at the stacks of boxes through Daniel's eyes. What would the prof think of his half-unpacked living space?

The eggshell walls were bare. Rumpled clothes poked out from his open closet. He kicked the pile inside and slid the door along the track. As Daniel surveyed the room, he tried not to let his shoulders slump. It could be worse. At least he had a bed frame. It had come with the house and sat low to the floor, but he had one.

He sat on the edge of the mattress and Daniel stood in front of him, loosing a bundle of rope. He draped the dark strands over his neck and tossed another three bundles aside. Each landed against the carpet with weighted softness and that *sound...*

He honest-to-God felt like there were butterflies in his chest.

Over the past week, Daniel had added to his makeshift collection. He'd never said as much, but Carver got the feeling he wasn't pleased with his tools. There were times when he'd sigh and pull at the fibers, like the lack of quality wasn't anyone's fault, but he still regretted the truth of it. And as he had every night, Carver watched in admiration as Daniel handled the ropes — how the natural tawny braids contrasted with the black he'd used the first time — and wondered what other skills the prof was hiding.

If this was his "travel kit," what toys did he keep at home? What might their nights be like if Daniel had everything he wanted at his disposal?

It surprised him how fast his views had changed. In the space of a couple weeks, he'd gone from a passing interest in less-than-vanilla encounters to planning his whole schedule around Daniel tying him up again. And maybe it was wishful thinking, but he'd noticed changes in Daniel too. When he'd first gotten to town, Daniel's personality had swung between extremes — at once the quick-witted academic and the bashful newcomer, too nervous to even ask if Carver was interested.

Now there was a certainty to Daniel, both when they were alone and at the bar. He tapped into a different energy when Carver was around — no longer frantic, though at times he was quick. It was more that Daniel was always exactly where he needed to be. He was fast when it was required, slow when that suited better. And when he looked down at him from over his glasses, ice blue eyes boring into his, Carver wondered for what felt like the hundredth time how he'd tripped and fallen into this with Daniel.

"You're quiet tonight."

The comment pulled him from his thoughts. "Am I?"

Daniel nodded. He shrugged and leaned back on his hands. He'd been kicking the question around for days, but he'd never said the words before. "I know what I'm gettin' out of this arrangement." Daniel smiled at the ropes in his hand, then lifted his gaze to meet his. He did his best to keep talking over the sound of his heartbeat in his ears. "But you? I don't have you figured out as much."

"I wondered if you'd ask." Daniel set his pocketknife on the nightstand, then patted the center of the bed. "It's a bit of a story. Okay if I get started?"

Carver nodded. He didn't trust his voice as Daniel reached for his belt. Normally, the man would watch as he undressed himself, but tonight Daniel laid him back and unfastened his jeans himself, sliding them to the floor along with his socks.

Daniel left his boxers on and thumbed the waistband of the dark fabric. "You want these on or off? There's merits to both."

"Why? What do you want?"

"I want to cut them off once you're tied and ready, but that's not what I asked." Daniel snapped the elastic against his skin. "On or off?"

He said things like that more often now, providing the smallest window into his own desires. Daniel's gaze lay heavy on him as he considered the question.

"On," he eventually said, pressing himself into Daniel's hand. "Since now I know there's options."

Daniel exhaled through his nose. "It's hard to believe you're new at this. You know exactly what you're doing to me."

He felt his face flush at the praise. "But you're not. New to this, I mean."

"Not really."

"How long?"

"On and off since grad school."

He snorted in amusement. "Weren't you like seventeen in grad school?"

Daniel lifted his left leg to the bed and placed the sole of his foot on the mattress. "I didn't jump in right away, but yes. Took some time to work up the courage to do more than watch." Daniel tied off a series of knots around his ankle. "There was this club downtown, not far from campus. They hosted play parties. I would borrow my lab mate's ID, drink club soda and watch the scenes. Mostly rope stuff at first, but I found it mattered less what acts were included. It was more about who was doing it."

"And people didn't mind you watching?"

"You might say that was the point. For some." He kept Carver's left foot flat on the bed, knee bent toward the ceiling as he wrapped the rope up and around. Once he'd reached the top of the leg, he spiraled back down. "It's been a long time since I've done so, but if you stay in a scene long enough, you start to recognize the players. The ones who really know what they're doing."

"Can't imagine that."

"There's not much else like it. Not that I've found. That sort of community...public vulnerability." Daniel huffed a breath. "People like to think they value communication, but rarely does anyone actually say what they want."

"Sounds like you miss it."

"It's not something I've made time for. Until recently." They shared a smile as Daniel finished the tie on his left leg.

"You ever been on this side of it?" Carver plucked at the ropes, running his fingers over the braided twine.

"I've bottomed before, but more as an exercise in understanding. Being tied doesn't do much for me." Daniel brought his right foot to the bed, ready to start again. "I don't need time to sit in my thoughts. I need a goal. An achievable end result." He pulled another bundle of rope from the ground, then decided against it. He rewound it tightly, looping the ends through in a way that held it together. "This, I can do. I'm better when I do."

"Better at what?"

Daniel laughed once. "At keeping my shit together. In all parts of my life." He paused, and Carver wondered if he'd continue. "That's one of the reasons Aminah was so supportive." Daniel tied more knots until his right ankle matched his left. "She wasn't interested in being tied, but she liked the aesthetics of it. She saw what it did for me. And she was so glad when I found new partners."

Neither of them had shared many specifics of past relationships. That sort of conversation was too close to The Talk, which Carver had a habit of avoiding at all costs. But he'd been watching Daniel work on his legs for a while and the hypnotic rhythm of his hands lulled him into speaking without thinking first.

"You quit everything when she disappeared, didn't you?"

Daniel's answer didn't come right away, but Carver could tell he'd heard him. His blue eyes stayed focused as he wound the rope toward his knee. "That's one perspective. It more feels like I never stopped. The next lecture. The next dig site. The next plane to catch." Daniel looked at him intently. There was more behind his eyes than Carver wanted to admit to seeing. "If you don't think about what you're missing, then you don't have time to miss it."

He swallowed against the lump in his throat. "I get that."

This would be the time where one of them should look away. Daniel seemed to be weighing his words. "You know, there's more to this than just rope. What we've been doing."

"How d'you mean?" To his mind, they'd already moved beyond "just rope." They'd already added different types of sensation play to the mix. What else was there?

"You like not having to choose," Daniel said. "Having me choose for you."

As always, the prof cut right to the chase. He stretched his neck and ignored the hot prickling in his cheeks. "Within limits."

"That's exactly what I mean." Daniel kept his hands on his leg and looked him right in the eye. "How would you feel about adding to this? Outside of the rope?"

The man's three weeks in town were almost over and Daniel was making plans? Wary interest stirred in his chest. "What're you thinking?"

Daniel examined his face, like he was looking for clues on how to proceed. "I might text you more. Tell you to do things. Ensure you're remembering others."

"Because that's something you like doing for people?"

Daniel caught his chin between his fingers. "I'd like doing it for you."

The intensity in his face was almost too much to look at. Carver felt a strange urge to laugh, but held it back. He coughed once. "Are you asking for permission to flirt with me?"

The prof smirked. "For starters."

"You are the strangest man I've ever met."

"So?"

None of this should have been as endearing as it was. He sighed and adjusted his hat, since for once, his hands were free. "Yes, Daniel. You can text me about more than grocery trips and rope. Anything else?"

Even he could tell there was more on Daniel's mind. But all he said was, "Not now," and returned to the ropes in his hand, so Carver followed his lead and sat on the bed, waiting.

"I'm almost done, then we'll have you kneel." Daniel pressed a kiss to the top of his right knee and resumed the tie. "I really want to see you in this one."

Hearing this was of special interest made him eager to please. He was curious about the sensation, what it'd feel like to kneel over the intricate pattern—and almost as badly, he wanted to see what his patience might get the prof to say tonight. It'd be embarrassing if the other man didn't seem to like it just as much as him.

Daniel excelled at candid praise, but that wasn't all. He had a habit of mumbling toward the end, sometimes even lapsing into other languages. Carver could well admit what that did for his ego, but he also wondered if he might recognize a word or two if he heard them again.

Daniel finished the ties on his right leg, then shed his own button-down. He folded it in half and placed it aside. The dim light of the bedroom revealed glimpses of Daniel's form as he helped him move on the mattress. He kept his focus on the lines of Daniel's arms as he guided him to kneel near the edge. The full weight of his body leaned on his shins and thighs, causing the ropes to bite into his skin. He shifted, adjusting to the sensation.

"Color?"

"Green," he said, knowing he'd probably get there. Daniel's hands plucked at the ties on his thighs and he shivered. It felt good. It always felt good. It was new to have this lack of movement in his legs, but he was willing to deal with discomfort if it got Daniel out of his pants faster. His body started to react to the restriction, to the soothing touches of Daniel's hands. And the ropes on his legs were still unfamiliar, but he resolved to grin and bear it. It'd be worth it.

Daniel was already hard and wet at the tip, holding himself just out of reach. "Can I —"

Not waiting for the end of the question, Carver reached his neck and swallowed him down. The professor's breathy moan was exactly as wonderful as he remembered. But while this was one of his favorite things, he couldn't lose himself in the rocking of Daniel's hips, the fullness in his throat. The ropes that usually felt so secure were holding him back in the wrong way.

He didn't like the numbness that crept into his legs, but he had goals here tonight. Things he wanted to hear and feel. If he could push through for long enough, maybe...

Without warning, the prof pulled himself away. He shifted on his legs as Daniel frowned. "Be honest, Carv. What color are you?"

He hung his head, glad his hat was there to hide his face. "Yellow?" He shifted on his knees again. "It's just... There's this tingling in my legs and—"

"You don't like it," said Daniel, quick to the point as always.

"I can try to—"

"Carver, stop." Daniel bent at the knees, leaning down until their faces were level. "Do you like this feeling? Yes or no?"

He let out the breath he'd been holding. "Not really."

"So what color are you?"

He licked his lips, not liking the taste of defeat. "Red," he said, ashamed and unsure why. This had never happened before. What came next? Was he going to leave?

Daniel pressed a hand to his face. When he dared look up, he saw eyes full of concern without a trace of anger. "Thank you for telling me."

Quicker than he could track, Daniel reached for his pocketknife and, in three easy movements, freed his left leg from the ropes. The immediate release of tension was jarring, but he knew he'd made the right call when he heard his own thankful sigh. Daniel repeated the same on his right leg, tossing the ruined ropes aside as he circled behind him on the bed.

"Lean into me," Daniel said. "Just for a minute. Please."

He felt silly about the whole thing now that his legs were free. The corners of his eyes pricked with wet heat and his throat was dry — but he didn't understand why. He was fine now. He didn't need to be coddled.

Daniel pressed soft kisses against his shoulder, sliding soothing hands all over his arms and back. In time, he relaxed into the strength of the man behind him. "Is there anything you want to talk about?"

Words rushed out before Carver knew what he was saying. "I don't want you to think — it's not that I didn't like the other stuff…" He huffed a breath in frustration. He'd never been good at conversations like this. "I don't know why that was different."

Daniel didn't sound upset at all. "Not everyone likes every tie. That's why there's thousands of them." He handed Carver the water bottle from his bag. "Drink some of this. How are you feeling now?"

"Kinda strange." Now that he'd had some time to come down, Carver tuned into the other sensations in his body — particularly the deep want he'd felt for days that was still unsatisfied. "Don't think I realized how badly I…" He shook his head. That was asking too much. "Never mind."

"Do you still want me to tie you?"

He closed his eyes, thankful that Daniel couldn't see his face. "Is it bad if I say yes?"

"It's only bad if you say something untrue." Daniel adjusted their positions so that his hat stayed on, pressed between his head and Daniel's chest. "There's plenty of ways to get to the same destination. Would you want to try a different option for your legs? Something you can lie down in?"

He opened his mouth to answer, but Daniel placed a finger to his lips. "Take a second to really think about it. Any answer is fine, so long as it's the truth."

He nodded and eventually asked, "Is that all right?"

"Of course it is." Daniel's hand rubbed his neck, just under the edge of his hat. "When you're ready, kneel on the mattress again for me."

This time, Daniel secured the tops of his thighs to his ankles, then had him lie on his stomach. He brought both hands behind his back and tied them together as well. As Daniel neared the end of it, he felt that floaty lightness rise in his chest. He didn't even mind that when he set his head down and pressed his cheek to the mattress, his hat tumbled off the bed.

"What's this one called?" he asked once Daniel was finished.

"It's a version of a hogtie. Do you like it?"

He struggled against his bonds. There was still a nice feeling of security in his legs — similar to being on them, but he didn't have to support all the weight himself. And with his arms secured behind his back, he was entirely at Daniel's mercy. Before, that might've felt like he was giving up too much control. Now he was simply thankful their night wasn't over yet.

"Yeah," he said in response. "This is better."

"Color?"

"Green. Definitely."

He heard the smile he couldn't see as Daniel stood from the mattress. The sounds of falling clothes sent a pulse of desire down his spine. He felt himself getting hard again, but even with his hips pressed into the bed, the tension in the ropes kept him from the friction he needed.

Daniel hooked a finger into the stretchy band of his boxers, still tight around his waist. He swore under his breath. "I meant to take these off you. I can pull them down, but—"

"Just use the knife."

"What was that?"

"You heard me." He arched his back, trying to press some part of himself into Daniel's hand. "Didn't you say you wanted to cut 'em off?"

"You'd let me do that?"

"So long as I don't walk away bleedin', I don't care." He tried to move again, unable to do more than twist in place. There'd been so much build-up at this point. He didn't know if he could wait much longer.

"Just be quick about it, man. I need..." He turned his face and huffed into the mattress. "If you don't get your hands on me soon, I'm gonna lose my mind."

Daniel exhaled slowly, shaky with anticipation. "All right. Hold still for me."

If before that moment someone had asked if he had a thing for knives, Carver would've said no. But he should've known better than to think in absolutes around Daniel. Not long ago, he'd have said the same about rope—and now look at him.

There was something intoxicating about how the sounds of Daniel's breathing mixed with those of his pocket-sized blade. The metallic *snick* of the knife opening. The coolness of steel against the small of his back. Daniel's breathy sigh as he stretched the material from his skin. The searing of the fabric ripping clean in half. It all made him ache for contact, had him biting into his lip as he fought to lie still.

By the time he felt Daniel's hands on his ass, he didn't have to be reminded that the man liked to hear him. He moaned as Daniel squeezed both cheeks, almost massaging, apparently fascinated with the sensation of skin-on-skin.

"I know we haven't really talked about this yet, but..." Daniel sounded like he couldn't catch his breath. "Carv, all I want to do right now is fuck you."

He'd have preferred to hide just how okay with that he was, but that hadn't ever been his luck. He groaned in longing. "Yes, I want that. Please, Daniel, I want that."

This tie didn't let him conceal anything. He was exposed in the best of ways as Daniel pulled the rope connecting his arms and legs — and *kept* pulling, using the help of his bindings to turn him onto his side. One of Daniel's hands started working in lube while the other ran the twisted line of his body — from the swell of his ass to the side of his torso, all the way up to where his shoulders pulled taut.

"You look... I can't even describe it." Daniel's hands shook on his skin. "You look so good for me like this. So good for me."

Why does he have to say these things?

He was certain he'd never blushed harder in his life. Then Daniel's fingers found his prostate — both crooked just right — and if anyone was keeping score, the sound that echoed off the walls in response probably counted as a scream.

Daniel kept on with it, easing off whenever needed to keep him on the edge, and not a single *fucking time* did the man reach around to touch his dick. He was so hard that all he felt was throbbing, a pulse that ran his entire body, but nothing in the world was going to make Daniel go faster than he wanted to. It could've been minutes or hours before the man stood, snapped on a condom and lay on the bed beside him. He held Carver's hips at an angle and lined himself up. They were both visibly shaking when Daniel caught his rim with the head of his cock, and it only got worse as Carver ground against him, up and down in a teasing motion.

There was *no way* he was going to last long enough for Daniel to really have him, but even this small bit was going to do it. It wasn't unheard of for him to come untouched. It just usually took more than one solid thrust.

Fucking overachiever Daniel. At it again.

He lost track of if he was doing anything for him, if he was still pushing back in a way that offered friction, but he turned his last shred of focus to the words tumbling from Daniel's lips. His mouth was pressed up against Carver's neck, breath blowing warm and humid against his ear.

"I don't—oh *shit,* that's...did you come just from that?" Daniel shuddered through an exhale. "Of course you did. So responsive. So good, so—fucking *shit,* Carver. *Scheisse—*"

"There. What was that?" he asked.

Daniel all but whimpered in his ear, "What? What are you talking about?"

"What you just said. What language was that?"

"Are you really asking me about languages right now?"

"What, that doesn't help?" Then he had a better idea. "How 'bout this?"

Carver pushed into his knees as much as the ropes would allow, arching his back into Daniel as he clenched around his cock.

"Fucking *fuck—*"

Yeah, that ought to do it. But Daniel still found a way to retaliate. He bit down on Carver's shoulder exactly hard enough, and as he thrust forward one last time, his hand slid down the vee of his hips to *finally* stroke the length of him.

He went off immediately, and he couldn't even be mad about it. It all just felt too damn good.

Things were never as dramatic the second time — when there was a second time — but it always left him twice as tired. He barely remembered what they'd been talking about when Daniel collapsed beside him, mumbling, "It's German." Then he laughed, good-humored and exhausted. He felt like he was missing the joke, but there'd be time to ask after that later.

Daniel only lay down a moment before he turned to his side and started untying the ropes. When he finished, they were both slick with sweat and opted to lie on their backs to let the overhead fan do its job. They passed his cut-up boxers back and forth to clean up, but more than that would have to wait. He doubted he could stay awake for the length of a cigarette.

"You know what's funny?" Daniel asked as they stared at the ceiling. "I can't remember the last time I spoke German. Guess it's an easy slip, considering the word."

"What's it mean?"

"Not much. It's profanity."

He shifted to lie more comfortably. "I'll take that as a compliment."

"You should." Beside him, Daniel pushed up to his forearms. "Look, I could bike back if you want me to." He sighed, abandoning his attempt to leave as he let his head fall to the pillows. "But I can hardly keep my eyes open right now."

"Just crash here."

There was a small pause. Not uncomfortable, but definitely there.

"You sure?"

"It's no big thing." He could see how it might seem otherwise, but he didn't have the energy to worry about it, at present. He turned on his side away from Daniel and dragged the sheet over his shoulders. "Pretty sure I snore, but you can fuck off to the couch if you need to."

"Not a problem," Daniel replied through a yawn. "I sleep like the dead."

The last thing he heard was Daniel roll over beside him. Then there was nothing but dark.

* * * *

When Carver woke, he knew at once that it was early. Weak morning light peeked between his plastic blinds. He didn't often see this time of day. Especially not when he worked as late as he had this week.

A voice behind him said, "I'm glad we got to do this before I left."

Memories from the night filtered into his sleep-fogged brain. He rolled to his back and saw Daniel, seated at the foot of the bed, bundling the last of the rope they hadn't thought to put away. He was dressed in the clothes he'd worn last night. His hair made it obvious he hadn't been awake for long.

"The rope stuff?" he asked. "Or the sleepover?"

Daniel breathed through a laugh. "Both, I guess." He flipped his messenger bag closed. "I need to get home before my morning class. Do some laundry. Find time to pack."

He swallowed and considered his words. "I thought you had another couple days."

"I do," Daniel confirmed, keeping his eyes on the floor. "But they're the busiest of my trip. I've got public talks on top of the lectures, and I need to make the rounds with the faculty. Make sure they like me enough to invite me back sometime."

He shifted up, sitting so his back leaned against the wall. "You gonna need a ride to the airport, then?"

Daniel nodded. "Monday afternoon, I guess. Yeah."

"Might have Martha's car back to you by then. Parts came in yesterday."

"That'd be great."

They were both silent for longer this time. He didn't know what to say as Daniel watched him, observant as ever. He wouldn't mind if Daniel reached for him, maybe kissed him goodbye. But he wasn't holding his breath.

"Do you work this Sunday?"

He shook his head. Daniel looked to be weighing his words. "Can I see you again before I leave? You could come by my place for once. I'll make you dinner."

Carver laid all the way down and pulled a pillow over his face. "There's no way you can do all this kinky shit, speak thirty languages *and* know how to cook. Don't even fuckin' say it."

"Fourteen. And is that a yes?"

He laughed into the pillow. "Sure. It's a date."

Chapter Nine

Daniel

For all Daniel had made his life about travel, he never remembered how long it took to settle in a new place. He was usually lucky to find his landmarks much before he was leaving. But though he'd only been in Fairview two and a half weeks, he felt more established than he had in years.

His thoughts had grown much quieter now that he had Carv to play with. A corner of his mind was always preoccupied planning—working out the next tie, dreaming of the sounds he might coax from the mechanic. He was everything Daniel wanted in a rope partner without even realizing it. Not to mention the sex was incredible, and how long had it been since *that* was a priority in his life? So while it was true that his last days in town were some of his busiest, he had little difficulty completing his academic work. His colleagues noticed his shift in mood too, though they'd only been colleagues a short time.

His schedule didn't allow time to visit Carver at Jeanie's, but they stayed in consistent contact over the next two days. Check-ins, mostly. Once, he asked Carver to send a photo of himself. He'd joked there wasn't much point since he was wearing clothes, but eventually complied.

Maybe it was greedy to try for this on such a deadline, but they were approaching a precipice, one he'd only reached with a couple partners before. He still shivered when he thought back to Carver's slip in speech...

"Well, yes, sir."

"We didn't discuss that."

"Discuss what? Manners?"

There was far more than manners that Daniel wanted to teach him. He almost wished he could rework his schedule to stay in town longer. Wouldn't be hard. As per his travel routine, he had multiple flight plans to get back east. It was a level of preparedness that had served him well many times, though it was laced with a thread of guilt now. Just like anything that touched on those last days before Aminah was gone...

"Why'd you cancel your flight, Henning?"

"You must know what this looks like – "

"Sorry to say, but you're a person of interest. We'll keep searching, but we can't let you leave..."

He shook the old words from his head and dug his phone from his pocket. He only had a few minutes before his next meeting, but he was anxious to try his latest idea.

He started easy, picking up where they'd left off yesterday.

Did you eat today? Or are me and Jeanie going to have to team up on you?

At this time of day, Carver was normally at his shop and more able to answer quickly. He still didn't know how the business was doing, but it wasn't long before Carver's response arrived.

Don't you dare. She's got enough ammo without you helping.

But did you eat? he followed up. Carver was too good at dodging important questions.

Yes. Yesterday was just busy. Ran out of time.

Busy why?

The answer arrived in the form of a photo. Martha's old sedan was up on blocks, hood open and torn apart. He smirked at the screen.

If you're trying to make me feel bad for asking, it won't work.

Sure, genius. How's your busy day going?

He sent back, *Waiting for yet another meeting to start,* then took a steadying breath. He gripped the phone tighter and sent the photo he'd taken moments ago. It wasn't anything special—just him sitting at his desk, drinking one of his collection of beverages. But Carver would remember that desk and everything else they'd done in his office. With any luck, it might encourage the man to exchange more photos with him.

He got his wish. The next message was a picture of Carver beside an open toolbox. He wore a dark gray mechanic's shirt and khaki work pants. His hands, arms and the side of his neck bore marks of grease and dirt. And as always, his straw cowboy hat sat perched atop his head.

Here goes nothing…

He typed out, *You should take that off. When's the last time you felt the wind in your hair?*

He hit send before he could talk himself out of it, snapped the phone closed and pushed it into his pocket. There was no telling how Carver would respond to a request like that, even if he'd agreed to trying "more than rope."

He knew what he *wanted* Carver's response to be. More than anything, he longed to see him with his hair down again, those strands of burnished gold falling to his chin—how he'd finally see his entire face without the shadow of a brim. But thinking about that would only make him later, so Daniel pushed the thoughts away and set off for his meeting across campus.

Only once he'd returned to his bike an hour later did he allow himself to check for a response. Another picture waited for him, but he still didn't get what he wanted.

True to form, Carver had dodged the most important part of his request. His hat was off, all right—and perched on the corner of his toolbox. Carver wasn't in the picture at all.

Smartass…

He checked the time and did some mental math. He'd found Carver's shop on his own once before. And while he was just as likely to get lost this time, he moved faster on his bike than on his feet. It flew in the face of what he'd been chiding Carver about earlier — he should be eating his own lunch right now — but he didn't care.

At present, there was only room for one thought in his mind. Because for the whole hour since he'd sent that photo, Carver thought he'd gotten away with this.

The mechanic didn't know how wrong he was. But if Daniel had his way, he was going to.

* * * *

Carver's red truck wasn't in the lot, but he spotted the man's motorcycle in the nearest parking spot. There was also a truck of indeterminate color, somewhere between blue and gray. The thought of other people at the shop made him pause. Maybe he'd make this a casual hello and not the thing his hindbrain kept asking for.

When he pushed the door open, he saw two of the only people he knew in the state. The private investigators he'd met with Martha were in the corner of the shop's waiting room. The dark-haired man sat against the wall and thumbed through an outdated magazine, a bland attention in his features. The blond stood beside him, looking at the few hanging photos, his hands shoved in his pockets.

Shit, shit, shit...

It was quite the pivot from the motivations that had brought him here. Should he say something to them? It was probably the polite thing to do. "Hey. It's Everett, right?"

The blond man's brow creased in confusion. "I'm sorry, have we met?"

Daniel was about to explain when another voice chimed in. "Of course you have," Colt intoned. "He's that professor who came past. Martha's tenant. Just got a haircut." The man looked at his partner. "You sure you used to be a detective?"

Somehow, Everett's response of "Shut your fuckin' mouth" sounded fond. Daniel tried not to pry into the couple's conversation and plucked at the strap of his messenger bag. "Is, uhm…is Carver around?"

"He's in back," Everett said. "Still working on the bikes. Since someone couldn't get 'em working."

Colt sniffed once, but his eyes didn't leave the page. "Not a bad thing to have someone check your work."

Everett grinned. "Look at you. Next you'll be asking for help when you need it. Then hell might actually freeze over." He took a seat beside his partner and squeezed the man's knee. Colt didn't move, but a half-smile curled his mouth as he turned another page.

Daniel sat a few chairs down and rummaged in his bag for a notebook. He didn't have anything to work on at present, but he also wasn't up for unexpected small talk. As he pulled the notebook free, a colored flyer fell out. He bent to retrieve it, but Everett was faster.

"What's this?" Everett plucked it from the ground. "'Ancient Advancements?'" He chuckled. "Ain't that an oxymoron?"

"Plenty would rather you thought so."

Both detectives turned to him and he tried not to sigh. Although it'd be easier to talk about work than invent something they had in common.

"It's just the lecture title," he explained. "My research focuses on ancient irrigation systems. Designs that work with local climate and topology, not against it."

Everett nodded along, looking impressed. "Not what I expected from some college professor."

"Most anthropologists focus on a people or place, not an idea. But Indigenous cultures have long held the keys to living with the Earth instead of on it."

"Well, thank God for you eggheads who're gonna save the world," Everett joked. "On behalf of us regular folk, we appreciate it."

"That's really not it." He kept his eyes on his empty notebook. This was deeper conversation than most expected in passing, but Everett had said the right combination of words and Daniel knew he wouldn't be able to let it go. "The world is burning around us and I'm, what? Supposed to be in a library somewhere? Reading about the peoples we all but eradicated that would've kept this from happening?" Frustration bled into his tone. "My research might be a drop in the bucket, but I refuse to be useless."

Colt looked up from his magazine and nudged Everett with his elbow. "See? He gets it."

"You wanna ruin his morning with your sunny optimism, then?"

"And let you off the hook?"

"Don't know why you'd start now." Everett patted Colt's leg twice and stood. "Lemme find Carv for ya. Make sure he didn't fall into anything back there."

Once Everett's footsteps faded in back, the shop was silent. No music played in the waiting room, leaving only the sounds of cranking metal and the turning of glossy pages. Daniel didn't mind the quiet, but it didn't stick around for long.

"Henning, hmm?" Colt said, skimming the page in front of him. "Feel like I should give you a card."

"How's that?"

"The name sounded familiar when you came by, but I couldn't place it." Colt closed the magazine and looked straight at him. "You were still students, yeah? When your girl disappeared?"

Heavy fists pounding at his door. Police and hotel staff shoving into the room. Angry, elevated voices demanding answers to questions he didn't understand.

"There's someone here. Don't move!"

"Aminah Bashir. Where is she?"

He could barely sit up in bed for all the firearms pointed his way. "What do you mean, where is she?"

God, but he was tired of having this conversation. He hadn't come here for a history lesson—quite the opposite. Only out of long-formed habit did he manage to keep a straight face. He closed his notebook and abandoned the pretense of busyness, meeting Colt's stare across the waiting room. The man's dark eyes held a touch of sympathy, but no pity.

That more than anything kept Daniel from causing a scene. People who'd never experienced this sort of trauma were always full of pity. But those who knew? Those haunted by their own tragic failings? They looked at him exactly like Colt was looking now.

Daniel breathed deeply as he rubbed his forehead. "I'm surprised you remember. Most don't. Not outside my field, anyway."

Colt tilted his head. "Most people aren't paying attention. Hard to forget, you ask me. Big news at the time."

"Yeah."

"They ever find her?"

He swallowed hard. "No."

Colt pulled his magazine open again. "Typical," he spat under his breath. "Cops are useless when it counts. No matter the country."

The frankness of the statement surprised him — and seemed to fly in the face of the little Carver had told him of the detective. "Weren't you police yourself?"

Colt snorted. "That's how I know what I'm talkin' about."

The sound of approaching conversation pricked his ears and Daniel hesitated. Maybe it wasn't too late to dodge out of the door — except Everett was already in back, getting Carver's attention. But after talking about Aminah…he hadn't expected to deal with that today. His nervous system was on high alert, looking for danger seven years gone. And he'd never considered himself religious, though he'd studied plenty, but Daniel was ready to thank whatever trickster god was responsible for Carver turning the corner — just as work-worn as his photo, minus one key element.

Carver wasn't wearing his hat.

The room faded to fuzzy background as Carver talked with the detectives. Daniel couldn't follow the conversation or the inside jokes, but he was glad for the way they made Carver smile, how his brown eyes warmed with laughter. His crooked grin creased a dimple into one of his cheeks. Daniel knew he was openly staring, but he didn't care. There was no way he'd be able to stop. No sense in wasting energy trying.

Then Carver noticed him, standing aimless in front of the line of chairs, and took a moment to look him up and down. He didn't know what his face was doing —

he hadn't thought to school it. He'd been so lost in the pain of his past, then so quickly reminded of his present desires. It was one hell of an emotional whiplash. His head still felt like it was spinning.

Carver looked away, a light flush on his cheek, and retied his hair at the base of his neck. For the brief moment it hung free, Daniel had to fight down a sigh. A warm ember of something bright flared in his chest.

He did that for me.

He hadn't even made it a formal request. Just suggested it. And Carver had complied—however cheekily. But that could be dealt with. It was why he was there, after all.

In plain sight of the other men, Carver winked at him.

Yes, something *definitely* had to be done about that.

When it became clear the room was waiting for him to speak, Daniel realized he'd missed a question. "I'm sorry, what?"

Everett shared a look with Colt, then repeated, "I asked what brought you in."

"Oh. The car I borrowed. Just checking on progress."

"That sad excuse for a vehicle." Everett shook his head, then clapped Carver on the shoulder. "Best of luck, man."

Colt nodded at the mechanic. "Thanks for making time."

"Not a problem."

"And I'll be callin' about that other thing in a day or two," Everett added. "Just waiting to hear back from some agencies—"

"That's fine," Carver said, cutting him off. "We'll talk soon."

Colt guided Everett out through the door with a hand on his back. Carver waved in farewell, then circled the intake desk. Without the sounds of machines or idle chatter, the room was completely quiet. he could almost hear the rushing of his blood, pounding in his ears —

"So," Carver said, "why're you really here?"

Everything felt too raw to play any games about it. "You took your hat off," he answered honestly. Like that explained things. Hopefully, Carver would know what he meant.

The mechanic smirked and filed a handful of papers. "I don't always wear it, you know."

"Just usually."

Carver shrugged and made his way back around the desk. Daniel swallowed hard as the man stood in front of him, but despite his best efforts the question slipped out. "Why'd you do it?"

Carver repeated the up and down he'd given him a moment ago — slower this time. Really taking him in. Seeing the effect of his little prank seemed to embolden him, and out came the answer he'd been craving.

"Because you asked me to."

Scheisse…

He closed his eyes and took a steadying breath. When he opened them, Carver was walking backward, holding his gaze in invitation as he turned the corner.

He'd never ventured beyond the sterile waiting room before. He had no knowledge of what a shop like this should look like, but to his limited understanding, the machines seemed to be in good shape. Four bays with lifts sat in line with rolltop garage doors. Two motorcycles were propped near the furthest wall and

Martha's sedan was in the closest bay, the engine raised above the hood by a hook in the ceiling.

In the time it'd taken to survey the room, Carver had picked up a wrench and sat on a low rolling bench. He'd also lost his dark shirt and wore only a ribbed white tank.

He exhaled slowly, grasping at straws. "What's that?"

Carver was only a few inches off the ground. His stretched-out legs straddled the red piece of plastic and kept the casters from rolling. He chuckled as he said, "It's called a creeper."

"What a name."

"Seems fitting." The mechanic swung the wrench on his finger. "You plannin' to watch me or something?"

"I don't know what I'm planning. Didn't really get that far."

"Well, if you have any ideas, feel free to share with the class." With that, Carver rolled himself beneath the car.

"I feel like that should be my line," he called after him.

"Lemme do another for you, then." Carver cranked the wrench in his hand and removed a piece of the car's undercarriage. "Oh, hey there, Carver," he said in a mocking tone. "Nice to see you. I know I said I was busy, but I'm here because..."

"That picture you sent. Of your hat. You did it on purpose."

"Did I now?" Carver tossed a sheet of metal out from under the car. The look on his face was anything but innocent.

"You knew what I meant. I wanted to see you, not the hat."

Carver rolled farther beneath the car. "Should've been more specific there, Teach."

"Don't call me that. You're not my student."

"What should I call you, then?"

It was too intentionally phrased to have been a mistake. Daniel marched to the car and set his leather shoe atop the rolling creeper and kicked. Carver wheeled head-first toward the center of the shop, but caught himself quickly. Almost like he'd expected it.

Still, it was enough to jostle him from underneath the car. Carver looked up at him, practically on his back, but his eyes were bright with amusement.

"You're teasing," he said.

Carver took his time sitting forward, sprawling his legs again. He pulled a shop towel from his back pocket and ran it over his hands. "Why not? Said dirtier stuff in my life for less." He tossed the towel aside and met his eye. "Sir."

Fucking fuck, he's trying to kill me...

Carver tried to roll forward on the creeper again, but Daniel stopped the corner under his foot easily. They held each other's gaze as he leaned forward, catching Carver by the neck. He took his time fitting a hand across the man's throat. "We're going to talk about this later. But right now..."

He couldn't find the right words. The feel of Carver swallowing beneath his hand was too distracting.

"I just want you," he said instead. "Is that all right?"

Carver laughed and the sound buzzed against his palm. "I gotta spell it out for you?" He leaned into the hold on his throat. "Some genius."

Daniel regripped to hold the side of Carver's face and pressed his thumb across his lips. "Really can't have you talking like that."

"Of course you can't," Carver managed to say. Keeping eye contact, he caught the edge of Daniel's thumb with his teeth. And bit down. "So do something about it."

That was enough permission for now.

"Get off that thing." His voice was already harsh in his throat. "On your knees. Right now."

"That's more like it."

He gripped Carver's jaw tighter, but the man only smirked. For once, the mechanic had full use of his hands, meaning Daniel's fly was down and open in no time at all. Carver pressed him back by the hips until his legs hit the taillight of Martha's car. Together they steered Carver's head forward until he sank his mouth down on his cock.

Oh, shit. That feels...

So much, so fast—Daniel honestly had to catch his balance. Carver was there to help, forearms pressing against his thighs. He didn't know where to put his hands—well, he knew where he *wanted* to put them. It seemed like that might be okay...

Gently, he rested one on the top of Carver's head. "Look at me."

Carver complied, not pausing his ministrations. He continued to swallow him down, but Daniel wouldn't be distracted. Not from this.

"Do you want me to hold you here?" he asked. "Tap once for yes, twice for no. The truth."

There was a pause, then a single firm tap to his side. Carver nodded as well.

Daniel sucked in a deep breath and closed his fist around the small bundle of blond at the man's neck. He went limp with pleasure, falling heavier against him, ceding control to the hand now guiding his movements. And perhaps sweetest of all, when Daniel pulled on his hair, Carver made a sound he hadn't heard in weeks — since the only other time he'd reached for this.

He hadn't known better that first time. But now, understanding the trust this required? What a gift to receive this from him. This man who did everything by himself, for himself — he was letting Daniel give him this. Minutes ago, he'd been so out of sorts, but now? Watching Carver on his knees, Daniel knew he'd never been more grounded.

God, he was just incredible — taking it all so well. He seemed blissed out already, and if Daniel wasn't trying to drag this out, he'd have told him so. The only thought in his mind was that Carver deserved *everything*.

A distant part of him recognized that was dangerously close to feelings. That probably warranted exploration.

Shit, shit, shit…

"What was that?"

"Nothing, *schätzchen*."

He heard the word leave his lips, died inside and plowed on ahead. Nothing for it, now.

"Don't stop," he said, thumbing down Carver's lip. "I want you to come while you're gagging on my cock."

Carver whimpered in response. Yeah, he'd thought that might be the reaction.

Daniel took his time making good on his promise, sliding in and out of perfect wet heat. He paused at the end of each thrust to feel Carver's throat contract. "Was this what you wanted?" he asked, sliding himself along Carver's tongue. "When you sent me that stupid picture?"

Another single tap. So he *had* done this on purpose...

"Did you know this is all I've thinking about?" he asked, chasing his breath. "Getting you by the hair, giving you exactly what you'd asked for?"

Carver gripped the base of his own dick hard — trying so desperately to wait, to do as he'd been told.

"Touch yourself," he told him. It was time to finish this. He gathered his self-control and pushed completely down Carver's throat, not moving back. He looked him right in the eye and said with a smile, "I'll wait."

He kept still as Carver swallowed convulsively around him. He counted the seconds in his mind and *fuck*, but Carver was impressive. He backed off to let him breathe, but Carver was close. Wanting to make good on his word, he pushed past his lips again. He tugged Carver's hair by the roots and held himself as still as he could.

Carver gagged — the sound mingling with percussive moans as he came in his hand. Only then did Daniel allow himself to thrust in and out more shallowly, to give the man proof of just how good he'd been.

Carver took most of it down, pulling off to let the rest paint his cheek obscenely. The jolt of desire that inspired was going to have to *wait*. It'd be hours before he could so much as think again.

Once he'd caught his breath, he spotted Carver's towel on the ground. He plucked it up and handed it over. "Here."

The mechanic was still glassy-eyed as he swiped the cloth over his face. That seemed to take the last of his energy and he slid down the fronts of Daniel's legs to sit down. Carver pressed his head against the car and chased his breath. "Fuck."

He had to agree. But, unfortunately, this had all taken longer than Daniel had hoped. The large clock on the wall told him there was barely enough time to get to campus, so as much as he wanted to slump beside Carver on the concrete, he stood on his shaky legs and fastened himself up.

"Sunday?" was all the question he could manage.

Carver nodded at his feet. Not wanting to risk a kiss, he squeezed the man's shoulder and was on his way.

As he semi-confidently navigated back to his office, Daniel couldn't help but laugh. Perhaps hysterically, but it was ridiculous. In the space of a couple weeks, he'd gone from never having sex at work to crossing off both of their places of employment. From that perspective, that only left the bar on the list. He didn't think Jeanie would be too keen on that, no matter how much she liked Carver.

Still. Now they'd started, he would've liked to get them all before he left.

But there wasn't time. He wouldn't be able to get away again before Sunday, though clearly there was *much* for them to explore here. He'd never have thought Carver would bait him that way, though maybe he should've. The man had taken to rope like a duck to water. If he was already riding the line of submission like that? After two days of texting? Daniel regretted not trying this sooner. Who knows where they might've gotten?

Regardless, Carver deserved something for this. Whether he knew it or not, that had completely turned his day around. He was grateful—maybe too much so. That had to be the reason, right?

Schätchzen? Really?

He couldn't believe he'd slipped so badly. This was why it was best that he kept to his plans. It was why, as tempted as he'd been, he hadn't canceled his flights on Monday. They'd agreed to a casual experiment before they'd explored these deeper dynamics.

It was one thing to play a role for a person. It was quite another to fall for someone.

Obviously, the two weren't mutually exclusive. Easily blended. Not something he'd done before to much effect, but with Carver...

He had to stop thinking about what ifs and maybes. He should be satisfied with what they'd been able to share. Before he left, he'd set Carver up to keep exploring on his own. He owed him that. And for his first couple weeks away, he'd check in to see how that went. He'd make sure his leaving town wouldn't drop him. Beyond that, he'd have to take Carver's cues and see.

But until then, Daniel had a plan. And it hinged on making Sunday a night to remember.

Chapter Ten

Carver

He'd riled Daniel up good at the shop—and successfully distracted the man from Everett's big mouth. Sure, it had been thanks to Daniel he'd gone forward with this in the first place. But if all Everett confirmed was that he had no living family, he didn't want to talk about it. Wouldn't *that* be a note to end Daniel's trip on.

Hey, thanks for the advice. Now I'm a hundred percent sure I've got no one. Have a good flight.

On principle alone, Carver refused to be that depressing.

But distraction had only been a part of his motivations during Daniel's latest visit to the shop. Before they'd met, he'd kept to the vanilla side of the hookup scene—with a few noteworthy exceptions. He'd just never thought it would be his thing. Now, it was obvious why. In the past when he'd considered this at all, he'd assumed he'd fall on the dominant side of the bargain. He was usually the one to initiate at the bar. It was a rare thing when someone tried to pick him up, not just flirt in the hope of drinks.

He'd never considered the other side until Daniel had crashed into his life. He hadn't known there were people who craved taking control the same way he craved giving it up. And the power that came with knowing he had something the man wanted…that for a couple hours, he didn't have to do or be anything specific… He could just sit there and feel — and not have to keep a lid on his reactions…

It was too easy to please Daniel, to rile him up and get the response he wanted. So what if it was always going to be temporary? It was so rare he found a place to rest his head, a moment of not having to be in charge. Last time, he'd uprooted his whole life expecting it would last.

He wasn't doing that again. He'd learned his lesson well enough.

* * * *

Harahan, Louisiana
Summer of 2013

"I've got it all figured out," Derek said, arms full of papers. Didn't notice that he was working under a pick-up. Or that Denise was ringing up customers from their busy afternoon.

"What d'you mean?" he asked, rolling out from under the truck.

"C'mere, Will. Just take a look."

He heaved a sigh and shoved off the creeper. Derek spread no fewer than twelve brochures across the truck's hood, all emblazoned with the Fairview College logo. He held a booklet in his hands and flipped through the pages.

Many sections were highlighted. Derek had spent time on this.

He swallowed hard as he listened to Derek excitedly talk him through The Plan. "I know we'll be in different classes, but it'd be just like old times. Us in school together. If you started your bachelor's now, even if you took time to work, we'd probably graduate at the same time. My doctorate will take me five years at least, and..." Derek trailed off. He looked up from the catalog in his hands. "Don't you want to know how to really set something like this up?" He gestured to the small, two-bay shop around them. "In a bigger place? Where you could do more business?"

If they had any more business, he and Denise would need to hire somebody. "Think we're set up all right for now."

"For now, sure. But isn't there..." Derek checked the office window, ensuring no one was near. He tugged them around the corner to hide from all possible view. "I'm not just asking for you. I'm asking for me. This program...it's harder than anything I've ever done. And if I don't finish in five years, that puts the rest of my plan in jeopardy."

"You really that worried about it?"

Derek shrugged at the floor. "But if you came with me...it'd be like bringing a piece of home. Having somebody to come back to. Someone who gets me." Derek caught his hand and rubbed the back of his knuckles, not commenting on the grease. "Isn't there a part of you that wonders what this could be? Someplace else?"

The words caught in his throat. Was Derek finally willing to talk about this? "I thought there was no 'us'," he said carefully.

"Of course there's an 'us', Will. I've always..." Derek sighed, taking both his hands in his own. "Just come with me."

He felt the beginnings of a smile in his cheek. "You really mean this, don't you?"

Derek nodded. "Yeah. I do."

He double-checked they were still alone and pulled Derek in for a kiss. There was still the awkward stutter — still worried someone would see them, like Denise didn't already know. But he didn't pull away. Derek pushed through his nerves and properly kissed him back.

When they broke apart, Derek was smiling. "So? You'll come?"

He'd always been a sucker for a smile.

"Of course."

That had been the worst part of it. Even years later, Carver knew that Derek had meant that. He'd been genuine in wanting to see what the world could be like — what *they* could be like, outside of Harahan. But Derek had never let go of the fear of being "found out." He was never willing to "risk it" and God, it was exhausting being thought of as dangerous. Like being with him at all was a burden.

It had taken far, far too long before Carver had realized the truth. It didn't matter if Derek had meant it. "Wondering" had gotten them out of their small town and landed them in another, but it wasn't enough to build on. He'd uprooted his whole life to move with Derek to Fairview. And whenever he'd try to do something like what people might do as a couple, Derek had acted like it was a chore. Like he was doing him some kind of favor.

His dad's visit had sealed the deal, but their relationship had long gone sour. Carver just hadn't had the heart to throw it out yet.

* * * *

Fairview, Louisiana
Spring of 2015

Derek's ain't-shit father was coming to visit, and in the weeks preceding the trip, Derek closed up even further. If he so much as bumped into him when they were in public, Derek had something to say about it. God forbid he show any affection in the privacy of their own home. They had to "practice" for when the all-important Kurt Patterson was there.

Didn't matter that his father had missed most of Derek's childhood once he and Denise had split. Apparently, his paternal opinions mattered more than anything they'd built in the last year. It was the same reason they'd leased a two-bedroom apartment even though it was more expensive. Because they needed separate bedrooms for the four times a year they had friends over – the few they even had of those.

Not a bit of their time in Fairview had gone as Carver had hoped. He'd traded away his shop for a stack of books he didn't care about and tests he barely passed. It burned to think about. So he didn't let himself. If he did, he'd have to do something about it and he wasn't ready to give this up yet.

He kept his head down for the first leg of Kurt's visit. He "went to bed" early in avoidance and woke in the small hours. After a few days of the pattern, he was plenty conscious on the side of a thin wall when he heard the sound of his name.

He hadn't meant to eavesdrop, but as he was the topic of conversation, he didn't feel bad for long.

"What about Will?" Patterson Senior asked. "How's he doin'?"

"Fine, I guess. He works at this bar a lot. We don't see each other much."

"I was surprised when your mother said you were roomin' together."

"He doesn't have any family, Dad. He needs a cheap place. It made sense."

"Well, that's nice of you. Considering."

"Considering what?"

"Oh c'mon, don't get all PC-police on me. I always figured your friend for a faggot, but living with him's a different story. You gotta be careful, son..."

Derek laughed like something was funny. The sound rang too true for his liking. "It's not like that. He's just my roommate, Dad."

The silent tension held until Kurt asked, "He gonna want to come with us tomorrow?"

"Nah. Alehouse isn't really Will's scene."

He didn't know how long it took to unfreeze his feet, to remove his hand from the door handle and sit on his unfamiliar bed. He'd never been so angry before. This sort of hurt...it was different than any other he'd experienced. This was visceral. Bloody. Like he'd been hollowed out alive.

Denise knew they were together. She'd congratulated him on the shop's last day of business. What'd Derek care about his dad's opinion anyway? He was paying for Derek's school, but still. Was how Derek felt about him really so awful?

Rejection and shame ate at him over the course of the day. He was glad to be working a double at Jeanie's. If he was working, he wasn't thinking. Thinking was dangerous. He worked himself into the ground on purpose, hoping it'd be enough to let him sleep. Derek's father would be leaving tomorrow. He just had to get through one more day. With any luck, both Pattersons would still be out. He could sleep through the rest of the visit and wake in his usual life.

He took care unlocking the apartment door, not wanting to wake anyone. Derek's father was passed out on their couch — apparently too drunk to make it back to his fancy hotel. Carver rolled his eyes and made for his room, which shared a wall with Derek's. Not something that was usually a problem.

Because usually when Derek made sounds like that, Carver was in the room with him. Not locked outside, listening.

His vision went hazy. His ears started to ring – not so loud it blocked anything out. Just sort of mingled with the heavy sighs, the peals of feminine laughter. The overt, rhythmic thumping that had bile rising in his throat. Then, there was nothing but numbness as he shook out an old duffel bag – the same one he'd used between fosters as a kid.

Didn't take long. He'd packed on autopilot before.

Not three minutes later, he was downstairs staring at his bike. He had no plans other than leaving, no certainty on where he would go. Of course, he wound up at Jeanie's. Without a word, she welcomed him in. The next couple days, as Derek blew up his phone with questions, she said all the right things. Made all the right jokes. That and a steady stream of booze helped numb him enough to function.

After he was certain Derek's father was gone, he returned to the old apartment once, when he knew Derek to be in class. He and Jeanie loaded his stuff into a truck he'd saved from scrap. He left his key and a three-word note on the kitchen counter.

Don't call me.

Of course, the note hadn't worked. But a new phone number sure had.

Carver knew well and good why these thoughts were plaguing him. But drawing parallels between his no-good ex and this curious professor wouldn't do him any favors. He'd already made up his mind on how this weekend was going to go. Good sense wasn't about to talk him out of it.

Though Daniel didn't drop by the shop or the bar, he stayed in frequent contact. Jeanie had a field day with that. He didn't need her pointing out how often he checked his phone—he knew. Like one of those pathetic dogs with the bell, he looked at the damn thing every five minutes for a word from Daniel. He'd developed a twitch in his thigh waiting for the notification to vibrate.

He couldn't help it. The sorts of questions Daniel asked made him wonder if the man had something special in store. People didn't plan things for him often. He was surprisingly charmed by the whole thing. And if having that meant sending hatless photos and calling Daniel something kinky? Shit, why not?

If he was buying a ticket to this ride, he'd take it as far as it would go.

* * * *

Fairview, Louisiana
End of September 2019

"It's open," Daniel called, a bit muffled through the door.

For all the times he'd driven the professor here, Carver had only ever sat in the driveway. Daniel's rental was a small one-floor house, but well cared for. Variegated brownstone covered the front. A small set of wooden stairs led to an open porch. Window boxes held flowers and assorted greenery, though he doubted that was Daniel's doing.

He stepped inside and was met by the scents of cooking spices.

"Smells great," he called out, though it was downright annoying how many things Daniel was good at. He removed his shoes in the hallway, but hesitated at the hooks on the wall.

It wasn't really that big a deal. He didn't need the hat inside. He lifted it from his head and went to find Daniel. He walked through a small living room into the adjoining kitchen. Daniel stood behind the stove, cracking pepper over a large pot.

"What're you making?"

"I know Septembers are warm here, but out east, it's the start of soup weather. Guess I had a craving for it."

"Sounds nice."

"Just trying to use what I can from the fridge. We'll see what happens—" Daniel turned to face him and froze. "You, uhm…" He cleared his throat. "You look really nice, Carv."

He looked down at the clothes he'd chosen for tonight. It probably was Daniel's first time seeing him outside of work uniforms. He wore a light-blue dress shirt—buttoned, though rolled at the sleeves. A coffee-brown belt was threaded through the only jeans he'd saved from grease and spilled tequila. He had the urge to tug down the brim of his hat before remembering he wasn't wearing it. Instead, he pushed a bit of hair behind his ear. Shit was always falling out when he tied it back.

"Nothin' fancy." He shrugged. "Just had time to clean up a bit."

Daniel's smile was almost enough to bring him to his knees right there. Instead, he watched the man finish the soup and helped slice up some bread.

"This is really good," he said as they dug in at the table. And he wasn't lying—chicken and mixed vegetables, with pieces of rice-shaped pasta. "What's these bits in here?"

"Orzo. Makes it a little heartier." Daniel ripped a piece of crusty bread. "And I had half a box in the pantry."

He swallowed another bite. "Can't remember the last time I had a meal like this."

"What do you normally eat?"

He dunked a chunk of bread in his soup. "Bar food after my shift. Or whatever else is fast."

Daniel nodded. "I'm pretty much the same. I don't cook unless there's a reason."

"A reason, hmm?" He looked up and caught the professor's eye. Seemed like there was something he wanted to say.

"Actually, I wanted to talk a little, if we could." Daniel turned his wine glass in place on the table. "The last time we…when I visited your shop."

He didn't hide his smirk. "I remember."

"Thought you might." Daniel circled the top of his glass with a finger. "You called me something."

He winked across the table, earning him a laugh. "You seemed to like it."

"I do." A light flush reddened Daniel's cheek and he looked down, pleased. "But I want you to know what it means. To me, at least." He took a short sip of wine. "It's a trust thing."

"How so?"

"Honorifics vary from person to person. What they like. What they don't like. How they want to feel. It's all important to consider." Daniel's blue eyes zeroed in on him. "If you're going to call me Sir, it means you trust me. It means you're willingly ceding control in accordance with the boundaries we've set. It's not a responsibility I take lightly. So I don't use the word lightly either." Daniel scanned his face, gauging his response. "Now, do you still want to call me Sir?"

He didn't think he could say it aloud. To be so blunt discussing this…it was still something he was getting used to. He started to nod, but Daniel shook his head once. "I need you to say it."

He ignored the heat in his cheeks and popped a piece of bread into his mouth. He considered as he chewed, but he'd known his answer before he'd arrived. Nothing he'd heard had changed his mind. "I agree. It's all good with me."

A bit of seriousness faded as Daniel let the breath fall out of him. "Thank you. I feel better about that now." He took a longer drink of wine and finished the glass, but didn't reach to refill it. "This goes both ways, you know. If there's something I should call you…"

"Like what?"

"I don't know. A first name, maybe?"

The comment caught him off guard. Daniel was clearly joking, though there was curiosity in his voice. Carver wasn't sure what to tell him.

"You know the name that matters. It's not…" He searched for the words and came up short. They were all tied to stories he didn't feel like telling. "I don't use my first name. Had a couple. None of 'em were me."

"See, this is important information to have." Daniel's good humor turned downright boastful as he leaned forward, helping himself to more bread. "I think I know how you feel about praise. But correct me if I'm wrong."

Was the man determined to have him blushing all night? "No, you, ah..." He cleared his throat. "You got that pretty right."

"I'm glad." They ate some more before Daniel pushed his bowl away. "*Can* I call you something? If it's all the same to you?"

"What're you thinking?"

Daniel removed his glasses and cleaned the lenses with his shirt. "It doesn't have to be your name. Could be anything. An embarrassment. An endearment. Or —"

He fought the urge to itch his neck. "How 'bout you go with what feels right and I'll tell you if I hate it?"

Daniel pointed with his folded frames. "You'd better. That's part of the deal."

Carver nodded. He'd learned that lesson with the futo. He wouldn't forget again.

"One last thing?"

He wasn't quite able to hide his annoyed sigh, but he met Daniel's gaze across the table. "What?"

"Blindfolds. Yea or nay?"

Sweet Lord, what had Daniel cooked up for him tonight?

His pulse picked up the pace in excitement. He found himself licking his lips and noticed Daniel watching him do it. The undercurrent of tension that had ebbed and flowed throughout dinner had all built to this question. To his answer.

"Yeah," he said. "That'd be fine with me."

"Perfect." Daniel swiped his crust around his bowl. "Finish whatever you want of that. I've got something to show you in..." He replaced his glasses and flipped his phone open. "Twenty-one minutes."

Why is he trying so hard to impress me?

He asked the obvious question. "What happens in twenty-one minutes?"

Daniel used his own trick against him and winked. "Guess you'll have to wait and see."

When they'd finished clearing their plates, he followed Daniel through the mud room and out of the back door. The professor pulled a maroon cardigan over his light tan polo, then he extended his hand. "Come outside with me."

He considered not taking it—didn't seem like the kind of contact they engaged in, but he didn't want hurt feelings this close to the end. Cautiously, he fit their hands together. It was a little strange. He'd never held hands and walked…well, anywhere before.

Daniel tugged him forward and led them out to a temperate night. The fenced-in yard was mostly clover and tall grass. A row of flowering bushes ran in a line behind the house. The front porch didn't wrap around, but in the middle of the yard was a large, thick blanket. Beside it sat a small telescope, pointed toward the sky.

He didn't know why, but the thought of Daniel planning this—having everything timed and set up just so—had him swallowing down nerves. "This something else you study?"

"I do have hobbies." Daniel squeezed his hand before letting go. "Let me show you."

Carver doubted the prof had a hobby he couldn't give a lecture on, but he enjoyed listening to Daniel regardless. He took turns between orienting the lens of the telescope and pointing out constellations, rattling off names from different cultures throughout time. Eventually, Daniel abandoned the telescope and lay on his back, showing him all that could be seen with the naked eye.

For his part, he watched and listened. The last time he'd looked at the stars was probably some planetarium trip in grade school. Made him feel small in the best of ways, if more than a little old. He wondered who else was watching the sky, from how many different places and angles. He'd never look at the moon again without thinking of this. Maybe that was the point—a constant reminder of Daniel, even after he'd gone.

Caught in his thoughts, he didn't notice when Daniel's musings on Mars went silent. He turned to his side and found Daniel's head tipped his way, just watching him.

"What?"

"Nothing. I can't look at you?"

"Didn't say that."

Daniel kept staring, that know-it-all glint in his eye. He was the picture of contentment as he opened his arm. "Come down here with me."

That sounded like more than an invitation to stargazing. He should be careful—even if Daniel weren't leaving tomorrow, this was dangerous territory. He stretched out at an angle to rest his neck on Daniel's chest. The man's arm landed across his collarbone and he let himself melt into the feel of it, to commit this night to memory. The wetness of the grass. The beginnings of a cooling breeze. The sweetness of bonfire smoke over the fragrance of calla lilies. Probably some neighbor burning brush, but he found himself glad for it.

Daniel picked up the star talk and rested a hand near his head. As expected, the man kept to the stray bits of hair that refused to stay in their band. His whispered check-in was mostly unnecessary, and Carver didn't stop himself from enjoying it. He closed his eyes and leaned into the touch. He breathed deep and slow as possible, allowing himself to relax.

For a while, they lay together in comfortable silence. He listened to the music of the late-night nature, the gentle hum of birds and insects often blocked by noise. When Daniel spoke again, his voice was softer.

"This trip…Fairview's been nothing like what I expected." He breathed through a laugh. "I'm glad I overpaid you to drive me home."

"Which time?"

"Every time. I'm sure I'll see it in my bill. For the car I never drove."

Carver swatted his side. "Would've been done sooner. If someone hadn't distracted me."

"Well, we both know I'm not apologizing for that."

Daniel tucked a bit of hair behind his ear. He tried to keep his eyes on the stars.

"I wanted to thank you."

"For what?" he asked.

Daniel looked at the sky. "I'd forgotten what it could be like. To try. To reach for something new."

There was a gentle tug at his temple as Daniel rolled a section of hair between his fingers. "I know you're new to this, so I wanted to be clear. If you want to keep exploring rope on your own…you should do it. There's different communities to connect with." Daniel brushed a thumb down the side of his neck. "You deserve to have what you want."

He cleared his throat, surprised at how harsh it felt. "Don't know if that's likely."

Daniel turned him by the chin until their eyes met. He wondered if the man had heard what he'd left unsaid.

Not now that you're leaving.

Was it his imagination, or did the prof look a little sad about that? Blue eyes fell to his lips as Daniel traced the lines of his mouth. He looked desperate all of a sudden. Like he'd been holding something back.

"Carv, I really want to kiss you. Can I?"

He almost laughed, then shook his head instead. "Why d'you still ask me? When you know the answer?"

Daniel pushed to his forearms and rolled to the middle of the blanket. "Because I want to know," he said, not stopping at the easy answer. "Because I think you're tired of always playing this part." Daniel kept a hand on his chin, gently tipping his face up. "Because I need to know you want this. So can I kiss you?"

Carver knew he could play this off, make a joke and brush past the offered tenderness. But nothing about the way Daniel looked at him seemed funny. He leaned in, ran his nose along the other man's and whispered, "You can kiss me."

Daniel smoothed a hand through his hair and grasped the back of his head. He pulled their mouths together and Carver's breath caught in his chest. It was hard to keep still as Daniel tugged the band in his hair.

"Yes?" came the gentle question.

He nodded and his hair fell free. Daniel's contented sigh was warm on his face. He followed the man's urgings and rolled on top of him. A light breeze helped toss the hair out of his face.

"God, you look good like that."

The breathless compliment left him lightheaded. He wanted so much from this last night together. He kissed Daniel deeply and worked his jaw wider, teasing with his tongue as the man buried his hands in his hair. And

Carver let himself lean into it—didn't hold back the sounds that always happened when someone combed over his scalp like that. His limbs grew heavy as he pressed his hips into Daniel beneath him. There wasn't a rope in sight, but he felt tied to the man in ways he'd tried to prevent. In ways he was tired of avoiding.

"Pull harder," he said into the kiss.   Daniel did so immediately, tugging at the roots as he secured their mouths together.

It was too good. Carver let himself moan. Couldn't even care they were still outside, in full view of anyone who cared to look.

"Oh," Daniel whispered, traces of laughter in his voice. "That's a *thing* for you–"

He spent his time on top hiding his face in Daniel's neck, only then realizing he'd never had the chance to explore him like this. Making up for lost time, he kissed over Daniel's pulse and nipped his ear for good measure. "You knew that already."

"Maybe I did. Maybe I planned for it. In case you ever let me get this far."

"What d'you mean?"

As if in answer, Daniel tugged his hair again. He made the same desperate sound, allowing it to echo from his throat.

"You're not even hesitating. Just letting me hear you. Carv—" Daniel caught his face between both hands and held him still. He leaned their foreheads together. "I want to tie you again."

All the blood in his body rushed south.

Daniel asked, "Will you stay with me tonight?"

This answer, he knew instantly. "Yes, Sir."

* * * *

"Did you buy new ropes just for this?"

"Of course I did."

Daniel stood near the bedroom door, organizing different lengths of thick red rope. The braided strands caught the light from the table lamps with a subtle sheen. Were they made of a different material? And what was the thinnest rope for?

"Go kneel by the bed for me," came Daniel's voice at his ear.

He suppressed a shiver and nodded. He turned to leave, but a hand on his arm kept him still. "Pants and shirt off. I'll take care of the rest."

As he shed his clothes, Carver surveyed the room. The mattress was probably a queen—they'd have plenty of room later. For now, he followed Daniel's instructions and knelt on the beige carpet. It provided some cushion for his bare knees, which might be helpful. No telling how long he'd be on them.

Daniel returned quickly. He'd left his sweater downstairs and lost his shirt as they entered the bedroom. Now he stood behind him, his own chest bare, running hands over the back of Carver's neck and shoulders.

"Playing like this," Daniel said, his voice calm and collected, "is best with extended aftercare. I don't want you to drop because I gave you what you wanted."

"What's different this time?"

"Just enough, I think."

Daniel removed a hanging pot from over their head. Now that he thought about it, that wasn't a great place for a planter. So close to the end of the bed, dead leaves probably fell on his feet and blankets.

"Martha sure likes her plants, don't she?"

"The ones downstairs are hers. This…" — Daniel paused — "is my addition to her collection."

"Why?"

"I needed a plausible reason to install this."

Daniel set the plant on the dresser to their side and he got a better look at the hardware above them. Had Daniel grabbed the first hook he saw at the store? Or was it that hefty on purpose?

Daniel rigged a long length of rope through the metal. Probably the latter, then.

"We've never done suspension," he said.

"We're still not doing suspension." Daniel gave the rope a hearty tug, lifting his feet from the floor. "Though we probably could. But this will be enough to release your full weight into it. You won't have to hold back."

He swayed on his knees. Daniel petted his head, righting his balance. "How are we so far?"

Motherfucking green.

He told him as much, though his choice of words made Daniel chuckle. "Good. Turn sideways a bit."

Angled this way, he could see Daniel in profile. Multiple lengths of the dark red rope lay across his neck. The color stood out against his fair chest, which had its own smatterings of light brown freckles. "I'm going to tie a chest harness on you first. Then your arms, behind your back." He gestured above them. "I'll attach the harness to this point, but you'll stay on your knees the whole time. You'll be able to lean into it differently. I'm told it can feel like flying."

The description certainly piqued his interest — almost as much as the photos Daniel had sent over the last few days. "Sounds like a lot of work."

"It will take some time. But there's plenty to keep us busy while you wait."

He heard the quick flick of a pocketknife behind him, and before he knew what was happening, Daniel had cut his gray boxers from his hips. Then a different sort of coolness slid down his lower back, down his ass — until it started to push inside.

It wasn't difficult. The small plug slipped easily in place and he sighed. This certainly would give them options tonight.

He got one last look at Daniel before a soft, padded fabric was pulled over his eyes. A hand remained on his shoulder as a confident voice said low in his ear, "Color?"

"Green."

"Safe word?"

He thought back on their text conversation. It was a ridiculous word — almost as bad as the cocktail — but maybe that was the point. "Long Island."

"Good. And you'll use it, if you need?"

"Yes, Sir."

"You're getting good at that."

He heard Daniel kneel behind him, felt the warmth of the man's chest press against his back. Daniel's arm circled his neck and he knocked his fist against his collarbone — a deep, thudding comfort that Carver felt down to his toes. Daniel's voice moved to his other ear as he told him, "I want you to relax. Don't worry about the time. Just be here with me."

He swallowed hard and nodded. He was glad the thick eye mask hid the bulk of his face. It was a release he hadn't expected, not having to control his expression. Permission to hide, in a way. It felt good.

They continued breathing in their own natural patterns, syncing up and falling out in equal measure. Daniel squeezed his shoulder twice, letting him know he'd be stepping away, then the soft, braided texture of rope pulled around his middle. The first loop fit snug beneath his arms. Daniel wrapped the strands around him three times—embracing him from behind as he passed the rope to himself. He listened to Daniel's competent hands tie knots he couldn't see, then it was the circling motions again, leaving him with two thick bands horizontal across his chest. Even when Daniel moved to his front, it still felt like being held.

He'd seen Daniel's hands move fast before, but tonight, he was going so slow. The subtle touches were hypnotic. Daniel stayed gentle even as he adjusted the lines, pulling rope over his shoulder to continue the work on his front.

"Do these itch like the others?" Daniel asked. He passed the ends under the lower rope on his chest. It sat high enough on his ribs that it didn't restrict his breathing, which meant he couldn't blame the tie for why he shuddered his response.

"N-no. They're softer."

"Do you like them?" A quick twist in the center, then Daniel set the rope over his other shoulder. He was behind him, finishing the harness, when Carver answered, "Yes. I do."

Carver could tell Daniel was smiling as he responded, "Good. They're yours. I want you to keep them." He could also tell when the smiling stopped. "They deserve to be used more than once."

It wasn't until Daniel was tying his arms that he managed to ask, but he had to know. So much talk of what he'd do once Daniel was gone... Why was he stuck on that now? Hadn't that always been part of the deal?

"Why're you goin' to so much trouble with this? Really?"

Daniel's sigh landed warm over his shoulders. The sharp rasp of pulling rope punctuated his words. "I meant what I said before. About exploring this more on your own. The responsible part of me wants you to have what you need, whether I'm here or not." He cinched down the knots at his wrists, leaving his arms stacked one over the other, bent at the elbows behind his back.

"How 'bout the rest of you?" he prompted.

Daniel plucked at the lines, sliding fingers beneath important points. Could the professor feel how fast his heart was racing? "If I can't be the one providing it? Then I want to leave an impression."

Daniel twisted a hand in his harness and he gasped. The lines around his middle tightened, holding him fast. "There's plenty that will want you. None of them will deserve you." An arm pulled tight across his neck and *goddamn,* but Daniel's hands were everywhere.

"I want to set the bar so high you never settle for less."

Fuck me…

He might be the one of them not wearing any clothes, but with that answer? Sure felt like Daniel was the one getting naked. This unbelievable man really wanted to be here. Doing this, with him. *For* him.

The urge to touch him was immediate. Overwhelming. And completely unachievable. He struggled against the bonds, but his arms stayed folded behind his back. Adrenaline and need raced down his spine, but they only made him harder. In their own ways, for their own reasons, they were both letting themselves have this tonight. Felt like pushing on a bruise, but there was a sick comfort in the pain — in wanting to see how bad it could get. Just for the knowledge of it. Some proof that he'd had it at all.

Daniel's hands moved from practical checks to the slower slide of intention. The lead attached to his harness like a hook in his ribcage, hauling him up, and the burden of holding his own weight eased. His knees stayed on the carpet as Daniel tipped him forward. Quite the sensation when he couldn't see a damn thing — and it did feel a bit like flying. Like he'd joined the stars himself. As time passed, he sank into quiet darkness, the only sounds in the room both men's elevated breathing.

Daniel kept at least one hand on him at the start. As he allowed his head to fall forward, he noticed Daniel less and the ropes he'd tied more. His whispered check-ins were frequent, as they always were. He half-suspected Daniel asked so often just to tell him how good he was doing.

He was once again thankful for the thickness of his blindfold as Daniel's hand thrummed the end of the plug while the other closed around his cock. He arched instinctively, but again, there was nowhere to go. His throat was scraped and ragged from the near-constant sounds Daniel was pulling from him. He kept timing the pleasurable tugs on the toy with restrictive pulls on the ropes. The back and forth of sensation was making him desperate, fresh sweat collecting at the nape of his neck.

Then Daniel hiked his forehead back, forcing his chin up and out. And *fuck*, but that felt good. So close to what he wanted. He tried to wrangle his thoughts into speech. "Can you…"

"What, Carv?"

He licked his dry lips. "My hair." He couldn't manage more words than those, but Daniel seemed to get the picture.

"I'll do you one better." The prof gathered his hair and twisted it into a band. Then he ran a thinner rope around his neck, allowing him to feel the size as it dragged over his skin.

Was he going to tie his *hair* up into this mess? He made a pitiful sound of need.

Daniel tugged twice on his small ponytail. "Yes?"

The words flowed easy as water. "Yes, Sir."

That earned him a kiss, long and deep, until he was chasing Daniel's lips. "You're doing so well, Carv. So good for me." He trailed kisses down his neck and whispered, "Such a good boy."

He swayed on his knees again, his spine entirely limp. Had anyone ever called him that before? It was silly, right? An embarrassing turn of phrase.

So why did it feel like something had cracked his chest wide open?

Daniel caught him by the hips and pulled him back to kneeling. With a quickness he rarely showed, the prof tied his hair to the ropes at his back. When Carver tilted his chin down, the rope pulled with lovely tension at the base of his neck. There was enough slack that he could control the pressure, but doing so forced him to hold still. Which he wasn't capable of doing at present, since Daniel hadn't stopped teasing him with that toy the whole damn time.

Daniel's grip stayed firm around the base of his cock, applying solid pressure and denying any release.

He was only interested in the slow, shuddering shocks that built with each stroke of the plug against his prostate. Already, Daniel had eased him through two smaller peaks of pleasure that he didn't usually bother with. But the compounding effect...he couldn't argue with the results.

Beads of sweat dampened his blindfold. He couldn't ever remember being this worked up. The rope twisted in his hair as Daniel applied more pressure. He keened and groaned, almost unable to speak.

Daniel hadn't said a thing about him coming yet. Hadn't told him not to, how he wanted it—not a word. What was he waiting for?

"I can't..." His voice caught in his throat as Daniel mouthed at the pulse in his neck. He timed the kiss with another squeeze of his inner thigh, the base of his cock. How was he supposed to last through all this?

"I can't fight it anymore," he groaned in defeat. "Please, let me...oh *God*—"

"Please what?"

Fucking *goddamn*, Daniel sounded worse off than he did. Like he'd been shouting. Like he was fighting off a precipice much like his own.

Then Daniel did the one thing he hadn't all night— he stopped. He held his hands perfectly still, clutching him close, but no longer teasing anywhere. "You can have it, Carv," he whispered low. "Just ask."

Carver tripped over his words trying to get them out faster. Wasn't time to feel embarrassed. He needed this too badly. "Please, Sir. Can I—can I come?"

The grip on his cock finally loosened, lengthening into a full stroke. Daniel bit down on the meat of his shoulder and removed the plug, replacing it with his own lubed fingers, and was he shaking? How long had he been shaking? He wanted to curse, to say words of any sort, but he was beyond language. Only sharp cries spilled from his mouth, no matter how he tried.

"*Now.*"

All that existed was Daniel's desperate voice — the way it buzzed in his chest, a plea and a command all at once. His eyes slammed shut behind the blindfold and he came into Daniel's hand, thrusting through the pleasurable sensations. The prof eased him through it and loosened the tie on his hair, allowing more movement in his neck.

He hung his head forward and tried to catch hold of his breath. Behind him, Daniel pressed his thumbs into the muscles of his shoulders, releasing the tension.

"Carv," he said. "You're incredible."

He could barely process the rest. He was too maxed out on sensation. He remembered Daniel freeing his arms and massaging down his limbs, then he held the man's waist while he detached the harness from the rigging. Daniel was quick to meet him on the floor, his sure hands loosening the ties around his chest. And all the while, Daniel kept up a whispered hush of praise. He'd have missed it if not for their close proximity.

"Amazing."

"You did so well."

"You don't even know how you look right now…"

"Just beautiful. So beautiful, Carv."

Daniel took a break from the ropes and removed the band from his hair. He ran his nails over his scalp in soothing circles. "I can't believe you were so good for me. Thank you."

Was he crying right now? Actually crying real tears into this padded mask? Had Daniel planned for this possibility, when he hadn't cried in years? How was a person supposed to respond to *that*?

Because yes, there was a warm wetness in the corners of his eyes. His exhausted sighs mixed with fragile laughter. His body felt wonderfully heavy. He'd needed every part of that more than he could've known.

Shit. This here needed another name. Couldn't just call it "sex." He'd had sex before—maybe more than his share—but he'd never felt anything like that. Not even his other encounters with Daniel had wrecked him like this. So when the prof returned to unraveling his work, he allowed himself to stay limp. He accepted the caresses of Daniel's hands and gave over full control.

When all was undone, Daniel sat on the carpet and leaned his back against the bedframe. Carver regained conscious awareness of his body curled into the other man's side, arms slung around his waist. A water bottle sat beside his discarded blindfold. He'd remembered the lighting was dim, but it seemed brighter as he blinked his eyes open.

"Hey, now. There we are."

Daniel peered into his face, like he'd been looking for something and only now found it. "How are we doing?"

Seriously?

"Daniel. What the fuck?"

The prof was already grinning—and doing a shit job hiding it. He so clearly knew what he'd done, the smug bastard.

Daniel passed him the water. "Might need you to be a little clearer."

He shook his head and took a long drink. "Don't think I can. The fuck did you just do to me?"

Daniel chuckled. "I think it's called catharsis." He pushed a hand over his hair again. "You let go of something there. I don't know what it was, and I don't have to." Daniel brushed a thumb over his cheek. "But I was glad to witness it. That was… I mean, you were—"

"You gotta stop with the compliments. Gonna give me too big a head."

"I've got to get them in while I can."

It was definitely a joke, until it wasn't. Neither of them said anything for a while, then Daniel started running hands over his body again, holding him from behind. And that decided things.

Carver reached his arm to catch Daniel's neck in a backward embrace. He was still choked up from his earlier release of emotion, but something had shifted into place for him now. A clarity on what he wanted, what he had to make himself ask for—just once before this was over for good.

"Don't tell me you're gonna make me feel all that and leave me wanting here."

Daniel shifted where he sat, laughing in his ear. "Have I ever?" He kissed the back of his neck. "What do you want? Tell me."

"I don't think I'll come again, but I don't care. I still want you." He pressed back against Daniel's still-insistent erection, knowing the man wouldn't have said a thing if he hadn't asked after it. And yeah, maybe he also knew he wasn't talking about just one thing here.

He exhaled low and slow. "I don't want to be done with this yet."

Daniel held him a little tighter at that. He pressed against the small of his back, obviously needy as he asked, "You're sure?"

"Daniel—"

"Okay. On the bed, then."

With help, he made it to the mattress and set up on all fours. Daniel snapped on a condom and still took his damn time about it, ensuring all was as it should be before he pressed inside. They'd had bits of this in their couple of weeks together, but they both knew Carver was too strung out to be the focus this time. Which meant he had one last chance to hear Daniel devolve into his own pleasure, those mumbling shouts he recognized but would never understand.

"*Schätzchen*, fuck—*fuck*, Carv. *Du fühlst dich so gut*, I swear…"

"I can't… *Ich will nicht gehen*, fucking *fuck* —"

Daniel shoved him flat to the mattress, but he pushed back up on his forearms—turning as much as he could to watch the show. Daniel locked his arms around his torso much like the harness from before. He twisted his face and neck up to kiss as he fucked into him, over and over until he stiffened behind him. Daniel's movements were sharp and precise, but somehow he was still the one being praised.

"God, Carver…just amazing."

For once, he felt like it.

Chapter Eleven

Daniel

Carver fell asleep in no time at all. Daniel would've followed if not for that bit at the end. Instead, he found himself lying beside an adorably snoring mechanic, staring up at the ceiling with too many thoughts in his head.

He let go a long sigh and rubbed his eyes. He was thankful that Carver didn't speak German — and more than a little frustrated at the sentiments he'd almost expressed.

"You feel so good…"

"I don't want to leave…"

There was nothing keeping him from saying that in a language Carver understood. There was no mandate forcing him away from Fairview, aside from the looming reality of their very separate lives. But he couldn't help but think… If he could just do the right thing here, if he could somehow be useful enough, maybe Carver's current feelings—whatever they were—would grow. Like his had.

Daniel shook his head. That sounded desperate even in his own mind. There was no favor he could do to make Carver want a long-term, long-distance relationship. Once he landed back east this evening, he was in for a stint in his dusty apartment, where he was supposed to spend the rest of the semester writing articles. After that, he'd be traveling for much of spring. It left little time for a social life. Carver deserved more than being pieced into the holes of his schedule.

He slept fitfully for the first few hours, getting up in the night for water and biological necessity. When he returned to the bedroom, the sight of Carver sleeping almost knocked his feet from under him. He leaned against the doorframe for balance and watched him a moment. While the feeling plucked at heartsore strings, neither was he able to keep a smile from his face.

It had been nice to have this again. Even just once.

Carver seemed almost peaceful with a pillow tucked under his arm, blond hair a mess on the sheets. He didn't know how long he stood there looking, but it was enough to feel embarrassed about it. So when a sleep-scratched voice said his name into the quiet, Daniel jolted in surprise, sloshing water down his front.

He entered the room and scooped clothing from the floor to dry his chest. "Just getting some water. You need anything?"

A muffled grunt of dissent told him no, so he finished what remained of his beverage and returned to his side of the bed. With Carver awake, he didn't know what the etiquette was here. The only other time they'd actually slept together, he'd been out the whole night. Was it okay if he just—

"Daniel. It's your bed. Kick me out or get in here."

If those were his only options, he knew which one to pick.

* * * *

When Daniel woke again, it was to an alarm he didn't recognize. Then there was grumbling, shuffling and a bit of frantic searching before Carver complained beside him, "Jeanie, I told you I can't today. I gotta — oh." He cleared his throat. "Everett. What's goin' on?"

It was an abrupt awakening, but he'd certainly had worse. Daniel blinked his eyes open and reached for his glasses on the nightstand. Once his brain engaged enough to realize Carver's outburst meant he was on the phone, Daniel shuffled to sit up in bed, unsure what he should do. He didn't want to eavesdrop, but he couldn't help being curious.

It was impossible to decipher the topic of conversation from Carver's one-word answers and conversational sniffs, but he watched as the other man pulled at his hair, reading his obvious nerves from body language. Carver sat on the edge of the bed, his back hunching further the longer he was on the phone.

"All right. That's ah…" Carver cleared his throat again. "Need to sort some things here. Can I call you back?"

He paused to listen, then nodded. "Yeah. Thanks, Everett." Carver set his smartphone aside and stared at the floor, pulling his hair in front of his face.

After a silent minute, Daniel prompted him. "Everything okay?"

Carver shook his head, like he'd forgotten anyone else was there. He pulled his hair back and tied it up. "Yeah."

"Something wrong?"

Carver looked over his shoulder to catch his eye. "That was Everett. He's in Harahan. Right now."

"Where's that?"

"Small town outside of New Orleans. I lived there for most of high school."

High school…didn't he meet his ex in high school? Is he worried about going back? Running into him again?

"What brought Everett there?" he asked, hoping Carver would share.

The man pushed out of bed and tugged on his jeans, as he had no boxers to speak of. "Said he found records that proved I was born there. Some contact of his just confirmed it."

"Oh." Was that it? Just a birth certificate? "Well, that's interesting."

"I guess." Carver zipped his jeans. "He said I should come, if I could. That he'd rather talk face to face."

Daniel followed the mechanic's lead and started pulling into clothes himself. "What, he wants you to meet him now? Like, today?"

Carver nodded.

"Why?"

"He wouldn't say. But if it was nothin', he would've just said so." Carver's blue button-up hung open on his shoulders as he sat on the edge of the bed. In unfamiliar clothes and with his hair down, Carver looked more lost than he'd ever seen. "Gonna be honest," he said. "I don't really know what to do."

If I canceled that regional flight in Mason, I could fly direct from New Orleans later this week…

He circled the bed and bent down to Carver's level. He wasn't sure if physical contact would be welcomed, so he kept his hands to himself. "Well…I think you've got two choices. Do you want to go meet Everett? Or would you rather leave it alone?"

Carver tipped his head in frustration, like he knew the answer, though he wasn't thrilled about it. "If he's found something, it sort of feels like I have to."

Daniel nodded, having made his decision. "Good. I'll come with you."

"Hmm?"

"I'll reschedule my flight. I'll go to Harahan with you."

Carver looked concerned at his sudden change of plans. "I'm not asking you to —"

"I know you're not asking." He cut Carver off and decided to take the risk, placing his hand on the other man's shoulder. "We can make the trip today and I'll fly out of New Orleans tomorrow. Or the next day." He shrugged and smiled. "When you travel as often as I do, you get the tickets you can exchange. It's really not a problem."

Concern faded to uncertainty in Carver's face. "You're sure?"

He dared a step further and brought his hand to Carver's other shoulder. He rubbed both with his thumbs and caught the man's eye. "You deserve to know where you come from. If you want to know."

Carver nodded. "All right. Fine."

He smiled, more relieved than he planned to admit. "Great. Then let's go."

* * * *

Carver
Harahan, Louisiana

They made a quick stop by the house to pack a bag. He called Jeanie once they were on the road and filled her in. For the few hours of their drive, he and Daniel listened to the radio. He appreciated that they could sit comfortably in silence together. At present, he wasn't up for forcing small talk.

No offense to Everett, but he'd never thought the man would actually find something. What did it mean that he was born in Harahan? Why did Everett want to meet today with so little warning? He did his best to keep his thoughts under his hat, which he adjusted on his head more often than necessary. Near the exit, he rolled down the window to light up a smoke, but found Daniel's hand over his.

"Don't."

"Excuse you? This is my truck."

"Come on. You so clearly don't smoke."

That caught him off guard. "What d'you mean, I don't smoke?"

Daniel looked at him over the top of his glasses, then returned to watching the scenery out through the window. "You smoke because bartenders are supposed to smoke. Or for an opening with your cheesy lines. Or to make people leave you alone."

Well, fuck him for paying attention. "And this don't count as that?"

Daniel removed his hand. "Fine. Do what you want. But I think you'd get more out of a toothpick." He opened the glove compartment in front of him. Inside was a stash of plastic-covered picks, the same as they stocked at Jeanie's.

"That's what you actually do when you're stressed," Daniel said. "You chew right through them."

His first reaction was surprise, but frustration followed. Where'd Daniel get off, knowing him this well so fast? He grabbed his pack from the cupholder and lit up regardless. They were almost there. He needed something to settle his nerves.

He pulled into the only diner in town and parked beside Everett's sedan. He'd expected to see it. But the navy Oldsmobile beside it? That box of a car he'd put up on blocks too many times before? Everett said he'd found a contact that knew his family, but there was no way... It couldn't be.

"You've got to be fuckin' kidding me."

"What?"

He ignored Daniel's question and tossed his half-smoked cigarette at the ground. He climbed from the cab and, sure enough, Everett was in the window — sitting across a square table from someone he'd never thought to see again.

Daniel circled the truck and stood in front of him. "What's wrong? You okay?"

The real answer was no. Hell no, in fact. But he was going to have to pretend. He was too angry not to address this now that he was here. He maneuvered around Daniel and pushed through the door to the diner, blowing past the host stand. No one stopped him. It wasn't until he stood beside their table that Everett noticed he was there.

"Hey, Carv. Glad you made it —"

But he wasn't looking at the blustering detective. He was looking at the woman across the table — more gray than brown in her hair than he remembered, but her eyes were just the same.

He swallowed hard and hoped his voice was steady. "Hi, Denise."

"Will," the older woman said. She looked him over from head to toe and smiled, only a bit sad. "You look good."

He clocked Everett's and Daniel's reactions to the name. He rolled his neck and stared at the floor. "Mostly go by Carver now," he corrected.

"Of course." Denise looked down at her hands, folded on the table. "I'm sorry for not tellin' you. I didn't know for sure till this investigator called—"

"Let's start at the beginning, ma'am," Everett chimed in. He motioned for him and Daniel to sit. "Might be easier to follow along."

He and Daniel took the open seats at the small square table. Everett opened a folder and passed over one of those important, official pieces of paper he grew up doing without—his birth certificate.

"Where'd you find this?" He asked, reading the only unknown name on the page.

Layla Carver. That was my mother's name.

"City records, here in town. Pretty easy once I knew where to look," Everett explained. "Not sure how much of this you know, but your mother gave you to the state pretty young. She..." He rubbed his hands together. "Well, there's no delicate way to say it. You ever heard of Safe Haven laws?"

Growing up like he did? Of course he had. He shrugged and Everett continued. "In the state of Louisiana, a mother's got sixty days to relinquish her child and face no criminal charges. The child goes to foster care until they're adopted."

"If they're adopted."

Everett acknowledged his correction, then flipped through a small book of notes. "You were relinquished at a fire station on the outskirts of New Orleans, so I checked nearby rural hospitals for births within sixty days of surrender. Gave me a smaller pool to start with than a big city. And it paid off." Everett reached across the table and tapped the corner of the document. "Came up with that certificate and your mother's name. Once I had that, it was simple. I think you know Harahan's a small place."

Carver nodded at the table, at the unfamiliar page in front of him. Then, for the first time since he'd arrived, he met Denise's gaze. "How'd you get mixed up in this?"

It'd only been five years since he'd seen her last, but Denise seemed older somehow. A little less hardy. A bit more frail. "The detective was calling around looking for folks who'd known your mother. I volunteer at the high school, answering phones. When I heard who he was calling for..." Denise shrugged. "I wanted to help."

"Did you know her?"

Denise seemed to expect the question. "Not well, but yes." Her sad smile turned momentarily fond. "Layla was a sweet girl. Real quiet. I knew her to say hello to growin' up, but we got closer senior year. She was a better reader than me. Always got A's in English." The older woman sighed, and the sadness took over again. "She left after first semester and never came back. Then her parents moved at the end of the year. Folks talked about what happened, but nobody knew. You know how it goes."

He decided to ignore how his throat was closing at the smallest similarities with this unknown mother of his. English hadn't been so bad. Wasn't hard. Just read the book and write the paper.

Did my mother think that too?

He coughed once, regretting his next question before it even passed his lips. "Is that why you always looked out for me? Because you knew who I was?"

"I suspected. I didn't know for sure until..." She waved a hand at Everett. "But you looked a bit like her, when you were younger. Especially when you grew out your hair. She had beautiful hair." Denise met his eyes again and reached for him across the table. "But it didn't matter either way, Will. I was happy to have you as part of the family." She squeezed his hands, pulling back before it could become an issue. "Derek never had many friends growing up, and I always wanted more kids. But I was divorced by then, and it just never happened."

The longer Denise talked, the more he glances he stole across the table to Daniel. The professor was putting the pieces together about the significance of the person beside them. Which probably meant he was in for *more* discussion of this once she left. What a joy that was like to be.

The table was obviously waiting for him to speak, but the fuck did they want him to say? He held out long enough that Everett interjected, clearing his throat as he closed his notes away.

"There's a bit more for us to talk on, but it can wait. And I haven't eaten yet. Daniel? You, ah…" Everett gestured to the professor, then pointed to the counter up front.

For once, he was grateful for Everett's ability to read a room. It took Daniel a moment to pick up the obvious cue, but he got there eventually. "Oh. Yeah, sure." He turned his attention to Carver. "Do you want anything?"

He shook his head. Food was the last thing he needed. He felt nauseous and pissed off, which was not a great combo. And if they left him alone at this table with Denise, there was no way he was getting out of talking about Derek.

God, *fuck* this town already. This was supposed to be his last day with Daniel. Not some trip down a shattered memory lane—

"How are you, Will? Really?"

Everett and Daniel stood over by the menu, but it was a small place and they were early for the lunch rush. Wasn't really such a thing as "out of earshot." Carver wasn't sure if that made it better or worse, but he put his elbows on the table and rubbed his forehead.

"I guess it's a lot to think about. Makes me see some things differently." He tugged his hat down on his head, then sat back and crossed his arms. "But it doesn't really change much."

Denise nodded and for a moment, he thought she'd leave it there.

"That's not all I meant."

Fuck. Here it comes...

"I know what you meant. I'm fine."

"You still in Fairview?"

He nodded. Denise took a long drink from her water. "Derek is, too. It's taking longer than he thought to finish his program."

He'd gone a whole year without confirming that knowledge—and many more before it, avoiding campus like the plague. He shifted in his seat, determined not to speak. If Denise had something to say, he'd listen, but that was about all the grace he was willing to extend, at present.

"I've asked him about what happened, but he won't talk to me. And I know I've no right to ask, but...whatever your fight was about? I'm sure you can get past it. Things happen, in relationships—"

Never mind. This? He wasn't doing *this*.

"All due respect?" He leaned forward, both hands on the table. "You don't know what you're talkin' about."

Denise's kindness was only ever outshone by her blindness. She'd never seen Derek for what he was—a coward.

He stood beside the table, ready to leave. "If you want answers, you can ask your son. Because I don't have 'em for you." He chewed his toothpick between his back teeth. It calmed his nerves a fraction, but he was still seething mad.

Wait, where'd he get a toothpick from? He didn't grab any from the car, and there weren't any left on the table. He looked over to where Everett and Daniel were "reading the menu." Daniel caught his eye, noticed the pick and smirked.

He mouthed the words, "Told you."

The prof must've put one on the table before he left. And, like muscle memory, he'd opened it right up and started chewing. Carver couldn't help the smile that threatened at the corners of his mouth, so he flipped the pick over and started chewing the other side. Anything to keep from thinking about how it felt to have someone notice his habits like that.

Beside him, Denise was nodding and standing herself. "I shouldn't have asked. I'm sorry, Will."

He caught her hand and took a deep breath through his nose, doing his best to think beyond his impulse to cut and run. He couldn't leave things like this. Not with her.

He held her hand a moment, then gave it a short squeeze. "Look. I appreciate all you did for me, I just—"

"Please don't apologize, dear. Every bit of it was my pleasure. Even the hard parts." Denise reached for his arm and patted it sweetly. "I really do hope you're well. That your detective friend finds what you're lookin' for."

He nodded, not wanting to risk his voice. Sure felt like it was breaking.

Denise gathered her purse from the table and headed for her Oldsmobile. He watched her go—and barely had a moment to collect his thoughts before

Daniel and Everett were back. He let the other men handle the small talk until their food arrived. The waitress handed a sandwich to Everett and a similar plate to Daniel. She also handed him a Styrofoam container that, if he had to guess, was something the prof planned to make him eat later.

Everett asked between bites, "You doin' okay, Carv?"

He reached for the sweet tea that had accompanied "his" to-go order.

"Just peachy," he said. He took a long drink. "So. She the reason you wanted to meet in person?"

"Part of it, yeah. But not all." Everett pushed his sandwich aside and reopened his notes. "I didn't want to assume, but I thought you might want some privacy for this. So we can wait if you want—" Everett darted a glance to Daniel, but Carver waved it away. Honestly, it'd save him time if Daniel heard it all from the source.

"The name Layla Carver doesn't show up many places once she left Harahan. Never married. Never owned property. Aside from her death certificate, it's mostly just this." Everett opened another file on the table. This one contained an adoption record, but the year was wrong—2000? He had been in middle school in 2000.

"This ain't mine. For lots of reasons."

"You're right. It's not." Everett produced a death certificate with the same year. "Layla Carver died in childbirth, a little over a decade after having you. She gave the baby up for adoption, through an agency this time. A girl." He waited a moment before adding, "Your half-sister."

No fuckin' way…

Had Everett really done the impossible? He had…family?

"Where?"

Everett looked pleased to have surprised him. "Still in Louisiana. She was adopted by a couple in the suburbs. Gretna, if you've heard of it. Not far from here."

"And you reached out to them. That's why you wanted me to come in person."

"I didn't confirm nothin', but yeah. I talked to the adoptive parents. Floated the idea, in case you were interested." Everett wrote an address on a napkin and slid it across the table. "If you want to meet her, the family's amenable."

What a Monday he was having. "What's her name?"

"On the birth certificate, she's listed as Caroline Carver. I think the family changed it, though."

Carver kept staring at the table. He wasn't sure what he wanted to do, what he was supposed to do—or if those two options had anything to do with each other. Beside him, Daniel chimed in for the first time since Denise left. He asked Everett, "Could you call them again? Does he have to decide now?"

"Of course not. But the family wanted you to know that they never made a secret of the fact she was adopted. Seemed to think it might be good for her to meet you."

He tried to gather his thoughts to respond, but Everett gave him an out. He stood with half his sandwich in hand and gathered his files with the other. "I'll just see what they say. I'll text you." He nodded in farewell to Daniel, leaving him and the professor alone.

Daniel started with the same question as Everett had. "So. How are you doing with all of this?"

He leaned his forearms on the table and pushed his thumbs into his eyelids, rubbing lightly. "It's a fucking lot at once, I tell you." Seeing Denise, and now this...it was too much. "This is all your fault, you know."

"My fault?" Daniel asked from behind his sandwich.

"Fine, you and Everett. But still." The toothpick in his mouth was nothing but slivers, but he kept at it. "Not sure what to do now. Was never very good at waiting."

Daniel pushed his own sandwich aside. "How about you give me the tour?"

"Of what?"

Daniel waved around them. "Here. Harahan. Every small town's got a claim to fame, right?"

"You're sittin' in it."

"Oh." Daniel's false enthusiasm vanished. It made him smirk as the prof tried to recover. "I mean, I've seen worse."

He raised an eyebrow and Daniel amended, "What? I've obviously seen better, but the point stands. Could be worse."

Now that they were alone, Daniel moved his chair closer to the corner of the table. That meant it wasn't much of a reach when he slid the demolished toothpick from his mouth, placing it on the table with one hand as he held up another from the glovebox. "There's also fries in the box. If you'd rather chew something edible."

His stomach audibly grumbled. There went his excuse. He rolled his eyes and opened the box. Once he did, the professor returned to eating himself. They were mostly through their meals when Daniel asked the question he'd been sitting on. "So, Denise. She's—"

"Yep."

"Your ex's mom?"

He nodded. Daniel blew a long sigh from his lips. "How was *that*?"

"You had to've heard most of it." Daniel shrugged, conceding the point, and Carver figured the man might as well hear the whole thing. "I haven't seen her since I left for Fairview. Haven't spoken to anyone with the name of Patterson for five years."

"No contact, hmm?"

"That's life. Closed doors and unanswered questions." He ate a few more fries. "But Denise is all right. Ain't all her fault that her son turned out to be a shit partner."

Daniel nodded. "Can I ask another question?"

"Got a feelin' you're gonna."

Daniel smiled, but he looked genuinely curious. "What's wrong with the name Will?"

"God, don't call me that."

"I won't," the prof was quick to say. "But I expected something worse. With the way you played it up."

He shook his head, making his way to a patty melt he didn't remember smelling so good. "It's a nickname. An old one."

"A nickname for…"

He sighed. Since it was easier, he slid the file with his birth certificate across the table. Daniel opened it, skimmed the page and looked up with wide eyes.

"*Wayland* Carver?"

"Mm-hmm. Try growin' up with that."

Daniel looked like he didn't know how he was supposed to respond.

"Don't you dare say you've heard worse."

A short laugh escaped. "Oh, I won't."

He took another bite of his melt and pulled the file back across the table. "Only thing she ever gave me was my name, and I always hated it. Made me feel like an ass growing up, but the kids always teased about it." He waved it away and took a swallow of sweet tea.

"One year, some teacher called me Will and I let it stick. Better than catching grief for no reason."

"You know, in German mythology, Wayland the Smith was a master craftsman. Made all sorts of weapons and armor for heroes. He killed some kings' sons and made his escape with a winged cloak."

He raised an eyebrow. Was there anything Daniel didn't know? "I think Layla had somethin' less fantastical in mind. Somethin' closer to the Jennings variety."

His phone buzzed on the table. A text from Everett, already.

Tomorrow morning work for you?

He showed his screen across the table. Daniel shrugged, like it didn't matter either way, but he knew what the prof would say if given the chance to express his opinion. He'd say this was why Carver had reached out in the first place, that he shouldn't stop now. All the annoying, accurate things he probably needed to hear.

But Daniel didn't say any of that. He stole two fries from his to-go box and winked. "I mean... We could get a room."

He huffed a laugh and texted Everett back.

All right. Meet you there.

* * * *

Daniel
Gretna, Louisiana

He had convinced Carver into giving him an abbreviated tour of Harahan since they'd made the trip. It took all of a half hour, and that was with Carver really stretching it out. There was only so long a person could look at marshland, churches and a singular post office.

They had spent the rest of the afternoon finding a hotel with a shuttle to the airport. Once they'd retired to their room, Daniel had rebooked his flight. Afterwards, he scanned the titles of various articles he should've finished long ago. He opened one and started skimming. Maybe he'd get a head start on that.

He looked up from the small hotel desk and noticed Carver staring into space again. He sat on the corner of the bed nearest the door. True to form, there was a frayed toothpick in the corner of his mouth. He'd been quiet today—which made perfect sense. He'd had to confront a lot at once with Denise. And the more he heard of that story, the more he realized how committed Carver had been to leaving that relationship behind.

Carv hadn't even known that his ex was still in school. How little of his own town was the man living in for that to happen? Was that why Carver worked so much? Not just to support his shop, but to have a reason to keep his world small?

Still, he couldn't help but be grateful for the extra time. He'd learned more about Carver's past in the last eight hours than the three weeks he'd spent in Fairview. And if he'd been afraid of falling for the man then…

He closed his laptop and circled the hotel bed. He lay down atop the comforter and looked to Carver, unmoved at the foot of the bed. "Hey."

The straw cowboy hat swiveled his way. "What?"

"Come lie down with me." Carver hesitated and he specified, "To sleep. You look exhausted."

Maybe it was the power of suggestion, but Carver yawned as he scratched the back of his neck. "Yeah. I feel it."

Daniel opened his arm to the side but didn't say more about it. He'd follow Carver's lead on what he needed from him. It felt like the least he could do.

Carver set his hat on the nightstand and kicked off his shoes. He shuffled close and leaned against Daniel's side, also staying above the covers with his clothes on.

Daniel found the remote and asked, "Is the TV going to bother you?"

"No."

He scrolled the channels for something in the "not mind-numbingly terrible" department. There wasn't much, but it gave him something to do. He landed on a nature show about a river in Brazil. Two commercial breaks in, Carver had settled beside him and was lying down more comfortably.

If Carver was going to meet his half-sister tomorrow, he couldn't help but think the man should take time to sort out his feelings.

"You know," he said, pushing blond strands from Carver's dark eyes. "You never told me why you don't like people touching your hair. Or why you decided to let me."

"Do I have to?"

"No. But I'm curious."

Carver didn't answer right away, so he returned his attention to the show.

"I'll trade you," came his eventual reply. "Story for a story."

"Okay. You have one in mind?"

"I do." Carver sat up to look at him, suddenly intent on this. "And you're goin' first."

"All right. Shoot."

"What's with you and German?"

Oh, no…

He managed to choke on his own spit in surprise, but Carver had a smile on his face, and really, that was all that mattered. "Beg pardon?"

"You've slipped into it a few times when we're together." The mechanic crossed his arms over his chest. "So what gives, genius?"

He was going to have to find a way to explain this now. He muted the television and did his best to think. "It's hard to explain. Different languages have certain…associations, I guess? They evoke different feelings."

"What's German feel like?"

Did he know what a personal question that was? Though at this point, turnabout should be fair play. He'd certainly learned some personal things about Carver today. "It's a comfortable language. Like a thick sweater. It was the first I learned after English." He took off his glasses and set them aside. "My parents both have some Germanic ancestry. They used to speak it when I was a kid and didn't want me to hear them. So of course, I had to learn it."

Carver smirked. "How long that take you?"

"Kids pick things up fast."

Carver gave him a meaningful look and he continued with his story. "By the time I was five, I understood most of what they were saying. Though they didn't catch me listening until I was eight. That's when they started encouraging me to learn other languages as well."

Carver looked impressed—then annoyed that he was impressed. It was nice to see his face again. He'd been ducking to look under his brim all day.

Carver licked his lips. "That's cute and all, but it doesn't really answer my question."

"Then be more specific. 'What's with German?' doesn't give me much to work with."

"Fine." The mechanic pushed onto his knees and leaned forward, making a show of looking him in the eye — because he knew what that did to him. "I want to know what cracked you up so bad the night you stayed at my place."

It took a second to remember which time Carver was talking about. To his mind, that was hardly a slip. Compared with what he'd said at the shop, or last night, even? But from Carver's point of view, he supposed his burst of exhausted laughter would be more memorable than a few mumbled words.

"People don't usually find me that funny." Carver leaned closer and openly stared at his mouth. "Not when they're in my bed."

God, he wanted to lean closer and take what was being offered. Instead, he grinned at Carver's blatant attempt to coax this from him with sex. Because as nice as that would be, the man needed to process all he'd learned today — not run toward distraction full force.

In lieu of leaning forward to catch Carver's mouth in a kiss, Daniel gave the best answer he could think of. "I guess it just made me laugh. Of all the languages I'd spoken that day, it was one I hadn't touched in weeks that broke through with you."

Saying the words aloud, he worried he'd told Carver everything and nothing all at once. He leaned back in bed, unmuted the nature show and waited to see what followed.

In time, Carver lay beside him again. Clearly pretending to watch the show, but it allowed Daniel to start a proper head massage for him. Despite his efforts to keep it back, Carver sighed contentedly.

"Your turn." He smirked and borrowed the Carver's eloquent phrasing. "What's with your hair?"

"Feel like mine's is boring compared to that." Carver breathed out through his nose, not lifting his head. "I had a foster mom that kept my hair super short. Said it was easier to clean. My scar was pretty fresh, and I was always the new face in school. Just made life harder than it had to be."

He couldn't help but brush a section of golden hair away from his forehead. To his eye, Carver's scar was hardly visible, but he wasn't about to try to tell him that.

"Whenever I could," Carver continued, "I would grow my hair out. Kept it long through high school till I signed up for the service. And started growing it back the second I was out."

"So it was always long with your ex?"

"I guess so." Carver was silent a long moment. When he spoke again, his voice was softer. "He used to play with it, like you do. Until he didn't."

He'd been holding back asking about Derek all day, but no more — not when the mere mention of him made Carver sound like *that*.

"You know that was his loss, right?"

"It should've been." Carver sniffed in disagreement. "He got to keep on living his life. I got to start all over. Again."

Daniel swallowed down what he wanted to say and considered the time they had. He ran his fingers through the top of Carver's hair once more. "New beginnings can be a good thing. I've made a life out of them."

"Yeah?" The mechanic yawned against his chest. "I'll hold you to that."

"You should."

It wasn't the only time he'd made this claim with Carver. But it was the first he heard the man laugh as he responded, "Probably."

Chapter Twelve

Carver
Gretna, Louisiana

He woke early and long before Daniel, who still lay where he'd fallen asleep. With the man's arm around his middle, he wasn't sure if he should move. But if he was going to meet Everett and his "family" this morning, it wouldn't do to be late.

He dressed as quietly as he could, though it didn't seem to matter. Daniel didn't flinch when he dropped his keys on the bathroom tile, or when he stubbed his toe and cursed before covering his mouth with a hand. All that had been half an hour ago. Now he was sitting in his truck in a convenience store parking lot, listening to an unfamiliar station on the radio.

He wasn't supposed to meet Everett for another fifteen minutes, but he needed a moment alone to think through what he was doing. He'd tried not to, but ever since he'd read Everett's file, he'd been imagining what this unknown sibling of his might look like. Would she be anything like the yearbook pictures of Layla, likely donated by Denise? Would she know more about their mother than even Everett had uncovered?

It was strange after living his whole life alone, this accidental connection he somehow had to another person. He hadn't even met her yet, but he felt changed by it. Fractionally less alone.

Then he pulled into his supposed-sister's neighborhood, and that tiny hopeful feeling evaporated.

Was *this* where she lived?

Carver parked on the road beside the large house and tried not to openly gape. A three-car garage and exposed brick to boot. This was easily twice as big as any place he'd ever lived. Probably more. He didn't know how long he sat there staring, but by the time he realized he was doing it, he was spitting frayed wood from his mouth.

He checked the time. Five minutes until Everett was supposed to arrive. He obviously thought this was going to go well, or he wouldn't have offered to be there, right? Except the former detective didn't know his history with people like this—people like Derek's father, with enough money to never struggle a day in their lives.

Maybe he'd be better off doing this alone. He didn't need an audience if this went south.

He took a deep breath and climbed down from the truck. As he approached, he noticed details of the house he couldn't see from the road. The front porch wrapped around the left side, mostly hidden by a flowering tree. He'd also missed the swing and the young woman rocking on it, arms crossed over her chest as she stared.

Had she been watching him sit there this whole time? He didn't know if that boded well or not. He kept climbing the stairs and stopped where the porch started to curve. He faced the long bench as it swayed. "Caroline?"

"That's not my name."

Her arms didn't uncross. Dark brown eyes stared back at him.

"Right."

Nothing like a strong opener…

"I don't really use mine either," he tried. "The name she gave me."

"Why? What'd she name you?"

He winced his way through it. "Wayland."

She considered that for a moment, then looked away. The wind blew honey-blonde hair off her shoulders, but she bundled it up and pulled a beanie over her head. "I'm Harper."

He nodded where he stood. Approaching for any reason didn't seem like a good idea. "Harper. It's nice to meet you."

"So, you're him? My 'brother'?" She uncrossed her arms to make air quotes around the word, then settled against the wooden slats of the swing. "Never had one of those."

"Don't know 'bout all that," he said. "But we're family by blood."

"Blood doesn't mean family."

Harper tilted her head as she examined him. He recognized the appraising look from all sorts of folks who thought they were better than him. It wasn't any easier to stomach knowing she was probably right.

"This here?" She pointed at the house beside them. "This is family. The people who've been here my whole life. Not some woman who gave me up for adoption. Not you."

He was long past his last idea on what would be good to say. He was trying to find a way to leave when Harper asked into the quiet, "You live around here?"

"No." He cleared his throat. "I'm in Fairview. A couple hours away."

"What do you do?"

He shoved his hands in his pockets and leaned against the porch railing. "I'm a bartender, mostly. Work on cars at my shop when I can."

Harper sniffed at that last part and something about it rubbed him raw. What'd she think happened to her parents' ritzy cars when they weren't in one of their three garages? Could he really be related to this brat?

"I'm shit with cars," she said. "Took auto shop sophomore year. Only time I ever flunked a class."

"You're probably good at loads of things I'm not."

"Don't act like you know me."

"I know I don't, all right?" He cut himself off before he could match her energy any further. One second she wanted to bite his head off, the next she was making small talk. He couldn't follow it. "Look, if you didn't want to meet, we don't—"

"I didn't. But my parents said I should." Harper stood from the swing and marched over to him. She barely came up to his shoulder, but she carried herself like she was taller. "I'm doing this for them. Not you."

The sort of loyalty she was talking about wasn't anything he'd ever experienced. He wasn't going to find kinship here, and it was becoming more difficult to stay cordial with her.

"If this is your idea of generosity, you can keep it."

"Hey. I didn't know you existed until yesterday. When my mom finally told me what was goin' on." Harper extended her arms out at her sides. "So, here I am. You found me. Congratu-fuckin'-lations." Her hands fell to her hips. "Now what?"

That was the question of the hour, wasn't it? How'd this get away from him so fast?

"I haven't thought about this any longer than you, all right?" He tried to take a calming breath, but it didn't seem to be working. "What do you want?"

Harper's attitude dropped as she stared him in the face. He stared right back and it was impossible not to notice their similarities—of stance, eye color, even temperament.

"What if I don't want anything from you?"

He sniffed once and adjusted his hat. "Fine by me."

"Shit, you give up fast," Harper called as he descended the stairs. The porch swing creaked back and forth as she kept on. "Must be one of those family traits."

Why had he thought this would be a good idea? With *his* luck? Why hadn't he left well enough alone?

Everett's sedan turned the corner just as he reached his truck. He dropped his keys, growled in frustration, then climbed in the driver's side as fast as he could.

Everett barely made it out of his car in time. "Carv! What's goin' on?"

He turned the ignition with a hard crank of his wrist. "If this is how you repay favors?" he yelled out of the window. "Stay the hell away from me."

"Hey, man, wait!"

He lit up a cigarette—because fuck what Daniel said, he *did* smoke when he was stressed.

"Don't call me."

He revved the engine, forcing Everett to dodge out of the way. The man could take his "help" and shove it up his ass. He had places to be. Shifts to work. And goddamn, did he need a drink.

He swiped his eyes with the back of his wrist and made for the hotel. He had a bag to pack, then he planned to be gone. That family shit wasn't in the cards for him.

Once, he'd made peace with that. He'd just have to do it again.

And it'd all be so much easier once a certain professor was gone for good.

* * * *

Daniel

He was midway through editing an article when Carver shoved through the door, mindless of the noise or how the handle slammed the rubber stopper. He swiveled where he sat in the mass-produced office chair and removed his glasses.

Not an encouraging sign...

"Sooo." He folded the frames aside. "How'd it go?"

Carver glared at him. "Don't start with me."

He cursed under his breath. "You want to talk about it?"

"I never did." Carver rounded on him, pointing down to him in the chair. "You're the one who wanted to talk about it. You and Everett. So fuckin' *thanks* for that, man."

He'd seen Carver frustrated before, but he knew from experience it took time to make him snap like this. Something must have really gotten under his skin. "That bad?"

Carver sat on the bed and leaned his forearms on his knees. The brim of his straw cowboy hat covered much of his face. He was acting like this was his own fault, like how he was feeling was somehow wrong.

"Her prefrontal cortex isn't fully developed," he explained. "I wouldn't take it too hard. She's processing new information, recontextualizing her whole life—"

Carver snapped his head up and cut him off. "What I don't need is some lecture on why I should've expected this."

"That's not what—" He stopped himself before he could make things worse. He wished he knew more about what had happened. He was shooting in the dark and clearly missing.

He took a few cautious steps closer and, when he thought it'd be accepted, placed a hand on Carver's arm. "I'm just saying, you might give it more time. You're both adjusting to new information. I bet she'll come around."

"I'm not even sure I want her to. She's…" Carver bit off the end of his sentence, then tried again. "She's had everything handed to her. She doesn't need a fuck-up like me in her perfect life." His shoulders slumped as he covered his face with his hands. "This is why I didn't want to do this."

He hadn't thought of it that way before. He'd assumed Carver wanted to know about his family for the obvious reasons—for money, if not connection. He'd never considered that what Carver was looking for was somewhere to belong. His heart ached the longer he thought about it.

"I'm sorry if I pushed you—"

"When's your flight?"

The stark question made his blood run cold. Carver froze beneath his fingers and stared pointedly at his hand.

"Tomorrow morning," he said, placing his hand back in his pocket. "I didn't want to rush, in case things with your family —"

"Stop worryin' about me, all right? I'm not your project, Daniel."

"Who said you were?"

Carver stood and made for his duffel in the corner, shoving clothes and toiletries inside with impressive haste. "Don't pretend." He scoffed. "You're not gonna fix me before you leave. And fuck you for thinking you could." He mumbled to himself as he zipped up his bag, "Such a hypocrite. Like you got it all figured out..."

"Carver, wait —"

"Just go back to your life already. And leave me out of it." Carver slung the duffel over his shoulder. His dark eyes were red at the corners.

"Don't call me."

Carver slammed the door as he left. The sound echoed in the silent hotel room.

Of course, his first impulse was to do exactly what he shouldn't, but Daniel knew the sound of a hard line when he heard one. And nothing Carver had said was untrue. Leaving was always going to be a part of this. He couldn't help that his own feelings had gotten tangled into this, but if Carver's hadn't...

Maybe it was best to leave well enough alone.

He convinced himself to take that approach for all of ten minutes before he was on the phone, making a different sort of call. His ride arrived quickly and, as usual, his many bags made the cab driver give him the eye, though he loaded them all himself.

The driver asked, "Where to?"

He handed over a handwritten address. "It's a bit of a drive."

"Not a problem. Where you going?"

He leaned against the headrest and sighed. "Fairview."

* * * *

Fairview, Louisiana

He paid the cab to wait at the end of Carver's driveway. If this didn't go well, he'd need a ride to…somewhere. He'd decide where later. One thing at a time.

It took a few minutes of knocking before he heard movement inside. He didn't let up until the door swung open. Carver stood there, beer in hand, with a look of frustration and begrudging surprise.

The mechanic plucked at the tab on his can. "The fuck are you doin' here?"

"You said not to call."

Carver crossed his arms, entirely blocking the entry. "Technicalities aren't gonna get you far. You're just proving my point."

"I'm not trying to fix you," he said adamantly. If nothing else, it was important Carver heard that much. He kept trying to catch his eye, but the man kept his gaze on his beer. "I was never trying to 'fix' you. Just let me explain—"

"You don't need to talk. You need to listen, Daniel."

The man sounded calmer than before, but that didn't mean all was well. Those hours in the car had given him plenty of time to reflect. Maybe Carver had done the same. He fought against his instinct to debate and tried to listen.

"You think you know what this is about, but goddamn, are you focused on the wrong thing." Carver took a long sip from his beer. "This ain't even about what Everett found. Not really." He pointed with his can. "This is about you."

About me?

He hadn't expected that. He kept himself from moving closer by crossing his arms. "How do you mean?"

"Daniel," the mechanic said, annoyed and exhausted in equal parts. He set his beer inside and returned to the small porch, closing the door behind him. He pressed his palms together and sighed, like he was really breaking this down for him. "The first thing you did on this trip was walk into a P.I. office. And all you came away with was keys to a shitty car." Carver angled his hands down so his fingertips pointed at him. "You, Mr. *60 Minutes*, with the girlfriend who's been missing for years. But did you do anything about it? You give her case to them?"

Carver's dark eyes pinned him to the concrete. He wasn't sure he could move, let alone talk.

"But I should," Carver continued. "I should bring my normal-ass shit to Everett. Let him dig on it. And for what? To have some snippy kid tell me we ain't family?" He waved his hand in frustration. "And *then* you tell me I should give her time? When you ain't done a thing but run from your own past? I mean, come *on*,

Daniel. Fix your own life before you're tellin' me about mine."

"I didn't..."

Words failed him as he considered Carver's point. Aminah's disappearance was a familiar pain, like a limp he'd learned to live with. He hadn't thought...not even when Colt had mentioned it at the shop...

Carver breathed out slowly and leaned against the house. He rested his hand on the doorknob. "You don't have to pretend to care about me or my family shit. We had some fun. Think we both needed an escape for a while. But it doesn't go deeper than that."

"What if it did?"

He met Carver's gaze for a long moment. In the fading light of evening, the shadow of his hat kept him from seeing much. More than anything, he wanted to know what the man was thinking. If there was some way past this at all...

Carver nodded to his cab, still waiting in the driveway. "When's your flight, Daniel?"

But the man's walls were firmly in place. Carver had already decided how this was going to go. Any late-game realizations from him were simply that—late. And that made them his to deal with.

He cleared his throat. "I told you. I leave tomorrow."

Carver turned away. "Then I think that's all there is to it."

He closed himself inside the house as the light clicked off on the porch. The turn of the lock made Daniel nauseous. He'd thought...but no. Must have gotten it wrong.

If that was how Carver felt? How he really saw him? There was nothing he could say in any language to change it.

Part Three

UNTREAD

Chapter Thirteen

Daniel
October 2019

Like hell was he paying for the long return to Gretna, so Daniel had the cab drop him back at his small rental. He didn't have a plan for if Martha showed up—or better yet, whoever her next tenant was. All he wanted was someplace quiet to review his memories of the last three weeks.

Apparently, there was much he'd missed.

Through the clarity of hindsight, he could see Carver's point. He'd grown attached to the man faster than expected. Faster than he'd meant to. And that had spawned a deep desire to help him find what he was looking for—what he'd hoped would be a positive family connection. He wanted Carver to have people around him that cared. That was why he'd interfered in Harahan, though it hadn't been his place.

He'd pushed harder than he should've for a casual, time-bound experiment. There were plenty of conversations he'd skipped in the hopes of helping before he left. But Carver had never asked for that help, or his opinion. And it hadn't stopped him.

After hours running it over, he didn't like what he saw at all.

The next day, he slept through his many alarms and missed his flight. Didn't even bother canceling— though he instantly regretted that. It was an expensive mistake to make, and not his first time making it. That was a clue as to how he was really doing. He'd lived with himself long enough to know when he was cornering himself into change.

"Fix your own life before you're tellin' me about mine..."

Maybe tomorrow would be the day he gave Everett and Colt a call.

But, first, he called Martha and explained he was extending his trip. She hadn't rented the place out yet, so he signed a new lease through the end of the semester. He could write in Fairview just as easily as out east. She even offered him use of the car that he'd barely gotten to drive.

"The mechanic called yesterday," she'd said. "He offered to drop it by the house."

"What time?"

"Likely before noon. But he didn't seem too sure."

As much as it killed him to do so, Daniel made sure he was gone all day. He holed up at the library as soon as it opened and got zero writing done, but he ran into an officemate who seemed excited he was still in town. Before he knew it, he was in the dean's office, accepting an offer to guest-lecture through the end of the fall semester.

It would give him something to do, at least. Less than a week without direction and he was already losing track of his days.

When he returned to the house that evening, Martha's sedan sat in the driveway. He found the keys under the visor and a note beneath the wipers.

No charge, Martha. Tell Everett to stop calling.

He moved through the next day on autopilot, splitting time between his office and the library. It was only when he locked his bike on the porch for the evening that he realized he could've driven to work. He indulged the maudlin impulse and sat in the driver's seat.

Without prompting, his time with Carver played again in his mind.

"You're a lot."

"C'mon, genius…"

"I'm a good kisser…"

"What's with you and German?"

"Come on, Daniel. Fix your own life before you're tellin' me about mine…"

He walked briskly back inside. He biked to work the rest of the week.

He bought extra calendars at the campus bookstore to combat his foggy mind, but they all wound up different amounts behind. According to his office, the desk at his rental and his junker of a phone, somehow today was Sunday, Tuesday and Thursday at once.

Maybe not technically accurate, but the feeling was just about right.

On a day that might've been Wednesday, his empty fridge got the better of him. He searched online for stores other than the one Carv had taken him to and printed off directions. It was an extra twenty minutes away, but it was the least he could do. Carver had been clear about not wanting to see him, so he wouldn't. He could fix that much.

Without anything to fill his evening, he dragged his feet as he wandered the store. He hated grocery shopping—too many choices, too much light and people were always in a hurry. He could never find what he needed without trekking down three different aisles first. He was staring at a shelf of variously flavored beans when he heard a voice he didn't expect.

"Well, hey, smart guy. Sorta thought you'd left."

Jeanie stood beside him, considering a can of hickory smoked. She didn't turn to face him, but she didn't need to. He felt plenty on display with just the corner of her gaze on him.

"I'm still around," he said, aiming for casual. "Not much time for a social life since I'm staying all semester. They sort of expect me to work now."

Jeanie sniffed. "Lame."

He grabbed a can at random and started reading a recipe for dip. "How about you? Business been good at the bar?"

"Things are steady this time of year. Near Thanksgiving, it'll be a ghost town. Then again for Christmas." Jeanie set a can in the basket on her arm. "Come mid-January, we'll be booming again. You get used to ebb and flow here. If you stick around long enough."

Whatever was in his hand would just have to do. He couldn't find it in himself to care about beans any longer.

"So. You gonna ask about him, or what?"

There it was—the question he'd been waiting for and dreading in equal parts. He adjusted his glasses and stared at the floor. "No, I'm not."

"Why?"

"He doesn't want me to. I'm trying to respect that."

Jeanie angled his way and looked at him for longer. "Seemed like y'all were close, for a time."

God, this is awful…

"Yeah, well." His throat was closing up despite his attempts to clear it. "Things change."

Jeanie put a hand on his cart. "Look. I got very few details about how things went with this sister of his, but I know it wasn't pretty."

"Jeanie—"

"I only know what I've seen, but I don't think you need to be such a stranger with him. Fairview's a small place. You're gonna run into each other. No matter how careful you are."

He nearly laughed at that. "I thought you knew Carver. The man's successfully avoided his ex for years."

Jeanie's eyes widened. "He talked to you about Derek?"

No. He wasn't doing this. He needed to get out of there.

"Not much. And not willingly." He started to push his cart forward. "I'm only staying through December. He doesn't need to know I'm here. So I'd appreciate you keeping this to yourself." He gave Jeanie a look until she let go of his cart. "Carv doesn't need to lose another hometown. Certainly not because of me."

Somewhere behind him, Jeanie called, "See you." He didn't want to lie on his way out, so he didn't return the greeting.

He'd only gotten half the items on his list, but he walked straight to the checkout and didn't look back. He put his handful of bags in the backseat, spared a moment's thanks he hadn't made it to the refrigerated section and decided to test the repairs on Martha's ancient sedan—for what was maybe the real reason he'd stayed in Fairview at all. It took time to reverse the directions in her shaky cursive, but within the hour he was parked at *Harkan & Kane Investigations*, marching into the office before he could talk himself out of it.

Colt sat at his desk and looked up at the sound of the door. He seemed unsurprised to see him, glanced down and turned a page of notes.

"Took you long enough."

He followed the detective in back as Everett called from his own desk, "Anybody gonna clue me in?"

"Don't bother," Colt told him as he opened the door to a conference room. "He'll figure it out eventually."

Once he was across the table, he told Colt the whole story, sparing no detail. He told him how he'd delayed his flight out of Berlin for a day, how they had rescheduled it together over the phone since they'd bought the ticket with grant funds. He told Colt how the last time they'd ever talked, Aminah had complained about the hotel's orange juice at breakfast. How when he'd arrived at their hotel in Malaga late, presentations had already begun so he'd given their talk himself.

And he told Colt how once he'd returned to their room for a nap, that was when the others at the conference had taken his questions on her whereabouts seriously. How he'd woken to police at his door, weapons in his face, and the horror of realizing *no one* seemed to know where she was...

"You're doing good," Colt said when they paused for a break. "Need some water?"

He took the offered glass and drained it. "Thanks. I needed that."

"Go back to your last phone call for me. When you rescheduled your travel."

The white lie barely tripped him, but he deserved a corner of privacy in this. Colt didn't need to know he'd stayed in Berlin because of a play party. He'd certainly never shared those details with police, who had already looked at him sideways—and that was *without* the knowledge that he tied people up for fun.

"I ran into some friends in Berlin and wanted to stay an extra day. I needed help because we'd used grant funds to book our travel. Aminah took care of the Foundation documents, tracking expenses, all of it. I could never keep the forms in order."

"Which foundation you talkin' about?"

"The private group that funded our grant. Heartland Educational Foundation."

Colt's hand froze mid-sentence in his sketchbook. He breathed deeply once, then continued writing. "All right. Think you know what's coming now."

He'd talked to too many detectives to hope he'd only have to tell it once. "From the top?"

Colt nodded, and he started the story again.

* * * *

Everett
Mason, Louisiana

That professor of Carver's kept Colt busy in back for hours. Daniel looked exhausted when he left, but Colt rounded his desk, ready to go. Like he'd found a line of something powdery and hadn't thought to share.

It wasn't often a case of theirs revved him up like that these days. He watched Colt scrawl lines of black over the stark white of his sketchbook. "What you got over there?"

"Nothin'." He didn't stop writing.

Everett scratched his nose. "Well, nothing's got your brow scrunched up like it does when you're in the thick of it. So c'mon, don't hold out on me."

Colt tore a stack of pages from his sketchbook, then produced a blank file and took his time with the label. To his eye, it read *Heartland Educational Foundation*. Colt placed the pages inside and unlocked the bottom drawer of his desk.

That can't be good...

"So. It's a third drawer kind of file."

Colt stared at the open cabinet. "I doubt it. It's just..." He didn't finish the thought. He didn't need to.

Everett rested his hand on his partner's neck and squeezed. Colt sighed, but it did nothing for the tension in his body. Though he slouched against the chairback, Colt's spine was still ramrod straight.

"Heartland again, hmm?" he asked.

Colt tapped his thigh in anything but an idle fashion. "I just need to check somethin'. Scratch an itch."

"There anything you wanna tell me, Col?"

Colt covered his hand with his own and said nothing further. It was a familiar silence. He'd learned not to push this one.

"Well," he said, dropping a kiss to the top of the man's head, "make sure you don't scratch that itch open, now. I think we've both had enough of you bleedin' all over the place."

Chapter Fourteen

Carver
Fairview, Louisiana

A number he didn't recognize called him three times that day, so on the fourth, he picked up to see what the hell they wanted.

"What?"

"Is this Carver?"

It didn't sound like Jeanie. "Who's asking?"

The voice on the other end shook, as if unsure. "His sister."

The word stopped him in his tracks. *Harper?*

He paused his work on Colt's motorcycles and stood, pacing the length of the garage. "Last I checked, I didn't have one of those."

"That's fair. I didn't..." Harper paused and took a breath. "I shouldn't have met you when I did. I was mad. Which doesn't really make sense, but I was."

That was quite the assessment for nineteen years old. He hadn't figured that for himself until much later in life.

"Doesn't have to make sense to be true," he agreed. "Look, I'm sorry I disturbed your life. I should've — "

"Just shut up a second, okay?"

Mostly out of shock, he did.

"*I'm* calling to apologize," Harper said, emphasizing the word. "Not you. There's nothing wrong with wanting to know about your past." He heard the creak of a swing in the background and wondered if she was on the porch. "I don't like to think about my bio-mom. She's just this big blank in my life. She died because of me."

He'd learned that much from Everett, but that was a hell of a way to put it. "She died giving birth to you. Big difference."

"Whatever."

He didn't know what to say, but for the moment they seemed okay with each other. Maybe a direct question would be a safe way forward. "Why're you callin', Harper? How'd you even get my number?"

"That P.I. left his card with my folks. I asked for you at his office and said I was family." She sounded rather proud as she added, "Nice ladies at the desk will do a lot if you say it's for family."

He couldn't help but laugh. "I feel like I should be worried you know that."

"Probably." She paused again and he heard more swinging. "I never had a brother. It's just me and the twins."

"Twins?" Was there *more* family he didn't know about?

"Chill out," Harper told him through the phone. "They're my younger sisters, not yours. My parents' biological kids." She chuckled lightly. "I think I'm all you're gettin' from this genetic lottery."

"I'm not complaining. I never had anyone before so…probably good to start small."

"Yeah. Makes sense."

He cleared his throat, a little embarrassed at all he'd just shared. "I gotta get to work soon, but if you wanted to talk sometime…"

"That's kind of why I'm calling. You live in Fairview, right?"

"I do. Why?"

"I took a year off after high school to work and save some money, but I want to apply in the spring. It's a small campus, but they've got a great history program."

He considered all he'd learned in Harahan — namely that Derek was still finishing his program. "You lookin' for a tour guide?"

"More a couch to crash on. For a college visit." She added, "I mean, we'll see. Dorms are fucking expensive."

He laughed. "That's quite the plan you're making."

' "Don't pretend you don't already like me. I'm kind of great."

"Yeah? Prove it."

"My favorite book is *Lord of the Rings*, Han absolutely shot first and I refuse to drink a martini if it's not made with Smirnoff or better."

He made an involuntary sound of disgust. "If your idea of acceptable vodka is Smirnoff, I don't know if I can claim you after all. Thought your parents had money."

"Hey. I could've said Skol."

"The words 'Skol' and 'martini' should never be in the same sentence." He shook his head. "You need to come by the bar where I work. Sort you out."

"I'm nineteen."

"I might know a guy. And the owner too." Some role model he was, but hey. He was new at this.

"Well, shit." Harper laughed. "Are they hiring?"

"Probably. People leave Fairview. It's what they do." He looked at the shop clock and swore under his breath. He was definitely going to be late. "Let me know when you've got your visit scheduled, I guess. I'll take you around."

And he would, even with Derek still in town. As long as he stayed in the car, they should be fine. It was worth the risk if Harper was interested. He caught himself smiling until she added, sweet as you please, "Thanks, Wayland."

Unlike the other times people teased about his name, he laughed — full and loud. Because he had the perfect response.

"No problem. Caroline."

"Ugh. Asshole."

"Don't dish it out if you can't take it, small-fry."

Harper groaned. "Your nicknames need work." She didn't say another word before ending the call.

He looked down at his screen, still laughing as he saved the number. Then he received a text that made him wish he'd waited.

I saved your contact under Wayland. Three middle finger emojis followed.

Real mature, he replied.

He hit send, but didn't close the app fast enough. His gaze darted from the row he'd been careful to focus on — and the conversation he kept meaning to delete.

Daniel got points for following directions, at least. He hadn't heard a word since the man had followed him back to Fairview. Didn't even know what state Daniel was in. All he'd ever gotten for a home address was "East Coast." He had no idea if the professor would ever be back in Fairview. Even if he was, with how they left things, Carver doubted it'd be for a social trip.

It was a bittersweet truth in the wake of this call from Harper, but he'd shut that door with Daniel on purpose. Didn't matter if regret was now in the mix. At this point, he'd be better off letting it stay closed. He didn't need another smartass trying to plan his life — while taking none of his own advice.

He'd seen that movie. Didn't like the ending.

The day after his visit to Harahan, he'd ignored Everett's calls all afternoon. He worked a double at Jeanie's and drank himself to sleep, intending to keep that schedule for as long as he could. He worked five days in a row before Jeanie forced him off for three. Worst thing she could've done for his mind, but the day and a half he'd spent unconscious kept him from complaining too loud. Of course, that left more than a day to wander his small house, where every room held a different dangerous memory.

Even pissed off at Daniel, he wanted him. The man was halfway across the country and still poisoning his usual well. He wouldn't be halfway through asking a guy to dance before he heard the professor's mocking in his ear. Then he'd be lost to the memory of the moment it all flipped, the way Daniel had kissed him against his own wall, how he'd gotten a hold of his hair and pulled...

Even if he did manage to find some company, without putting too fine a point on it, he was pent up in more ways than one. In ways the average hookup wouldn't be likely to help. He'd kept the bundles of red rope that Daniel had used with the hard point, when he'd blindfolded him and sent him into outer space. Nothing else was scratching the itch, so he decided to look up a few ties. Didn't do much besides frustrate him in a new way.

Daniel had made this shit look easy. No way he'd be able to figure out the complicated patterns on his own. But once the thought was in his mind, he wasn't able to shake it. His next day off saw him tying up his own wrist, securing it around the leg of his bed as he lay across the sheets. He pulled against the tension until the bite was just right, sliding a slick hand into his boxers as he tried to relax into the memories.

The first time he'd tied him... Daniel fucking himself on his lap while the rope kept his hands away...

The night he'd changed Daniel's plans when he broke up that bar fight... The desperate way he'd pushed him flat against the couch...

On the bed, right here, when he'd tied his legs, cutting the clothes from his body just to have him faster...

The way Daniel would lapse into German near the end, like he'd done something so right, the man forgot what English was...

Adding the rope was enough to finish him off, but any relief was momentary followed quickly by a rush of shame. He didn't have that anymore — that safe place to land, where he knew he'd be taken care of. How did someone go about finding this on purpose? Did he even want it, if it wasn't with Daniel?

The answer to that scared him more than all the rest.

* * * *

After he'd spent some weeks texting with Harper and her yuppie parents, she arrived at his door with a rolling suitcase and a matching bag over her shoulder. He shook his head as she walked inside. "You movin' in already?"

"What?" She didn't look up from her phone. "I like options. Sue me."

She'd parked behind his truck, so it was easy to take her keys and drive them around in her car. No way was he going to be as obvious as he'd been driving Daniel around. And yeah, maybe there were some less practical reasons too. It was an older model, but it wasn't often he got to drive around in a Lexus. Not bad handling for a luxury brand.

He felt a little silly waiting in the car as Harper went on her tour, but he'd take silly over sorry. Two hours later, he picked her up from the admissions building.

"You putting miles on my car while I'm gone?"

"Whole bunch," he said with a wink. "It's nice."

Harper buckled her seatbelt. "My mom upgraded last year, so I got her old one."

Old one? This car was barely five years old. He and Harper might share some DNA, but their upbringings had been worlds apart. Not having much to add to the topic of luxury vehicles, he asked after her tour. Harper didn't say much as she scanned a brochure.

"I got scholarships and *still*," she complained, "tuition's so expensive."

If Harper was driving a Lexus and worried about paying for college, the prices must have gotten even steeper since he'd been paying it. He shivered at the thought. "You've done the official tour. You down to take mine?"

Harper nodded, so he drove them down the side streets with free parking at certain hours. They rode past the bookstores that had better used stock, and a diner down the street that served giant portions for cheap.

"You seem to know your way around," she said as they turned from campus. "Did you go to school here too?"

"A little."

"Just a little?"

He shifted in his seat. "My ex studied philosophy there. Doctoral student."

"A doctorate in philosophy? Jesus." Harper pulled at her black beanie. "I know we're still getting to know each other, but I gotta say. That doesn't sound like your speed."

"Yeah," he agreed, flicking on the turn signal. "Derek was a lot. In too many ways."

Harper turned to him with a look, but didn't say anything. In time, she shrugged and opened her brochure again.

Did I just come out to my sister?

"Derek, huh?"

He adjusted his grip on the wheel. It'd been a long time since he'd had to think about this. "That a problem?"

"Are you kidding?" Harper snorted in amusement. "My family might have money, but it doesn't automatically make us assholes."

296

"Guess they usually go hand in hand, in my experience." He stopped at a red light and, once it turned green, hit the gas. Something whirred and clanked under the hood as he accelerated. "That's the second time it's made that noise."

"Just ignore it. It's always making sounds like that."

Carver took a moment to look at the dashboard. There were too many lights on for a kid with matching suitcases. "So you've got college money, but not 'fix-your-Lexus' money?"

"Shut up."

"That sounds like it's coming from the engine. You shouldn't wait on that."

"Is this what I've got to look forward to? Lectures about my car?"

He'd already made the decision and started driving toward his shop. "You'll thank me later. Gonna have to wait for those burgers I promised at Jeanie's."

"Why? Where we goin'?"

He smiled. "Somewhere you might actually learn something."

* * * *

The first thing Harper said when they pulled into his shop was, "Are you gonna kill me?"

The accusation caught him completely off guard. "*What*?"

Harper looked at the concrete building which, at this time of day, did cast its share of long shadows. She nodded slowly, as if coming to a conclusion. "This place is a crime scene waiting to happen. You could rent it out to film horror movies."

"Yeah, alright. C'mon, already."

The kid kept her mouth shut until they got inside. Harper stood in the middle of the waiting room and whistled through her teeth. "Seriously, Carv." She picked up a magazine from 2011. "This is fuckin' bleak."

"I'm still fixin' up the shopfront, but the tools all work fine." He tossed her keys over and waved toward the back. "Gonna get your hands dirty. Be good for you."

He opened a garage out back so Harper could pull into the bay. Once he got the hood open, it didn't take long to find the problem. "Lucky for you, it's not the water pump or alternator."

"What is it then?"

"Power steering." He wiped his hands on a shop towel. "Grab me a funnel and I'll swap it out for you."

Working together, they drained the old fluid and had it replaced in minutes. He made Harper drive around the block to see how things sounded. When she returned, she jumped from the car with a grin. "That sound is gone!"

"Good. Should fix one of the lights on your dashboard, at least."

"You wanna take a crack at the others?" Her smile was genuine, but he wondered if there was more to it. She'd been talking about money an awful lot for someone who'd always had it.

"Your parents have you paying for the car yourself?"

Harper shrugged and leaned her against the taillight. "It was my idea. I want to help out more, it's just...expensive."

"Life is expensive. Best get used to it."

"Super helpful, Carv."

He looked up in time to catch her half-hearted middle finger. He flashed one back until Harper smiled. "I did just save you about a hundred bucks in labor."

She pushed off the car and handed him the keys. "Maybe next time I'm in town, you can show me how to change the oil?"

Carver turned to shelve the funnels and fluids they'd used. "Business has been slow. I'd probably be free if you did."

Harper was looking at her phone again when he joined her by the car. "You know, I tried to search for your shop. I couldn't find anything."

"So?"

She looked annoyed, but kept on talking. "Did you know you're the only auto shop within ten miles of campus?"

"Yeah," he scoffed. "For all the good it's done."

"Because no one knows what this place is. You've got no online listing. Not even a sign out front. I'm talking basics here." She turned her phone so he could see the screen. She wasn't wrong. Guess he thought those things got updated automatically. "If you don't put yourself out there," Harper said, "people won't know to look for you."

Carver dug a toothpick from his pocket and placed it in his mouth. "You know how to do any of that?"

"What? Use Google?" Harper gave him a look, then put her hand out, palm up. "Give me your phone."

"Why?"

She didn't put her hand down until his phone was in it. She walked across the lot and turned to face the shop, snapping a few pictures before she climbed in the passenger seat. "Consider this me paying you back."

By the time they pulled into Jeanie's, the shop's listing was live. He'd need Harper to show him how she'd done all that, but for now, it was up. Something off his "to do" list that had never seemed to get done.

She handed back his phone once they pulled into the lot at Jeanie's. "I didn't know if you had an email, so I made you one. I saved the password on a note in your phone."

"I have an email. I'm not *that* much older than you."

"Well, now you have two." Harper smiled. "Burger time?"

"Yeah. You bet."

With that, she left the car and darted inside Jeanie's. He shook his head and, before climbing out after, took a moment to look at the listing she'd made. None of today would've happened if he hadn't gone after his past. Now his present included burgers with his sister and best friend. Wasn't hard to see a future with all that too. He'd never thought he'd have something like this. That empty place he'd carried inside his whole life felt less so, maybe something approaching full. But the warm feeling in his chest wasn't entirely guilt-free. He should call Everett, at least. Mend some fences for how things went in Harahan. Maybe he'd give them a deal on the work for Colt's bikes. Most of all, he wanted to tell Daniel, but that impulse faded fast. He couldn't. Daniel wasn't in his life anymore — even though Harper was, largely because of that pushy professor.

It seemed strange that Daniel didn't know. Stranger yet that he wanted him to. He scrolled through their messages again. Maybe he'd text, one of these days. Let him know how it all shook out. He could smooth over how they'd left things in case Daniel came to town again.

He leaned against the headrest and sighed. Like that was ever going to happen.

Chapter Fifteen

Carver
Late October

"Please say you can cover last minute."

He rolled over in bed and rubbed the sleep from his eyes. He pulled the phone away from his ear and checked the time. It was barely three PM. The bar was bound to be dead.

"Jeanie?" His voice was thick in his throat. "You need somethin'?"

"This migraine's been kicking my ass all day, and the new server I hired called in sick. But it's Simone's day off, so I really don't want to—"

"'Course not." He owed Simone too many favors already. He wished Jeanie hadn't waited so long to call. He could hear how tired she was. "How soon?"

She sighed. "Faster would be better."

"Fifteen tops, okay?" He'd take the world's fastest shower and ride his bike over. He'd make better time that way.

The slate-gray sky had threatened rain all day. Even at speed on his motorcycle, the air was thick and wet against his skin. Stop signs were optional as he flew down the back roads, and it wasn't long before he was trading his helmet for the cowboy hat in his tank bag.

"Hey, I'm here," he said as he pushed through the door. "You don't have to stick around, I got things—"

He looked up and saw Jeanie. But she wasn't alone.

She was serving the only customer in the place, seated at a booth along the left wall. A brown-haired man with glasses that he was nervously adjusting on his nose.

Daniel...

What was he doing here? When had he come back to town? Questions raced in his mind until the moment he met Jeanie's eye. She had the decency to look guilty as she filled a pint beneath the tap. He watched her pour off the foam and set the glass on the lacquered wood top.

She arched an eyebrow. He crossed his arms over his chest.

Without a word, Jeanie slid the beer down the bar like there someone waiting to stop it. He had to jog up fast to catch it, and even still, it was a close thing. He didn't much feel like cleaning glass on top of this ambush, so he fit his hand around the beer as Jeanie returned to the register.

He took a long pull and set it down half empty. Daniel's gaze had been on him since he'd entered and maybe it was cowardly, but he hadn't been able to look back yet. He stared at Jeanie instead and hoped she'd read his mind. It'd be great if his stomach would quit clenching quite so hard.

She poured another beer and walked it over on a tray. "Table four," she said. "I'm on my break."

"Jeanie…"

She squeezed his arm and tossed a towel over her shoulder. Then she walked into the kitchen, leaving him and Daniel alone in the barroom.

He didn't know how to feel — blindsided was about all he could come up with. The familiar urge to escape prickled at the back of his neck. He could leave if he wanted. He could finish this beer, jump on his bike and ride back home. Jeanie wouldn't push him past that. If he wanted, he could put this professor and all his mind games in the past.

And if he hadn't just texted Harper about that business page she'd made, he might've done it. But there was more to his life now. Something resembling family. He wouldn't have found that without Daniel's meddling, frustrating as it was at the time.

"If you don't put yourself out there, people won't know to look for you."

The kid had been talking about his shop, but the advice still seemed to apply. He took a steadying breath and scooped Daniel's beer from the tray, carrying it along with his own. He stopped at the edge of his table.

"What are you doin' here, Daniel?"

Blue eyes lingered on his face, then dropped to the empty glass on the table. "Oh, you know. Just a long day. Thought I could use a drink."

He couldn't help the smile Daniel's sarcasm inspired. "What, they don't drink out east?"

"Trust me, they do. But I never got that far." Daniel shifted in his seat, turning to face him as much as the booth allowed. "I sort of missed my flight. The college offered me work through the semester. I took it." Daniel closed his computer. His mouth creased into a pained sort of smile. "It's good to see you."

It wasn't fair what that simple comment did to him — made everything inside itchy, like he couldn't get comfortable in his skin. He set Daniel's beer on the table and looked at him from under the brim of his hat. Their eyes met and he wondered if Daniel was remembering the same night he was.

He slid into the booth across from Daniel. "Jeanie put you up to this?"

The prof turned his fresh pint in the ring of condensation from his empty. "We ran into each other a bit ago. She called a few days after. Offered…" He waved his hand, as if unsure what to call this. "I should've said no, but obviously, I didn't." Daniel stared at the table between them. "I wanted to give you space. Like you said."

He couldn't help the laugh that followed Daniel's comment. "I'd say you did all right. Didn't even know you were in town."

The professor brightened a bit. He took a sip of his new beer and Carver followed suit. "Jeanie mentioned you might be getting a roommate."

He nodded. "For a bit, next spring. Just till she finds her own place. It's uh…" He tapped his thumb against the edge of his glass. "It's been good. She texts a lot. Helps with the shop some, too."

Daniel looked pleased to hear it, though he still teased, "If she sticks around, you might have time for the little things. Like getting a sign."

His smile widened. "You sound just like her."

Neither of them said much for a time. He didn't know what was going on in Daniel's brilliant head, but his own average mind was teetering between extremes. He wanted to thank Daniel for his help just as much as he wanted to tell him to leave. And more than anything, he'd like some clarity on just what it was they'd been doing here. Everything had happened so fast, then it was over. He wanted answers about what they'd shared. How a person might define a relationship like theirs.

He pulled his hat down on his head. "So. When's your flight this time?"

"December twentieth."

"And you thought, what? We'd pick up where we left off? Just push the end date a couple months?"

"That's one way of putting it."

"What's another?"

Daniel leaned forward and lowered his voice, an intense sort of gleam in his eye. "Another is that it's been three weeks since I've seen you, and I don't know how that can be the same as what we spent together. Not when it feels like so much longer." He huffed out a breath and gripped the edge of the table. "Another way of putting it is I miss you, for whatever that's worth. I wasn't the one putting limits on us. If you wanted things to go otherwise..."

He heard what Daniel left unsaid.

Just ask...

Conflicting feelings rioted inside him. He wanted what Daniel seemed to be offering, but something in his gut kept him from believing it was real. His throat was dry and his words came out harsh. "What am I supposed to do with that?"

The professor's voice regained its usual steadiness. "You can do whatever you want with it. I just wanted you to know." Daniel pushed aside the mostly full glass in front of him. He flinched, like he'd considered reaching across the table, but folded his hands in front of him. Carver's arms were still locked across his chest, but the more he watched Daniel's hands, the more the insides of his wrists pricked with heat. He rubbed one against his arm, hoping for relief.

"I know I pushed about your sister," Daniel continued. "I'm sorry. It was selfish to force your timeline, I just... I wanted to see things go well." He shrugged, a sad smile breaking over his face. "I can't help that I like taking care of you, Carv. Whether you asked for it or not. So, yes. I'm in town for a couple more months. And for my part, I'd rather spend that time with you than without."

Daniel looked at him sincerely, like it took everything not to be touching him in some way. "After that, we'd have to see—I'm never going to stop traveling, but..." Nervous energy took over until he looked him square in the face. "Isn't there a part of you that wonders what this could be? With more time?"

He had to close his eyes against the echoes of his past, when a different college boy had looked at him with hope, asking questions of what could be if they were brave enough to take the leap.

The last time someone had asked him that, he'd spent a year of his life trying to fit a mold that chafed him. Wasn't this more of the same? Just moving the chains down the field?

"I've wondered about a lot," he said. "Doesn't make any of 'em good ideas."

For the barest moment, it looked like he'd slapped Daniel across the face. But one blink and it was gone, a cool neutrality in its place. "Right," he said to himself. "Okay."

Daniel slid his laptop into his messenger bag and pulled the strap over his shoulder. He took two steps toward the door before turning back to the table. "You can call, if you want. If you change your mind." He laughed once, though little was funny. "Even if you don't. I still don't know many people, and...well. You know where to find me."

"Still at Martha's?"

"Yeah." Daniel pulled a pair of familiar keys from his pocket. He examined them longer than necessary. "The car works great, by the way. You..." His voice caught, but Daniel forced himself to finish. "You do good work."

With one last look, the professor pushed his way out of the door. All the oxygen in the room might as well have gone with him. Carver folded in half where he sat, pressing hands to the table and his forehead to his hands, grateful for the way his hat covered the whole affair. At the sound of someone sliding into the booth, he found the strength to lift his head. Jeanie was staring at him, looking pained.

"How's the headache?" he asked.

She worked her jaw and jerked her head at the door. "After listening to that? About the same."

Just as he'd thought. That wasn't her migraine pain face. That was her "you're in for it" face. Because of course, Jeanie had been listening.

"If I'm about to be lectured, can I finish my drink first?"

"Be my guest."

He took his time draining the last third of his beer. Jeanie raised an eyebrow once it was empty. "You done?"

He wiped the foam from his mouth. "Yeah. Think so."

"Great. Because it's past time you stopped acting so fuckin' scared."

He set his empty on the table. "There she is."

Jeanie ignored his interruption and cut right to the chase. "Look, Derek was shit. We know this."

He tipped his head in acknowledgment, though she was pointing out the obvious. "And?"

"*And* there's plenty of shit out there," she said. "No one's arguing that. But this professor of yours—"

"He's not mine, Jeanie."

"I think he is. Or he could be." She met his eye. "If you'd let him."

"Yeah? For how long?"

He didn't realize he was going to say it until the words were in his throat—with surprising volume, in fact. If he hadn't bitched to Jeanie about all manner of woes before, he might worry how she'd take it. As it was, her eyes only softened. She reached across the table and covered his hand with hers.

"Why's it matter how long it lasts, sugar?" He moved to push her away, but Jeanie stood and slid into the booth beside him, taking proper hold of his hand. "You remember that hurricane party when Nate was blowin' through? When I was dating that girl from the Quarter?" She knocked into his shoulder. "We sandbagged her house with that little rat dog of hers."

"God, I forgot all about that. What'd she call it?"

She laughed through the name. "Mitzy."

"Yeah. Damn thing never shut up."

Jeanie nodded. "Mitzy's like plenty of us here. Once you've survived a storm or two, you're always lookin' for signs of another. Even when they're not there."

"Don't you dare make that little dog make sense to me." He picked up his glass, forgetting it was empty, and set it down again in frustration. Jeanie placed a hand on the back of his neck and rubbed.

"Relationships don't last forever. I'm not sure they're supposed to. Caring about people means you'll get your heart broke most of the time, and it's only ever worth it because of shit like this." She gave him a gentle shake. "Be honest. If you never saw him again, is that gonna make the time you shared mean any less?"

He hated it when Jeanie made sense. He leaned his head against the booth and sighed a half-hearted, "Fuck you."

He tried to look away, but Jeanie ducked her head until she caught his gaze. She nuzzled her way under his arm until he set it around her shoulders. "You feel better now?" he asked.

Jeanie smiled despite herself. "I think so."

"Good." With his free hand, he nudged his glass until it sat in front of her. "Because if I'm not workin' tonight, I'm gonna need another. Need to deal with all the knowledge you just dropped on me."

She flicked his ear as she left, but she took the glass with her. Not a minute later, they were staring out through the window, watching heavy air condense to water drops on the glass. When their pints were empty, he squeezed Jeanie's hand so she'd budge over. He kissed the top of her head and headed outside. Any more quiet reflection would have him too drunk to drive home.

He took his time riding back, never turning right where he could take three lefts in a row. He'd never thought of himself as a cautious person, but...maybe he was. Maybe he had been for a while.

Even being intentional about it, he still arrived home too soon. He walked straight for the fridge once he was inside, cracked a fresh beer and sat on the edge of the couch. His plan the whole ride over was not to think about Daniel anymore for the day. The surest way to stick to that was at the bottom of a box of beer, except that did nothing for the time before unconsciousness took over. He struggled to find any peace as he turned it all over in his mind.

"Beautiful. Just beautiful, Carver."
"I want to set the bar so high you never settle for less."
"Do you still want to call me Sir?"
"You can have it. Just ask."

He leaned against the cushions and sighed. "Fuck me."

Dark clouds had gathered in the brief time he'd spent indoors. Fat drops of water spattered his face as he looked skyward. More of Daniel's words played in his ear.

"When's the last time you felt the wind in your hair?"

He held his eyes closed and shook his hair out of its band. The rain felt good. Cool and clean on his scalp. And with that, he'd made his decision—timelines be damned.

Whether they had three weeks or two months before this ended, Daniel was worth taking the chance.

* * * *

Daniel

He'd done his best to go to the bar with no expectations. No preconceived notions. No attachments or hopes. Of course, he'd failed miserably. But he supposed the thought had to count for something.

He'd been scrolling emails he had no intention of reading when Carver had walked in unawares. Their eyes met for the briefest moment before Carv had retreated to the bar and his friend, but that was all it took for any lingering doubt to vanish. Daniel knew what he wanted as soon as he saw him again. There was nothing for it but to tell him, no matter the outcome.

The way they'd left things wasn't a total loss. Neutral footing was a step in the right direction. Maybe with time, he'd call.

The short drive to his rental had done nothing to settle his thoughts. Alone on his porch, he stared at his silent phone. Perhaps he should take a page from Carver's book and find some distraction. He'd yet to return that telescope, since no one had asked for it yet. It wasn't until he'd set everything up that he remembered the overcast sky. This level of cloud coverage would certainly affect visibility. Never mind that the sun was still out, no matter how dark things seemed.

So, fine. No distraction, then. If he needed a night to sulk and wallow, he'd let himself have this. The intermittent showers didn't need to deter his plans. If he was going to commit to lovesick melodrama, might as well go all the way and sit out in the rain.

Then he heard the flare of an engine, the skid of tires over pavement, and decided he should really be done with this. He was so deep into wishful thinking that he'd actually heard a motorcycle. Heavy drops fell faster and he covered the telescope, trying to keep it dry.

Still, he heard it. The sound of that bike. And it was getting closer.

He looked up in time to wonder if he was losing his mind after all, or if that really was Carver riding up to the house, parking in the driveway, striding up the stairs —

Oh, God.

"What — is something wrong?" he sputtered. There had to be a reason he was there. "Are you —"

Carver took the stairs two at a time and tugged off his helmet. His hair was a perfect mess. The sight caught him speechless.

Carver marched right up to him and, never breaking his stride, pulled him into a kiss. Blond stubble scratched his chin as the man sighed into his mouth. He'd worried he'd never hear that sound again. Carver pressed his palms to his cheeks and held the sides of his face. His whole body tensed in surprise, but the relief that followed...

Incredible. Just incredible.

He met Carver's kiss and the man relaxed in his arms. The unbidden, unhindered sounds he so adored echoed from Carver's throat and he wanted to taste them on his tongue. He wanted to make him do it again. He wanted so much so quickly, Daniel wondered how he'd stayed standing this long. He slid his arms under Carver's until they circled his shoulders, resting a hand on the back of his neck to reach for that perfect mess of blond —

Carver pulled back as suddenly as he'd started. He pressed their foreheads together as they swayed in the rain. "For however long you're here?"

It was a start. It was so much more than he'd hoped.

"Please?" he asked, pulling Carver's chin close. The cool scent of rain clung to his clothes. "I know it's selfish, I just...I just want more time with you."

Carver leaned into his touch. "Me too."

He pressed closer, holding Carver as much as possible. He opened his mouth beneath the man's lips and didn't stop himself from tasting, from teasing at the edge of his kiss. Because Carver was letting himself react in the most beautiful ways — an obvious shiver as he tilted his head at an angle. The way he swore and held on tighter as Daniel licked over his pulse.

The reality of what was happening hit him like a drug. Carver was *actually there*, was really being this raw with him. To encourage the behavior, he let himself be moved—shoved, really—against his rental house. Carver kept kissing him, senseless and desperate, and while the cool rain kept them from combusting with need, there were better places to continue such wonderful ideas.

He nudged Carver away with his nose and plucked at his sopping T-shirt, snapping the wet fabric against his chest. "You're soaked. You should take this off."

"You don't wanna help with that?"

Carver dipped low to kiss his neck. He fought to maintain resolve on moving them inside. "Don't tease me, *schätzen*. In with you."

He fumbled with the door, but Carver did as he asked and didn't notice his slip. Or if he did, he wasn't asking about it.

"You've called me that before."

Or maybe he was.

Shit, shit, shit...

He tried to school his face as he closed the door behind them. "Have I?"

"A few times." Carver leaned into his space, not letting him out of the entry. His mouth was so close, but Carver held his lips away. "What's it mean?"

He gripped the sides of the man's neck and steered them toward the nearest surface. He didn't care which—so long as it was close. "What do you think it means?"

"Sounds like 'shithead' to me, but I don't think that's somethin' you'd say. Even if you thought it was true."

He laughed and leaned forward for a kiss. "It's nothing. Come here and I'll—"

"No, Daniel." Carver pulled back to look at him. Desire shone in his dark eyes. "Stop talkin' around it and tell me. What's it mean?"

If they were going to make this work, they had to deal in equal measures. And if that meant letting Carver in on this secret…what else could he do? He'd been caught out. He could only hope it wouldn't scare him away.

"Sweetheart," he said, holding his eyes closed. "It means sweetheart."

Carver didn't speak, but he froze beneath his hands. That wasn't an encouraging sign.

"I didn't—I can stop, if you want," he rambled. "It just sort of…" He blinked his eyes open and shrugged. "Just sort of happened."

Carver still kept his eyes closed. His lips were pressed firmly together, parting to allow one question. "Did you mean it?"

He asked honestly, "Which time?"

Carver tightened his hands on his hips. "Start with this one."

Nothing for it, then…

"Yes, I meant it. I mean it." He wished Carver would open his eyes. "I can't help but care about you."

There was a rasp at the edges of Carver's surprised sigh, the only bit of evidence the man had heard him at all. He kept still until Daniel touched his cheek. "Carv?"

The sound of his name woke him to action. He met his gaze hungrily. "Don't change a thing."

Carver wasted no time pushing him against the door, and he was reminded of why rope was often necessary if he wanted to stay in control. But he'd let them have this a moment longer. He was rather enjoying the show.

"Take this shit off," Carver whispered against his mouth.

He tugged the collar of the other man's T-shirt. "You first."

He'd only meant to pull the thin cotton aside, but if Carver wanted to rip it down his back like some comic book hero come to life, he wasn't going to complain. Carver shouldered out of the garment as he stared him down, pulling open his pants with an easy motion. Daniel held his gaze as he removed his own top layers. Right as Carver reached for his chest, he caught him around the waist and flipped their positions.

He forced Carver to face away from him and moved both hands above his head. Then he kissed down the back of his neck, across his shoulders, before reaching around to pluck at the man's tenting boxers.

"Carv, I want to..." He grasped him through the fabric. "Can I—"

"You fuckin' better."

He spit in his hand and slid his fingers down Carver's ass, teasing. "Stay put for me."

He swiftly hit his knees, tugging boxers and denim down with him. He might not have any rope at hand, but there were other ways to keep Carver from moving. For instance, if his legs were shaking, he wouldn't be able to walk much of anywhere.

With this plan in place, Daniel broadened his teasing caresses. He wasn't going to stop until Carver was losing his mind. He kissed down the side of his hip, trailing lower, until he pried his cheeks apart to bury his tongue inside. Carver's high-pitched whine cut him to the core. He teased and prodded with mouth and fingers, the heat at Carver's core a stark contrast to the chill of his skin. He squeezed the man's thighs as he worked in circles, nudging into that bundle of nerves every fourth or fifth stroke.

The muscles in Carver's legs jumped and his stuttered breathing grew harsh, but it wasn't just the sounds he was after this time. Daniel wanted to watch the man writhe apart. The two of them had always been on a clock, could never afford the time he wanted to take, but now? Now, he meant to. Carver wasn't leaving this house until he'd had him in every way possible.

Except then, a desperate groan broke his name in two perfect pieces, and the request that followed... He was helpless to fight it.

"*Dan*-iel, you gotta—" Carver huffed between breaths. "I can't take any more teasin'. I want your hands."

"Want them where?" He nipped the side of Carver's ass with his teeth.

"Up here. My throat. My mouth." Carver's knees wavered. He braced his forearms against the door. "Please, Sir."

That was the only combination of words that could've gotten him off his knees. Daniel stood and wrapped an arm around Carver's middle. He pulled his hips back so he could grind against the cleft of his ass, then placed his hand at Carver's throat, applying enough pressure for him to feel secure. He set Carver's feet, then reached his other hand for his mouth. He pushed two fingers down his throat and Carver bucked against him, moaning around his fingers as he reached for himself, desperate for release—

Daniel hiked up his head, moving his wet hand to fist Carver's cock. "Let me." He stroked him once, long and slow. "Please let me."

Carver nodded and he reminded the man to breathe. After a few shuddered sighs, they both were ready for more. Daniel alternated between stroking his cock and teasing his sensitive rim, all the while ensuring his other hand never left Carver's throat. He didn't press or crush, but held with intention, caressing the sides.

He stroked his cock again and the man whined his name—*there* it was. Carver was getting close. Daniel gripped him at the base and his legs began to tremble.

"You can take it." He dropped a kiss on Carver's shoulder. "I know you can."

Carver was biting the flesh of his own forearm, bracing against the door to keep himself standing. So he kept teasing, kept on holding his throat, kept pressing his hips against the warm body in front of him.

"You're doing so well," he whispered, timing his next promise with a precise stroke of his prostate. "Ride this out without falling and I'll fuck you until you come."

"*Shit*—" Carver focused on his breath. "Yes, Sir."

He kept on stroking, not letting up until Carver seized against him. His legs shook so hard that Carver's belt rattled against the floor, but he rode out the orgasm without coming, just as he'd told him to. Carver's forearms were still against the door, keeping him upright—though leaning was perhaps a better term.

With his head dipped low between his arms, Carver looked wrecked already, but he knew the man would be twice as responsive now. He brushed Carver's hair off the back of his neck and ran his thumb over his Adam's apple. "That was amazing. You're so amazing."

"Front pocket." Carver huffed, not missing a beat. "You promised."

"I did." He leaned down and searched through Carver's pockets. He found a condom and a pack of lube and joked, "These for me?"

"Yes. For you."

Something about the way Carver said that made him wonder. "Have you picked anyone up since you thought I'd gone? You don't have to answer." If Carver told him this, he wanted it to be his choice.

"No. I haven't."

He hadn't expected that. He had no claim to it. But he wanted it.

Mine...

Oh, how he wanted it.

He turned Carver's head and caught his mouth in a kiss. "I can't believe you."

He pressed his palm into the small of Carver's back and set to opening the packaging. He loosed his own pants and boxers, fitting the condom on as Carver mumbled, "Please." He used the lube to finish getting him ready with his fingers, then he pressed his lips to the heavy pulse in the man's neck. It sped and thrummed against his mouth as he worked the tip of his cock inside. He sank closer and closer until he settled against Carver's ass.

"*Fuck*. You feel incredible." He wrapped an arm across his torso. "Tell me how you're feeling. Can you come from this?"

Carver's voice was delectably harsh. "Yeah. Might need a little —"

He didn't wait for him to finish the request. Daniel reached around their bodies and took Carver in hand. He was thick and hot against his palm, pleasure-damp and desperate as he hardened at his touch. Carver sighed brokenly, so close to losing control. He tried to move his hand aside, like he meant to finish this himself—but that wouldn't do.

"Let me. I want to."

He wasn't usually the one of them begging, but he didn't care right now. He rolled his hips into Carver's again and again, pulling out an equal pressure on his cock. And maybe it shouldn't feel like a risk, but he wanted to say it again, to know that Carver understood, that he might even reciprocate—

"*Schätz*, I'm close."

Carver moaned at the endearment, and how'd he ever think he could last past that noise in his throat? All semblance of time and language left him as Carver groaned, desperate huffs of pleasure punctuating every thrust.

"*Scheisse*," he cried out. It was all too much. He screwed his eyes shut. "*Schätzen*, fuck, I'm coming, *fuck*—"

Carver squeezed his inner muscles around him, holding him transfixed within the tight heat of his body. He emptied himself with a groan, pressing kisses and praise into his skin. And he didn't know what language he might've been speaking by then, but Daniel knew what he meant to say.

Thank you…

I can't believe you…

Goddamn it, Carver. I love you.

Once coherent thought returned, he pressed a kiss to the top of Carver's spine and pulled away. He could've sworn the point of going inside was finding somewhere comfortable, but they hadn't managed it—not that Carver seemed upset. Affection mingled with pride in his chest as Carver slumped against the wall. Not a thought was spared to clothe himself or do anything but catch his breath.

He followed the other man's example and slouched to the floor. He threw an arm around Carver's shoulders and pulled him into his chest, leaning their collective weight against the front door. "Was that okay?"

The question was instinctive, and it seemed Carver's laughter was, too. "More than."

He grinned. He felt better than he had in days. "Next time, there'll be a bed. I meant for there to be a bed."

"I didn't."

He looked down and caught the glint in Carver's dark eyes. They laughed as they settled against one another, both content to stay where they were for now.

"So...just this," Carver said in time. "That's still something you want?"

"What do you mean?"

"Didn't make it to the rope this time."

He shrugged, though he was glad for the chance to clarify this point. "It's not always about the rope. Or the names, lovely as they are." He kissed the side of Carver's head. "I told you. I want more time with you. What we do with it..." He pushed a bit of blond hair aside. "I'm open to any of it."

He didn't expect a response, but when it came, it stole the breath from his lungs.

"So this would be, what, a relationship?" Carver laughed nervously. "Are you my dom now?"

Oh fuck, I want that.

I want you to be mine.

He took three even breaths before he asked, "Is that something you want?"

Carver leaned his head against his shoulder. "I've never had a long-term relationship worth a damn. Let alone somethin' with those sorts of..." He searched for the word. "Dynamics."

All of that was more than fair. Daniel shifted to sit more upright. The pose allowed him to see Carver's entire face. "What are you doing December nineteenth?

"Why, you got plans?"

"I do. Dinner, with you."

His answer didn't seem to bring Carver any clarity. "You not gonna eat until then, or what?"

He looked down his nose at the other man. "I mean I don't want to leave without us discussing…us. And if we feel it's going well… I could find a reason to come back to Fairview." He reached his hand for Carver's. "Maybe there wouldn't have to be goodbye. Just 'see you later'."

Carver interlaced their fingers, moving so both their hands rested on Daniel's knee. "All right. It's a date."

The words felt warm in his chest. He ran his thumb across Carver's knuckles. "Now. Would I be correct in assuming you don't work tonight?"

"You would be."

He smiled. "Then there's time for a nap first. Up you get." He tugged Carver onto his feet.

"What comes after the nap?"

He kissed him softly, smoothing a hand across his stomach. "If you're lucky? You."

Chapter Sixteen

Daniel
December 2019

Over the course of the next several weeks, Daniel cut down his visits to Jeanie's to once or twice a week — because there was a difference between a sprint and a marathon. Since they'd agreed to give this a go, they didn't need to meet at the bar anymore. He'd had Carver over for dinner multiple times, both with and without a "dessert course" that included their favorite hard point.

Carver invited him over on his off days too, no longer needing the excuse of a hookup to request they spend time together. They split their time between his rental and the mechanic's small house, and both parts of their relationship continued to grow. Carver still liked being tied, still liked when he took control. There were nights they leaned hard into their budding dynamic, providing them each the surrender or control that they craved. And it was lovely how now, when they put themselves back together, neither one of them felt compelled to leave. Their old, contrived excuses were more like jokes when they traded them.

It was comfortable. It was different. It was all surprisingly simple.

On what had become an average Thursday, he was in his office reviewing exam questions when his phone buzzed twice. A text. He smirked, expecting to see Carver's name on the screen.

I've got something. Come by the office if you can.

He didn't recognize the number, but the directness of the message made him feel like he should. He stared at the words and wracked his brain for what this could be in reference to. When the thought came, it hit like a blow to the chest. He pulled a white business card from his wallet and took note of the handwritten number.

It was Colt. Saying he had something.

Had he actually *found something* about Aminah?

His stomach swooped low and his face went hot. His whole body reacted to the news in increasingly unhelpful ways—his skin itched and he felt like shivering, but the sweat on his palms made him fumble his phone. He set it down before he broke the thing, then placed both hands on the desk.

Not enough deep breaths later, he sent a response.

When?

He was staring at the clock on his phone, but he couldn't have told how much time passed if he tried. He was frozen, transported back to those first days after she had disappeared. The desperation and guilt—the back-brain terror that had paralyzed him as the authorities made him tell his story over and over...

"Why'd you change your travel plans?"

"Weren't you supposed to land yesterday?"

"And she didn't give any indication something was wrong?"

"Who was she traveling with?"

"Why weren't you there again?"

"You've got a habit of changing your travel last minute. Why this time? What was so important you'd risk missing your talk that day?"

The only thing that pulled him from his thoughts was the buzzing in his hand — another message from Colt.

I'm out of town starting tomorrow. Don't want to do this on the phone.

It was like Colt was *trying* to stress him out with these responses. He quickly pecked out, *On my way* and threw anything he could think of needing in his messenger bag. He had to turn around for his keys when he was halfway down the hall, but eventually, he made it to Martha's sedan and paused, hands on the wheel as he breathed.

This trip would make tonight much later than he'd planned, but he didn't have a choice. He couldn't keep living with the shock of recurring grief — every time he spoke at a new school, whenever someone recognized either of their names...

Seven years of wondering was more than enough. He turned the key in the ignition and started the drive to Mason.

* * * *

Carver

The idea for tonight had started small at the tail end of Harper's visit. The two of them had been at the bar with Jeanie, and as they'd just come from it, his shop had been the topic of conversation. Weeks later, Harper was sending him quotes from custom sign places in town. Now the finished product stood in the corner of the lot, easily visible from the road.

The angular design glowed in neon that resembled the signs at the bar—Jeanie's contribution. The bright yellow border shone around two lines of blue text—*Carver's Auto, Repair & Detail.* The pink and orange sky made quite the backdrop. He pulled his phone from his pocket and lined up a good shot, staring at it for longer than was necessary.

He was adding the photo to the business page when Harper joined him at his truck. She jumped to sit in the bed beside him and handed him an open domestic. "From Jeanie."

He nodded his thanks. "Lookin' real good around here."

"It's less depressing than it was," Harper teased. "The grill's almost ready, and your P.I. friend brought the meat. When's Professor Hot Stuff getting here?"

He rubbed his forehead with both hands. "You have *got* to find another name for Daniel. I'm serious."

Harper quirked an eyebrow at him. "You still call me small-fry."

"What of it?"

She gave him an obvious look, like what she'd said was explanation enough. "So I'm absolutely gonna call your boyfriend Professor Hot Stuff. Them's the breaks." She took a sip of what he hoped was lemonade. "I don't know what to tell you."

He sighed and turned his phone over in his hand. Still nothing.

Harper wandered back to Jeanie at the grill and he watched the small group from afar. It was a quaint celebration. He'd never done much like it before. To him, having even three people set time aside for this felt excessive, like he was trying to be the center of attention. Wasn't a comfortable feeling. It was the same reason he couldn't enjoy birthdays.

But there was nothing obligatory about the three people conversing in his shop parking lot. Harper had turned on some music and was playing sous chef to Jeanie. Everett poured ice over a small cooler of bottles, though it looked like he was sticking to the Arnold Palmers they'd set out for Harper.

"You need help with anything?" Everett asked, not knowing any better.

"Unless you're gonna cook this a perfect medium-rare," Jeanie said, not looking up, "you can kindly fuck off, Blondie."

Harper was immediately snickering. Everett looked at her in shock, then over his shoulder to catch his eye. "*I'm* Blondie?"

Everett pointed to where he sat in his truck bed. All the attention made him wish he hadn't left his hat inside. He bundled his hair up for something to do.

Harper piped up, "We'll workshop it. But for now, yeah. It's sticking."

"Say no more," Everett conceded, throwing his hands up as he backed off the grill. "I'll be over here, minding my own damn business."

The sounds of laughter and music mixed to a pleasant background. He should go join them, instead of sitting here worrying. But he stayed where he was, his mind still reeling for an answer to Harper's question.

There had to be one. Daniel could be absent-minded and forgetful at times, but he'd never been intentionally cruel. He'd have a reason for missing this. He wanted to hear it. It felt like begging for disappointment, but he texted Daniel the picture of the new sign with a message.

Not bad, huh?

He pocketed his phone and planned to have that be his only outreach. Except by the time he was standing, his phone was already ringing. Daniel had called back immediately.

He put the phone to his ear and circled the truck, ensuring there was plenty of distance between his conversation and his guests.

"Carv," Daniel said. "That looks amazing."

"I think it'll do."

"I'm really sorry I'm not there. I wanted to be."

He kicked the toe of his boot into the pavement. "You wanna tell me where you are?"

"I do, but...it's a lot to explain." Wherever Daniel was, the dull tones of speaker announcements filtered over the line. "I'm actually in Mason right now. I'm at the airport."

Well. He hadn't expected *that*. He inhaled through his nose and let it out slow. And he was glad he did, or he wouldn't have heard Daniel say, "I never told you, but I asked Colt to look into Aminah's disappearance. He got in touch today. He might've found something."

"Are you serious?"

"Yeah," Daniel confirmed, though he didn't sound happy about it. "Colt said he might need me to…verify things. Identify if…you know." He trailed off, not finishing the sentence.

"Right." He had no clue what to say. "Fuck. I'm so sorry."

Daniel breathed through a tired laugh. "I suppose in a way, it is your fault. I only told him because you suggested it."

"So it's my fault you're takin' your own advice?"

"Well, when you put it like *that*."

Daniel's sarcasm knew no bounds. He shook his head at the pavement. "How long you gonna be gone?"

"Colt seems to think only a few days, but there's no telling how long this will take."

"Sure." He wanted to say something reassuring, but his whole body was still on high alert.

Even through the phone, Daniel seemed able to read his mind. "I'm going to do everything I can to be back for our dinner."

That was the thing. He *was* worrying about their dinner, despite how selfish that made him. The date of the thing didn't matter. Logically, he knew what Daniel was doing was important. They'd reschedule.

And also, they'd spent the last two months trading the date of December nineteenth like their own private joke. Daniel had taken to calling it their "performance review," which was probably funnier to people whose jobs required such things.

"Don't worry about it," he said, trying to be encouraging. "It's not important —"

"It's all important. I promised we'd talk, and we will." Daniel paused, then added, "Don't go filling your dance card on me yet."

Another announcement played in the background. "How're you doin' with all of this?"

Daniel sighed. "Doesn't totally feel real. It's like I haven't been able to catch my breath since he told me."

"Yeah." He felt so useless, here on the other side of the phone. He couldn't do anything and he wanted to comfort Daniel. Was this what life would be like once he was traveling again?

"Well, if there's anything I can do, let me know."

"Anything?"

He recognized that shift in tone. Despite their serious conversation, his body responded eagerly. What could Daniel want in *that* way when he was about to be across an ocean?

"What're you thinking?"

"I wasn't planning on international travel today, so I don't know if my phone will work once I land. I'm not sure when I'll be able to call." Daniel's voice became hushed, like he was cupping the phone to his mouth to keep from being overheard. "But if I knew you were waiting for me…"

Oh.

"How d'you mean?"

Daniel's voice was already harsh with want. "You know exactly what I mean."

If he closed his eyes, he could almost imagine Daniel was there, responding to his lip in person. Because he did know what Daniel meant by waiting. It was one of the newer power plays they'd added to their dynamic. On nights Daniel wanted to tie him, he'd leave a bundle of rope in plain sight. When Carver was ready, he'd remove his shirt and hat and kneel beside the bed — for as long as Daniel deemed necessary.

They'd worked their way up from shorter increments, once going so long as half an hour, but the thought of waiting days for Daniel — on or off his knees — that was quite the escalation. The potential payoff was huge, but so was the risk of disappointment.

"Fifteen minutes. Before you go to sleep," Daniel said. "Send me a picture of you kneeling. Even if I don't get it right away, I'll know you're doing it."

"And that'll help you?"

"*Yes.*"

It wasn't often his voice wavered like that. Daniel sounded pained, but he pushed through to explain. "I need something else to think about. Or I'm going to lose my mind." He breathed heavily into the phone. "Will you wait for me, *schätzen?*"

Every time Daniel called him that, it was like a shiver down his spine. Like a firm grip twisting in his hair. He swallowed hard, knowing how he wanted to answer despite his reservations. If he was going to be *this* open with Daniel...

"It's not a responsibility I take lightly..."

He nodded at the ground, decision made. "I'll wait for you. Sir."

"Thank you."

Daniel's relief was cut off by another announcement. There were the sounds of people shuffling to stand, then Daniel was saying, "I've got to go. I'll call when I can."

And it wasn't until much later, when he was alone in his small one-bedroom, that Carver realized what completing this task for Daniel would really mean. Sending pictures of himself, blatantly submissive, out into the void? Without even knowing if he'd get a response?

He held tight to what he knew of Daniel and their last two months together. He set up the camera timer and hit his knees.

Trust was terrifying. But he was willing to try.

Chapter Seventeen

Colt
Malaga, Spain

From the moment Daniel had told him the name of his patron, Colt had been thinking about this moment, right here. Didn't have to look further than the Foundation's board of directors before he started seeing familiar names. He'd said it before, though he hadn't known how true it would prove until now. The Edwards' family money had legs.

Every time he came across another connection, the thoughts needled him like mosquitoes, keeping him up in the night. The more he learned about the makeup of the sprawling operation, the more intermingling he found between Edwards' family businesses and Heartland's many causes. Staffing services, educational grants, housing commissions — all programs that dealt with people in need. All places someone looking for easy marks might start hunting.

He'd told Everett a hundred times they hadn't gotten them all at Foxland. Someone had helped Keith turn his sick hobby into a goddamn growth industry — someone smart enough to cut and run when the story broke early. Was it really that big a stretch to think they'd met through legitimate business? He wouldn't know for sure until he followed this trail to its end.

The fact the professor had agreed to accompany him would make things easier. Lend him some credibility. He caught Daniel's eye where he sat by the door, then adjusted the small white flower he'd set on the table — the agreed-upon signal with his contact. He set the stem beside a beverage that might've been a guess, but it was a good one.

The door to the café opened as Colt took a sip of his coffee. He forced himself to focus through the haze of sensations the beverage provided. If he hadn't been watching closely, he'd have missed the woman behind the older couple at the door, chatting as they walked inside. She wore a brown-patterned headscarf with a simple blouse and pants, keeping her head low as she searched for the flower. Her eyes widened when she found it, just as dark as his own with a similar suspicious stare.

Colt closed his sketchbook and folded the flower inside. When the footsteps stopped by his chair, he pushed a glass of orange juice across the table.

"Fresh squeezed," he told the woman. "I asked."

In the corner of the café, Daniel stood amazed. "Oh my God. Aminah."

* * * *

After Daniel's expected—though no less helpful—outburst, they left the café as discreetly as possible and followed Aminah a few blocks. She turned into a public garden with a pond and a winding path. They walked for minutes in silence before she sat at an empty bench. Colt approached her first, noting how Daniel lagged behind.

"How'd you find me?" Aminah asked, watching the dancing streams of water that jumped from a small fountain.

Later, Colt would show her all the messages he'd found in which online groups, how he'd compared the syntax of posts from known usernames to those he'd found after the date of her "disappearance." How he had realized she was using her connections to search for intel on Heartland. But he didn't know how much time they'd have before Aminah spooked, or before Daniel shook out of the haze he'd been stuck in since the café. So for now, he sat beside her, leaving plenty of space between them on the bench. He pulled out a page of printed messages and turned them so she could see.

She skimmed the words and sighed. "I was afraid of that."

"You were careful," he said. "Don't think anyone would notice if they weren't lookin' for you."

"Why would anyone have been looking for you?"

Daniel seemed to have found his voice, though he stood away from the bench and wouldn't look at Aminah. Her gaze stayed steady on the fountain, so Colt turned and said, "Because of what she knew."

Aminah nodded. "I volunteered with the Foundation during my program. I worked with others applying for grants. Helped get the word out about different opportunities." She picked at the corner of her headscarf that rested over her shoulder. "I met a lot of students, many who got their work funded because of me. Over the years, we compared notes and found discrepancies in the funds we should've received. By the time I was ready to graduate, just from who I'd talked to, I estimated fifty thousand dollars was missing from what had been promised."

The figure was closer to seventy-five by his last count.

"And that wasn't all," Aminah continued, crossing her arms as she spoke. "Those annual fundraisers they'd throw…all the galas and dinners. There wasn't a woman I knew through the Foundation who hadn't been solicited, harassed or worse from some boss in a suit. That place was rotten to the core and everyone knew it. But no one said anything. They all wanted the money more." She chanced a glance at Daniel, but he wasn't looking at her. She turned back to him and Colt nodded, encouraging her to keep going. "I decided that once I'd graduated, I'd find a way to use the information. I wanted to know where the money had gone, who was responsible. And I didn't want my work affiliated with Heartland anymore."

"So what stopped you?" he asked.

"The only thing I cared about more than my work." This time, her gaze lingered on Daniel long enough for him to notice. "I never told anyone, but…my parents are undocumented. Someone at the Foundation found out. At the start of our summer of conferences, I got a call on my room phone. Before you flew out to join me."

Daniel took off his glasses and rubbed the bridge of his nose. "You never told me any of this."

"I couldn't. I hoped if I just ignored it, maybe stayed quiet for a little, it would go away." Her eyes went hard as she explained, "The voice on the phone said they'd arrest my parents if I did anything to harm the Foundation's reputation. The next morning, I had a job offer in my inbox. It required an NDA."

He snorted once. Couldn't help it. "Carrot and stick, all in one."

"I got two more calls that summer," Aminah said. "Both were followed by job offers in the morning. And it was always when we were scheduled to speak at different conferences. When I was alone."

The professor paused, considering his next question. "Did you get a call the night I changed my travel?"

Aminah nodded. "That worried me more than anything. We'd made that change at the last minute, but they still knew about it. That's when I knew they were watching too closely to risk going public. If I went home, I'd always be looking over my shoulder, wondering if this was the day they'd take my family away for good."

"And if you accepted a job with them," he chimed in, "you'd have to sign away what you knew."

"My work would never belong to me, and I'd never find the answers I wanted." A wry smile fought for space on her otherwise sullen face. "No matter what I chose, they'd taken my life without firing a shot."

"So you decided to haunt them."

Aminah's dark eyes flashed over to his. "I refused to choose between my dignity and my family. I resolved to lay low until it was safe, then find a way to use what I knew."

"Except that never happened."

"Sounds like you know." He tipped his head in acknowledgment. Aminah waved at the messages in his hand. "I tried. But I couldn't reach out to anyone who'd known me before, and it was hard to get new people to talk when I couldn't share anything about myself. When I was just some username on a screen."

He closed the messages in a folder and placed it inside his sketchbook. All this aligned with what he'd figured. It was time to talk business. "Do you still have evidence of what you found?"

"With all it's cost me?" Aminah sat up straighter. "Of course I do."

"Where is it?"

"Safe." She leaned against the bench. "Why do you want to know?"

Colt swiveled to sit in the other corner and matched her posture. "Without gettin' too far into it, I think your bad guys know my bad guys. And I think all of them don't want the dirt you've got getting out." He unfolded his arms and tried to look approachable. "I think we could help each other."

"How?" The question came from Daniel, but Aminah arched an eyebrow that said she agreed. He was going to have to be careful about how he phrased this. He hadn't even talked to Ev about this yet.

"Yours isn't the only story like this I'm lookin' into. Soon, I'll have a file full of tales like yours to show to people that matter. And however that plays, lots of folks will be running scared. Gonna provide a lot of leverage that could yield a lot of answers. Maybe right a few wrongs along the way." He leaned forward on his knees and met Aminah's eyes. "If what you've been through makes you want a piece of that? I'm willing to do whatever I can to help." He breathed through his nose and made his final request. "In exchange for a copy of your files."

Aminah thought for a long moment, never once breaking eye contact. "One condition. My family can't be a part of this. Their safety is the whole reason I stayed away so long."

He couldn't help but smirk. "I've been thinkin' about that. What we need is information. A way to tease the line on this." He pointed to Aminah. "They had reason to keep an eye out for you back when. We need to know if anyone's still lookin'. And there's a lot less reason to bother a dead girl's parents than a missing one."

Daniel blew a sigh from his lips. "I grew up on German literature and even I think that's bleak."

Aminah looked over to Daniel. "We could say you hired someone to look into my disappearance and they found a plausible cause for death. Closed the case overseas."

"We print an obituary," he said, ignoring Daniel's sigh of protest. "And see if anyone comes looking." He waited for Aminah's attention to make his next point. It was important she know the risks. "You might have to move on a moment's notice. It's a lot to ask a person to live that sort of life."

She laughed humorlessly. "I've done it for seven years. I'm willing to try something new."

He nodded and returned his sketchbook to the backpack slung over his shoulder. From the second pocket, he retrieved a fresh legal pad. He clicked his pen.

"Tell me everything you know about anybody with the name of Edwards."

* * * *

Daniel

Colt and Aminah talked a long while on the bench. Even though he was standing in earshot of the whole thing, if someone had asked what they'd been talking about, Daniel wouldn't have been able to answer. He couldn't stop staring at her.

She was alive. *Really* alive. Even in his wildest dreams, he'd never have thought it possible. He kept cycling through shock, relief, overwhelming joy, then the crash of pain when he realized what this really meant.

He'd worried for years that her disappearance was his fault. And it was. If he'd been there that night instead of staying in Berlin, she wouldn't have gotten that call. None of this would've happened.

The thought sent him reeling each time it washed over his mind. He felt completely untethered. Like he didn't know which way was up. More than he had in the last two days, he wished his phone would work. The fact that Carver was waiting for him was the only thing he was sure about.

He hoped he could be sure about that. Or he really didn't know what he'd do.

He was staring at his phone and wishing for service when Aminah joined him by the pond. They watched a gaggle of ducks swim around the fountain. There was so much to say, but none of it fit into words.

"It's okay if you're mad," she said. "I would be. You should be."

He sighed, unable to hold on to his anger. "It's hard to be mad at bravery. You did what you had to. I just... I can't believe I didn't know all that. I'm so sorry."

"I chose not to tell you about the calls or my parents. You can't do anything about what you don't know."

It felt like getting off on a technicality. He didn't like it.

"Where'd you go? To hide?" He looked at her a long while, overcome with residual worry. "I searched everywhere I could think."

"I'm sure you did."

He took a ragged breath and tried to collect himself. "So, where were you?"

Aminah looked out at the park. The ducks quacked happily in front of them. "I went hiking, at Pico del Cielo. And a few other places."

He shook his head. "No wonder I didn't think of it."

Aminah reached for his arm and he caught her hand, squeezing lightly. She returned the gesture, rubbing over his knuckles with her thumb. "Can I ask how you're doing?"

There was no possible way to answer that. "Bit up and down, at the moment." He cleared his throat and looked at their held hands. "I kept on with our research, you know."

"I didn't. It felt too risky to keep tabs on anything from…before."

"We've been able to keep digging at our original sites. And added new ones." He caught her eye and couldn't help but smile. "I do a version of our talk anywhere that will take me. Sometimes, they even listen."

"I would expect no less from you." Aminah turned to face him and reached for his other hand. He gave it to her and swallowed against the lump in his throat.

"I know there's no way to apologize for what this did to us. But I do truly hope that…as much as you can, you've gone on with your life."

How was he supposed to have this conversation? It was too much. Aminah reached up and caught his face in her hand, cupping his cheek. "It wasn't wrong to act as though I'd died. It's what I wanted you to do." Her gaze fell to his mouth. "Hated that it was necessary. But I really thought it was. Even more so now, after talking with your friend."

They looked at Colt, still seated on the bench. He flipped over a page of the legal pad and continued to write.

Daniel took a deep breath and stopped trying to fight back tears. "I'm sorry it took me so long to look for you. And I'm sorry I couldn't help back then." He pulled her into a cautious hug, thankful to have her return it. "But I will now. We're going to figure this out."

Aminah said into his chest, "I hope you're right."

* * * *

Richard Edwards
Mason, Louisiana
December 2019

"More coffee, sir?"

He nodded, not looking up. One of house staff filled the china cup by his hand, then left him to eat in the garden. Winter was one of the better times to be back home in Mason. The weather was cool enough to sit outside while still being warmer than anywhere else the business might take him.

Chicago and New York were dreary this time of year. There was nothing better than Louisiana sun to start the day.

His phone buzzed on the table and he set his newspaper aside. It was a bit early for anyone to need him yet. He wiped his mouth and tapped the screen. There were two texts from an unknown number.

The first was a picture of a newspaper much like the one he'd been reading. He zoomed in to see an obituary, circled in pencil.

Aminah Bashir (27), reported missing in 2012, has finally been laid to rest. She is survived by her parents and partner, Daniel. The family credits a private investigator with bringing closure to a difficult seven years.

Private services will be held. Donations can be made in her name at...

The rest was cut off from the image. The second text held one word.

Problem?

It was the decades of practice that let him keep his breathing steady. He didn't need more than that single word to know who was contacting him. There were different sorts of business that required his attention — both savory and less so. Such was the burden of his position.

He folded his napkin in thirds and wiped both corners of his mouth. Handling this directly was below him, but overseeing its completion did fall on his shoulders. Such was their deal. He didn't like it, but he didn't have to. Business was business, and he'd do anything to protect the family.

Keeping a deal with the devil meant never forgetting his due. To the known, unlisted sender, he responded.

No.

And once he'd finished breakfast, he used another phone to make a call that couldn't be traced. This had to be done correctly. The right message had to be sent.

"I need to know who did this," he said. "And I need them to not do it again. Whatever you think is right."

Richard couldn't tell if it was paranoia or a hunch, but he'd know soon enough.

Chapter Eighteen

Carver
Mason, Louisiana
December 19th

He pulled into the lot at Harkan & Kane Investigations and waved at the glass wall of the office. This late, the only car in front of the strip mall was Everett's sedan. The neighboring Cash for Gold and Dollar Store were both closed for the night.

He checked the time and decided to start unloading on his own. Wouldn't be long before Daniel was supposed to arrive at Edwards Regional Airport. They'd spent just under a week apart, but he was anxious to see the man again. By the time he'd parked the now-functional motorcycles, Everett stood on the sidewalk, shaking his head.

"Awful kind of you to help with those."

He popped out the kickstand on the second bike, leaning it beside the first. "Don't mention it."

"I was gonna say we owe you one, but I think that's how this all started."

He chuckled and reached in his pocket for his smokes. He sparked the lighter and inhaled, then offered the pack without meeting the other man's eye.

Everett reached for a smoke and leaned into the offered fire. "Don't tell Colt." He exhaled and faced the empty lot. "You hear anything 'bout how it went?"

"Not really." He ashed his cigarette and looked down the empty street. "How 'bout you? Any updates?"

Everett shook his head. "Gonna have to see."

He'd hoped for some shred of information before he saw Daniel again. He didn't know what to expect. He hadn't received a response to any of his evening pictures, though he'd sent one every night. He'd held up his end of the bargain.

Everett angled toward him, sighing out smoke. "Look, I don't know about your genius, but mine can be a bit one-track-minded. Especially when it's important."

He laughed in earnest. If anyone could sympathize with how he was feeling, it'd be Everett. "How d'you deal with it?"

The former detective tossed his half-smoked cigarette aside. "Fuckin' habitual, at this point. I just try to hold down the fort. He's gonna realize he needs help sooner or later." Everett crushed the cherry under his foot, grinding it into the sidewalk longer than was necessary. "Still. Wish he'd looped me in on this. International travel and I've got no goddamn clue…"

He leaned back on his heel and looked the man up and down. "That was actually good advice."

"Yeah?" Everett itched his neck. "Well, I get there eventually."

"Guess we'll have to call it square. On the helping each other front."

"Pretty sure that's just what friends do, man." Everett clapped him on the shoulder, then reached in a grasping manner. "Speakin' of which, let me get another cig. Don't know who I'm kidding putting the damn thing out."

He offered the pack again as Everett turned from the road, using his body to block the breeze that kept the lighter from working. He was down to his last drag when he noticed something rolling down the road. A dark town car slowed to a stop, no hazards or turn signals in sight. Seemed odd, but maybe Everett was expecting another client.

"You know that car?"

Everett turned over his shoulder. "Can't say I do."

Something about it tripped him. He hadn't spent long in the Army, but he'd trusted his gut long before the government put a weapon in his hands. "You sure?"

Everett looked again. "I don't think so."

The car's back window lowered. Metal flashed in the fading sun. And while common sense said that couldn't be the muzzle of a gun, instinct told him otherwise.

What in the actual fuck…

"Holy *shit*," He pushed the other man toward the office. "Everett, get down—"

Gunfire roared behind them as they dove inside. The bullets came fast, one after another—semi-automatic, which meant a wide spray. He rolled behind the nearest desk and looked for better cover. He pulled his hat down instinctively and curled in on himself.

Best he could tell, Everett was half-hidden behind a cabinet to his right. He leaned out to see what was happening and only caught shattered glass. The shots kept up for no more than ten seconds, then nothing. His ears rang something awful, but that sounded like screeching tires to him. Whoever it'd been, they were gone now.

"Everett?" he called out.

"Here. You okay?"

"I'm fine." He rolled to the other side of the desk. "The fuck was *that* about?"

What he saw left little doubt.

"Good thing we ain't keeping score." Everett tore his shirt off his shoulders and wrapped the fabric around his thigh. It didn't stop the steady flow of red that leaked from his leg. "You need to get me to the hospital. Fast as possible."

He wiped blood from his own forehead, but there wasn't time to inspect it. He got Everett's arm over his shoulder and loaded him in the truck. Luckily, no bullets had punctured the tires.

"You know where you're goin'?"

"Yeah. Ain't far."

He avoided the carnage of the building and backed the truck out of the lot. It wasn't only Everett's office that had been hit. The Cash for Gold storefront seemed just as smashed up, though the convenience store on the other side was fine. Was this some random act of vandalism? Or something much more pointed?

He didn't know if Daniel and Colt had landed, but they needed to know what had happened. He couldn't figure this out on his own.

"Not gonna be able to pick you up after all," he told Daniel's voicemail as he drove. "It's Everett. There's somethin' weird going on... Just stick with Colt, okay? And meet us at Mason General."

* * * *

Daniel

They were in sight of the airport doors when he felt a buzz in his pocket.

Finally.

Between the revelations, arrangements and deviations of this trip, Daniel had never managed to get his phone to be more than a useless brick. Now that he had signal again, he flipped the screen open to view his message thread with Carver.

He'd been wondering about this for days now. Had the man really done as he'd asked?

It took some time to load, but there were four pictures in total—one for each of his days away. The timestamps varied, some earlier than others. But even the nights he'd worked late, Carv had taken the time to do this. He'd set up his phone, knelt beside their bed, removed his shirt and hat and *waited*. All because he'd asked him to.

The rush of need that inspired made his throat run dry. He'd missed Carver before, but now? Not even the surprise he'd tucked away for their dinner seemed like enough.

He looked at the photos again and found a voice note, timestamped two hours ago. He scanned the lot of the small airport as they stepped outside, but Carver's red truck was nowhere to be found. He hit play on the message.

"There's somethin' weird goin' on here..."

He's at the hospital? Because of Everett?

Daniel's stomach fell into his feet. He stopped Colt with a hand on his shoulder. "You have a message like the one I just got?"

"Haven't checked."

"You should."

He'd watched Colt keep a straight face through a lot recently, but whatever he heard when he put the phone to his ear bled all color from his face. Colt closed his eyes and bit the inside of his cheek. He tapped his thigh.

"Not again."

Was this a common occurrence for him? He didn't get a chance to ask as Colt pulled out his keys and started for the parking lot.

"We gotta go. Now."

He had to jog to keep up. "What's going on?"

"This is way too fast. There's no way they could've…"

"Wait." The thought stopped in him in his tracks. "You think this is because of —"

The sentence caught in the back of his throat, like if he said the words aloud, that would make it true. Had someone really been watching for news of Aminah so closely? After all this time?

Colt waved him on toward his truck. "I know it is. Just got that feelin'."

* * * *

Mason General sounded like a large operation, but the brick building was no more than four floors and sat comfortably in the center of town. Daniel still would've found a way to get lost if it weren't for Colt, who seemed more at ease navigating the place than he'd expected. Like he'd spent time in these halls before.

The first doctor they found, Colt knew by a first-name basis.

"Rachael. Do you know if —"

"He's all right," the dark-haired woman said. She motioned for them to follow and they fell in step behind her. "We put him and his friend in the same room so police could talk to them. Stapes left an hour ago." She paused at the end of the hall and pointed out a door to their right. She consulted her clipboard, then raised her eyes to Colt.

"Is it all right if…" She gestured his way. Colt nodded and she returned to her notes.

"No more than surface cuts and abrasions on a Wayland Carver." Her hazel eyes moved to Colt. "Everett had a gunshot wound in the leg. He'll be fine in a couple weeks, but he's going to need physical therapy."

Colt nodded, breathing slow with his eyes closed. "Thank you."

"I thought you were takin' things easier these days."

Colt and the doctor stared at each other, saying nothing — and he was slow to catch on to cues at times, but even he felt like a third wheel the longer he stood beside them. He pointed at the door he assumed was Carver's. "Is it okay if I…"

The doctor nodded. "They can each have one visitor. Go ahead." He held the door open, but the former detective wasn't behind him. He heard the doctor say, "We should talk, Colt. Just for a second."

Daniel was more than happy to give them privacy. All he cared about was how Carver had ended up in this mess. Inside the small room were two occupied beds. The dividing curtain was pulled back, allowing both men to see each other. Carver sat sideways on a thin white mattress and pulled at the gauze on his arm.

He's okay.

Relief stole his breath, making it hard to speak. "Hi."

Carver turned at the simple word, more of an understatement than a greeting. He was halfway to his bedside when the door opened again. Colt made a direct line for the other blond in the other hospital bed. One of Everett's legs was propped on a stack of pillows, but otherwise he looked fine.

Colt demanded in a worried tone, "The fuck did they do to you?"

"I'm alright, Col. Honest to—"

Everett fell quiet halfway through his sentence. With the look Colt was giving him, Daniel didn't blame him. He turned to Carver and scanned his body for injuries. "Are you okay?"

Carver nodded. "More or less. But I've got no idea what happened. It was like somethin' out of a movie. This town car pulled up and—"

"You saw the car?" Colt asked. His intense gaze shifted to Carver.

"Now hold on," Everett interrupted, scooting up in his bed. "We were just shot at in the plain light of day behind whatever mess you all chased across an ocean." He pinned his partner with a look of his own, but Colt only stared at the floor.

Everett looked at him expectantly. "One of you gonna tell us what's goin' on, or what?"

He shrugged at Colt, who gave him the go-ahead. This wasn't how he'd pictured this conversation going. He stood at Carver's side and rested a hand on the back of his neck. The man sighed, releasing some of the tension in his body. Watching the effect of his touch on Carver did more to steady him than anything had a right to. Which was good. He'd need all the help he could get explaining this.

"Aminah's alive. She was never missing, she disappeared. She's been in hiding."

"This whole time?" Everett asked. "What from?"

"She'd been gathering evidence against the private group that funded our research. They tried to threaten her into silence years ago, but she was two steps ahead of them." He turned his attention back to Carver and the only opinion he cared about. "She disappeared on them and took her evidence with. She's kept her head down ever since. Apparently, for good reason."

Colt piped up from the corner. "No one should've put this together so fast. It all but proves my theory."

Everett asked what they were all thinking. "Which theory would that be?"

"Someone from Heartland's been watching for news of Aminah," Colt explained. "Even if her body or luggage turned up, someone might've found the files. Her computer was never recovered." The man's leg started to bounce as he shook his head. "But Aminah's got no ties to Louisiana at all, let alone the Edwards family. There's no reason one line in an obituary would've sent someone here that fast—"

Everett finished his partner's sentence. "Unless someone's been watching us too."

Colt nodded. "We've always known Keith was working with someone."

"You think he met this someone through Heartland?"

"I think they work with Edwards' businesses too often to count it out." Colt scratched his nose in thought. "Even if Aminah's files don't give us the guy we're lookin' for, that's not the only reason the information is useful. If we collect enough secrets with enough of the right names, we won't have to find a thing. Richard's gonna tell us himself."

"You have *got* to be fuckin' kidding." Everett shook his head at his partner. "You want to blackmail Richard Edwards? The richest man in the state?" He pressed his head against his pillow in disbelief. "Is that what you've been locking away in that drawer of yours?"

The longer the conversation continued at the other bed, the more Daniel felt like they should give them some privacy. He caught Carver's eye and mouthed, "*Are you cleared to go?*"

Beside them, Colt sighed. "I was trying to protect you."

Carver nodded in response to his question while Everett cajoled his partner. "Like it or not darlin', I'm in this with you. We do for each other. Fifty-fifty. Whatever you do or don't wanna call that, that's how it is. And you're not gettin' out of it, all right? So quit tryin'."

The room stayed silent for a long while. Daniel caught Carver's eye. He seemed similarly affected by Everett's proclamation. It made him even more desperate for home. They'd spent enough time chasing their pasts. They deserved a chance to talk about the future.

Before any other conversation started, he reached his hand to Carver. "You drive your truck or your bike over here?"

"The truck." He cleared his throat. "I would've been here waiting, except…"

"I know." He pressed a quick kiss to his forehead. The images he'd barely had time to appreciate were suddenly all he could think about. "If we leave now, we'll be back in Fairview with..." He checked his watch. "A whole forty minutes before midnight."

"I guess it is still December nineteenth."

"So it is." He extended his hand as Carver stood from the bed. "Let me drive you somewhere for a change."

"You know where you're going?"

"No. But it doesn't matter." He smiled at Carver and winked. "I never feel lost when I'm with you."

* * * *

Colt

He wasn't sure when Daniel and Carver slipped from the room, but when he looked up next, he and Ev were alone. There was a hurt look on his face that had nothing to do with his leg.

"I just don't understand why you didn't tell me what you were up to." Everett sighed and reached for his hand. "I always thought if we were gonna go back on Edwards...we'd do it together. Or at least talk about it first."

"I know."

"You can't just do this shit without me. It ain't fair. And I can hear you thinking already, so don't try it. If you disappear on me again—"

"You'd be better off."

"Like hell." Everett gripped his hand tight enough to hurt. "Col, there aren't words for what you mean to me. I'm not lettin' anything take you from me. Not even you."

"You don't..." He cleared his throat and tried to breathe past his overwhelming senses. Everett burned bright as the summer sun before him, but the taste of copper and grief was strong in his mouth. How was he going to explain this?

"You still don't get it, Ev," he confessed, voice low. "I *can't* lose you. I haven't..." He rubbed the red-winged blackbird on his arm. "There's been like three or four people in my life that I ever...and I've lost 'em all." He looked Everett in his blue-fire eyes. "I'm not losing you, too," he rasped. "It'd break me for good."

"As far as I'm concerned?" Everett asked, leaning close. "Any plan that's got you away from me counts as losing you. And I'm not doing that either. So c'mon over here already."

Colt waited for him to scoot as much as the bed would allow, then fit his arm around Everett's shoulder. If they leaned close, they'd both be able to fit.

"If they used you to send a message once, there's good odds they'll do it again."

"So we stay quiet," Everett told him. "For real this time. We follow all your paper trails and keep things under our hat until we're ready."

"They'll still be watching."

"We'll take other cases. Show them there's nothing to see."

This was just what he'd been afraid of. Everett's bright outlook had a tendency to make him blind. "It's risky. You know that, right?" He looked down at the top of Everett's head. "Being close to me? Only ever brought people grief, historically."

"Was never any good at history," Everett replied. "Too many dates to memorize."

He breathed a laugh despite himself. It was weakness to stay. But he couldn't follow his better logic this time.

"We're in this together, Col. I love you too much for anything else." Everett tilted his head enough to look him in the eye. "Okay?"

He didn't want to admit it, but Everett was right. It was the only way.

"Okay, Ev."

Everett reached for a remote and flipped on the grainy television. He stopped on anything with a laugh track, but didn't watch much for long. "Rachael said she can prolly spring me tomorrow. I've got to stay tonight. Let 'em run their tests and such." He turned the television off. "You should go home, get some sleep."

Colt took the remote from Everett's hand and put the sitcoms back on. "Not a fuckin' chance."

They stayed side by side despite the narrowness of the hospital bed. Everett's breathing soothed him better than any music. And maybe it was their proximity to yet another near-death experience, or Rachael's pointed reminder to change Ev's emergency contact before they left. But he took his partner's hand and fit their fingers together. For once, Rhett was right about something — it didn't matter what they called it. They'd be trading off posts at each other's bedsides until one of them wasn't there to do it.

Everett looked at him warmly, if a bit confused. He tried to keep the gravel from his voice as he kissed the man's knuckles.

"In sickness and in health, right? Ain't that what you're always on about?"

"Col. You bein' serious right now?"

He pulled Ev into his side and held him close. "Yeah. Think I am."

Chapter Nineteen

Carver
Fairview, Louisiana

It was strange, getting driven around in his own truck. He'd done his best to stay awake and keep Daniel company — and more importantly, keep the man on course. But it had been a good long while since Carver had been shot at, so he was only somewhat surprised to be roused from an against-the-door nap by Daniel, petting his head.

"Hey. We're home."

That wasn't a word he used often. Wasn't often it felt appropriate. But it sounded right in Daniel's travel-weary voice, here in the driveway of his longer-than-anticipated rental.

He allowed himself to wake slowly, holding his eyes closed. "What time is it?"

"Eleven-forty-five."

He sniffed in amusement and started to sit up. "Don't think there's any places gonna be open for dinner this late."

"Let's not make assumptions. I was supposed to have more time, but—"

"Daniel." He laughed through the man's name. "I appreciate the gesture, but it really doesn't matter right now." He yawned and stretched in his seat. "We gotta get you back to the airport in the morning anyway. Let's just get some sleep."

"We will. But if I'm honest, I've thought of nothing but this since you followed me back from Jeanie's. Since before that, even." Daniel held one of his hands in both of his own, an earnestness on his face that he hadn't seen before. "If I have to leave you tomorrow after everything we've just been through, then please. Humor me tonight."

What could he say to a request like that? He swallowed hard and nodded. "All right."

Daniel looked like he'd handed him a gift. "Wait five minutes, right here. Then come inside."

"Okay."

Daniel left the driver's seat and headed toward the house. Carver pushed his head into the seat and sighed. Of course, he'd been thinking about this too. Even more so while Daniel was gone. But as he watched the professor unlock the door in excitement, his own anticipation grew in kind. Whatever Daniel had planned, he was on board. Funny how that quirk of his had brought him so much worry before.

He'd spent so long fearing that Daniel would turn out to be like Derek, and they had their similarities, sure. But only on the surface. Where Derek had made plans to change him, Daniel's only supported him. He introduced him to things he never would've considered. Things he wasn't sure he could live without, now he'd had them.

He checked the clock. Three minutes left. It felt longer than the past four days combined. But he waited out the time in mildly anxious silence, chewing on a toothpick for something to do. When he opened the front door, he heard Daniel moving in the kitchen, along with the metallic clang of something falling to the floor.

"Fucking *fuck*."

He smirked. That was definitely one of Daniel's favorites. He kept on through the kitchen and paused beside the kitchen table, where Daniel waved at an assortment of items.

"What's all that?"

"It's our date. Or what I could salvage of it." The professor pointed to an empty pot. "I promised you dinner. I was going to make soup again. Mostly what I have to offer from that is bread."

Daniel handed a full baguette to him and he laughed. He tore off a piece from the top and raised it in cheers. Anything was better than hospital food. He took a bite as Daniel moved onto the next item — a blanket he remembered well.

"If it was a clear night, we were going to look at the stars again."

"What if it wasn't?"

Daniel tugged a DVD from beneath the folded fabric — something called *Cosmos*. "We would've watched it on the couch. Still need a blanket for that." Then Daniel moved to the item that had caught his immediate attention, running a hand over bundles of rope the color of earth and sand.

"I got these with tonight in mind. I was going to rig you to the point with the blindfold again. Watch you fly." He closed his eyes as Daniel described it. He could already feel himself relaxing, a lightness in his chest that he'd never experienced before Daniel showed it him.

"And this..." He opened his eyes to see a thin, square box. "This I've wanted to talk about since the first time I ever tied you." Daniel held the box in both hands, took a breath then set it down beside the ropes. "But I'm getting ahead of myself. I know it's only beer and bread, but will you sit with me?"

He did as Daniel asked and sat in the nearest chair. The other man sat beside him, keeping them both on the same side of the table. For a day that had included international travel and the unraveling of nefarious plots, Daniel still looked better than he had a right to. His brown hair had grown some in the last few months, just enough that when he pushed his hand through it like that, the length on top swept across his forehead.

"Do you know why I almost left? That first night at your place?"

How could he forget *that*? He remembered their first kiss whenever he walked through his own front door.

"Not really," he answered. "You never told me. And I never asked."

"I almost left because, even then, I knew I wouldn't be able to keep casual with you." Daniel looked at him in that way he did sometimes, like he'd never seen him before. "You fascinate me, Carver. I can't help but want to know what you're thinking, how you're feeling. And I didn't think you'd want that from me. So I was going to leave." Daniel smiled, full and bright. "Then, you did what you've done every single day since I met you. You turned my resolve on its head and showed me just enough of yourself that I had to stay."

Daniel looked almost embarrassed as he continued to speak. "I know how I get. When I attach to someone like this…they become my sole focus. Which is why I probably pushed with Harper."

Carver found his voice for this. It was important that Daniel know. "You were right."

The professor met his eye. "I was an ass."

"So was I. Think we're square on that."

Daniel laughed, but he sounded strained. He reached a hand for his neck and stroked the side of it. "This is what I'm talking about. You're so quick and you don't even see it. You've worked so long for everything you've got, and you act like it's nothing. Like you're just some average person." Daniel pushed his fingers through his hair, loosening the band in back. "Like you're not the most beautiful man in every room you walk into."

Daniel had always had a way with words, but he was outdoing himself tonight. Carver wasn't sure how much of this he could take. He blinked back the wetness in his eyes and tried to focus as the prof kept talking.

"You told me when we first met that you weren't the type for long-term relationships. That you genuinely preferred keeping your romantic life simple." Daniel looked at him over the top of his glasses. "Now I know what I think about that, but I'm not making the same mistake twice. Because this was my honest attempt at casual and I swear, I fell in love with you faster than I ever have before."

He was finding it hard to breathe by the time Daniel slid the small box in front of him. "You can tell me no, and I'll stay gone for good. But if you tell me to stay…" The professor looked at him hungrily. "Make sure you mean it. Because I don't plan on letting you go."

Inside the box was a braided length of leather. Both ends attached to a small ring of dark metal, not more than a half inch across. It looked like a necklace. Something he might wear every day.

"Do you know what this is?" Daniel asked.

He nodded and cleared his throat. "I wouldn't mind you tellin' me, though."

"It's a different kind of collar. Meant more as a reminder than others we've used. It's supposed to be less obvious. Something only you and I know." Daniel lifted the leather from the box and ran it between his fingers. "I bought the materials weeks ago. Whenever I had you wait—by the bed, the couch, any time you couldn't see—I would braid it. Bit by bit, until it was finished. I'd sit and wonder what it'd look like if you ever chose to wear it."

Daniel's gaze fell to his throat and he swallowed convulsively. The way the man was looking at him, too-blue eyes full of nothing but love—*goddamn*, had he really said love? Was that right?

His mind quieted as Daniel brought a hand to his face. "I want more than just your nights, Carver. I want your mornings and your afternoons and as many months as you'll have me." Daniel moved his hand to his chin, tipping him up. "I want to know that no matter how far I go, you'll be here waiting for me. And in return…" He leaned close, his voice full of emotion. "I will care for you in any way you ask. So tell me, *schätzchen*. Will you wear this for me?"

It was good that Daniel had him sit for this. Hearing that question, asked with all the frills and feelings he'd never admit to wanting, made all the muscles in his limbs give out. Daniel caught him with a hand at his side and pushed the hair out of his face. It was all too much for words, so Carver leaned forward and kissed him. Soft and sweet, the way Daniel would do after scenes — long before he understood why he was doing it.

He pulled away, taking time to memorize how Daniel looked just now. Like his next few words held all the answers to the universe. "Yes, Sir."

"Oh, thank *God.*"

Daniel threw his arms around him in a hug, which had the added benefit of holding them both upright. Relieved laughter turned to a sigh as the other man held him close, nudging their heads together. "Can I?"

He nodded and Daniel leaned away, unclasping a small latch in the back so it opened like a necklace. He lifted his hair off his neck as Daniel fastened the leather around his throat.

There was a weight to the ring that he hadn't expected. He tucked a finger underneath and ran it around his neck. Daniel was watching his every move, so he dropped his hand, making room for the other man to pluck at the loop at the hollow of his neck.

In hushed tones of awe, Daniel said, "You look amazing. I can't..." He stopped himself from reaching for him as his gaze fell to Carver's arms, following the lines of gauze and bandages from the hospital.

The prof smirked. "There were *so* many things I was going to do once I got this on you..." He looked at the rope on the table, then back his way. "How are you feeling?"

If there was a word for this, Carver didn't know it. Daniel had put this together, planned this whole thing for weeks — just for him. Just to make sure he felt cared for. To make sure he felt loved.

Loved...

That word was going to take some getting used to, but for Daniel? "I want everything you just said," he told him, making one request. "After we get some sleep. That okay?"

The kitchen clock beeped as Daniel kissed the top of his head. Midnight. Guess they'd made it in time after all.

Daniel traced the line of his collar with two fingers. "Of course," he said quietly. "You're worth the wait."

* * * *

Mornings at Daniel's were always better than waking up at his place. The prof at least tried to keep a full kitchen. More so once he'd seen how little Carver knew about cooking.

He was up early, ready for a full day of playing taxi back and forth to the airport. Daniel had rebooked his travel directly through New Orleans. It meant a longer drive and he wondered if all Colt had said at the hospital had influenced the decision at all. Personally, he meant to keep away from anything with the name of Edwards for a while. Just on principle.

Once they were down in the kitchen, he asked, "You got coffee somewhere?"

Daniel pointed without looking. "There's tea in the cabinet."

He shook his head. "Not enough for all the drivin' I'm doing today."

He went back to the bedroom to snag a fresh shirt from the dresser. Once he was dressed, he took in his reflection in the mirror on top. The collar really did look like a necklace, if a person wasn't looking for it. Catching that flash of metal beneath his borrowed T-shirt had him grinning at his own reflection. He tugged on his hat and grabbed his keys, pressing a quick kiss to Daniel's cheek as he passed through the kitchen.

"Be back in a bit."

"You better be," Daniel teased.

Early mornings and school breaks were the best times to be on campus. This morning being both, he took advantage of the emptiness and drove down streets he used to avoid. There were plenty of coffee shops he could've gone to, but he chose one across the street from a small blue apartment complex and parked his truck on a street he'd avoided for five long years.

It was almost like he wasn't in control of his body. He'd had the thought of wanting coffee from here so many mornings and ignored it. But not today. He wasn't in the business of ignoring things anymore. Because whether Daniel realized it or not, he'd called his bluff by going on that trip with Colt. The prof really had gone and fixed his own life. And much as he wanted it to be otherwise, he wasn't done addressing his own baggage.

He looked again at the coffee shop across the street. That'd be his second stop. He ought to do this before he talked himself out of it.

He opened the door to the apartment building and sure enough, Denise's information was good. The last name of *Patterson* was still listed on the middle mailbox. As he climbed to the second floor, flashes of the night he'd left played over in his mind. For as bad as things had been near the end, it still surprised him how much it had hurt. He'd never been angrier in his life and had none of the words to express it, no recourse but to cut and run.

He knocked on a familiar door and waited. He had the words now.

It was early, but he didn't care. He heard shuffling sounds inside before the door opened to Derek, still in his sleep clothes, wearing a look of genuine surprise.

"Will? Is it..." He cut himself off in disbelief. "Are you really — "

There was a time when having Derek finish even one of those sentences was all he'd wanted in the world. Today, he didn't give him a chance and looked Derek right in the eye.

"I don't need you to say a word. But I do need to say this to you." Carver took a deep breath and gave it to him straight. "How things went with us? That fucked me up for a long time. You asked me to be with you. I moved my whole life for you. And we could've had a real shot, if you weren't so scared of what you wanted."

Derek's arms slowly fell by his sides as he kept talking. Carver wasn't sure what he was going to say next — kept realizing the truth of what he'd said after he'd already said it. He was purging everything he'd held back since the day he'd marched down these stairs for good. "I get why you did what you did, but that doesn't change how wrong it was. And you deserved to know. Your actions had consequences, even if you weren't the one paying them."

Derek held his gaze in a look of shared history. He watched the other man break away first, then look forward again, game face on. "Is this you asking for an apology?"

"I don't want anything from you."

Fuck, but he really meant that. He almost laughed, it felt so good. He shook his head at Derek and stared him down. "Consider this notice served. I'm not livin' my life around yours anymore. And if that makes anything uncomfortable for however long you're staying in town, that's a you problem. You can get out of my way for a change."

From deeper inside the apartment, another voice called, "Who is it, babe?"

That sure sounded like a man's voice to him. Much deeper than the one he'd heard through the wall the night he left. Derek held the door closed enough to ensure he couldn't be seen.

"No one," he called behind him.

He worked his jaw. Typical. But that wouldn't be how this ended. He took a last look at Derek and all he used to want. "He know he's just your roommate yet?"

Derek's face lost all color.

"Will, that's not—hey, come on! You can't just say that and—"

He didn't catch more than that. The staircase wasn't long and, since he took them two at a time, that was all Derek got to say before the building door closed behind him.

The drive back to Daniel's was all the sweeter for the coffee in his hand and the muffins he'd bought because he could. He held the bag between his teeth as he pushed inside the house, setting all but Daniel's coffee on the kitchen table. He turned to where Daniel was burning something on the stove and caught him around the waist from behind to kiss. He kissed the back of his neck.

He could hear Daniel's smile in his voice. "What's that for?"

"I need a reason?"

"No. Unless there is one."

He placed the cardboard cup within easy reach of Daniel's hand. "I got us coffee."

"I can see that."

"There's this shop I used to love. From when I lived on campus."

"How was that?"

He leaned away from the stove and collected his own coffee. He took a sip. "I saw Derek."

Daniel spun around with a look of shock on his face, spatula in hand. "How was *that?*"

"Sort of amazing," he admitted. He hadn't been able to stop smiling all morning. "I'd thought of going back and tellin' him off so many times. Just never worked up the nerve." He noticed he was toying with his collar about a half-second after Daniel and he laughed. "You didn't tell me this thing gave you superpowers."

Daniel closed his eyes and set the spatula on the counter. "You're telling me that the first day in your collar, you went and told off your ex that you've avoided for five years?"

Well, when he put it like *that.*

"Guess so."

Daniel exhaled through his nose and turned the stove off mid-omelet. He recognized the sound of those mumbles, if not the words they created. "You wanna try that again?"

"You should learn that one. I say it often enough."

"What's it mean?"

"I said, you're *trying to kill me.*" Daniel strode over to the table and pulled his laptop out of his bag. Carver watched, his heartbeat picking up the pace every second.

"What are you doing?"

Daniel didn't look up. "Rebooking my flight."

"Are you serious? You can't—"

The prof didn't utter a word. He set his hand on the ropes still lying on the table. "You were saying, *schätzchen?*"

For most people, this would be a joke. A way of saying what they wanted while doing what they had to instead. He didn't realize how serious Daniel was until his eyes snapped up from his screen. "Why are your clothes still on?"

"Really?"

"Did I not sound serious? Or was it my lack of immediate action that's confused you?" In defiance of both those statements, Daniel quickly hit a series of keys, clicked twice then snapped the laptop shut. His hand tensed where it lay on the ropes.

"If you're not upstairs kneeling in the next sixty seconds, I will force you to the ground and tie you there myself."

Only Daniel could make something so rough sound like the reward it really was. He shed his clothes as he made his way to the bedroom. All the while, he could hear Daniel following—not more than five steps behind, for all he'd told him to wait. He'd thought Daniel might be a little impressed with how he'd spent his morning, but this went beyond anything he'd hoped for.

Once naked, he hit his knees, not able to get his hair up before Daniel was on him. The man twisted both arms behind his back, catching his wrists in a single line of rope. He loved when Daniel used those fast, competent knots, leaving him restrained in seconds.

"You're amazing," Daniel told him, his voice almost reverent. "I'm so fucking proud of you." He touched his collar from behind, twisting the metal loop so it tightened the leather around his throat. "Remember. It's whatever you want."

His eyes slipped closed. He surrendered to the floaty feeling in his chest. "Use my mouth?"

Daniel nodded. "Then what?"

The man could always tell when he was holding something back, but he wasn't sure how he'd feel about this...

"I want to fuck you. But I want my hands for that."

Daniel tipped his chin to the side, humming his approval. "Be good for me, *schätzchen*. And you'll get it."

He heard the soft shush of cotton pants falling, then hands were in his hair, pulling back what he hadn't yet wrangled. Daniel moved in front of him and took himself in hand, exhaling in pleasure as he slid his cock into his waiting mouth.

Carver moaned at the fullness, swallowing around him when Daniel paused deep in his throat. He held him there for a count of five before pulling him off again. The brief lack of air made him lightheaded. It was perfect.

"Why do you like this?" Daniel asked, more curious than judgmental.

He grinned, not ashamed to say it now. "Because I'm good at it."

"I'm not arguing that. But why else?"

He blinked his eyes open and leaned his head against Daniel's thigh. "You like watchin' me lose control." He kissed the other man's hip. "We do share some things in common."

"It's true," Daniel agreed, pushing him back down on his cock. "God, you take this better than you've any right to. It's like you don't even need to breathe."

Daniel let him work from there then reached for the bottle of lube and their favorite silver plug. Carver watched Daniel's sure hands ready the toy before he reached around his own back. He exhaled slowly, then bucked into Carver's mouth.

Like he wouldn't notice *that*.

That was the main reason he'd wanted his hands, why it was so important to impress and earn the privilege. For all the many things they'd tried in their time together, whenever he'd been inside Daniel, the man had done all his own prep. Hadn't let him help at all. And if just using his mouth was enough to get him speaking German? Who knew what languages he'd hear once he got his fingers inside him?

Daniel's thighs shook against his cheek. By the way his hand tightened in his hair, he could tell that Daniel was close. Wouldn't be long before his own hands were free to wander, to explore, to—

Daniel pulled him off, cursing. "*Fuck,* not yet. Not yet, Carv."

"Why not?"

"Because you said there was more you wanted." Daniel started removing the rest of his clothes as he stepped behind him. Then he hiked up his head by the grip on his hair, angling his neck to whisper in his ear, "You're gonna fuck me until I come all over your perfect chest. So there's never any doubt who you belong to."

Fucking hell, that's hot...

Daniel grabbed him by the arms and moved him onto the mattress. He lay flat on his stomach until the ropes fell to the floor. With the pressure off his wrists, his arms sprawled at his sides.

"Move over." The prof laid down on his back and set his glasses aside. "I want to watch you."

His face and neck flushed until he was literally hot under the collar—the only thing Daniel hadn't taken off. "You gonna lay there and tell me what a good job I'm doin'?" he teased. "That how this is gonna work?"

Daniel removed the plug and replaced it with two of his own fingers. He grinned. "Don't pretend. You love it."

He couldn't help it—he really did. He'd have to tell him, eventually. But for now, he took his time working Daniel open, kissing down the man's neck as he got what he wanted. He followed the light brown patterns of freckles with his lips, hardly noticeable unless Daniel let him up close. He mouthed along the man's collarbone and teased his prostate with two fingers, thankful for how his answering moans covered the words he wasn't ready to have heard.

And because he knew Daniel would love it, he let himself make all sorts of undignified noises, each earning him a cry of praise. He lined up at Daniel's rim and pressed forward, breathing through the sensations. When he was halfway inside, holding Daniel by the hips, the man hooked a leg around his knee and pulled him forward—bringing him in *much* faster than he'd expected. The prof wanted things surprisingly rough for how sweet and slow he liked his rope play, but Carver had never been one to disappoint. He wasn't about to start once it counted.

He followed Daniel's directions and enjoyed the tight heat of the body below him, the grip of their arms around each other, the words Daniel mumbled in languages he'd never heard before—and more than a few that he had.

"Now, *schätzen*," Daniel commanded in his ear. "Turn over now. *Right* now."

He rolled to his side, separating them long enough to get the job done. Daniel pushed onto his knees and threaded the abandoned ropes through their second-favorite hard point—right above the pillows. He made a loop like a handle and pulled, using the leverage to settle on top. Then the prof guided him back inside, sinking down until their hips were flush.

"Like this. Fuck up into me."

He placed his hands on the crests of Daniel's hips and set about doing as he was told. The muscles in Daniel's arm flexed as he pulled down on the rope, returning them to the satisfying pace they'd set before. He supported their movements as best as he could, chasing the shudder in Daniel's thighs, because he'd been close. He'd been *so close* and he couldn't wait any longer. He wanted it now, *now* –

"Please, Sir."

"Please what?"

"Let me taste you."

Daniel stroked himself with one hand as he rode, clenching those deeper muscles around his cock and *fuck*, but there was no way he was lasting past this. As he balanced on the precipice, Daniel's gaze fixed on his collar.

"Why?" Daniel demanded. He knew what the man wanted to hear.

"Because I'm yours." His legs locked up in pleasure, his hips, his stomach, *goddamn* – "I'm yours, Sir."

"*Scheisse*, yes. Mine. You're *mine*."

Daniel groaned and stroked himself to finish across his chest. Only once he was spent did he swipe a finger through the mess and bring it to his mouth to taste. He mumbled through harsh breathing, "Only mine."

He slammed his eyes shut as he shuddered up into Daniel, calling out his release so loud his throat would be sore tomorrow. For a couple of reasons. And as they fell atop each other, an absolute ruin of sweat and tears, there was no doubt in his mind that this was where he was supposed to be.

He'd always known that people left Fairview. It was just what they did. But if they had some place to come home to, then the distance hardly mattered at all.

Epilogue

Daniel
Fairview, Louisiana
January 2020

He stood in the door of Carver's shop and had to dodge the line at the desk. Harper was ringing folks up at the register, which meant Carver was either out back or down the hall in his office.

It'd only been ten days since he'd last seen his mechanic. He had proof of that in ten lovely pictures that had kept him company on his trip out west to Berkeley. Still, he was eager to get to the real thing. He was about to check the garage when Harper caught his eye.

No skipping the welcome committee, then…

"Hey, Professor Hot Stuff."

He tried to ignore the flush that always followed that nickname. He adjusted his glasses. "Charming as ever, Harper. Is Carver —?"

"He's in the office. Going over receipts."

"That means there were some. That's nice."

"What can I say?" She motioned to the line at her desk. "I'm good at my job."

He turned the corner and pushed the door slowly open. He wanted a moment to look at Carver before the man noticed he'd arrived. Sure, he had plenty of pictures for that. But even the best of his photos paled in comparison to reality.

Carver sat at his desk—pencil in one hand, calculator in the other. His hat was perched on the coatrack in the corner. Blond hair fell in his face as he scrubbed something out with the eraser. The rocking motion moved his shirt and he caught a flash of metal at his throat. Daniel's whole body buzzed at the sight of it.

God, I missed you.

He knocked on the door, unable to wait any longer. "Hey, stranger. You working tonight?"

Carver raised his head and smiled at the old joke. He pointed to his desk. "If this counts as workin'. More like torture."

"Your business is a success. Sounds awful."

"Let's not jinx it, all right?"

Daniel leaned his hip on the corner of the desk, giving Carver a look until he backtracked on the self-doubt.

"I mean, yeah. We've been doing pretty well. We'll see how the next month goes."

They'd been working on the pessimism. He nodded, accepting that answer, then Carver motioned for him to close the door. Once he'd returned, the man asked, "You hear anything from…"

He let the sentence trail off, but of course Daniel knew who he meant. He checked their agreed-upon public message boards for updates every day. "So far, there's been nothing but green," he told him. "Colt hasn't heard anything either. According to him and Everett, no news is the best we can hope for."

Carver nodded and his gaze returned to the pile of receipts on his desk. Since the door was now conveniently closed, he circled behind his chair and put both hands on the man's shoulders, massaging lightly. "How much longer, do you think?"

Carver sighed and pushed hair from his face. "An hour, maybe."

"Sounds perfect." As soon as the man picked up his pencil, he leaned close and stroked the back of his collar. "Be home in forty-five minutes and we'll do that tie I sent you."

"The one with—"

"Mm-hmm."

"Where I'd be—"

"That's the one." He pushed a piece of blond hair behind his ear. "That seem doable?"

Carver gave him a look he understood to mean, *I hate you.* But when he followed it up with a cheeky, "Yes, Sir," and gave him that sideways grin? It sounded more like that other four-letter word they got closer to every day.

Feeling satisfied that he'd made himself clear, he walked back to the door. "Good. Then I'll see you at home." Thank goodness Martha had let him keep that rental. He'd finally gotten the hard points exactly how he liked.

And while fifty-one minutes wasn't quite forty-five when Carver knelt beside their bed, it was still good. It was all unbelievably good. He touched Carver's braided collar and knew he'd never tire of telling him.

Want to see more like this?
Here's a taster for you to enjoy!

Out in Austin: Teddy's Truth
KD Ellis

Excerpt

Teddy tugged at the hem of his overlarge sweatshirt then discreetly scratched beneath the band of his sticky sports bra. As far as he was concerned, breasts were disgusting lumps of fat that hoarded sweat, bounced like painful beanbags on his chest when he was busy catching a football and strained the front of any button-down he tried to wear. He couldn't understand why boys were so obsessed with them. He personally couldn't wait to get the damn things cut off.

Hormone therapy had deepened his voice and given him a shadow of patchy fuzz on his jaw. Clippers had sheared him of his blond hair and his mother's Italian heritage had blessed him with broad shoulders and narrow hips.

It was unfortunate that it had also cursed him with breasts that not even puberty blockers had been able to thwart.

He wished he could blame her awful time-management skills on their heritage as well, but he knew better. The fault lay with either Jack or John—the bottle or the boyfriend, whichever she was currently in bed with.

He'd been sitting on the hard, concrete steps of the high school for almost an hour. It wasn't like he could call her. His cell was out of minutes, and hers was probably dead on the nightstand.

Just as the final school bus trundled back onto the parking lot and Teddy was about to give up on waiting, someone stepped up beside him, casting him in shadow.

"Stay there," Teddy ordered, craning his head back until he could grin at his best friend. "Perfect. Be my sun block."

Shiloh, still in his leotard, laughed and nudged Teddy's hip with his shoe. "If you don't think I shine brighter than the sun, then clearly I'm not wearing enough glitter."

"Shine as bright as you want, but just keep standing there. Fuck, it's hot!" Teddy gripped his collar and tugged at it repeatedly, trying to stir a breeze. All it ended up doing was wafting the stench of boob sweat up into his face.

"Well, duh, it's ninety degrees—and you're in a sweater." Shiloh rolled his eyes and dropped onto the curb beside him. "And it's not even pink."

Teddy opened his mouth, his usual response dancing on his tongue—that boys don't wear pink—but he swallowed it. Shiloh was currently in a hot pink leotard and pink Chucks.

Instead, Teddy shrugged and glared down at his baggy jeans and boring blue sweater. "You know why." It was hard enough getting people to call him Teddy instead of Thea. Or, worse, Theodora.

"I'm going to make you a shirt. It's going to be pink and fabulous. It's going to say, 'Call Me Teddy'. *And* it's going to be in glitter." Shiloh threw an imaginary handful into the air, then fell back to lie on the sidewalk, his arms flung out.

"With your handwriting, they'd probably think you wrote 'Daddy'." Teddy dropped back to use Shiloh's arm as a pillow.

Shiloh shifted but didn't pull away. He just rolled onto his side, his blond hair flopping into his eyes. He left his arm beneath Teddy's head, bringing their faces close enough that their noses nearly touched. "It's not *that* bad. Besides, you're clearly not a *Daddy*."

Teddy rolled his eyes. Ever since he'd borrowed Shiloh's laptop to finish up his college application essays—and forgotten to clear his search history after falling down the rabbit hole of kinky porn—Shiloh's teasing had been less than subtle. Teddy refused to be embarrassed, though, especially since the only reason he'd stumbled onto that website in the first place was because Shiloh had left three separate bookmarks for it.

It reinforced everything Teddy knew about their relationship. They were destined to be the bestest of friends—but nothing more. They were both too attracted to the same type of man—tall, dark and dangerous.

Still, knowing his friend was into the same kinks that he was didn't mean they needed to talk about it. He ignored the leading comment and switched back to the far safer topic of handwriting. "Remember when Mr. Carmine thought you wrote an essay on *Storage Wars*?"

"Hey, Mr. Carmine also thought you wrote an essay about Quasimodo."

"I did write him an essay about Quasimodo. Well, really about how the novel by Victor Hugo helped raise the money needed to restore the cathedral, and—" Teddy felt the beginnings of a spiel on gothic architecture creeping up.

Shiloh interrupted, "Yeah, buttresses...a rose window. I remember. I still think the gargoyles are creepy."

"You said buttresses," Teddy snickered, shoving Shiloh's shoulder.

"Teddy, can I touch your *buttress*?"

"Your hand can stay far away from my *buttress*, fuck you very much."

"It's like a butt fortress. I just want to invade your buttress! Why are you so mean to me?" Shiloh rolled onto his back and kicked his feet against the sidewalk like an angry toddler, except for the smile on his face.

"No, it's impregnable!" Teddy stuck out his tongue.

"Well, duh, you're a boy. Of course you're impregnable."

"Something tells me you don't know what that word means."

Immediately, Shiloh rattled off the definition. "Impregnable. Unable to be captured or broken into. Also, unable to be defeated or destroyed. But you have to admit that it sounds an awful lot like it means you can't make babies."

"And thank God for that," Teddy shivered at the thought of being responsible for a little, squalling, helpless baby. "I might miss wearing pink, but I won't miss *that*."

Teddy froze at the accidental admission. His therapist had told him that it was normal, that gender was a spectrum and that just because he still liked feminine things didn't make his desire to transition less valid. Still, it was the first time he'd admitted it to anyone except his therapist.

Shiloh sat up slightly to face him better. "You can still wear pink. You can wear whatever the fuck you want." Shiloh's voice hardened. "And if anyone bothers you about it, I'll cover their lockers in gay porn. Just say the word."

"The poor football players won't know what to do with themselves. Think of all the spontaneous erections." The few he'd dated had been far more interested in his ass than a straight guy probably should be — not that he'd obliged, since he refused to be anyone's dirty little secret.

Shiloh sighed. "It would be a beautiful gift to all of us."

A black Mercedes pulled up to the curb, barely parking before the driver was leaning on the horn.

"Impatient bastard," Shiloh grumbled. "I don't know why he's in a hurry. He gets paid by the hour."

"Well, that stick is so far up his ass it has to be uncomfortable sitting down." Teddy sat up and straightened his sweatshirt. The Becketts' driver was a homophobic dick. He didn't understand how the man hadn't been fired yet.

Shiloh pushed himself to his feet. "I bet he has hemorrhoids. That's probably where he rushes off to every night."

"Ew. You picture him rubbing cream on his ass?" Teddy teased.

Shiloh gagged, shoving Teddy to the side. "Gross. You're such a dick. I don't know why I hang out with you."

"Because you love me."

The Mercedes blared its horn again, a demanding series of honks that only ended when Shiloh threw a hand up in acknowledgment. "I gotta go. Do you have a ride?"

Teddy shrugged. "Yeah. She must just be running late or something. I'm sure she'll be here soon." He knew she wouldn't be, but he'd rather walk than listen to the driver sling slurs. He didn't understand how Shiloh dealt with it.

Shiloh hesitated on the bottom step, looking like he wanted to say something, but all he did was give a small nod and say, "Okay. See you Monday?"

"Yeah, see you."

About the Author

Gin Vane is your friendly neighborhood bisexual she / they, deconstructing heteronormativity one queer romance at a time.

As a lifelong reader of the genre, Gin refuses to compromise plot for spice and lives by the motto "por que no los dos?" Gin primarily writes MM and MMF, though she enjoys reading and writing lesbian romance as well. Gin lives for the slow-burn that scalds and loves a good character redemption arc. Their novels are always full of heat and often include elements of polyamory and BDSM.

When not at the writing desk, Gin can be found dancing at their pole and circus studio, knitting beside the most perfect cat, watching crime shows and Brit coms with her husband or cooking dinner with friends and partners.

Gin loves to hear from readers. You can find their contact information, website details and author profile page at https://www.pride-publishing.com

PUBLISHING

Sign up for our newsletter and find out about all our romance book releases, eBook sales and promotions, sneak peeks and FREE romance books!